I wasn't even a man when I took a life for the first time, although you couldn't say I was a child. If I'd ever had a childhood, it hadn't lasted long. My father, may he rot in hell, had seen to that. I took his life as well and that, too, happened before I was old enough to be considered a grown man.
I never regretted it for a second.
That path almost led to my own grave, and would have, if I hadn't stumbled across somebody who was as different from my father as day was from night. Sarge had seen the monster lurking inside, so he took control, gave me guidelines, rules, so I wouldn't be the monster my father had planned.
It worked. I restrained the worst of my rage and honed the skills that had been drilled into me—theft, stealth... assassination. The broken child ceased to exist and I became Spectre, an assassin spoken of in whispers, hired to take out the worst of humanity.
Then I was sent to kill her...and my world came to a screeching halt.

Tia

It's taken a long time, but I finally had a nice, steady routine. I stopped trying to conform to the neurotypicals of the world and found my *own* normal.
Normal went out the window when I walked into my kitchen and found a strange (**hot**), dangerous looking man drugging my new dog. It probably wasn't the smartest thing to leap at him like a banshee and attack, but that's what I did.
When my attempt to wreck the vehicle was averted, my kidnapper didn't hurt or threaten me. In fact, he told me he wanted to protect me.
He had to be crazy. But if he was crazy, what did that make me? Because I believed him. More, I found myself seeing something beyond the rigid, blank mask he wore. He kept trying to push me away, but I couldn't keep my distance.
He calls himself a monster...but when I look at him, that isn't what I see. I just see him...and I know he's meant to be mine.

SPECTRE

AN EROTIC ROMANTIC SUSPENSE

Shiloh Walker

Copyright

A Special Thank You

This book was made possible through the help of numerous patrons via my Patreon.
I want to thank all of them...thanks for sticking with me, and for believing in me.

Special thanks:
Samantha & Tricia for being my top tier sponsors.
And to Natalie for her generous sponsorship.

Additionally:
Mikaela had her name drawn to be included in the work, so...
THANK YOU!

And, last but not least,
a huge thank you to my patrons:

My Patrons

Samantha Anne Karp Hauser
Tricia M.
Natalie H.
A.J. Morrison
Anna Mae N
Candice
Carla
Cecilia R.
Clare
Debbie L.
Diana S.
Farah
Heather
Holly C.
Jill Brown T.
Julia F
Kathy D
Kerry
Larry Omans
Maggie Walker
Nicole
Noelle A.
Roger S.
S. Kayne
Serena M.
Suzanne C.
Tantris
Thaois G
Tracy F

Acknowledgements

I'd like to thank Kim from Salt & Sage Books for offering her insights on Tia's character and that of the children she teaches. Your help was so appreciated... and thanks to Erin for reaching out.

To Pam, AKA the WONDEROUS one, my long-time editor.

And to Angela Waters for such a gorgeous cover and for always working with me.

Dedication

Although it's going to be a long time (possibly never, and I'm okay with that) before he reads this, my nephew K helped inspire a number of things about this story, including Tia's occupation.
So, while he isn't going to read this any time soon (MAYBE EVER) ... this book is in part dedicated to K.
You are one of the loves of my life, little man.
Every time I think of you, you make me smile.

And although I haven't told her, bits and pieces of Tia's character from some of her physical features to her outspokenness were inspired by my niece, A.

She probably WILL read this. Yikes.

You're also one of the loves of my life, sweetheart.

Love and adore you. Keep writing.

Warning

This isn't a snuggly, comfy read. The male MC is hired killer, while the heroine is neuro-atypical. Some dark material is involved—the hero kidnaps the heroine. There's also violence when he goes on a rampage against those who put a contract on her. Also references of abuse (not against the heroine). Also very graphic, erotic scenes with minor bondage play.

Prologue

Hot blood gushed out under his hand as he collapsed against a wall. Meric Bach tried to find the energy to push himself upright, but he was fucking tired and the adrenaline that had fueled him for the past forty-eight hours was gone. It was as if all the epinephrine had pumped out along with the blood. He felt cold and he knew enough to know that was bad. He'd never been hurt this severely before, but cold wasn't a good sign.

Especially since it was July in Los Angeles and he'd been running for his life for more than thirty minutes.

Had he lost them?

Noise at the mouth of the alley caught his attention. Almost afraid to look, he clutched his weapon and squeezed his eyes closed in an attempt to clear them. It worked...briefly. When he lifted his lids, the dots dancing at the edge of his vision had eased and he darted one quick glance toward the source of the voice he'd heard.

Low and soothing, rich, the kind of voice he'd heard coming out of dive bars and even some of the fancier ones that he'd once been forced to visit with his father. Meric had come to dread the sound of music, because showing up at a bar rarely turned out well for him. He never knew what kind of sick shit that old bastard had planned for him when they went to 'visit' a friend.

Still, this voice didn't send prickles of warning down his spine or give him the urge to run. Maybe he was too close to dying for that. He didn't know. The voice drew nearer.

Meric tightened his grip on the pistol, the Sig Sauer P220 he'd stolen from his father. The man was dead now. Maybe that meant the weapon was his anyway. Could he inherit his father's shit even though he'd murdered the man? Even though almost everything his father had owned had been obtained illegally?

Focus! His father's voice, harsh and angry, always angry, barked at him from the farthest edges of his mind. *Your inability to concentrate will get you killed. You are useless, boy! Worthless!*

"You are dead, *arschgesicht*," Meric said without realizing he'd spoken the words aloud.

"No, son, I'm not. But if you don't get some help, I think you're going to be, and soon."

Meric jolted at the sound of the man's voice—the speaker he'd heard. The one with the low, musical voice. Wheeling his head around, he stared at the big black man in front of him. "Get it over with, *mistkerl*."

"*Mistkerl*, huh?" The man cocked his head, then, without warning, broke into perfect, flawless German.

Meric blinked, dazed. "Why does some American *afterlecker* from an LA gang speak German?"

"I could ask why you, an American kid, keeps insulting me in perfect German, or are you a German kid who speaks perfect English?" His gaze dropped. "More to the point, why are we standing here while you're bleeding and weaving on your feet? Let's go get you some help."

He took a step toward Meric.

Meric lifted the gun, a sudden influx of adrenaline lending him strength.

"Whoa." The man paused, holding up his hands. "Easy there. Easy, kid."

"Why are you fucking with me? Do it already."

Impossibly, the man's eyes went...

Meric frowned, because he couldn't identify it. He'd only ever seen cruelty, lust, anger...emptiness.

This big man with his broad face and broad shoulders and large hands had none of that in his eyes. In fact, if Meric had allowed himself to do so, he would almost have thought there was...gentleness. He'd experienced gentleness once, when he'd found a skinny, hungry young dog. He'd brought it home with him. Two days later, his father had found it and broke its neck in front of Meric. But in those two days, for that short period of time, Meric and the dog had each other and the dog had gazed at him with wide, soft eyes. It had been a stupid mutt, but a kind one.

This man's eyes had that same gentleness. But unlike that sweet, innocent, helpless dog, this man wasn't stupid.

"You're not with them, are you?"

"I'm not part of any gang, if that's what you're asking. Come on. I want to help. Let me take you to the hospital."

"No." Meric reversed the Sig, pressed it to the underside of his chin. "No. If I go to the hospital, I'm dead. I'm dead anyway."

Meric never saw the man move. One moment, he held the gun. The next...the man held him, pinned against his body and Meric no longer had the weapon. The feel of somebody bigger and stronger than him stirred dark, ugly memories.

"No..." Instinct took over and he panicked, driving his elbow back into a hard gut, then he drove his heel down on a vulnerable instep. Or it would have been vulnerable. Thick boots protected fragile bones. The panic screamed louder. "No..."

"Relax, kid. I won't hurt you. Fuck, son, somebody did a number on you. Relax."

Meric couldn't. He'd die first.

A thick, powerful arm clamped around his neck. Once more, blackness edged in. Just before he went under, he heard the man saying, "Sorry, son. This is the last thing you need."

* * * * *

There were certain constants in Meric's life. Things like a hard, lumpy mattress, waking to darkness, usually with the air too tight and close. He'd grown used to the hard knot of hunger in his belly and had even accustomed himself to sleeping when it was far too hot or far too cold. Rest was never easy to come by so it was crucial to sleep whenever possible. Stale air, foul smells, sirens wailing in the streets nearby— none of that fazed him.

He came awake in the blink of an eye, immediately on edge because *none* of that was present.

Instead of sirens, he heard seagulls.

Instead of the mold and damp of the hotel where he'd been crashing, he smelled the tang of salt air...and bacon. *Frying* bacon. And coffee.

His belly rumbled.

He went to cover the incriminating sound with his hand and encountered the thick, heavy padding of a bandage.

"It's about time you woke up."

The sound of that voice had him flinching and immediately he rolled out of bed, eyes searching for a weapon.

As the big man came around the edge of a wall, Meric braced himself. He had no weapon, nothing but his fists. There was a lamp on the table, but it didn't look heavy enough to do damage. Still—

"Your Sig's in the dresser drawer." The big man nodded to the simple, utilitarian stand by the bed. "You look better."

Meric snarled instinctively. "Where the fuck am I, and who the fuck are you?"

The big man cracked a smile. "You can call me Sarge. You got a name?"

"No."

"Your name's *No*?" Sarge's teeth flashed white against his skin. "Seems like a mean thing to do to a

6

kid. *No, don't do that. No, you can have some cookies.*"

The thought of his father giving Meric permission to have cookies was laughable. Only he didn't laugh. Meric stared at this man who'd told him to call him Sarge.

Sarge sighed and gestured to the dresser once more. "Like I said, your weapon is in there. It's not loaded. Magazine's next to it."

"Stupid of you," Meric said, curling his lip. "Leaving my gun where I can load it and shoot you."

"Well, I'm not seeing where you benefit from shooting the man who got you out of LA before the Crips got their hands on you." His brows rose over eyes that were a soft, translucent amber against deep-brown skin. "That is who you were running from, isn't it, kid?"

Meric said nothing.

"Hard to believe, kid like you taking out the head of a gang like that. How old are you? Sixteen? Can't be much older. What did you use? Wasn't the Sig. It's a fine weapon—you've taken care of it. But it don't have that kind of range. Last I heard, they're thinking Alfonse Jordan was taken out at a range of about five hundred yards. Cops found a spot that might have been where the sniper took him out. And the weapon. No prints, though."

He looked Meric up and down skeptically and gave a half laugh. "If it wasn't for the rumors I heard while I was doing what needed to be done to get you out of the city, I never would have believed it. Still not entirely sure I do. You're tall enough and you got serious muscle on you, but you're skinny as hell. And you took a man out at five hundred yards. At night."

"It isn't complicated if you know what you are doing," Meric said, annoyed by the dismissive tone.

"That a fact?" He rocked back on his heels and crossed massive arms over his chest. The pose caused his biceps to bulge.

Meric couldn't help but think how easily the man could crush him.

"Heard another rumor. Another sniper went down a few days ago. A close-quarters kill. Guy was something of a ghost. Worked as a mercenary after he was kicked out of the German Army for...authority issues." He narrowed his eyes on Meric. "Any of this ringing a bell?"

Much of it did not, but none of it surprised Meric. He remained silent.

Sarge sighed. "This man...his fingerprints ID him as Walter Kramer, German citizen, wanted by his country and a shitload of others for various crimes. His ID pegs him as an American, but the social security number, the birth certificate? Fakes." He shrugged. "Good fakes, according to my contact, but fakes, all the same. Kramer was something of a legend, though. As I said. Top-notch sniper, handy with bombs, and explosives, too. Not very picky about who he took out. Mean son of a bitch. Then he gets taken out in his fuckin' hotel room. You know anything about that...Meric?"

A cold fist of terror gripped the young man's insides, squeezing, squeezing...turning his bowels to liquid and his knees to putty. "What do you want?"

"Right now?" Sarge shrugged. "I want a plate of that bacon I finished frying up, some eggs, and coffee. I bet you wouldn't mind the same. Then we can talk."

Without saying another word, Sarge turned his back on Meric and walked out.

* * * * *

The walls were curved and looked like stone under a coat of somewhat fresh whitewashing. Peering up at the tall, round barrel of the building, Meric tried once more to make sense of what was going on, but as with each previous attempt, he failed.

Edging forward to the wrought iron railing, he peered over and looked down, spying a door that led outside. It had to. The light falling through was too bright to be anything but the sun.

Licking his lips, he gauged the distance, and his strength.

Could he make it before Sarge figured out what he was doing?

No, weakling. You can't. The voice of his father, although not welcome, wasn't incorrect.

He'd seen Sarge move. The man was big, powerful and fast.

Meric was still recovering from an injury and while he was fast, his strength was only a fraction of that of the man who'd brought him here.

Caged animals learned certain lessons—when to eat, when to rest, when to bide their time.

Meric had lived most of his life as a caged animal. He wasn't as strong as he needed to be to flee or fight. Unless he had no other choice, the best thing for him to do was to wait—wait, bide his time, grow strong. Then he'd strike.

"Decided to join me, I see." Sarge swung him a pragmatic look, one that made Meric think the other man saw see clear through him.

"I want some coffee." Meric gave the big man a belligerent look, pleased his voice sounded flat and emotionless, like his father's would have. No sooner had he thought of the mean fucker who'd fathered him than he found himself thinking about what Sarge had said—German citizen. Sniper. Handy with bombs. Wanted by the authorities in Germany and in other countries. Meric had never questioned his father about the numerous false identities, or the countless escape routes he'd been made to memorize every time the old bastard dragged him into a job. That had simply been his life. But he wasn't surprised to learn this information about his father, either.

"Just coffee, huh?"

The speculation in Sarge's voice pissed him off.

"Just coffee."

"Okay, okay." The big man held up his hands, then poured a cup of the steaming brew and set it in front of Meric. "Sugar or cream? I make it strong."

"No." He took a sip and instantly regretted it. *Strong* didn't quite define the potency of what he had just taken in. But he wouldn't relent and ask for something to smooth the way either.

Sarge whistled easily as he plated up a serving of breakfast and put it down in front of the chair opposite where Meric sat. Then he slid the rest of the bacon onto a plate with the two remaining eggs. Meric almost said something, but a memory of his father throwing away food in front of him loomed in his mind and he bit his tongue. Maybe if he didn't say anything, he could creep back in here later and grab a bite. The son of a bitch would probably make him clean up anyway. If that was the case, he could eat every fucking thing he found, couldn't he?

Sarge put the second plate down, tantalizingly close to where Meric sat and gave him a shrug. "Sorry, kid. Table's not that big. It's only me here." His pale amber eyes gleamed. "Well, usually. Don't mind the company, though."

Meric didn't respond as he drank his coffee and did what he could to study his surroundings.

From what he could tell, they were on the second level of the building—one that was constructed to be *round*. He didn't have much reference but he had the impression the structure was big, too. He was dying of curiosity but kept the questions behind his teeth. It was either that or lose his teeth—a lesson he'd learned early in life.

"It's an old lighthouse."

Meric shot Sarge a look.

"That's what you were wondering about, right?" Sarge grabbed a piece of bacon and crunched into it, chewing slowly and with obvious pleasure. He took the time to enjoy a second bite before continuing. "You can ask me anything you want to know. I don't mind. If it's something I don't want to talk about, I'll just tell you I won't answer. But there's no harm in asking."

Meric snorted and looked away, not fooled by the obvious bullshit.

"Anyway, it's not used anymore. There's a bigger, more advanced one close by. We're a few miles north of Gloucester, Massachusetts. My dad, his dad, his people have been running this place..." He paused and blew out a breath, skimming a hand back over his short, bristly head of hair. "Well, one of my great, great grandfathers—missing a great, great, probably, he was an escaped slave. Old John made it all the way up here to Gloucester around about 1824, long before the Civil War. The lighthouse keeper was Timothy Austin. He was a Quaker—their kind didn't hold with slavery, you know. Anyway, my several-times great-grandfather ended up being taken in by Austin. That old man was getting on in years, didn't have a family or anything. When he passed, he left the place to my ancestor. Been in the family ever since. We've been running it for years, right up until it was decided that a more efficient system was needed. My grandfather was lucky enough to know people with the right connections. Gramps bought this place before it even went on the market. It's been home to my family for generations."

Meric swung his head around and looked at Sarge. "Fascinating."

"Kid, you've got a game face that trumps men twice your age." Sarge started to laugh and smacked his thigh.

When Meric didn't share his amusement, Sarge's laughter faded and his smile was replaced by a frown. "Of course, maybe I shouldn't be so amused by it. I got a feeling it was a shitty life that made somebody as young as you so hard." He took another piece of bacon and demolished it. "Man, there is nothing like fried, fatty pig. You get me?"

Meric stared so hard at the crispy, golden brown piece of pork in Sarge's hand, his eyes unfocused. Jerking his head away, he blinked and forced his gaze to his coffee. "Whatever."

When he lowered it, the plate of food looked like it had been nudged closer.

Sarge was shoveling a bite of egg into his mouth. He caught Meric glaring at him and paused. "What? Do I have food on my face?"

Meric started to answer, then stopped. "It's nothing." Determinedly, he looked away, staring out the window in the curve of the wall past Sarge's shoulder. He thought he could make out a couple of inches of water.

And the sound...closing his eyes, he heard a rhythmic, rushing noise that was oddly...soothing.

No, he told himself. It *wasn't* soothing. Nothing about this shit was soothing. He needed to take in his surroundings and get out—and *not* find anything about the place remotely soothing.

The sounds of eating continued, not obnoxiously loud, but it was hard to miss the quiet rasp of a metal fork over a plate, the crunch of bacon. Paired with the rhythmic sounds of water, it was almost...peaceful.

Meric banished the thought, again and sipped his coffee, determined to make it last. If he drank it slowly enough, he could fool his belly into thinking he'd eaten something.

"You sure you don't want any of that?"

He glanced at Sarge and saw him pointing at the plate that sat a few inches from him. His belly gave a demanding gurgle. Face going red, he looked from the plate to Sarge, then dropped his eyes to study the empty plate now sitting in front of Sarge.

"I mean, if you're happy with coffee, that's fine. I

don't want to be greedy or anything, but if you're not going to eat it..." Sarge went to reach for it.

Meric didn't realize what he was doing until the tines of the fork narrowly missed Sarge's hand.

"Well. Okay."

Sarge gave him a measuring look as he leaned back in his seat, watching Meric as he started to eat.

A few minutes later, Meric's plate was empty.

Then another plate, laden with more eggs and two pieces of toast was placed in front of him.

He didn't question it, just started to eat.

His belly hurt by the time he was done. A cup was put at his elbow. He sniffed, caught a spicy scent.

"Ginger tea. Might help to drink it, unless you want a bellyache from all that food you put away."

He was thirsty, so he didn't argue.

When he was done with the cup, he finally looked at Sarge. "What do you want?"

"Who said I wanted anything?"

Meric snorted. "You didn't keep me alive, then feed me out of the goodness of your heart." He spat on the floor and muttered under his breath.

"Look..." Sarge sighed, giving the spittle on the floor a disgusted look. "First, I get you not trusting me. In your place, I wouldn't trust me either, but can you not spit on my floor?"

Meric's ears went red, then redder still as Sarge got up and grabbed a paper towel from the roll over the sink, wetting it, then coming over and kneeling on the floor a few feet from where Meric sat. *Stupid*, he thought. He could so easily attack. Kick him, strike the man. Right in the head, stun him, then attack.

Then Sarge looked up, gave him a flat look. "Don't try it."

Meric tensed, then forced his muscles to relax. "Don't try what?"

Sarge shook his head and finished his task before rising and tossing the paper towel into a trash can on the far side of the room. He washed his hands, turning his back to Meric—again, *stupid*. When he turned, he gave Meric a look that let him know he'd been quite aware of what Meric was thinking. He returned to his seat and sat down, annoyance still on his face. "Now...*second*...I don't want jack shit. I saw a hurting kid and decided to help. That's all there is to it."

"Bullshit—"

Sarge held up a hand as Meric went to spit again. "You spit on my floor again, son, you and me are going to have a problem."

Meric smirked.

Staring Sarge straight in the eye, he leaned over and spit on the spit on the floor.

Sarge sighed and lifted his gaze heavenward. He got up and gave the spittle on the floor a long look, then studied Meric. "I've got lasagna on the menu for dinner. Normally, I don't make guests clean up, but for that..." He pointed at the small, shiny little pool of fluid. "If you want to eat anything but peanut butter for dinner, you'll clean the entire fucking kitchen *and* that mess."

He walked out.

Meric smirked. Sure, the man was planning on making lasagna. And, yeah, sure, Meric was planning on *staying.*

Chapter 1

M oney wasn't the deciding factor when I took a job, but with some of them, if the payout wasn't adequate, I wouldn't touch them with a grenade launcher. It wasn't worth the hassle.

Right now, my current job was proving to be a shit show and, with every passing second, I was starting to think I needed to ignore my client's next call when it came, burn the phone and forget the whole mess.

The only thing keeping me from doing that was curiosity. Curiosity and boredom. Neither of those were good motivators, but I'd spent the past few months lazing on the beach in Cancun, with the odd, occasional, self-chosen target to alleviate the boredom.

I was ready to get back to the job.

So far, though, I had yet to see anything in eastern Tennessee that could possibly warrant my presence, although looks could be deceiving.

I was a prime example of that. To the casual observer—or even a trained one—I looked like a man in his late twenties or early thirties enjoying a day in a popular tourist destination, a backpack with moderately expensive and well-used photography equipment stowed inside. If somebody were to take a look—say law enforcement—they'd find that the Canon EOS 5D Mark IV's SD card already held several hundred pictures, mostly of scenery,

but there were other shots for variety. All three of the lenses showed signs of use, and I could detail which one was ideal for each shot. I'd initially started carrying a camera because it was a useful explanation if I was ever caught walking into odd places, but over the past decade, I'd develop a passing interest. One could even say it was a hobby, although I simply considered it a useful deception.

Paired with the casual clothing, stylishly overlong hair visible under the baseball cap and a pair of battered boots, I sipped my coffee and looked over a map as though searching for a prime hiking trail in the nearby national park.

My contact should have called ten minutes ago. If I didn't hear from him soon, I'd leave. So far, all this had cost me was time and the plane ticket, but the fat piles of money I had stowed in various banks, both in America and outside of it, made the cost of the ticket negligible. The client had offered to take care of travel, but that was a hard no.

Taking another sip of coffee, I glanced down the walkway, first left, then right, before using the sparkling pane of glass in front of me to survey the street. I'd finished my check and was looking at the time when somebody approached.

I took in everything about him out of habit and wrote him off as a nonentity. Not a threat, not a contact, not a problem.

The man settled on the bench next to me, heaving out a tired sigh before glancing at me. "Waiting on the wife?"

I gave him an affable smile even as I gave my surroundings another look then went back to looking over the map.

My companion spoke again, drawing my attention once more.

"Come here every year," the older man said, waving a hand toward the shopping center off to our right. He looked to be in his forties, overweight in the way a desk worker might be, with a friendly smile and thinning black hair. He had smile lines fanning out from his face and they deepened as he grinned at me. "You'd think I'd be used to the fact that she wants to drag me into every damn store. I could have stayed at the cabin and watched TV but here I am."

"Married life," I said, playing the part. I did that easily. I'd even put a gold wedding band on my hand prior to boarding my flight. It helped curtail flirtations and was another way to throw people off. Just another part of the role I played in life.

"You got it." He aimed a finger at me, gunman style and laughed, a deep-belly sound of rich amusement that seemed a little too much for such a simple comment, in my opinion, but I'd come to learn that there were simple people out there who were able to laugh at the smallest things. It puzzled me, but many things in life did. I'd stopped questioning those things, because the answers always eluded me. "You and the missus thinking about going on a hike?"

"I am." It caused a ripple of dark amusement to think about a nonexistent wife so the smile I gave was genuine. "She doesn't care for the outdoors unless she's enjoying them from the comfort of the passenger's seat. I'll just have her drop me off at the park."

The phone in my hand finally buzzed. I gave my companion a nod and rose, pacing a few steps down and putting my back to a wall as I opened the secure calling app, as well as another, one I'd specifically designed myself. It altered my voice so that no known software could use it for a voice match, assuming any of my possible employers were stupid enough to try. "You're late."

"Spectre!" The jovial voice came over the line, irritating me in a way the overweight tourist never could. "I had some business matters to attend to...you understand these things."

"I understand that you told me you'd call at 10:15. It's almost half past. The sort of work I provide requires accuracy at all levels. If you can't manage to contact me at the proper time, can I trust you to be accurate on other levels?"

A couple of young women went by and one of them

shot me a flirtatious look. I ignored it as I listened to the change in the breathing pattern on the other end of the line.

"I'm a busy man, Spectre."

"I know you are...Tommy." Dead silence. I couldn't help but smile. "I'll give you credit. Whoever handles your tech and security is decent. I'm better."

"I'm not amused," Tommy O'Halloran said, his voice tight.

"I didn't expect you would be." The leader of the Irish Mafia in Boston wasn't a man known for his sense of humor.

He'd taken over from his father at a young age, just six years ago, when his father suffered an abrupt, fatal heart attack. He'd only been twenty-four at the time. From what I could tell, some men in the organization didn't think he was ready for it. Tommy had taken the reins of control with brutal hands and swiftly silenced all dissenters. Humor wouldn't serve him. Shifting my stance, I braced a foot on the wall behind me as I gave the perimeter another slow look. "But I don't take jobs without knowing who I'm working for. That was made clear in the initial contact."

"You haven't agreed to *take* the job yet. This invasion of my privacy doesn't engender trust, Spectre."

"Then we can end this discussion now. You found me. I'm sure you can unearth other possibilities." I lowered the phone.

"Wait." Tommy's voice came out in a rough growl. "All right."

"The payout for this job is substantial."

"You already mentioned that. What is substantial, in your mind?" A cute brunette went bustling past me, laden with bags and I watched as she dropped down onto the bench I'd vacated, grinning at the man there. She leaned over and kissed his cheek before brandishing the bags. He looked at them with a wince. Calculating how much she'd spent, I decided. But then he leaned in and kissed her.

Human interaction could be fascinating.

"I'll transfer five hundred thousand in Bitcoin to you just for assessing the job. If you accept it, I'll send another five hundred thousand. Complete it in the manner I request and I'll send another million."

As the couple on the bench got up and wandered off, I blinked slowly, processing what Tommy O'Halloran had told me. "You're offering two for the job."

"It's an important job. And I need it completed soon. Within the next ten days."

Mind furiously working, I flipped through my mental file of everything I had learned about the O'Halloran family and could figure out only one issue important enough to warrant this level of urgency from Tommy.

"Does this have anything to do with your brother?"

"You seem to have a great deal of interest in my family," Tommy said in a testy voice.

"I don't have any interest. I simply believe in being thorough and taking all angles into consideration. And you haven't answered me."

"What the fuck does it matter? I'm offering two million on what will be one easy fucking job. Are you interested in *that*, at least?" Sarcasm punctuated his every word.

"My curiosity is piqued, but if it's so easy, why hasn't one of your men handled it?"

He didn't want to answer. I could all but hear the mental debate going on, but finally, he said, "The job can't be traced back to me in any way. My men are skilled, but they lack your level of skill. Your reputation, even your name, is all based on your ability to move in and out without being noticed. Rumor is, nobody even knows what you look like." He paused for a beat, then asked, "Is that true, Spectre? Has anybody ever even seen your face?"

A toddler, dressed in jeans and a bright-pink shirt with a bear cub on it, headed toward me, chasing a ball that had escaped her hands. Carefully, I caught it with my foot and nudged it back in her direction. She beamed at me and squeaked out, "*Baaw!*"

I translated it to mean, "*Ball.*"

"Somebody is looking at me right now, Tommy."

He grunted. "Look, I don't have time for this dicking around. Are you going to take the job?"

"You haven't given me details yet. I don't take jobs without knowing the specifics."

"You're as big an asshole to work with as people say. I'll text you an address. When you get there, let me know."

Chapter 2

"**I**t doesn't look like yours." A serious face lifted toward mine as I stopped at the table.

"It's not supposed to, Annie. Can I touch your shoulder?"

She frowned at me, considering the request. Finally, she nodded. "But if I don't like it, you have to stop."

"Deal." I rested my hand on her shoulder and eased in a bit closer, but not enough to invade her personal space.

Rhiannon Haggard, or Annie as she liked to be called, was older than some of my students, and hadn't been diagnosed until she was ten. She was fiercely smart and judging by the work on her canvas, she had a definite artistic talent, even if she wasn't pleased with how the piece was progressing.

Gently, I rubbed her shoulder as I gestured at the painting with my other hand. "Your piece shouldn't look like mine. It's your painting. It's supposed to reflect something about you. My painting reflects something about me. We're different people so why should our paintings look the same?"

"If this painting reflects me, then I'm a mess." Her round face—pretty, young and sweet—was dominated by her big eyes and an unsmiling mouth.

The lack of a smile didn't concern me. I couldn't even count how many times I'd been told to *smile* as a child, or had a teacher or other well-meaning adult ask why I was upset, all because I wasn't smiling. The smiles and reactions I saw from others had always confused me but by middle school, I knew I was the one who was different and I'd made an attempt—sometimes—to mimic those around me. It didn't take long to learn those little expressions led to fewer interactions from people who felt they should ask what was wrong... or just idiots who felt the need to tell a kid to smile for no reason.

I'd spent so much of my childhood trying to figure out what was wrong with me, then, later, I'd faked being normal, and it had been *so* exhausting. *Too* exhausting, at times.

Annie had been diagnosed a little later than some of my kids, but she had parents who loved her and were working to help her get the tools she needed.

I hoped she wouldn't have the same struggles I'd had—most of these kids wouldn't. I was glad they wouldn't always be wondering what was wrong with them, if they were broken.

I think *most* of the kids who attended my workshops already knew they *weren't* broken, that nothing was wrong with them, although I always reinforced it. I envied my kids a bit in that aspect. That reassurance was something I hadn't had until I almost an adult.

"You're not a mess," I told Annie as I gave her shoulder one last rub. She had sort of leaned into it, which I took as a positive sign. "You told me yourself that you hadn't done much painting before. You just need practice. Think about it—I didn't pick up a paint brush until I was fifteen. You're younger than I was."

Annie thought that over, then gave me a solemn nod. "So if I practice, when I'm older, I'll be even better than you are."

At that, I did smile, and Annie cocked her head to the side, studying me. I understood that well enough.

I was still trying to figure out people.

This thing I was doing—using art to help kids on the autism spectrum—could be completely draining. But when I got too tired, I made myself remember how it had been when that teacher put a canvas in front of me my freshman year of high school. I'd been behind, as always, struggling, as always, ostracized and alienated. Until she'd taken the time to help me find who I was.

"You just might," I told her, with a wink.

"I will be," Annie said with a decisive nod before turning back to her painting of a forest. Now that she realized she didn't need to try to copy mine, some of the tension relaxed from her shoulders and I moved on to the next student.

Even though I always made it clear that I wanted them to make something that was their own, there was inevitably a student or two who tried to paint as I had. But in today's class, it was just Alli. My second trip by her station showed the forest to be taking on its own life and I found myself pleased with the development. Judging by the gleam in her eyes, she was, too.

"Your mom and dad will be proud," I told her.

She considered the words. "Maybe. They want me to be normal."

My heart clenched at her words. How many times had *I* heard comments about shit like that?

Why can't you be normal?

Why are you so weird?

Even from my own mother, although God knows she had been *nobody's* picture of normal. And I'd loved her anyway. Even though parts of me still hated her.

Pushing old hurts and my anger aside, I thought of the couple who'd brought Annie in, of the conversations I'd had with her mother. "Your parents love you, Alli. They want what's best for you."

She didn't answer as she bent her head to her work.

I moved over to D'Shawn, a boisterous boy of nine who took my workshop once every couple of months. If his parents could afford it, he'd be there every week. He loved painting, and according to his mom, he might have a crush on me. He had high-functioning autism and was far more affectionate than many of the kids I worked with.

In some ways, he'd actually helped me because he always wanted hugs when he came in, but at the same time, we had to work with him, because he needed to learn the rules about personal space, not only with others in the workshop but in general.

"Ah...the Millennium Falcon." I wasn't surprised he'd deviated from the project I'd suggested, and it had just been a suggestion.

D'Shawn walked to the beat of his own drum in so many ways.

"The Millennium Falcon!" D'Shawn pumped a fist in the air and laughed. Small for his age, he sat on his knees on his chair as he wielded his paintbrush, eyes narrowed as he carefully finished one area of the famous spaceship. "Who is stronger? Luke Skywalker or Rey?"

"Oh, no, my friend. I'm not having this talk while class in going on."

"I think Luke is stronger. He's a lot older and—"

Carefully, I backed away, hands upraised. "Not here."

"Luke is way stronger," a quiet boy in front of D'Shawn said. "The Last Jedi was stupid. Rey hasn't even been trained. She's a dumb girl."

"That's it," I said firmly, moving to the front of the room. "Remember the rules for staying in my class. We show each other respect. No name calling."

The boy in question, Matthew King, frowned. "Rey's not even real. What does it matter if I say she's dumb?"

"There are females in this room who *are* real. Part of life is learning to respect the feelings of others. The way you say it, it's like the reason Rey's not strong is because she's a girl," I pointed out to him, wondering if I should let this go. But this was one of the lessons I wanted these kids to learn—the rules about respect and trying to think about others.

It had been be hard for me, learning those rules on

my own, never understanding why people either laugher at me or avoided me or just *stared* at me like I was wrong or broken. I wanted to help kids, kids like I'd been, so they didn't have to feel like I had.

"If you want to make a case that Rey wasn't a very good Jedi, you need to come up with something other than her being *a dumb girl*."

"She is a dumb girl." Matthew folded his face into stubborn lines. "She's a fake dumb girl, but she's still dumb. Girls *are* dumb. The reason my dad left is because my mom is dumb. She's a girl."

My face heated slightly and discomfort rose inside me, but I pushed it down. The kids in front of me were also uncomfortable and the girls, especially, were upset. Annie rocked slightly in her chair, while the youngest student in class, Andrea, sat in her seat and hunched over, arms wrapped tightly around herself. It was as if she wanted to shrink down so small, she disappeared.

"Maybe the reason your dad left was because you're dumb," D'Shawn said into the quiet of the room.

Matthew's face went red.

I lunged forward but if he hadn't tripped on his chair, I wouldn't have caught him in time. Panic was a bubble in my chest, one threatening to explode. I locked on D'Shawn's wide, startled eyes and used that to ground myself.

"Calm down, Matthew," I said. "Calm down."

Matthew, of course, wasn't in the mood to listen.

* * * * *

"What in the fuck do you mean he won't be able to come back? We paid $150 for this and he's only been here three days!"

Matthew sat on the ground next to his mother's car, rocking and humming to himself. His mother alternated between giving him concerned looks and fighting back tears, but at her husband's words—she stiffened. "*I* paid the fee, Matt. You didn't want to even bother with this, so don't act like you're out anything except the time it took you to come down here."

He turned on her and once more, that bubble of panic swelled in my chest. I wanted to lock myself in my studio, close the blinds, curl up on the big beanbag chair, and hide. Instead, I squared my shoulders. "Mr. King, Ms. King, this sounds like a personal matter between you and something that would best be discussed where it won't further upset your son."

"He's upset because you're kicking him out of the stupid workshop!" Mr. King whirled on me and jabbed a finger in my direction. "If you're kicking him out, we want the money back."

"There are no refunds once the student starts the class." Folding my arms over my chest, I stared at him. "Supplies have to be purchased and other costs factor in. I understand some children may have behavioral issues and I make accommodations with those families. I offer one-on-one classes for kids who don't work as well in groups with others. But it's included in the workshop terms that money won't be refunded if a child is removed due to violent behavior. Your son attempted to attack another student and before that, he was being disrespectful. I gave him several chances and he persisted. This decision is final."

He took a step closer, using his greater height to loom over me. My brain kicked on, listing all the psychological factors behind why men like him did things like this but it was still hard to stand my ground. "You are not going to cheat us out of our hard-earned money—"

"It's not *our* money," his wife said, grabbing his arm.

He spun on her.

I'd been holding my phone since he climbed out of the truck, eyes wide and angry, clearly looking for a fight. Now, as he knocked her hand away, I hit the *dial* button. I'd never had to call 9-1-1 on a parent before and I didn't want to do it now, but what if I didn't and he hurt her, or me, or—

The voice on the other end of the line cut off the mad ramble of my thoughts, thankfully. "*Nine-one-one, what's your emergency?*"

Sensing the man's attention turn to me, I rapidly gave my name and address. "I have an angry client here and would appreciate it if you sent somebody out."

"What the fuck are you doing, bitch!"

A car pulled into the drive. I recognized Annie's parents and relief now vied with panic for control.

"Ma'am, I'm notifying patrolmen in the area. Please stay on the line."

Matthew's father pointed a finger at my nose. "You stupid c—"

"What's the problem here?" Annie's father came huffing in our direction, his friendly face creased with concern, while his wife came at a slower pace, looking at King with distaste before shifting her gaze up to my house where Annie still waited with D'Shawn.

"Nothing, man," King said, looking over at Paul Haggard with a friendly smile that was a sharp one-eighty from the look he'd given me. "Just a little misunderstanding. Ms. Jenkins was explaining that she'll be sending us a refund since the program didn't work out for our boy, Matthew."

"No, I wasn't," I retorted, my cheeks heating even as anger and nerves vied for control.

King's gaze bounced over to me, narrowing.

I met his gaze. "If you think manipulating me in front of another parent will make me do what you want, you're wrong."

On the other end of the phone, the woman's voice softened, "Ma'am, is everything okay? A patrol unit is less than five minutes away."

"I'm fine," I said, even though I really wasn't. There was too much going on and trying to maintain an air of calm was taking everything I had.

"Are you sure?" the question came from Annie's mom, Mikaela, not the woman on the phone. Her gaze flicked between me and the Kings, mouth tightening slightly as she looked over at the father before sympathy made her eyes soften as she looked at the distraught boy.

"I'm fine, Mikaela. Thank you." The ache in my chest eased somewhat at her concern, and at the presence of the woman on the line who continued to murmur to me reassuringly. "The police are on their way out, too."

"There's no reason for the damn cops—" King snapped.

"I think you should leave," Paul said.

King puffed up his chest, glowering at the shorter, stouter man but Paul didn't back down an inch.

"Mikaela, I'll wait with Ms. Jenkins but why don't you go on up there and sit with Annie and that other kid? They look pretty upset." He smiled in his wife's direction but stayed at my side. "Ms. Jenkins and I have this under control, right, ma'am?"

I nodded at the clear question in his words, thankful beyond words for his kindness.

"Matt, you need to go," Ms. King said, sounding exhausted. She gave me an embarrassed look before moving over to crouch in front of her son.

My heart hurt for both the boy and his mom. She'd mentioned in her initial emails to me that she was in the midst of an ugly custody battle. I hoped like hell she won, because that man was toxic. Matthew clearly adored him, although I had no idea why. As his mom tried to talk to him, Matthew's rocking became faster and faster.

"Looks like the cavalry is here," Paul said.

Both King and I looked up and followed the other

man's gaze to the bend in the road where a cruiser had just appeared. King gave me a dirty look, then turned on his heel. Without saying a word to his son, he stormed over to his truck and climbed in.

"What a fucking asshole," I muttered without thinking about it.

"You can say that again," Paul said.

At the wealth of emotion in his voice, I found myself smiling. Looking over at him, I said, "Thank you. So much."

He blushed.

Chapter 3

The address I'd been given was on a winding road that would eventually meander through the Smoky Mountain National Park. It was dotted with a mix of residential homes and rental cabins. Some of the homes looked like a stiff wind might blow them off, while others likely cost in the high six figures, minimum.

All he'd provided was an address with instructions to text once I'd arrived.

His secrecy wasn't helping his case. I'd been there nearly an hour, waiting, going through the information packet he'd finally uploaded to a secure account. The taste in my mouth had gone from bad to worse with every passing minute.

Even before she came out of the cabin, I'd already made my decision, but the sight of her kept me locked in place. Or...well, it kept me from leaving.

I'd been doing this too long to be caught doing something so obvious as staring. I'd brought out a camera and set up like I was taking pictures of an empty stretch of land at the end of the road, using that cover to get in various angles of the entire area.

Through the lens of the camera, I was able to get the occasional look at her face and something about her features kept tugging my attention back to her. She was pretty, of course. But I'd had my share of women, ranging from homely to plain to attractive to beautiful. It wasn't her looks, or rather, it wasn't *just* her looks.

She had a jaw that was both strong and elegant and it was set in a firm line as she moved down the driveway to speak to a big, broad man who stood there yelling and gesticulating.

Other than a faint flicker of her eyes, which I caught through the high-powered camera lens, there was no reaction.

I frowned as the overweight tourist from town pulled up, both him and his wife climbing out of their car. The round guy went to the side of my would-be target, while his wife headed up to the house. I looked away, shooting a few more shots of the land and the neighboring trees, before casually looking back to see the woman sitting down next to a girl with hair the same rich, dark brown. There were other kids, too. I had noticed the unhappy one sitting on the ground by the vehicles in the large, double-wide driveway and two more had left since the woman had come out, urging the unhappy kid along in front of her.

When she put her phone to her ear, I grimaced because there was only one logical explanation. She'd called the cops. Packing up my equipment, I'd sat in my car under the pretense of taking notes, although I still watched her and the men with her, one clearly angry, the other hovering nearby protectively. Mr. Tourist from Gatlinburg played a nice white knight.

Still, my gaze went back to her. For a few moments, I forgot entirely why I was there. Human interaction, the play of emotions I could see over a person's face, had always intrigued me. Emotions, and my lack of ability to fully understand them, were so intriguing. But her face, serene and remote even as she faced a man who would likely inspire rage in others, never changed.

Another woman came into view. I'd caught glimpses of her as she shifted and moved, but mostly, she'd been hidden by the angry, aggressive man. Now she spoke to him and his obvious anger grew until I wondered if he might strike her.

As I scanned the area once more, a car turned onto the road.

A rare flicker of irritation roused, dying as fast as it

formed. The cops had arrived quickly. Seconds later, the prick noticed and backed down.

I found myself wondering what I would have done if he'd raised a fist to her, or even grabbed her. Would I have stayed here and watched?

That flicker of irritation returned and burned hotter, flaring into anger before I could snuff it out.

I was familiar with anger. It fueled the beast that lived deep inside me, one I had to keep tightly leashed. The violent emotion no longer filled me with fear as it once had, because I'd mastered it and knew how and when to let it out.

But I hadn't given it permission to slip its leash now, nor had I expected it to happen. A tremor racked me before I could stop it and I wrested the reins of control back from the enraged creature panting and straining for freedom, just under the surface.

Still, the hot spear lingered as I watched the driver do a three-point turn and whip his truck around. No. I wouldn't have watched.

By the time the cop reached the home of logs and sparkling glass windows, the prick was almost to the end of the block. Shifting my camera to his rear bumper, I took a picture of his license plate, then lowered the camera, calmly disassembling it before packing it away.

As I drove past the house, I allowed myself one last look.

Tommy texted me via the secure app but I didn't bother to pick it up.

I needed to be somewhere private before I spoke to him. And I needed to find out more about the woman...Tia Jenkins.

* * * * *

The connection was buried deep enough that it wasn't obvious at first glance, but within two hours, I had my answer.

Tia's brother was a cop. Not just any cop, either. He

was the cop who had broken open the case that had put Tommy O'Halloran's little brother, Brian, in prison. I read through the various articles and even obtained court documents, reading witness testimonies, and making note of certain details. Brian hadn't been running the operation. He was too green. But several of the victims had given testimony that he'd been the one to bring them in, promising high-paying jobs, help with school, modeling prospects. One testified about a friend who'd come into the US with her. They'd traveled from Russia on work visas after being promised jobs at a modeling agency via a website. Her friend had already been getting nervous on the plane, and when she started having doubts, her friend mentioned it on a text. When they were picked up at the airport, the friend had hesitated and suggested getting a hotel to think about it for a few days.

The driver agreed to drive her to a hotel, but first took the witness to the "agency". The girl saw her friend three days later, after her body was discovered by a couple of kids twenty miles south of New York City. An artist's rendering of her had been featured on the news. The only reason the witness had seen it was because she'd been out on her first *date* with an older man who had raped her six times in their two days together.

Brian had been the one to photograph her for the "agency's" website, which turned out to be a pseudo-escort site that pimped out virgins to the highest bidder. Her name was Inessa.

After Inessa's virginity was sold off for the sum of five hundred twenty thousand, her profile was transferred to a different escort site. Inessa had lost track of all her *dates* over the four years she'd been held captive. She'd stopped counting at four hundred twenty-three, a little over a year after she'd been kidnapped and forced into the life.

Her story stood out mostly because she'd escaped. Her last, and final date, had been driving drunk on their way from dinner to the hotel and when he'd wrecked, she'd crawled from the vehicle, bleeding, and flagged down a car, which happened to be the cop. The half-brother of the woman they wanted me to kill.

Curious, I looked up Inessa, wondering if the O'Hallorans had put out a contract on her.

The first internet search result had me pinching the bridge of my nose.

Internet Icon, Sex-trafficking Awareness Activist Commits Suicide.

One more mark against the O'Hallorans.

My phone rang.

The number had a Boston area code but it wasn't the same number Tommy had been calling from. Memorizing it, I looked at the second laptop screen and opened a second tab on the secure browser and entered the number. As it got to work tracing it, I went back to reading about Brian O'Halloran.

The phone stopped ringing.

A message popped up on the secure app and I opened it, reading it with little interest.

You've had time to consider the job. We should talk.

I debated answering. I'd rather never talk to the man again, but decided it would be wiser to keep him on the hook for a bit longer.

Spent some time observing her today, but had to leave early because LEOs came out. Will return tomorrow for additional surveillance.

I smirked, thinking about how that might burn Tommy's ass. When a text popped up a minute later, I congratulated myself for knowing him so well.

Why the fuck were cops out there? You were supposed to be good.

"Idiot."

They weren't there because of me. I'll finish background research and resume tomorrow, as I've said. Good night.

He texted again.

When I didn't answer, he called.

When I didn't answer, he texted.

After three rounds of this, he finally sent a tersely worded acknowledgment.

> *Probably best not to be in the area if cops are sniffing around. But I expect to hear from you by tomorrow or I'm pulling other people in. You're not the only game in town, Spectre.*

I didn't answer. I saved each of his messages to a secure cloud account then deleted them from the phone.

Instead of going over any more of the court case, I started a search on Mackenzie Bailey, Tia's brother.

I'd had limited dealings with law enforcement officers, and for good reason, but with the plan I had forming in the back of my head, it would be a good idea to know more about him.

Chapter 4

"**W**hy the fuck didn't you tell me you had an asshole hassling you at one of your classes?" Mac's voice, usually so easy and laid back, bristled with irritation and my immediate response was to end the phone call and pull my blanket back up over my shoulders and settle again into my comfort watch of *Thor: Ragnarök*. My favorite way to unwind after a bad day, or even a good day, was to binge watch as many Marvel films as I could. Sometimes, I even did it in order, watching the entire franchise from beginning to end.

It wasn't something I could finish in one evening, so I opted for a routine that would settle me without feeling *incomplete*—watching all three Thor films. That way, I could feast on the yumminess that was the Odinson brothers—Thor and Loki.

I paused the movie, refusing to miss one of my favorite interactions, Thor as he argued with Loki on Sakaar after being bought by the Grand Master.

"I had it under control, Mac," I told him calmly. My heart bumped hard against my ribs, because there had been a few moments when I'd been afraid, but nothing had happened, so why tell Mac and upset him?

My half-brother worried about me too much anyway. Why make it worse?

"You had to call the *cops*, sweetheart," he said, voice gentler now.

I could visualize him easily, standing in the middle of the loft he'd bought after winning all that money at the Kentucky Derby a couple of years ago. He'd won just a little over a million. He'd tried to talk me into going with him, but I couldn't stand the thought of that many people.

He'd made even more money when a publisher had approached him about writing a book detailing the events and trial that had made him somewhat famous for a while. They'd offered to set him up with a ghostwriter, but he'd passed, saying he could handle the work on his own.

The bright, open loft had a wall made almost entirely of glass and it offered a gorgeous view of Atlanta. On the few occasions I'd visited him, I'd loved standing there and staring out over the city. Mac had asked me to move in with him more than once, even setting up a bedroom and a studio for me in the massive loft, but I'd suffocate in the city. There was too much noise, too much chaos. I loved my mountains.

"Tia..." His voice had that edge of frustration in it and I jerked my attention back, reminding myself to focus.

"I called the cops so there wouldn't *be* trouble. I had it under control. The parents of another child showed up a few minutes before the cops did. Even if the jerk had gotten much more out of hand, I wouldn't have been alone."

"So he *was* out of hand!" Mac locked on that little tidbit. Typical Mac. Typical brother.

Even as I thought it, my heart warmed. We hadn't had each other in our lives until well past my sixteenth birthday. My mother died and I'd been forced to live with an aunt who hated me. I'd found the information about my father in a box of my mother's papers after Auntie Tanya dropped them on the curb for the garbage collectors to pick up. I'd waited until she'd gone to work that night, then gone outside and taken all the papers out, replacing everything with stacks of newspaper from around the house. She'd been going through all of Mama's things since she moved in and after I'd realized what she was doing, I'd grabbed as much as I could and hidden it in my room, in books, in my underwear drawer, wherever I could. A few days after I'd salvaged that particular stash from the trash, I'd found the birth certificate, and for the first time, learned my father's name. Thanks to the computers at the library, I was able to find both my father, Michael and his son, Mac...my half-brother. All made possible by that omnipotent, social media, big-brother corporation, Facebook.

My father and Mac had arrived at my doorstep the day after I'd contacted them, sending Tanya into a rage.

We hadn't had much time together, but I'd had Dad in my life for a while...and he'd given me a precious gift. Teachers at school had frequently requested conferences with my mom, but she'd blown them off. Tanya had done the same. My art teacher was the one who suggested I talk to my mom, then my guardian about getting evaluated for Asperger's. Her brother was on the spectrum, she'd told me, and I first started seeing signs of hope when I read about it. But my mom hadn't reacted well when I asked her, and I'd known better than to ask Tanya.

Dad hadn't just listened. He'd taken me to a psychologist and paid for the expensive tests out of pocket, ignoring Tanya's threats of suing him for violating her rights as my guardian. He'd still been in the process of fighting Tanya's claim of guardianship when he was killed less than a year later.

That gift, though, actually having the knowledge and understanding about why I was the way I was...I don't think I could ever make him understand how precious a gift it was.

And I had Mac.

He was always there for me. Even if he did live a few hundred miles away in Atlanta. Always there, always looking out for me. And sometimes, he hovered.

"Mac, I'm a big girl. I don't need a babysitter."

"I'm not saying you do, Tia. I just..." He stopped and sighed.

Closing my eyes, I rested my head on the back of the couch. "I don't read between the lines well, Mac. You know this by now. What's bothering you? You have to tell me."

"Fuck. I'd think it was obvious," he muttered. He said it in a way that made me think he hadn't meant to say it out loud at all.

Still, it stung.

"It's not *obvious* to me, jerk." Immediately after the insult left my lips, I regretted it. But I had a hard time admitting I was wrong. Hunching my shoulders, I waited for his retort.

It didn't come. "Tia, I'm sorry. I shouldn't have said that. I've just had a rough few days. Work shit, and that asshole Brian O'Halloran has a parole meeting next week. His fucking psychotic brother is pulling his normal shit again, too. The first thing that came to mind when I got the call was that some of Tommy's boys had been there hassling you."

I swallowed. "They still don't know I exist."

"You found me because Dad's name was on your birth certificate, honey. We call each other all the time. I visited you a few months ago. If he got somebody digging around in my history long enough, or trying to uncover my phone calls..."

"If you're trying to scare me, you're doing a good job, Mac."

"I'm not..." He groaned, frustrated. "I don't want to scare you, honey. I just... I want you to be careful."

"Maybe I should get a dog." The thought came to mind out of the blue but once the words were out there, hanging between us, I liked the idea. "Not a puppy though. Puppies are hyper. Like babies. I don't know how to take care of a baby."

"A dog wouldn't be a bad idea. Maybe I could dig around some, see if I can't locate somebody who has a trained dog who could be a companion and still act as a decent guard dog."

"I don't want some mean Doberman around here that would scare the kids, Mac." I frowned thoughtfully, trying to remember what I knew about dogs. It was very little, really.

My mom had been allergic.

My aunt had owned a mean little Chihuahua she'd called Princess. Princess bit my ankles and toes so often, I'd developed the habit of wearing socks and shoes if I wasn't in bed or in the shower One of the bites on the back of my right ankle had been deep enough to leave a scar. It had gotten infected, too, even though I cleaned it three times a day. My gym teacher had found me cleaning it in the locker room and sent me to the school nurse who had then called my aunt and demanded I go see a doctor. By the time I got to the doctor's office late the next day, I had a fever and the bite was inflamed and swollen. My aunt had yelled at me the entire way there for faking it, then bitched the entire time to the pharmacy *and* on the way home, blaming me for not taking care of it. Now that I was thinking about it, maybe a dog wasn't a good idea.

I told Mac.

"Is this because Princess bit you?"

"Yes." I rubbed my finger over the bite scar, wondering if that mean old dog was still alive. She'd been four when my aunt had moved into this house. I knew that because my aunt had celebrated the dumb dog's birthdays. Just after her sixth birthday, I'd turned eighteen and had asked my aunt if she and Princess would be moving out. She'd slapped me. The next day, I called Mac from my art teacher's phone and asked him if he could help me make my aunt move out, since the house had been left to me.

She'd left less than a week later. I haven't seen her since.

"Princess was a spoiled little shit, and a mean one. Exactly like her owner. We'll find you a well-trained dog who likes people, *and* one you like."

The calm confidence in Mac's voice soothed me, but still. "If the dog likes people, how can he be a guard dog?"

"Because that's what a guard dog does." A clicking noise came over the phone, followed by a sigh a few seconds later. "I have to take this call, Tia. Call me soon?"

"On Thursday, like always." I kept rubbing the scar, but the anxiety about a dog had lessened again. I'd research it tomorrow, then think about it. If Mac thought it was a good idea, it probably was. Right? "Good night."

"Good night. Love you, Tia."

A nervous knot tightened my throat, but I said the words. "I love you, too, Mac."

"You still sound like you're on your deathbed, confessing. You don't have to say it every time, sweetie."

"You do," I said stubbornly. Mama had been a queen when it came to weaponizing emotions, but I wasn't going to let her affect my relationship with Mac. As hard as it could be to say it, I'd damn well do it. "Good night."

Then I ended the call before he could say something else that I'd have to respond to.

The relationship thing could be draining.

But, as I snuggled back in to finish watching Thor and Loki, I found myself smiling. A little. Mac made me feel safe. Nobody else had ever done that. Not even my mom.

* * * * *

I didn't have classes on Wednesdays. I had a routine that I'd kept since graduating high school. I went to the aquarium in town. It was a giant tourist trap, filled with loud, boisterous kids, and sometimes, obnoxiously rude people, but it also had amazing fish and one of my only friends worked in the kids' area. Bianca always took her lunch break at twelve-fifteen and we walked across the street to the busy Mexican place.

"I heard you had some excitement at your place yesterday," she said after we ordered. She'd experimented, going with the daily special.

I didn't, ordering my usual—three tacos with cheese but no lettuce and a margarita. I'd never indulged in alcohol up until two years ago. Some mean bitch from the church where Mama had gone had come across Bianca and me while we were eating one Friday night. Bianca had been enjoying a margarita. I'd been drinking water. The woman had nodded at me and said, "It's good you don't drink. Your mama did and that's probably why you have so many problems, bless your heart."

The server had come by to check on us and both she and Bianca had gaped at the woman in shock.

Bianca had started to get up. I'd been flushed with embarrassment, but I hadn't known what to say. Bianca had given the woman a defiant look, then pushed the margarita to me. *"Tia's only problem is dealing with people like you who have a stick up their asses. Here, Tia. Have a drink. It won't remove the stick, but it can make them easier to ignore."*

I'd had a drink. Now, every time I came to the cantina, I had a margarita and dared anybody to say anything to me.

"A grouchy father who got mad when I told him his son couldn't come back to class." I looked at her for a few seconds, then glanced away. "The boy needs more than just art therapy—he needs the kind of help I can't give him."

"Like?"

"He's violent." I hated saying it. Too many people misunderstood autism and other disorders on the spectrum. Matthew had Asperger's, like I did, but his issues had more to do with his father than anything else. I'd bet my best set of charcoals on it. The ugly attitude he had was something a child learned. And he'd learned it very well.

"Ah. Yes, that would be a problem. Did the dad not believe you?"

"I don't think he cared. He learned it from his dad, after all. That's obvious." I picked a chip from the bowl and dipped it into the salsa. "He wanted his money back and I said no. I want to get a dog."

Bianca barely blinked, not fazed by the rapid topic change.

"Why?"

I couldn't tell her about the issue with Mac—and through him, Tommy O'Halloran. She was one of the few people who knew I had a brother, but I never talked about him and Bianca had her own boundaries. We respected those things about each other.

"Safety," I said honestly. "And a dog can be good therapy, too."

"For you or for the kids?"

I considered that, then said, "Both, although it was a safety thing first. But the therapy aspect came into play because of the children."

"So you're going to offer pet therapy, too?" She looked amused now.

I frowned at her. "No. But if a dog makes the kids want to pet him, that's...well, that's nice, right?"

Without waiting for her to respond, I launched into a lecture, giving her facts I'd learned over that morning, once I'd woken and decided I did like the dog idea. I caught the amused, patient look in her eyes, but ignored it as I continued to list facts. "I don't need an assistance dog, but it is fascinating how much the right sort of dog can help people on the spectrum, especially if they are capable of independence, but need an extra push. They can help their person get ready in the morning and pick up things that get dropped. The dogs can help students get to class and into their seat on time without getting anxious and do the same for adults who have jobs outside of home. They also help calm us down. I can use that." I thought about last night, and Mac's call. Then the episode earlier, what had precipitated it. "If I had a dog, I wouldn't have had problems yesterday."

"Well, that depends on what kind of dog you had."

Bianca's voice pulled me out of my distracted state and I looked at her. "Meaning?"

"Not every dog is going to chase away the jerks of the world, Tia." She took a sip of water before continuing. "Some of those little yappers..."

"Princess was a yapper," I reminded her. We'd been in high school together. She *knew* how much I hated Princess.

"Princess wasn't a dog." She waved a hand dismissively. "That foul creature was a hellbeast your aunt summoned. Probably her familiar."

I grinned. Bianca was one of the only people in the world who could make me smile.

Bianca winked at me. "She was also stupid. She liked to go tearing off at the fence when that one couple came in, remember? They had a German Shepherd? That big pupper could have *crushed* her head like *that*." She snapped her fingers. "What was his name?"

"Arnie."

"That's right. The guy wanted to name him Terminator and the wife said no. They settled on Arnold—Arnie. Maybe you should get a Shepherd. You seen them lately?"

"No." I looked away, a familiar sensation of anxiousness rising inside. "The house was sold after the fire. He... Tate, the husband. He was killed in the fire. They had another cabin, near Chalet Village. Two couples with young kids were up there. They kept trying to call them to check on them and nobody ever answered. He finally went up to see if they were okay. Dana never heard from him again. They found his body a few days after the fire. She was too heartbroken to keep either of the properties."

"Oh." Bianca's voice was soft and for a minute, neither of us spoke as memories washed over us. A couple of years earlier, wildfires from the forest around the town had all but destroyed Gatlinburg, leaving casualties and broken dreams in its wake.

Bianca had been in town at the aquarium working when everything went to hell. I'd been in Georgia visiting Mac and she hadn't realized I was gone. The panic we both felt when we couldn't reach each other was still enough to give me nightmares.

The quiet between us lingered, but unlike normal, it was uneasy and heavy. It left me feeling itchy and my heart started to beat too fast. My hands started shaking. I clenched them in an effort to still the movement but it was too late, Bianca saw. She pushed the food out of the way and covered my hands.

"Breathe," she reminded me.

"I am."

"Breathe more." Giving an encouraging smile, she waited until I followed the order.

I did so, even though it irritated me. The tightness in my chest didn't ease and she nodded at me to do it again. "Blow it out slower this time, Tia. You know how this works."

I glared at her even as I made myself drag in a deep breath through my nostrils, releasing it over a count of five. I wanted to be normal. I almost blurted that out to relieve the pressure in my chest, but I knew Bianca would want to comfort me and make me feel better. She couldn't fix this and we both knew it, although she'd insist there *was* nothing to fix, that I was perfect the way I was. And she meant it. But nothing she could say would make me *not* wish I couldn't be like other people. I just wanted to...tell somebody that. Just talk about it, so I could get it out, without anybody trying to fix it.

The idea came into my head, settling in with the rigidity of tempered steel. "I'm going to get the dog."

"Ah...okay. Just like that?"

"I've researched it. I've thought about it. There aren't any downsides if I find one I like and that likes me. I'll have a companion and security." Nodding decisively, I picked up my margarita and took a drink. "How do you shop for a dog?"

"Well..." She blew out a breath. "If you're not looking for a companion dog, you can always try the shelter."

A niggling reminder in the back of my head—Mac had said he'd look into it for me, ask around. But if he was worrying about Tommy O'Halloran and dealing with Brian O'Halloran's parole hearing, he had enough to do. Besides, a dog shelter had people who knew dogs, didn't they? And I could research more, figure out what dogs were good for security.

"Maybe I should go with you," Bianca suggested.

Pursing my lips, I studied her. "Why?"

"Think about it, Tia."

I made a face at her. "You think I'll end up letting somebody talk me into adopting half the shelter or something?"

"Well..." She arched her brows.

"All I have to do is think about the dog hair and I'll be fine. It might even scare me *away*." I sipped my margarita and glanced around, looking for the server. I wanted some water. My gaze landed on somebody sitting at the bar. A male somebody. One with a stunning face, carved cheeks, a mouth that needed to be memorialized on paper.

"Uh-oh."

I continued to stare at him. He casually glanced my way, eyes bouncing off me as if I wasn't there, which was how I preferred it because I wasn't sure I could handle it if such a flat-out beautiful man were to actually *look* at me.

"You've got *artist Tia* face on."

The man got up and he was lost to view. Disappointed, I looked over at Bianca.

She grinned at me. "Was he pretty?"

I didn't try to deny it. "Very." I leaned forward, wondering if I could see him out the window.

"I have to get back to work." Bianca went to pull her wallet from her purse.

"I've got it." I already had the money, with tip, in my pocket.

She scowled at me.

"I've got it," I said, giving her my best stubborn look.

"I'll let you get it. *If* you promise to wait for me before rushing off to pick out a dog. You're going to wait for me, right? I get off at three today. You look up the local shelters and we'll...figure something out." She pointed at me. "And don't go getting your heart set on going home with a dog today. You need to find one that *suits* you, otherwise you'll both be miserable and I'll cry if you adopt one only to take her back to the shelter. Which means *I'll* end up adopting her."

"Fine." I rolled my eyes and dumped the money on the table. "Now let's go. Maybe we can get a back view of the guy. He was *very* pretty, Bianca."

A few minutes later, the two of us casually strolled over the bridge, admiring the man as he crossed at the light, heading away from us, a weathered-looking canvas backpack slung over his shoulder.

We'd gotten close enough to see that the back almost put the front to shame and he'd glanced to the side once, giving Bianca a look at his profile.

"I agree. He's *very* pretty. I bet he's hung."

I burst out laughing. "Probably not. He's too pretty to have a body like that *and* be blessed in the phallic region."

"You never know." She leaned over and hugged me. "Remember. You promised to *wait* for me. No dogs without me."

I grumbled but nodded. "I remember."

* * * * *

I spent half the afternoon loitering in town, hoping for another look at him. Gatlinburg was a tourist town, after all, and if you sat and watched long enough, you could see the same people several times in the span of a day.

But I didn't see him. Finally, I headed back to the grocery store to take care of that errand so I could be done before Bianca got off work. I needed food but I wasn't putting off the idea of getting a dog. The more I thought about it, the more determined I was to *have* my dog and that meant I'd get her today.

So, of course, hours later, I headed into my house with a beautiful canine.

I named her Valkyrie because she was sort of standoffish—that made Bianca worry, but once I stared into Valkyrie's eyes, I'd been lost. I'd never felt a connection like that to anything or anybody, except painting.

Only this was different because Valkyrie looked at me with wide, wary eyes and once they brought her into one of the visiting rooms for us to get acquainted, she'd poked her wet nose into my hand, then let me pet her.

She was very fluffy and I already knew I'd be cleaning hair up all the time, but watching her prowl the house, sniff at doors, I already felt better.

Her previous owner had called her Trixie, but Trixie was a silly name for a dog and I didn't like it. I'd made a trip to the pet store and the staff there said she'd learn a new name since she was still young. I only had to be patient and train her. I might not always be patient, but I was determined and that could amount to the same thing.

I had told the shelter lady that I ran art classes for kids with Asperger's and autism and she'd given me a sad smile. Valkyrie, apparently, had been a companion for an older woman with diabetes who'd passed away a few days ago.

None of her children had wanted the dog, although they had said she was well-behaved and loved kids. I didn't understand why they hadn't taken the dog, but that just meant she was mine now. I'd introduce her to the children slowly, after she got used to me.

After we got used to each other.

I called to her.

She didn't look at me.

Reaching into my pocket, I pulled out the clicker the boy at the pet store had recommended and made it click, calling her name at the same time. Her ears went up and slowly, she looked at me. "Come here, Valkyrie."

She only stared so I used the clicker again and showed her one of the treats I had in my hand.

Her tail wagged slightly.

"Want a treat, Valkyrie?"

Her eyes moved to mine, then to the treat.

Slowly, she came forward, nose sniffing the air.

I gave her the treat and as she scarfed it down. I patted her soft, fluffy, golden-brown head. "Your name is Valkyrie now." Her ears perked and I gave her another treat. "Come on. Let's go out back again."

We went outside and she relieved herself, taking what seemed like forever. How big could a dog's bladder be?

When she came inside, I gave her the last treat in my hand, then swung by the kitchen to get more. This time, I put a handful of the bite-sized snacks in a baggie. The boy at the store had said I could keep some in my pocket, but that was gross. No, thank you. "Let's take a tour of the house, Valkyrie, then I'll set up your food bowl and you can eat while I get your bed ready."

We walked all through the house, her padding along at my side while I talked. It was weird, in a way, hearing my own voice so much, but she seemed to listen, looking up at me whenever I stopped and cocking her head as if to encourage me. When we reached the studio where I worked with the kids, her nose went to work and she walked around, sniffing the floors, the seats. "You smell all my kids, don't you?"

She continued her investigation and I went over to my desk and sat down. I sometimes sat there and sketched between classes. If she was going to sniff every square inch, I might sketch her then send a scan to my brother. Maybe it would keep him from freaking out when I told him I'd already bought a dog. As I went to sit down, I froze, staring at everything on my desk.

The hair on the back of my neck rose and it wasn't until Valkyrie bumped me with her nose that I broke out of that frozen state.

"Something looks off here, Valkyrie." I racked my brain, trying to place what it was. I knew how everything was supposed to be placed on this desk, down to where I'd left my charcoals when I called it quits the last time I used them. So what was out of place?

Valkyrie's faint snuffling caught my attention. I saw her smelling my chair. "Do you like how my butt smells?"

She flicked her ears and walked over, nose to the floor.

Her tail fanned the air gently and she looked placid and calm.

I looked back at the desk, still unsettled. Something wasn't right. What was it? What was it?

Chapter 5

I'd already made my decision.

Before I'd even received the first text from Tommy, I'd known I had no interest in killing the woman for him. But his parting shot, that final message had lingered with me until I finally banished them from my mind so I could sleep. I had no problems killing. It would be more honest to say that I enjoyed killing. It was likely a gift from my father, a contribution from both his genetics and his abuse.

Sarge had told me I wasn't a psychopath in the way my father was and over the years, I'd come to believe him, although if he hadn't found me when he had, it would have been too late for me. If I hadn't almost bled to death in an alley, if Alfonse Jordan's men hadn't caught up with me, then I would have kept going down that path until I was as twisted and fucked up as Walter Kramer had been.

He'd succeeded in making me into a monster, but Sarge had caught me before I was too far down the path and he'd redirected that hot, burning anger that had driven me to accept a contract on my father.

I wished I could say the anger was gone, lost to apathy and the serenity Sarge had tried to impart, but I'd be lying.

In this aspect, my father had succeeded. Rage was a monster inside me, one that often slept, but certain sights, sounds, scents—that was all it took to awaken that beast. He'd been clawing at the back of my mind ever since reading the witness statements from Brian O'Halloran's trial. If Tommy had realized what his actions would do, what he would awaken, he never would have called me.

The thought of him getting his hands on the

woman I'd seen earlier, hurting her, all to punish a cop who'd brought down serial predators, had teased the monster within into full wakefulness and the burn of anger had simmered under my skin ever since.

The anger was dangerous.

It had made me reckless already when I'd followed Tia Jenkins into the restaurant and sat at the bar while she ate lunch with a friend. There was something vulnerable about her. Gentle. Compelling. But at the same time, she seemed incredibly bold and that had been surprising.

Very little surprised me.

She'd seen me. Whether she'd realized I was staring at her, I had no idea, but she'd spent a good minute staring at me and it had taken a level of effort not to return that stare because what was *in* her gaze was something I wouldn't have expected, and something I needed to pretend I hadn't seen.

Hot, female interest.

The memory of it lingered with me throughout the afternoon as I went about my preparations and by the time I let myself back into the anonymous hotel where I'd stayed the last few days, I felt like I was walking on a razor's edge, and below me, flames waited.

I wasted little time analyzing it. I could do several things to alleviate the near palpable rage, but only one was viable right now. Had Tommy been within my reach, I could have just killed him. With the fury chewing away at me, I likely would cross a line, taking more pleasure in the act than I usually allowed myself, making him suffer, bleed, beg. But he was out of reach up in Boston and my current plans wouldn't let me leave Tennessee.

That also eliminated another avenue for purging the fury. A trip to the brothel I used in Germany would be the most effective manner, but again, it required leaving Tennessee...and the fucking country.

Down to the final option, I stripped naked and climbed into the shower, turning the water up so that it was painfully hot. Pain wasn't necessary, but it helped. Cock already hard, I wrapped my hand around it and began to stroke, cupping my balls in my free hand and squeezing, tighter and tighter until the pain helped blank out my thoughts, then I eased back and focused on the heavy weight of my dick, the way my hand glided over my skin, the heated splash of water. My breath stayed near level. My pulse barely sped up. Shoulders wedged against the narrow stall, I worked my erection and enjoyed the serenity of a blank mind.

Then I closed my eyes and a memory flash-danced through my head.

Tia. Tia Jenkins, the woman I'd been hired to kill. Standing a few feet away with her friend, a tiny grin at her lips and a blush on her cheeks. Thick, heavy curls falling around her shoulders, breasts rising and falling under an emerald green T-shirt. I'd never cared for the color green.

My father's eyes, like mine, were green, and the vain bastard had loved to wear shirts that same color and I hated anything that reminded me of him.

But seeing that rich, vibrant shade on her—it was lovely. Her light-brown skin glowed against it.

My cock jerked viciously.

My breathing sped up.

My heartbeat accelerated.

I tried to shove her image from my mind.

It didn't work.

The memory flash played on. She glanced at me, a nervous sort of glance, but a hungry one, her full-lipped mouth still curved in that tiny smile.

Fuck.

The orgasm spilled out and I came hard and fast.

Shaken, I looked down. I was still hard. I still hurt. "Fuck." I continued to pump and the orgasm dragged on and on while the thought of her smile, the way she bit her lower lip loomed larger and larger in my head.

Finally, the raging climax came to an end and I sagged back against the fiberglass of the shower stall, staring at the water puddling and swirling down the drain.

* * * * *

The hand job hadn't done it.

I changed into the sole set of clothing suitable for a workout and left the hotel, opting for a route that would take me up the nearest steep incline. I pushed hard at a pace so demanding, I was soon out of breath, the air burning in and out of my lungs. Once I reached that point, I slowed to a jog and caught my breath, then fell into an easier pace.

I couldn't run myself to exhaustion, not on a job.

But the fiery rage living inside dulled down to a simmer and I could think. By the time I returned to the hotel, I was able to push the beast back into the cage. After another shower, a quick one to wash the sweat from my skin, I dressed and lay down, setting my mental alarm clock to wake in three hours.

* * * * *

I woke clearheaded but somewhat bemused about my mental state from earlier. It was something I'd have to figure out, because I had a job ahead of me, one I'd assigned to myself. I finished my preparations for the night, then set about wiping down the hotel room. That morning, before I'd followed Tia to the restaurant where she'd had her lunch date, I'd canceled my plane ticket and used some of the cash I always traveled with to purchase a nondescript dark grey Honda CRV. I'd met the seller and a friend at a local restaurant and I'd seen his surprise when I arrived alone, but he'd relaxed after a few minutes of bullshitting.

Sarge had taught me how to blend and I did it so well, I might as well be a chameleon. We spent almost twenty minutes doing nothing talking and by the time I asked if I could look under the hood, both had relaxed and we kept talking while I checked everything out. Neither of them had even hesitated when I asked if I could drive it around the block to see how it ran, offering to leave my wallet behind as security. They'd waved it off and ten minutes later, I'd passed over two grand in cash, the owner signed over the title and I left.

I'd driven the rental back to the airport and used a rideshare app to get back to Gatlinburg. I'd have to burn the cover I'd used for this trip, but I'd selected one with that intent in mind already, so it was no loss.

The last order of the day had been a quick trip out to Tia Jenkin's house. I'd left the CRV in front of the vacant house, one I'd determined was a rental. The plan had been to do some simple reconnaissance. But upon discovering she wasn't there, I'd decided slip in and familiarize myself with the layout of her home.

That was what I told myself.

Now, thinking back to my walk-through of the painfully neat living space, I wondered why I'd lied to myself.

It should have been only an attempt to familiarize myself with the home. I'd spent far too much time wandering each room for that to be the case. She had an alarm system, which I'd disarmed from the back door with my smartphone, using an app I'd designed myself. It basically took the system offline, but the alarm company wouldn't realize it, because my phone was now working as a clone of the system. It would stop when I left and the system would carry on as if nothing had happened. She wouldn't receive a notification because as far as the system itself was concerned, nothing had happened.

As I gave the hotel room one final look, I slipped my hand into my pocket and rubbed my thumb over the surface of the business card I'd taken from the stack on her desk. The stack had been crafted in an *X*, each card alternating angles. I'd taken the top one to study it but instead of putting it back, I'd slipped it into my pocket and readjusted the position before leaving. Now, I tugged it out and gave it another look.

ART*x*

The lettering was in white, against a rainbow scribble that should have been chaotic, but managed to escape that effect somehow.

Below that was her name and smaller print, Art Therapy Classes & Workshops for Children on The Autism Spectrum.

It explained why she'd managed to stay calm while dealing with the prick, the day before. Maintaining calm would be a necessity for therapists.

Sarge had talked me in to seeing a therapist. Twice.

The older woman had reminded me of the aunt in the classic TV show about the sheriff, Andy Griffith. She'd been nice and sympathetic and the moment I realized she'd guessed what had happened to me, I'd told Sarge I'd never go back.

But that had been close to fifteen years ago. I was older and my scars were far better buried.

That hot prickle ran down my neck again, making the hair stand on end, while the ugly, coppery taste of rage flooded my mouth.

"Later," I told myself. I'd have time to indulge in that darkness later.

I had a job to do.

* * * * *

It was ten o'clock when I pulled onto the street. I had everything ready to go and planned to be on the road by midnight. Tommy, by now, knew I wasn't going to take the job. I hadn't talked to him, but he wasn't an idiot. He'd called half a dozen times earlier in the day, then sent a few texts. A span of nearly six hours had gone by with no contact. Ten minutes ago, he'd called again. I hadn't answered. I wouldn't talk to him until I had Tia safely out of Tennessee.

He couldn't have gotten anybody decent in place in such a short time. That's what common sense told me, but I had an unmistakable sense of urgency and I wanted to get this part of the job over with.

Some of the homes around me had their lights off already. Others, like the home of Tia Jenkins, still had lights on. I drove to the house next door, the rental I'd used for cover the previous day. I was using it again, only this time, I had a key. Using a credit card associated with this job's identity, I'd rented the cabin online and hauled in my duffel and an empty suitcase, freshly purchased from a shop in Pigeon Forge. Turning on a few lights, I did a walk-through, taking note of the windows that faced toward her house, closing curtains on other windows and going over the plan once more in my head. I brought up the website for her business and went to the *about* page, but it provided precious little data and nothing had changed since I'd read it last night.

She had classes tomorrow.

I felt a tug of regret for that. I didn't like doing things that might upset children.

After checking that the house was secure and as expected, I put the suitcase in the bedroom, leaving the lights on in there and in the bathroom. I also turned on the TV in the living room, keeping the volume muted. That done, I retreated into the kitchen and pulled out a pair of night vision goggles and checked the yard. I caught a pair of eyes glowing, close to the ground, the floppy long ears. A moment later, the rabbit turned and sped away, quickly lost in the grass.

After finishing my check of the area, I tugged the goggles off, opened the window facing her house an inch, then sat down to prepare and wait.

Maybe ten minutes passed. It was closed to ten-thirty.

Movement caught my eye and I looked through the large window in the kitchen that faced out over the backyard. I had the blinds open at a slant and the lights in the kitchen behind me were off. Still, I felt exposed. Although my dark clothes and naturally olive skin wouldn't stand out in the dim room, thermal imaging could pick me up with ease. I knew, because I'd used such tools myself.

It was paranoia, though. That was all.

The property backed up to a slope and the yard itself was a natural decline, allowing for absolutely shitty line of sight. I reached for the night vision goggles but stopped, staring at the back door of the property next door.

Tia Jenkins stepped outside, letting the door close slowly. She skimmed a hand back over her hair, loose now and spilling past her shoulders. As I watched, she stretched, reaching her arms up high over her head, spine arching. Her shirt rode up over her belly, exposing her skin while her breasts jutted out against the fabric of the shirt. I found myself wondering how soft her skin would be, what it would feel like to stroke my hands over those breasts, down to grip her hips.

She opened her mouth and for a moment, as I watched her so intently, it almost felt like she was speaking to me. But she was too far away. Frowning, I peered into the yard. She had a bright light on the porch, one that lit up the back yard so effectively, I'd already made the decision to put it out after I knew she was asleep. Her bedroom was near the front of the house so she wouldn't notice when the light suddenly went dark. The bright light, as it turned out, proved to be a blessing.

Earlier, I'd checked for any sign that there was another soul living in that house with her. There had been nothing, not even a goldfish.

But as I watched, a big, fluffy, light-brown dog

trotted around the yard, nose to the ground. She started toward the rental property. I blew out a slow, careful breath.

"What the hell?" I said as the animal edged closer, now maybe ten yards away.

The dog's ears flicked.

"Come on back, Valkyrie. That's not my property."

Her voice was faint and the dog lingered another couple of moments, still staring toward the window.

"Valkyrie!" She spoke more firmly and the dog turned away, obediently walking back to the house without a backward glance.

"Fuck." Skimming a hand back over my naked scalp, I looked at my small kit, then went back to work, just in case.

Chapter 6

There was somebody staying in the cabin next door. I'd seen the lights earlier.

I decided to blame Bianca. The place had sat empty for close to two months and now tonight, when I was trying to get adjusted to the idea of having a dog—so much hair—there was somebody else encroaching.

Valkyrie gave me a look of mild reproach as she climbed the steps. She sat on her haunches and regarded me with liquid black eyes. It was possible it wasn't reproach in her eyes. "You're not a mind-reading dog." I held out my hand, a treat already inside. She wagged her tail and came forward, delicately nipping it out of my palm. "Good girl."

I gave her a pat on the head, then looked over at the house next door where some unknown person would stay for the next day or so, at least. Most people stayed a minimum of three nights, because the rental company that had bought the house ran specials to get people to stay longer. Single night stays cost almost as much as two-night stays and two-night stays came with a free third night. "That house isn't mine. You have to stay in my yard—our yard."

Valkyrie's ears flicked forward, then settled back into place. I opened the baggie and gave her another treat. "We'll work on it." I knew she didn't understand but as I'd hoped, it was nice talking to somebody, or, well... just talking. "Come inside. It's time to get ready for bed."

Her nails clacked along behind me on the floor as I went through, checking locks and setting the alarm. In the bathroom, she lay on the microfiber rug in front of the tub and put her head on her paws, watching me as I brushed my teeth and washed my face, then grabbed my basket of hair stuff and went to sit on the bed so I could deal with my hair. Valkyrie watched with wide eyes as I brushed my hair, tracking each movement. It was weird, having her focus so intently on me as I brushed, then worked moisturizer through the curls, going through the routine that Bianca had helped me figure out.

My mother usually forced me to wear plaits clear up until eighth grade and then in one of her *moods,* as she'd always preferred to call her rages, she'd slapped me with a brush and told me I'd damn well learn how to take care of my own hair if I couldn't stop whining when she did it. My hair had looked like shit for months because I never thought about washing it and I tried to ignore the teasing and name-calling. Bianca found me in the bathroom hiding after a teacher had said something to me.

It had taken my friend forever to get me to talk.

Once she had gotten it out of me, she'd announced, in typical Bianca fashion, *we're going to figure this hair shit out.* I'd told her, *you're white. You can't help me with my hair.* She'd waved it aside, grabbed my hand and pulled me to the library where one of the few black school employees worked. Mrs. Alton, the librarian, had been on staff for what seemed like forever and she had *terrified* me, although Bianca loved her. Bianca had gripped my hand even as I'd tried to tug away and explained to Mrs. Alton the problem. Mrs. Alton's stern face had softened and she'd told us to come back after school if we could.

We'd left with several books and neatly typed advice from Mrs. Alton, and Bianca's dad had picked us up, then, because her parents adored her and spoiled her, he'd taken us to the store. He'd spent almost fifty dollars on stuff and I'd been clueless about it because I'd been too busy reading through one of the books, absorbing everything and trying to figure out if I could do those plaits myself, not the little girl ones like my mother always did, but something...prettier.

I never would have known about the money he'd spent either, if Bianca hadn't accidentally let it slip a few years ago. It had filled me with a weird mix of awkwardness and gratitude, something I'd talked to my counselor about. It was weird, but I'd finally come to see that even though I hadn't realized it at the time, I *had* had a family and people who cared about me— Bianca's family. It hadn't been just *because* of her that they'd done the things they'd done. They'd done it for me, too.

My awkward attempts to figure out my mess of hair hadn't gone well and I'd never learned the patience to let somebody else do it, mostly because I kept remembering too many hours listening to my mom rage at me, having her smack me with the brush if I moved even an inch.

Bianca had been good to her word, though. We'd figured the hair shit out and I'd been doing the same basic thing for almost fifteen years.

I finished moisturizing and pulled the curls into a loose pineapple updo, then grabbed the silk scarf from the nightstand. As I wrapped it around my hair, Valkyrie shifted, shaking her head.

A few stray dog hairs went flying. I watched them and reminded myself I'd known I'd have dog hair to deal with if I got a dog. Gathering up the hair supplies, I put them back in their basket and returned it to the bathroom, then got the Swiffer from the closet in the hallway. I loved Swiffers. They made life so much easier. I had three of them in various closets throughout the house. Five minutes later and the dog hair was taken care. Valkyrie gave me what I decided was a doggie smirk. As I put the Swiffer away, I looked at her and said, "We'll have to get you a brush. I bet if we brushed you well, we could get a lot of that extra fuzz off you."

She cocked her head and perked her ears.

"What did I say? Brush?"

Her tail swished and I smiled. "You know that word. Tomorrow. Come on. Let's go to bed."

I don't think I was imagining it. She gave a disappointed sigh but rose and followed me. Inside my bedroom, she looked around. Pointing to the dog bed, I said, "You sleep there."

She didn't move.

"Bed, Valkyrie." I pointed at the padded cushion we'd bought at the store and snapped my fingers. The clicker was annoying and I'd learned that she responded to the snap of my fingers, too. She did so now, clicking her way over to the bed and pawing at it, then she climbed into it, circling around and around. It looked like a ritual, which was something I understood, so while she finished, I moved over to the bed and climbed in.

I'd put Valkyrie's bed on the right side of mine, because it faced the window and I always slept facing the same way. I didn't like the idea of her watching my back. I could see her eyes glinting in the dark. Smiling at her, I said, "I hope you don't snore."

I also hoped I didn't have trouble falling asleep with her in the room.

Closing my eyes, I snuggled down under the covers.

Valkyrie made a snuffling sort of sound, a doggie sigh, then her breathing settled into a soft pattern so faint I could barely make it out.

It made me smile and I decided she wasn't the snoring type.

I'd sleep fine.

* * * * *

I was wrong.

But it wasn't Valkyrie keeping me awake.

I'd made the mistake of going through the day, including those mental snapshots I'd taken of various people. I did that a lot. Only one person had really caught my attention today.

Carved cheekbones, a perfect mouth. He'd worn a hat—I didn't like hats really, but I hadn't been able to make out anything about his hair so it must have been pretty short. What color was it, I wondered. His eyes?

Not that it much mattered. My attention kept wandering back to his mouth, the set of his eyes, even if I hadn't been able to make out the color. The breadth of his shoulders.

A shaky sigh slipped out of me. It had been way too long since I'd had sex, I decided. It was a complicated thing anyway, because getting to know somebody well enough to *want* to touch them, and let them touch me could lead to disaster, but the kind of guys who tended to be okay with taking their time were also looking for more than I wanted...from them, at least.

I needed a male Bianca.

If we were both bi, it would be a great arrangement, probably, but that was neither here nor *now* and it wasn't helping my current situation.

I started to slip my hand into my pajama pants, but stopped, remembering the dog. Easing closer to the edge, I peered at her. She was sleeping. I wasn't going to go to another room to masturbate in my own house. It wasn't like she could gossip about it, right?

Eyes closed, I slid my hand past the waistband of the loose cotton pants, past my panties, and downward until my fingers touched the curls between my thighs.

I bet he's hung, Bianca had said.

I doubt it, I'd told her.

And he probably wasn't but that was reality and right now, I was alone in my bed and I could imagine anything, including him in my bedroom, stripping his clothes off. And in my imagination, oh, yes...I decided he would indeed be hung.

I whimpered and slid my fingers inside my pussy while imagining it was him. My clit pulsed, hard and aching, as I stroked my thumb over it, pretending it was his tongue.

He was the one riding me through climax, while I bent over in front of him, his hands gripping my hips. In reality, I arched up against my own touch, sweating and straining toward climax. In my imagination, he said my name and whispered dirty things to me.

And in both reality and my imagination, I came.

When it was over and my breathing had slowed, I realized I was being watched.

Cheeks flushed, I turned my head and saw Valkyrie had sat up in her bed and was watching me, nose at work and ears up.

"Are you going to be one of those pervy dogs who likes to watch their owner have sex?"

I have no idea if dogs can roll their eyes, but it sure as hell looked like she did. Then as I sat up to go wash my hands and change my panties, she lay down and put her head on her paws, looking away from me, giving the appearance of boredom.

Amused, I said, "Nobody invited you to watch in the first place."

* * * * *

I was awake.

Lying in the bed, I tried to figure out what had woken me. Eyes closed, I listened. Everything was utterly still and silent. As always. I started to close my eyes, then stopped, pushing upright. Valkyrie's bed was empty. I snapped my fingers but didn't hear the familiar click, click, click of her nails. I tugged the scarf from my head out of habit as I slid from the bed.

It was a little past midnight.

Absently, I glanced down the hall toward the back door.

I froze.

It was too dark.

The bright light that illuminated the backyard wasn't on. An odd sensation tickled the back of my throat. I stepped back, thinking about the phone I'd left by my bed. "Valkyrie?"

I heard a faint whimper.

Forgetting the phone, I rushed forward, following the sound. Faint light filtered in from the kitchen. I always left it on and was relieved to see it. But then I saw my dog. "Valkyrie!"

I lunged for her, skidding to my knees. "No, no, no, no..."

I pulled her head into my lap, already shaking, rocking back and forth. "What did I do wrong, girl? Did I do something wrong?"

The floorboards creaked behind me. The cabin, made of wooden beams and sparkling glass windows and plank wood floors, had a habit of creaking and groaning and I'd become familiar with the various sounds.

This particular noise was the sound of somebody walking across the floor. Their footsteps were soundless, but the relatively new boards still creaked and groaned as they accommodated a person's weight.

My breath froze in my chest.

"You didn't do anything to the dog," a calm voice said behind me.

My entire brain went red hot and I understood, for once, what people meant when they said they saw red.

"You hurt my fucking dog." Easing her head down, I bunched my muscles. "Didn't you?"

There was no response.

With a sound I didn't even recognize, I surged up and spun, my hands clasped together. It was blind instinct. Mac had taught me basic self-defense and I had sucked at it. Every time he came at me, my instinct was to freeze and I couldn't stop it.

Instinct drove me now, too.

A tall, lean man stood behind me. At my blow, he jerked back.

I moved again, blind to everything but the need to hurt.

"Tell Tommy O'Halloran he can suck dick!" I shouted at him, swinging again.

This time, he caught my wrists and jerked me against him, pivoting and moving. As the world spun around me, terror threatened to overtake the rage, but from the corner of my eye, I saw Valkyrie. She whimpered again and lifted her head slightly, a thin sliver of her dark eyes showing as if she wanted to look at me. I howled. Or tried to. He clamped his gloved hand over my mouth. His other had my wrists clamped in front of me. Somehow, he'd also managed to swing me far enough into the kitchen so that I was pinned against the cabinet, my lower body all but immobilized.

Burning shock went through me. His body, hot enough that I could feel him through his clothes and mine, was all long, lean muscles. I could feel his breath in my ear, his lightly stubbled cheek rasping against mine.

It had been a couple of years since I'd let anybody get this close to me.

You didn't let him. Make him get away, inner logic dictated.

But I couldn't and the panic started to set in. A keening noise tried to well up. I couldn't breathe. He'd hurt my dog. I was trapped. He'd hurt my dog.

I bit him.

Behind me, he tensed. But the hand over my mouth didn't move even as I bit down harder and harder.

"Your dog isn't hurt. Merely drugged. She'll wake up. Will you please take your teeth out of my hand before you tear a chunk of flesh out?"

I bit harder. He'd *drugged* my dog?

"For fuck's sake." He leaned more firmly into me and let go of my hands. Oh, big mistake. I swung back, trying to punch him, but nothing effective landed. Logic intervened as I remembered where in the kitchen I was. Stretching out a hand, I barely managed to wrap my fingers around the handle of one of the knives in the chopping block.

Something pierced my neck.

I jerked away, but not fast enough. *Drugged!*

I swung back with the knife. It wasn't one of the bigger ones, but it was sharp. A fillet knife. His sharp intake of breath, followed by a guttural swear was like music. He let me go and backed away. I spun around, brandishing the knife.

He had his hands up. "Put it down, Ms. Jenkins. The medication will hit soon—"

"Fuck..." I stopped, because the word sounded wrong. My *voice* sounded wrong. "You drugged me."

Emotion flickered in his eyes. "Just enough so you'll sleep."

"Great." I blew a raspberry at him, swaying a little. Bracing my hand on the counter behind me, I said, "So I won't be conscious when you kill me? Or are you taking me to Tommy so he can do it?"

"I'm not taking you to Tommy."

"Liar." My throat thickened. "Just...leave my dog here. Okay? My brother will call me tomorrow. He alwash...*always* does." I blinked hard, trying to clear the dots from my eyes. "Leave the dog. He'll take care of her. If you didn't *kill* her. There's no reason for that fuckface to hurt me *and* my dog."

"I..."

I swayed again, the dots at the edge of my vision finally connecting to form clouds.

He was talking. I couldn't make out the words, but I heard his voice. Why was he trying to sound reassuring?

"You're a motherfucker," I said, smiling suddenly. It must be the drugs. That was the only thing that made sense. Why else would I smile?

I looked down and saw the knife in my hands. It was wet and red with blood. "I stabbed you. I hope it hurts."

Mac would be sick once he figured out Tommy had gotten me. Just sick.

A sick, desperate, determined thought hit me.

I was dead anyway. Tommy had sent this son-of-a-bitch after me. But I had the knife. I still had control, for now. And I didn't have to let Tommy win—I didn't have to let him hurt Mac the way *he* wanted to, did I?

Sheer impulse driving me, I looked at the man's startlingly pleasant face and smiled even wider. "Tell Tommy to fuck off."

Wrapping both hands around the handle, I pointed the tip toward my belly.

Chapter 7

"**F**or fuck's sake." She struggled harder and I let go of her hands to focus on sedating her. Her body was wild and hot as lightning. I tried to ignore it as I pulled the syringe out, but I couldn't. Her warmth, her scent...her softness. She swung backward and I wrapped my left arm around her upper body, pinning her torso to me.

She moved far faster than I expected. She also didn't display anywhere near the fear she should have. Everything about her threw me off, including how she'd managed to grab one of the cheaply made butcher knives I'd noticed on my initial walk-through of the house. I hadn't noticed that because of my insane reaction to the feel of her moving against me. *That* never happened. Locking my jaw, I pushed the plunger on the syringe and tried to ignore her wriggling, struggling warmth.

Sick fuck. She's scared and fighting and you're getting a hard-on.

But even my mental castigation wasn't enough.

In the blink of an eye, I went from detached and focused on the matter at hand to focusing on *her*, the round, lush feeling of her ass as she shoved against me, the flex of her legs as she fought. If my brain had been where it needed to be, instead of being suddenly tied-up with my wayward dick, I would have noticed the knife sooner.

As it was, I barely had time to shift before she made the wild plunge backward. She drove it into my thigh and the blade pierced flesh in a way that it went in through the lateral area, like she wanted to peel away the top layers of skin and muscle a bit at time before exiting.

Instinctively, I jerked my leg straight back just as she wrenched her hand forward to attack again.

The pain hadn't hit yet but it would.

I'd also made the fatal mistake of loosening my hold a fraction, giving her the chance to turn.

Ignoring the first bloom of pain, I evaded as she made an awkward attempt to lunge. I grunted, then swore.

She swung around and glared at me, the cheap knife wet and gleaming red.

It would have been laughable—me, standing there bleeding while she started to sway, holding a butcher knife that likely had never cut anything tougher than my own skin.

"Put it down, Ms. Jenkins. The medication will hit your system soon—"

"Fuck..." The word came out too thick and slow. She cleared her throat and rapidly blinked her eyes. "You drugged me."

For some insane reason, the befuddlement in her voice, the anger, it bothered me. Blood spread up my neck to stain my cheeks red.

"Just enough so you'll sleep."

What the fuck. Why am I explaining myself?

"Great." She sagged backward and made a rude sound, blinking owlishly as she stared at me. "So I won't be conscious when you kill me? Or are you taking me to Tommy so he can do it?"

"I'm not taking you to Tommy." That was the *last* thing I'd do.

"Liar. Just leave my dog here. Okay? My brother will call me tomorrow. He alwash...*always* does. Leave the dog. He'll take care of her. If you didn't *kill* her. There's no reason for that fuckface to hurt me *and* my dog."

Her voice was thicker now and something that might have been tears lit her eyes along with the anger.

Shit. Something hot and uncomfortable settled in my gut, even as rage started to fester and flame in the back of my head, a toxic, deadly mixture. *Tommy, you don't know it but you're already dead.*

"I'm not taking you to O'Halloran, Tia." I frowned at the sound of my voice forming her name, but I couldn't take it back. I didn't even want to.

"You're a motherfucker. I stabbed you. I hope it hurts." She gave me a wobbly smile and her lids drooped. Then, a second later, she looked back at me with a bright, almost fevered smile. "Tell Tommy to fuck off."

I was almost too late.

Lunging forward, I caught the blade right before she would have gutted herself, closing my hands around hers and engaging in a brief tug of war. She screamed, the sound ragged, raw and desperate. I got the knife away and hurled it across the room.

She swung wide at me, missing by inches, then stumbled, almost falling. I caught her and felt a fresh rush of hot blood flow down my leg. I needed to get my leg dealt with and bandaged, but I couldn't yet. Not until I knew she wasn't going to do something foolish.

"You miserable fucker," she mumbled, growing limper with each passing second. She glared at me, more emotion showing on her face now than I'd seen. "You're a miserable fucker. Are you going to hurt my dog, too?"

"No." I brushed her hair back from her face, not even aware of the action until it was already done. "I won't hurt the dog."

"Okay." She relaxed, oddly enough. "You're still miserable and I hate you."

"I understand. You're safe, Tia. I won't hurt you." Her lids drooped low and she sighed, the sedative finally taking hold.

* * * * *

By the time I managed to deal with my leg, the dog was stirring. I hadn't planned on the animal and the sedative I preferred to use was short-acting. I hadn't brought anything else into the house with me and I'd already spent far too much time here.

I couldn't risk trailing blood through the house looking for a first aid kit, so I improvised. That was something I excelled at. The entrance wound bled steadily enough that a bandage alone wouldn't do it. I'd found super glue in the meticulously organized kitchen drawer and used it to seal it the best I could. Then, using a pad of paper towels as a makeshift bandage, I hunted down a first aid kit—she'd have one. This neat house, the organization, I had no doubt of it.

The kit, under the sink in the bathroom, looked like something a pro would be proud to own and I was able to bandage it properly.

I lingered only long enough to take care of the blood in the kitchen, using bleach and paper towels that I flushed one by one. There was no way to know if I'd gotten everything but at least there was no obvious sign that a man had bled like a stuck pig in here.

Even though the injury hurt, I found myself smiling as I opened the door to Tia's closet. I didn't get surprised often and hadn't ever had a woman throw me off balance.

Don't spend time wondering over it right now. You have to get her away from here.

Her and the dog.

We needed miles between us and this house, well before Tommy sent in somebody else. He wouldn't waste any time once he realized I wasn't taking the job.

Stepping into the oversized, walk-in closet, I almost turned around and left. It was too big, an airy, feminine space that instantly made me feel out of place and out of my depth.

Organized with ruthless precision, there were built in drawers of soft peach, open shelves stacked neatly with T-shirts, grouped by color. Sweaters were folded on another set of shelves and also organized, not only by color, it appeared, but by material as well. There was a section for dresses, organized by season and color, and by length and occasion as far as I could tell. A few dressier pieces at one end, with the rest of them casual, all marching in a perfect rainbow.

Jeans stacked on one shelf and below them, another set of stacks, all cotton and various shades of colors. More pants, I assumed. Judging by her organizational craze, she wouldn't be putting shirts over there.

Moving deeper into the managed chaos of color, I spied the shelf where she kept a couple of duffels and below that, four weekend-sized suitcases, the sort one could take on airplane. None were the plain, solid-color people typically saw. Instead, they were patterned with outdoor scenes. One showed a wintry landscape, while another depicted a beach and one looked like New England in the fall. I touched that one with the tips of my fingers, thinking of Massachusetts, the lighthouse Sarge had left to me when he died.

Pushing the thoughts aside, I acted on instinct and grabbed the one with the winter landscape. I wasn't surprised to feel the weight of it. I don't know if she'd been planning a trip or if she routinely kept suitcases packed. But it was convenient. Putting it on the bed, I flipped it open and checked. Several pairs of jeans, socks, underwear and bras. Inside a packing cube, I spied a couple of sweaters. Judging by the colors visible, at least two.

I closed it, then went into the bathroom. It wasn't a surprise to find a toiletry case packed and ready to go. Grabbing it, I looked around but didn't see anything I might be missing. I was almost to the kitchen when a thought occurred to me. I brushed it off. But after two more steps, I stopped and swore.

"You're going to get your ass caught over this." I gave both Tia and the dog another quick look. The dog was stirring restlessly, but that was all. A few more minutes, easy.

Jogging to the studio, I grabbed a couple of sketchpads and several small boxes of drawing supplies she'd left on her desk. That would have to do.

It took more time than I liked to get everything in the car, including the dog's collapsible wire dog crate. It erected easily and I shoved the cushion in there while keeping half an eye on the dog and the other on the neighborhood. It was still quiet. I'd backed my vehicle into her driveway, careful to keep my face averted to avoid doorbell cameras. I'd already disabled Tia's. I would take her computer and hopefully find a way to access the account. The phone wasn't coming with us. It would stay here. I hadn't been caught on the device but erasing the timeframe for which it was disabled would slow things.

If I couldn't access the account, in the end it wasn't a big loss.

As I approached the dog's crate, she opened her eyes groggily. The soft brown reminded me, again, of a small, silly pup.

Stop. Do the job.

"Hey, girl," I said. "Sorry about this."

I gave the dog another dose of the sedative, a heavier one. I'd have to access more, but I had an acquaintance close to St. Louis. He'd stock me up and I could finish the rest of the trip.

I was too pragmatic to waste time on hoping but I found myself disliking the idea of having to drug her the entire ride. And I wasn't talking about the dog, although I didn't like that idea either.

Up front, Tia slept, although thanks to the sedation, it was more like unconsciousness than sleep.

She wouldn't stay that way much longer but I had

enough time to get off this mountain and out of Gatlinburg.

That would be enough for now.

Chapter 8

I've had crazy dreams before. Odd dreams were perfectly normal for me. I mean, things like waking up in school naked were commonplace and I'd had hundreds of dreams that involved me walking up the sidewalk that led to my aunt's house, ringing the doorbell and just...waiting.

She never answered in the dream and I'd gotten plenty of psychobabble analysis on why. I have things I want to say to her but I don't relish the confrontation so until I work up the nerve, that door will stay closed.

Many dreams were lucid, too. I could control the aspects, either completely or to a large extent and those were the craziest dreams, because they were so vivid.

As vivid as this one.

But I couldn't seem to control anything right now.

I *had* to be dreaming, though. Nothing else made sense. Sounds were too clear, scents too defined, the feel of the seat under me a tactile torment, hard and worn, with a spring jabbing into my right butt cheek. And I was *cold*. Not all of me, really. My feet. They were freezing.

I had socks on, but they weren't the really warm sort that would chase away the chill and since this was a lucid dream, I could just open my eyes and go to my room and get those socks. Right?

My lids didn't want to lift and my limbs wouldn't move.

So, the logical explanation was that I wasn't dreaming.

After what felt like an eternity, I finally found the strength to open my eyes and sat staring out into blackness. My mind didn't register the puzzle of that and I sat there, confused and with an aching head while my toes turned into little stubby, icy twigs.

"Go put on some socks," I muttered to myself. "Then you won't be cold."

"I thought you were waking up."

The sound of another voice had me freezing, and not because of my frigid feet, either. Heart hammering somewhere near my throat, I tightened my fists involuntarily. That was when I noticed something else that didn't fit with the dream scenario. I couldn't move my hands. Adrenaline flooded me and the fog laying over my brain fell back. Whipping my head around, I found myself staring at the profile of a stranger.

Not a *total* stranger—he was vaguely familiar. A few seconds passed as my memory lined up and things fell into place.

Fuck.

"I'm not dreaming," I said in a flat voice.

"No." He glanced over at me. "You're not."

I jerked my hands up, or that was my intent. Struggling against a band for a few seconds, I resisted the rising panic and managed to calm myself only through sheer will. Staring at the distant taillights of a semitruck far ahead of us in the night, I breathed in deep and slow. "Did you at least leave my fucking dog alone?"

He blew out a sigh that sounded tired.

I wanted to punch him. Looking over at him, I smiled. "Does your leg hurt?"

"You've got a mean streak." He smiled at me, glancing away from the road for a second. "I think I like that."

"I don't give a fuck what you like."

He laughed.

It sounded rusty, like he rarely bothered with laughter and humor and other human emotions. It was also deep, warm and oddly...inviting. I shoved the thought away even as it formed. The fucker was kidnapping me and taking me to Boston, where Tommy O'Halloran lived. This was all to get at Mac and I was *not* going to be one of those people with Stockholm Syndrome either. I also was *not* going to be used to hurt Mac. It didn't matter what it took. I wasn't going to let it happen. Resolutely, I made up my mind, gaze focused on the rapidly disappearing taillights. "How far are we from Boston?"

"We're not going to Boston."

"Uh-huh." He'd bound my hands in my lap by simply securing them together at the wrist with something, then pulling the seat belt strap over them. Nothing complicated and if I was patient, there was no reason I couldn't get them free.

"We passed by a rest stop," he said. "There won't be another one for some time but as long as the next one isn't busy, you'll be able to get out and use the facilities. I'll get you something to drink as well."

"Oh, wow, thanks so much." I put as much sarcasm into the words as I could.

He made another low, rusty laugh.

I made another attempt to ignore the odd tug in my chest, looking instead at the dashboard. The digital clock read a little after five. It had been almost eleven when I'd gone to bed and I don't think I'd been asleep long when something woke me up. We'd been driving...maybe five hours? Couldn't be much more than that. I did the calculation in my head, trying to figure out how close we were to Massachusetts. I hadn't ever been there, but I'd been to Philadelphia with Bianca. We'd eaten messy cheese-steaks, visited museums and walked until our feet hurt. It had taken ten hours to drive there and Boston was at least a couple hours north.

"Are we heading to an airport?" I asked. I sounded calm. I normally did. Emotion didn't always reflect in my voice and that was something that threw a lot of people who didn't know me. I'd learned it wasn't an unusual trait among some aspies, but the knowledge hadn't helped relieve the frustration it caused me when people got uncomfortable around me because of it.

Now it felt like a blessing. *Not* showing this guy fear seemed to be a good thing. I mean, books always touted not showing the bad guys fear.

"No, Tia. We're not going to an airport." There wasn't any sound of frustration or irritation in his voice, which really didn't do much to settle my nerves. I couldn't decide if I wasn't hearing anything because I was lousy at identifying such emotion or because the emotions *just weren't there*.

With another look at the clock from under my lashes, I decided it didn't matter. If he was taking me to an airport, it would have to be a private one because no way would I get on a commercial flight and he had to know that. If he planned on driving me the entire way to Boston...well, we were about a third of the way there. The sooner I disabused him of the notion that I'd go meekly along, the better. So I had to deal with the problem of my hands and I had to do it without him noticing.

The answer was simple and it came to me as I sat there wiggling and fussing in the seat. Each time I moved, he'd glance at me. I felt the speculation in each look. I let each movement become more and more restless, pulling my hands closer and closer to the seat belt every time I shifted in the seat, grumbling as I did so.

"What's wrong?" he asked after fifteen minutes.

I'd moved no less than five times in that fifteen-minute span, each time with progressively more irritation.

"There's a broken spring in the seat that's jabbing me in the ass and I have to pee and my shoulders hurt," I said, trying to emulate the whiny tone I'd heard on TV shows. I didn't do it very well.

He didn't even look at me as he answered, "I told you we'd try for the next rest stop. It's under forty-five minutes away now."

"You try crossing your legs for that long," I snapped at him and wiggled again, half-twisting in the seat this time, my body turned away from him so he couldn't see what I was doing. Almost there. I couldn't see the taillights of the truck and there were no headlights behind us.

He sighed. "If it's that dire, I can pull—"

With a last, determined twist, I pulled my hands free and lunged for the steering wheel, mind already calculating possible impacts and damage. He was going seventy. My fingers brushed the steering wheel as he swore and slammed a hand against my chest. I struggled harder, desperate. Fingers curled around the fake leather wrap, I managed to wrench it toward me a fraction.

He shoved me back into my seat, a powerful hand splayed between my breasts as the vehicle swung and veered. Next to me, he swore once more, then went silent.

My heart lurched up into my throat.

Behind me, I heard a faint, weak whimper. Confused, I looked back as the SUV tilted precariously. My heart did the same thing as my gaze landed on something tucked in the back of the vehicle. Something I hadn't seen. A dog crate. Heart twisting, I closed my eyes.

The crazed motions of the car steadied. Next to me, my kidnapper breathed hard.

I wasn't surprised when the vehicle slowed, then came to a stop altogether. He curved a hand over the back of my neck and tightened it menacingly. "What in the fuck was that?"

"Why did you bring my dog?" I asked. I hated the

tremor that worked its way into my voice.

The hand on my neck tightened, then loosened. To my surprise, he stroked his thumb over my skin. "What?"

"You don't fucking need my dog!" The words exploded out of me and I jerked away, cringing against the seat as I turned to glare at him. "I don't know you, I've never done a damn thing to *you* or Tommy O'Halloran. But my brother's a cop and Tommy's little brother is in jail because my brother is a *good* cop and caught that slimy son of a bitch. Fuck the fact that Brian O'Halloran is a perverted, scum-sucking piece of shit. But my *dog* is a *dog* and has nothing to do with *any* of this. I just got her! Why did you bring her!?"

He drew back, studying me with shuttered eyes for a long moment then looked straight ahead at the dark road. After a moment, he pulled the vehicle back onto the road. "Behave yourself and your dog will be fine."

"Yeah." I curled my lip at him. "Like I'd trust you."

He smiled humorlessly. "You can always try to crash the vehicle again. I didn't think to tie her cage down. If we crash into a tree or anything else going seventy miles an hour, we're all more than likely dead...but she'll become a projectile inside a metal cage. Think about that the next time you feel the need to grab onto the steering wheel."

My stomach cramped at the mental picture and I almost vomited.

* * * * *

The sky had started to lighten when we pulled off to the exit for the rest stop.

I noticed it when we got out but I was so focused on my overly full bladder that I didn't think about it until we were back at the car and I was holding Valkyrie's leash so she could do her business. She was wide awake and alert and I wanted to tell her to bite the leanly muscled figure who stood too close. But even as I tried to figure out how to make those wishes known, he pulled something out of his pocket and held it out to her. "Treat, Valkyrie?"

Her nose twitched.

I glared at him. "What are you doing?"

"Giving her a reward for good behavior," he said, his unreadable eyes meeting mine. "She waited until we stopped instead of pissing all over the car and she hasn't snapped at me. She's a good dog. Don't good dogs deserve rewards for good behavior?"

I glared even harder.

The right corner of his mouth twitched in a half smile. "Would you prefer to give her the dog treats?"

"I'd *prefer* that you let me go."

"I'm sure you would." His lids drooped and he held out his hand, several treats in the bowl of it.

After a few seconds, I snatched them away and turned toward Valkyrie. She delicately nipped each one from me, her tail fanning the air slowly. "At least you're not wagging your tail for him, you big traitor."

The tail moved a little faster.

He shifted next to me. "We need to get going."

I ignored him, lifting my eyes to look at the eastern skyline where the sky was breaching the horizon and painting it with hues of pink and gold.

"Tia."

My belly went all hot and tight. Nearly an hour had passed since I'd woken up. So, six hours. Boston was twelve or fourteen hours from Gatlinburg, max. Would I see another sunrise? I'd never been a morning person and found myself suddenly bitter at the idea of not seeing another.

He took my elbow and I jerked away, backpedaling. "Leave me alone!"

"We're going," he said implacably.

Half wild, I looked around. Why weren't there any of those heroic, burly truckers around? Or even a skinny one who'd glance over and cause a distraction?

There was *nobody* but us.

Fingers wrapped firmly around my upper arm, he started to walk. "We're going."

I resisted, but although I considered myself fairly strong, I didn't slow him even a bit. I told myself to fight harder, but his words from earlier lingered. *Behave yourself and your dog will be fine*.

"You're a bastard," I said as he opened the door and waited for me to climb in.

Vivid green eyes met mine, set under straight, golden brows. His scalp was bare although I could see the faint growth stubble, far lighter than his brows, indicating that he likely shaved his head. The severe look only drew attention to the intense color of his eyes. "I am. You'd do well to remember it." Illuminated by the streetlights, his features on stark display, he leaned in closer and said softly, "Trust me, Tia. You've never met a bastard quite like me before. So stop fucking with me."

Fear lurched inside. I shoved it down because really, what did it matter at this point? "Why? I already know what's coming. Seriously, I'd probably be better off making you mad enough that you snap my neck." I gave him the most derisive look I could manage. "Assuming you know how. Anything you dream up will be better than what Tommy has planned."

He placed a hand on my throat, thumb resting in the hollow, where my collarbone notched together. He pressed lightly, eyes boring into mine. "And what makes you so sure of that?"

"Because you might be a professional killer, but he's a raging, psychotic pervert on a power trip and he wants my brother to pay for the fact that *his* brother is in jail." My voice shook. but I didn't look away. "It kind of sucks to be the pawn in the middle."

"Do you want to call your brother and tell him to back off the O'Hallorans?" His thumb pressed a bit more gently.

"No!" Disgust curdled inside at the very thought.

"Why not?" His voice silky now, he moved in closer and murmured against my ear. "Brian O'Halloran has already served five years. He's a young, stupid, arrogant fuck and he gets his ass kicked in prison on a regular basis. One might say he's already done his penance. If you told your brother to back off, maybe Tommy would do the same...and you'd be left alone."

I couldn't suppress my shiver and I had no idea if it was because of how close he was, or his words. He was too near and it was unsettling. I wanted to lie to myself and say it was only because he was dangerous and taking me to Tommy, but a sick, twisted thing inside me knew otherwise.

"Brian O'Halloran sold girls as young as *eleven* into prostitution," I said, voice shaking. I was disgusted with myself, and *him*. "He should rot in jail the rest of his life."

My kidnapper drew back, an odd, enigmatic look on his face. The hand on my neck lingered longer, then stroked. There was something too...*tender* about the touch and my brain couldn't process it. Baffled by all of it, I stared at him. I stared at him so hard, trying to figure him out that I didn't think twice when he took my hands. At least not until he had me half-restrained already. I jerked. "Hey, you son of a bitch!"

"We've established that," he said calmly, ignoring my struggles.

Behind us, Valkyrie made low, unhappy noises in her throat. Why the *fuck* had I put her up?

He bent low and put his face in mine as he finished securing the zip tie around my wrist. "If I could trust you not to be stupid, I wouldn't do this. But I have a few matters to tend to. I'm not going to all of this trouble so you can send us careening off the road at seventy miles an hour."

I spit in his face.

I didn't even think about it. I just did it.

A muscle twitched in his jaw but he tugged something from his pocket and wiped the saliva away without any other reaction. A moment later, he bent over me. He had another zip tie. Breathing hard, I watched as he fastened the seatbelt, then secured my wrists to it. His eyes flicked to mine, icy green and remote. "I'm not going to have you splatter us all over the interstate."

"I guess you have other women to kidnap after you're through with me."

He moved away without answering and I jerked uselessly at my wrists. The door was still open but even when I sensed him next to me, I didn't stop struggling.

He cupped my chin.

I jerked away.

Inexorably, he forced my face back to his.

"What do you want?" I snarled.

Instead of answering, he put something over my mouth. It took a few seconds to figure it out. He'd *gagged* me—there was tape or something over my mouth and I couldn't even *speak*. While I was still fuming and struggling to comprehend what he'd done, he gestured to the horizon where the sky had finally given way to dawn. "The sun rises in the east. Pay attention, darling."

Chapter 9

S ometimes, boy...you can walk too close a line. If you don't have a clear focus, something to center you, it gets real easy to stumble and lose your balance.

Sarge's voice was so loud in my ears right now, it was as if he was right there, talking to me. I could almost imagine he was, too. Under most circumstances, I might have appreciated it. He'd been dead five years but not six months had passed before I'd started to lose the sound of his voice. Not his words. Not the rules he'd drilled into my head. I might as well have those carved into my flesh. He'd made sure I understood them and if nothing else, I'd keep to them out of respect to him for saving me, keeping me alive.

Respect, son? Is that all you got for me?

At the driver-side door, I paused and dragged a hand down my face, frustrated. Of all the times for the old bastard to rise up to haunt me, *now* wasn't the time.

I sucked in a breath, scraping my nails over the light stubble on my cheeks, then stopped as a scent teased my nostrils. Hers. My blood was already running far too hot because of her, far too close to the surface. Those big, dark eyes locked on mine as she glared at me, her fear hidden behind a mask while her anger lay naked for me to see. It was a subtle thing, that anger, her emotions almost muted, but...not.

Her features were smooth, hardly revealing anything. But her eyes...they showed so much.

Light splashed over us and I looked up to see a vehicle approaching. Jumping into action, I climbed into the SUV and looked over at her. Tia had her head bowed but as the truck neared, I saw her tense, awareness blooming. "Don't go doing something to attract attention, Tia. It's not worth it."

Her eyes flicked to mine, a pithy *fuck you* there, plain to see.

Humorlessly, I smiled. Once I was on the road, I glanced back over at her. I was tired of the fear in her eyes. It shouldn't bother me, but it did. "The sun rises in the east, right?"

Her brows came together and she stared at me, confused.

Shrugging, I shifted my attention back to the road. "If we were heading toward Boston, wouldn't we be heading northeast?"

She made a muffled sound behind the tape I'd put over her mouth and again, that pang of guilt surfaced. "It won't be for long," I told her. "Somebody will call soon and I can't have you interrupting and making things worse. Once I've dealt with a couple of matters, I'll take the tape off."

She screamed at me. There was no other way to describe that sound.

Clenching my hands on the steering wheel, I kept my eyes glued to the road. I wasn't going to hurt her. I knew that. Soon, she'd figure it out.

She's still scared, you prick.

I knew she was. I couldn't do anything about it.

Ahead of us, the horizon was still mostly dark, the road west not quite ready to greet the day. My phone rang before I could think of anything else to say that might make her feel better.

I was relieved, though. This was one of the two calls that needed to happen before I could take that tape off her mouth. Picking up the phone, I accepted the call and put it on speaker. "Hello, Tommy."

"Spectre, you finally decide to answer the fucking phone," he said, his voice silky.

Next to me, Tia stiffened and her breaths came faster, harder. I hoped she didn't pass out, but I couldn't worry about that now. "I was taking care of some matters, Tommy. I wasn't aware you'd put me on retainer. Sorry if you had that impression."

"I hired you to do a fucking *job*, you cunt."

"That's not entirely accurate, now is it? You sent me to *evaluate* a job. I had yet to decide if I'd take it. I haven't given you an answer yet. The last time we talked, I hadn't made up my mind." A car sped past me on the right and I could see another pair of headlights in my rearview mirror. We weren't exactly in any sort of early-morning rush, but there were more cars on the road than I liked considering I had a woman restrained with duct tape over her mouth in the seat next to me. "I've made up my mind, though. Would you care to hear my answer?"

Tia had gone still—deathly so.

"I've already sent another team down there, you stupid bastard. Maybe if you're quick, you can get in on the action, but the money won't be even *half* what it was going to be. I'm not somebody to fuck around with, you get me?'

I laughed, some of the icy-cold rage I'd felt since reading up on Brian O'Halloran leaking into the sound. "You never did ask what my answer was, Tommy."

He snorted, but abruptly demanded, "What the fuck is your answer?"

"It's *no*." At his snarl, I laughed again. "And your men are going to have a hard time doing any sort of job when they can't find her. Who did you send? That stupid fuck, Ben Leary and his ham-handed brother Griffin? Those two couldn't find their dicks in the dark with a flashlight and the guidance of a paid professional."

The rasping sound of his breath made me smile. "What are you up to, Spectre?"

"That's easy, Tommy. I took Mac Bailey's sister out from under your nose. She's out of your reach...where you can't touch her."

He bellowed, the sound loud enough that the dog in the back jumped, rattling the cage. Next to me, Tia swallowed. I heard it, the audible click in her throat.

"You dirty feckin' bastard," he rasped, the faint Irish in his words thicker now. "I'm going to find you and rip your balls off for this."

"Stupid boy." I allowed myself a small smile, relishing his fury. "You can't find me. The only way you'll ever get close is if I'm breathing down your neck...and when that happens, it will be because I'm about to tear it open."

I disconnected the call, then picked up the phone and punched in another number.

"Bailey speaking," an easy voice said, clear and alert, despite the hour, the words softened with the lazy drawl of the south.

"Mac Bailey."

"That's me."

I looked over at Tia. She was staring at me wide-eyed.

"You're going to want to listen to what I have to say very, very well, Detective Bailey. It's regarding Tommy O'Halloran."

I couldn't see the man, but I felt the way he snapped to attention, as though a string connected us through the phone line.

"I'm listening. Didn't catch your name, though," he said. The easy drawl was still there, but the sharp undercurrent made it clear that only an idiot would underestimate this man.

"I didn't give it. Nor will I. A few days ago, I was contacted by O'Halloran about a job. It concerned your sister."

"What?" The word came out clipped and harsh, all attempts at being casual gone.

In my mind's eye, I saw a mental picture of him. I'd done my research, watched the various interviews of him, seen him on the stand in news recordings as he testified against Brian O'Halloran and the other people involved in the trafficking rings. Dark-gray eyes, deep-red hair, lazy smile to match the lazy drawl. Those eyes had gone hard as onyx as he described the conditions of the victims. They'd be hard like that now—harder perhaps, because Tia was his sister and he loved her.

Love. How much did that affect one's actions? I didn't know, but it had to be considerable.

"Tommy O'Halloran has grown tired of trying to intimidate or pay you off when it comes to his brother. He is ready to try more...definitive, damaging tactics."

"Listen, you prick," he said, voice coming lower now.

He must already be at the station, I decided, and was looking for privacy. I cut him off, because I needed to end this. Tia still sat there with tape over her mouth and the fear I felt bleeding from her was suffocating me.

"I think I told you to listen," I said shortly. "I'm not your real problem. He hired me to kill your sister. I...declined and she's effectively out of his reach. He's going to react very badly to that."

"What the fuck do you mean she's out of his reach?" he shouted.

No attempts at being quiet now.

"I have her with me." I looked over at her. She sat with her head slumped, shoulders rising and falling rapidly. I could make out her lashes moving rapidly, too. Focusing back on the road, I continued the conversation. "He won't be able to find her. But he may well come after you, guns blazing."

"Are you telling me you *kidnapped* my sister?"

"Yes." There was no point in lying.

"You called a fucking *cop* and told him you *kidnapped* his sister?"

"There's no point in going to this trouble if Tommy then directs his attention toward you and *you* end up dead and somehow his brother gets out of prison early," I pointed out.

"You kidnapped my sister, but give a rat's ass about some piece of shit human trafficker sweating away down in a federal lock-up in Georgia? *And* you want me to believe Tommy O'Halloran hired you to kill her, yet you didn't because...why?"

"Let's say Tommy missed his mark with me, Detective Bailey, like he missed his mark thinking you could be bribed. I have to end the call now. I'm sure you'll attempt to track it. Give it your best shot, although I'm going to say upfront—you're wasting your time."

"Wait—"

Next to me, Tia surged forward, jerking against the seatbelt and zip ties.

I ignored her, and Bailey's protest. "I'll touch base with you by this time tomorrow and hopefully, I can let her talk to you then."

I ended the call, then turned off the phone. There was a truck pull-off ahead and a quick look showed it was empty, save for one lone truck at the very front. Pulling in, I quickly removed the phone's SIM card and battery. Rolling down the window, I tossed the battery out and gave Tia a look. "Just in case you get ideas." I dropped the SIM card into the cup holder for disposal next time we stopped and shoved the phone back into the pocket of my cargos. Leaning closer, I reached for the tape on her mouth. She jerked back. "You want me to take that tape off or not?"

Her nostrils flared, eyes wide.

"The longer it's on, the tougher it will stick."

She closed her eyes, then sagged, sinking closer.

Carefully, I caught the edge I'd left peeled in and tugged. It came off easily enough although as soon as it cleared her mouth, she jerked her head, ripping the rest of it. I swore. "Damn it, Tia!"

"You son of a bitch! What kind of game are you playing!" she shouted.

Up ahead, a light in the truck went on.

Fuck. Without thinking, I caught the back of her head and yanked her against me, my mouth coming down on hers. At the same time, I freed the seat belt. Then, grabbing a knife from a cargo pocket, I cut the zip ties away. It took only seconds. Tia was frozen in shock.

She finally jerked away, managing to get a few bare inches between us. From the corner of my eye, I saw a shadow descending from the truck.

Determinedly, I pulled her back to me and whispered against her ear. "There's a trucker up there. He heard you. I'm not going to hurt you, but you won't be safe from Tommy O'Halloran as long as he's after you. If he gets you, you won't die right away, but you'll wish for it. You'll beg for it. And you'll do it for a long, long time before he finally kills you. So for now, you're stuck with me. I don't want to hurt or kill an innocent man, but if you push me..."

"Asshole," she said, voice shaking.

"Yes. Remember that." Then, brushing my lips over hers, I grabbed her and pulled her into my lap. She was stiff with shock as I rubbed my mouth over hers, breath coming hard and fast.

She was pissed off, angry and scared.

I was becoming the monster Sarge had never wanted me to be, because the predominant thought in mind...

Fuck, she feels amazing.

Chapter 10

You are not going to do this Stockholm shit!
My mind recited over and over and over as his mouth skimmed mine, as he slid one hand up my knee and his free arm went around my back, a firm brace that didn't imprison but also didn't allow for much movement, either. His taut body was hot and hard and strong, the wiry strength the kind I would have found fascinating any other time. I could see myself wanting to draw him, watch him when he wasn't looking so I could commit the lines of him to memory.

But this wasn't *any other time*.

The hand on my knee slid higher, along my side and my breath caught. Tensing, I braced for him to grab my boob, but he grazed by, going completely past and to my horror, my nipples drew tight and throbbed in resentment. My pulse was slamming by the time he curved his hand over my neck and tugged me in closer, arching my head back.

In the dim light, I couldn't make out the green of his eyes, but to me, they seemed darker, so much more intense, so much more dangerous as he bent over me.

"He's ten feet away. You decide what happens, Tia."

He kissed me, his mouth absurdly gentle and such a distraction that I couldn't figure out what he meant. Ten feet away? Who? O'Halloran? I'd finally figured out we were heading *west*—then that phone call.

His tongue came into my mouth, past the paltry barrier of my parted lips and a startled groan left me.

I didn't like kissing.

I mean, I never had.

I'd put up with it with one or two of the guys I'd dated, and there had been *one* guy I'd been somewhat serious about who had actually been somewhat decent at it so I'd grown to...well, not hate it.

But I never *liked* it.

Except that weird noise just now? It had come from me. His tongue toyed with mine, teased, then withdrew and he caught my lower lip. I shivered as he bit me and that was when I realized my fingers hurt. I'd reached for him, my left hand clutching at his shoulder and my fingers all but sank into the hard pad of muscle there, as if I was trying to leave permanent impressions on his skin.

He lifted his head a bare inch and in the ever-growing light, he stared at me. He had a faint glitter in his eyes that I hadn't seen before. I had no time to process it, either, because his mouth was on mine again and the arm he'd wrapped around me had shifted. Now he played his fingers over the small of my back and I shivered, the light touch far more erotic than if he'd dipped his hand between my thighs.

"Everything okay?"

I jerked in surprise.

The man holding me—*my kidnapper*—let go. His hand fell from my neck. He stopped kissing me. His head sank back onto the padded headrest and he gazed at me from under lashes that I could now see were tipped with gold. We touched all along the right side of my body where I pressed against him—my ass, hip and leg. But he wasn't holding me. His left hand still danced over my lower back but it was a gentle stroke, not at all restraining.

The look in his eyes was clear, his words echoing in my head. *He's ten feet away. You decide what happens, Tia.*

Without looking away from him, I swallowed, then answered, "Yeah, everything is fine. My...boyfriend and I are...or *were* having an argument. Hope we didn't wake you up or anything."

Even to my own ears, my voice sounded stiff.

"You sure?" the guy called out. "You're not in trouble or anything?"

I half turned, glancing over my shoulder in the dim light. "Yeah. He's just being an asshole. Don't know why I expected anything else, but I'm not in trouble. Thanks, though."

"All right, honey. If you're sure." The taut silence lingered and I knew he was still waiting.

"Yeah, I'm sure. Thank you, again. I mean it." The hand on my spine slid higher, then back down to play with the bare skin where my shirt had ridden up.

I stared straight ahead, listening to the gravel and trying to slow my heart. There were other problems, too, like my stiff nipples, abraded by the worn fabric of the T-shirt I always slept in, my pussy, aching and wet beneath the pajama bottoms. I squirmed on his lap and he made a low noise, not quite a groan, but louder than a sigh, under his breath and I realized something—Bianca had been right.

He was most *definitely* hung. I could feel the throb of his cock against my hip like a brand and I had the insane urge to turn, shift so I could straddle and rock against him, cuddle as close as I could and ride him until this ache abated.

But I couldn't do any such thing.

However, I didn't have to *acknowledge* my aching pussy, my wet panties or the crotch of my pajamas, even the tight buds of my nipples. I didn't even have to acknowledge *him* or what had to be a fantastic cock.

"He's climbing back into his truck."

I scrabbled back into my seat and hurriedly dragged my seat belt on as if that alone would undo what had just happened.

"Thank you," he said softly.

"Why?" I stared stonily out the front window.

He put the SUV into drive before answering. "I

already told you I didn't want to hurt or kill an innocent man. But I would have."

"You could let me go," I said sourly.

"But then I'd be killing you, in effect." His voice was quiet, but the words were steel. "I meant what I said about Tommy O'Halloran. If I had to choose between hurting or quickly and painlessly killing an innocent man, or letting an innocent woman be raped and tortured, then murdered? There's no question which one I'd choose."

* * * * *

Hours later, I squinted against the bright light and stirred, waking to silence.

A confusing, sweaty mass of dreams had plagued me and my head ached.

A cold nose poked my bare arm and I looked over to see Valkyrie nudging me through the gap in the front seats. My heart hitched a beat and I looked around. Where was—

The hope inside deflated before it could really form and I blew out a breath, staring straight ahead instead of out the window at him where he stood patiently.

Seconds ticked away into minutes. My bladder panged urgently. After we'd gotten back on the road, he'd given me a bottle of water. I'd wanted to ignore it, but the taste of him lingered and I had to choose between the lesser of two evils—accepting water from the devil or having that reminder of his kiss on my lips. One drink had made me aware of how thirsty I was and I'd guzzled the whole thing. It had been replaced by another and he'd said, "The sedative can make you thirsty."

I'd tried to ignore the water, again.

I'd held out maybe a half hour.

Now with thirty-two ounces of fluid straining my bladder, I knew I couldn't ignore him forever.

Valkyrie nudged me and whined low in her throat. It sounded questioning...and a little plaintive. Maybe she'd give me an out. "Did he let you pee yet?"

Her ears pricked.

"You have to go pee?"

Her tail thumped twice, hard.

"Okay." I went to open the door, but he beat me to it. The temptation to shove against the paneling so it crashed into him was strong, but I elected not to. For now, I was trying to figure out everything and it seemed smarter to *ignore* him. Opening the door for my dog, I let her jump out and bent to take the leash he'd left coiled on the floorboard. After snapping it onto her collar, I straightened and turned. He'd moved closer and my face heated as his eyes jerked upward.

He had *not* been looking at my butt, had he?

Ignore him, Tia, I reminded myself.

Why was that so much easier said than done?

It was a puzzle I couldn't figure out. Walking a few steps away from the car, I looked around, trying to be subtle. After a few seconds, I realized there wasn't any point to that. Save for a low, squat building off to the side, we looked to be in the middle of nowhere. Curiosity burned inside but I kept the questions trapped behind my teeth as Valkyrie sniffed at the grass, trotted around for a few seconds, then finally squatted. She looked at me with big doggie eyes and I huffed out a breath. It felt like she was rubbing it in. I was going to have to ask the asshole to use the fucking toilet.

Once she was done, I turned to glare at him.

He stood ten feet away, his back to me.

And there was somebody walking toward him.

My breath lodged in my throat, a mix of apprehension and hope mingling. Before I could make up my mind on what to do, he turned and gave me a deliberate look.

I had absolutely no idea how to read that expression, but I knew one thing—I wasn't going to find any white knight here.

The bubble of hope popped and I looked over at Valkyrie as she came to stand next to me. She nosed my hand and I rubbed the top of her head. "My normal life isn't like this, you know. It's boring. I like it that way."

As voices drifted closer, I tightened my grip on the dog's leash and started forward.

Chapter 11

Leo Wallace, with his shock of wiry white hair and snapping bright-blue eyes was a hard man to peg. His face was smooth, almost as ageless as Sarge's had been before cancer had eaten him up inside. If it wasn't for the white hair and the knowledge in those eyes, he could have passed for a man in his forties, easily. But he'd looked the same when Sarge had introduced me to him and that had been more than a decade ago. He moved a little slower and there were more lines around his eyes and mouth, but he didn't look like a man in his mid-sixties. At least not until you looked into those eyes.

"How are you doing, son?" he said, holding out a hand.

I gave it a quick shake, aware his gaze had drifted past me to linger on Tia.

I heard her approach but even if she'd been silent, I would have known. I'd been keenly aware of her for the past four hours and hadn't breathed easy until she'd fallen into a restless sleep outside of Belle Rive, Illinois.

Even then, I hadn't been able to block her from my thoughts. Every sound she'd made—the low, soft moans, her occasional sighs—had been torture. It had been even worse when she'd slid into something that had to have been an erotic dream, her hand going between her thighs while throaty moans escaped her lips.

I'd wanted to pull over and stare, watch. Would she climax? Was she thinking about that kiss? But even as I considered that last thought, I'd been disgusted with myself. She'd responded, yes, but that didn't mean anything. She was in this situation because I'd forced it on her, no other reason. Reacting to her the way I had only proved how much of a monster I'd let myself become.

And yet...I couldn't block out the sound of her soft moans. When I licked my lips, I still tasted her.

It was a relief when she'd drifted back into a quieter sleep, although I continued to check on her. If she'd started to wake at any point in the past hour, I would have had to drug her again because I couldn't risk her figuring out any information about Leo, but I'd been lucky on that part.

I'd blindfold her when we left. I'd already made that decision. If she didn't fight, I didn't want to force a needle into her skin. Still, I was about to ask Leo for more. He'd gone to veterinary school after leaving both military and government employment in his late thirties and ran his own part-time business out here in farm country. The same drugs were often used to sedate both people and animals and he'd been my supplier for a long while. But I saw the way his mouth went tight and how his lids flickered.

"You didn't forget those rules, did you, son?"

"If I did, you think I'd come here?" I replied. We both knew that Leo might have given up killing after he'd finished the job in Mexico, but he kept a loaded weapon close at hand, tucked out of sight because he never doubted that one day his past might catch up to him. It had almost happened once. That was how we'd met. "I know all about that Barrett you keep tucked away in there."

A faint smile cracked his face but it faded as he shifted his attention to Tia.

"What's a Barrett?" she asked.

"Nothing you need to worry about, ma'am," Leo said, giving her a polite smile. "That's a gorgeous dog you have. Okay to pet her?"

Tia frowned and then looked down at the dog. "He wants to pet you."

I shot Leo a sharp look, warning him not to say shit. She was...unique. Different. Amazing. But I had a feeling not everybody would see what I saw.

Leo never even looked at me. He simply waited for Tia to respond.

After a second, she did, with a shrug. "I don't think she cares."

Leo hunkered down in front of Valkyrie, his wide, nimble hands stroking over the dog. She leaned into him, clearly recognizing a true animal lover.

"She's a Golden Shepherd?"

Tia cocked her head. "Yes."

"Thought so. I've seen pictures of them, but never had the pleasure to meet one." Leo looked back at Valkyrie, smiling. "You're a beauty, aren't you?"

"She knows it, too," Tia said, her voice softening some.

I told myself I didn't care. I knew I lied.

"Nothing wrong with a lady knowing her worth, I always figured." Leo pushed upright with a pop of his knees and a grimace. "Why don't we go inside? I imagine you wouldn't mind using the facilities...?"

"Please. I'm about ready to have a very embarrassing problem."

The two of them strode toward the utilitarian building that acted as both Leo's home and a small hospital when needed. I trailed behind, figuring Tia would feel better with some space...and wondering what she'd tell him when she had five seconds alone.

That was about all she had, too. As I came inside, I heard a door slam in the distance and Leo winced as he sat down. He focused his gaze on me and in a flat, hard voice, he said, "Sit down, Meric."

The tone made me think of Sarge. With a faint smile, I did, holding the older man's blue eyes. "Are you going to ground me?"

"You're going to tell me what the flying fuck is going on." He delivered the words in an icy tone.

I thought of how he'd stood with me over Sarge's grave, tears rolling down his face.

"She's in trouble, Leo," I said calmly.

"You'll have to do a lot better than that." He jabbed a finger at me.

I considered it, then reached down and unzipped the pocket on my right thigh, pulling out my personal phone. The one I'd been using for all contact with Tommy, and with Mac Bailey, had been a burner. A high-end one, bought with cash on my last trip to Seattle and activated when I'd last been in Washington. That had been nearly nine months ago and since then, it had gone unused until I'd decided to look into the job that had been sent my way through a labyrinthine online network, one so complex I wasn't even sure I could undo it now. The data was stored in an anonymous, secure cloud network and I was aware of his growing impatience as I logged into the site. I was also aware it wouldn't take Tia much longer to finish in the bathroom. He'd deliberately taken the chair facing the part of the building divided off for his living quarters and I knew why, too.

"Today, son," Leo said.

"I'm in. I need to pull up the data." I tapped on the icon, went to the very first contact, sent five days ago, then opened it. The email, sent anonymously, opened and the text, a few words and a figure, were visible.

Sliding it over to Leo, I asked, "Are you still paying attention to organized gang action around the country? For...old time's sake?"

He'd picked up the phone, but paused now, gaze lifting to mine. "Certain things never change."

"I received the job request while I was in Mexico, taking some down time. I didn't receive any identifying information at first. Just that. The offer and the payout."

He squinted at the phone's screen, then reached

into a pocket, pulling out a pair of glasses. "Damned old eyes. Fuck. That's what I thought it read. Who was the target?"

"She's either still using your...facilities...or trying to climb out the window."

"Won't work." He sighed pragmatically. "I've got this placed locked up tighter than a virg...well." His lids flicked, then his gaze returned to mine. He never had been one to talk crass around women.

I smiled. I'd already known she was back there, despite my comment. I'd felt her, like sunshine on my skin—angry sunshine.

"Who put out the offer?" Leo still watched me, but the ice had faded from his eyes.

"Tommy O'Halloran."

He sighed and rubbed his finger along the side of his nose. "How the hell did a nice girl like that run across him? She ding one of his over-priced, ugly cars or something?"

"You're most definitely still keeping tabs on the criminal element." I heard the scrape of a shoe behind me but didn't turn. "Let's flex your mind a bit more. His brother Brian is in prison."

Leo's mouth spread in a wide grin. "Yeah, I know about that, son. Ran into a couple of cops he couldn't buy or scare away...shit." The smile faded and he cracked his neck, then looked behind me. "One of them your dad? Boyfriend? How are you involved in all of this?"

She stopped pretending she wasn't there and stormed closer, giving me a sullen look before answering. "I'm *not*. He's delusional."

"Her half-brother is the detective who brought Brian down."

Leo looked from me to her. "Why are you here, son? You want me to keep her under wraps so you can go kill that fucker?" He looked at Tia with an apologetic smile. "Sorry, ma'am."

"Apology not accepted." She stared at him, her gray eyes cool and unblinking. Other than a faint line between her brows, her expression appeared calm, but I knew she wasn't. Her voice had a knife's edge as she said, "What exactly do you *mean*, keep me under wraps? I've had enough of being carted around and treated like an idiot child."

I went to say something but Leo shifted on his stool, giving her a thorough appraisal. Something about his expression had me hold my silence.

"You're right. You shouldn't be treated like an idiot child. Come here, Tia. I want to show you something." Leo gestured to the spot next to him.

I was mildly surprised when Tia actually came and settled there on a stool that had been out of my sight behind the tall worktable. He gestured at the end of the table. "Hand me the laptop, son. Tia, you hang back there listening to us for a while. You probably heard this smart-ass reference organized gang activity?"

As I turned the laptop over, Tia shifted on the stool and flicked her gaze back and forth between us. "What's your point?"

"When I got out of the military years ago, I did a stint with the FBI. It was before I got married. Only did it for about five years. Too much shit. Decided I'd do what I'd originally planned to do when I was a kid—work with animals. I learned quite a bit about my particular area—organized crime and gang activity." He flipped open the laptop as he spoke and began tapping away. Behind the lenses of his glasses, his eyes were as sharp as they'd been when I first met him. "That knowledge served me well later on. Somebody...close to me got involved with a bad element in Mexico. He was young and arrogant. Not a bad man, just stupid. Loved to gamble and made some bad bets, borrowed money, then more money..." He sighed and looked over at Tia. In that moment, all his years showed. "He tried to run. He had a wife and a daughter. They caught up with him, killed his wife, threatened to do the same to his baby girl. She wasn't even two. But before they killed her, they'd find a sadistic bastard with specific depravities. That was when I showed up, along with a friend and his protégé. We killed everybody there and got the poor fool and his little girl out. It was too late for him, though. They'd broken him. He committed suicide not long after. His little girl was put up for adoption." Leo paused and lifted his head, staring off into the distance, eyes dry and unseeing, glittering with suppressed emotion. "And I still watch them, waiting to make sure none of the ones who knew what had happened are able to find her, track her down. To do that, I have to stay in the thick of things."

He cleared his throat and glanced at me.

I rose from the stool and went to the small refrigerator tucked in the far corner. It held mostly water and the Mello Yellos he loved. Grabbing one of those, I took it to him, popping the top before sliding it over.

He nodded, taking a drink and offering a faint smile. "Thanks. Throat got dry there, son. Now, then, back to what I was saying." He looked down at the computer and flexed his hands. Soon, he was tapping away at the keys at a pace that made me wonder how fast he'd been when he'd still been active. "If you want to keep up with what's going on with organized crime, gangs and Mexican cartels, Tia, you have to keep an eye on the big picture. It doesn't work to watch one small group, or even the ones most closely associated with the one you're concerned about. You never know when something going on over in China is going to have an effect on the drug trade coming out of Mexico and when that, in turn, will have a ripple effect clear up in Massachusetts."

He looked at Tia, studying her over the tops of his

glasses. "You're a smart woman and by the look in your eyes, I can see you're following."

"I already *know* Tommy O'Halloran is after me." She crossed her arms over her mid-section and hugged herself. "I'll go to Atlanta, stay with Mac."

"I imagine you already know there are...problems with that idea." Leo gestured with one hand. "You're in this situation because Tommy O'Halloran's brother was involved with some bad folks working in the Atlanta area. Some street gangs have organized almost to the same level as organized crime groups. One of them was involved in the human trafficking ring that your brother helped bring down. Brian O'Halloran was in the area working with them. They had ties to another gang in Boston which is how the...partnership formed. It wouldn't be a stretch to imagine Tommy reaching out to them and asking them to deal with you if they knew you were in the area."

She scoffed, shaking her head. "So you think I'm going to hang out here in Missouri the rest of my life?"

"If I know my friend, it won't be necessary." Before she could respond, Leo nudged the computer closer. "I also think you need to be aware of what Tommy O'Halloran is capable of. Your brother knows. I know. M— My friend knows."

He glanced at me, grimacing.

Tia didn't seem to notice, though.

She was staring at the computer screen and as I watched, the blood drained out of her face.

I reached for the computer.

She snatched it away, still staring at the screen. "What is this?"

I rose and went around the table and took the computer. Her fingers had gone limp and I didn't have to do much more than tug. Her face was a sickly ashen gray and she looked at me with stark eyes and blinked slowly, as if her lids were weighted down.

Swearing, I looked at the screen. When I saw what was on it, I almost threw it down and smashed my heel into it.

Instead, I shoved it at the old man and turned back to Tia, cupping her head and urging it downward. "Take a couple of deep breaths."

Half-expecting her to refuse out of stubbornness, I braced for her to sway off the stool, maybe lose consciousness. She didn't. Her body shuddered as she breathed in and out, then she shoved up against my hand until I let go. "I need to walk."

She wobbled as she stood, but steadied almost immediately. Voice sharp, with a high edge to it, she demanded, "What the fuck was that?"

"That was Marta. She was a young immigrant from the Ukraine. She came to America thinking she'd won an international nursing scholarship." Leo crossed his arms over his chest, watching Tia, unfazed.

If he hadn't been a friend of Sarge's, and if I didn't need his help, I'd hurt him for putting that look in her eyes.

"Instead of meeting the presenters at the airport as expected, she was picked up by two of Brian's...girls. One of them is his on-and-off-again girlfriend. Her mother runs an escort service that's a front for a prostitution ring. Everybody in Boston knows it but every time the FBI gets close to shutting it down, O'Halloran gets wind of it and somehow his lady's mother is able to clean house just in time. Several of her clients are high up in the echelon of Boston government and society, so bringing her down will be problematic. It was her idea, the FBI thinks, to stage a phony scholarship contest to bring in new young women from other countries. For more than a month, Marta was forced to work as a prostitute but one day, the back door to the home where they're all kept was left unlocked. She slid outside and ran. The building was being watched by FBI agents, of course, and they followed from a distance, then approached once she was safely away. I wasn't able to get into all the files, but..." Leo looked away. "My best guess is that SAC— Special Agent in Charge—was determined to get a bust this time and he put her in harm's way. A few days later, she went back in, wearing a wire. But Tommy knew she'd talked to the FBI. When she got back inside..." He lifted a shoulder.

"They did that to her." Tia swallowed and looked away. She sighed and it was so deep, her whole body seemed to move with it, shaking slightly as she let the explosion of air leave her lungs.

"You can't expect them to be any kinder to you. If you go to Atlanta, your brother *could* protect you. He *could* request assistance from the local FBI or the state police. But their protection will only last so long and Tommy O'Halloran hasn't been brought to court even once, only his brother."

She shot me an angry glare. "I don't want to live my whole life *hiding* because of that fuckhead."

"You won't."

"I don't know what else you think will..." She stopped then, understanding dawning. Her lids flickered and she swallowed nervously. "You're planning on killing *him*. Aren't you?"

I didn't answer.

She laughed, the sound a little hysterical. "There are *laws* about that kind of thing!"

"Those laws never stopped him."

Chapter 12

You're planning on killing him. Aren't you?
There are laws about that kind of thing!
Those laws never stopped him.

I don't know why those words were still lingering in my head. It had been eight hours since we'd hit the road and driven steadily west.

He'd blindfolded me when I'd climbed into the car and I'd been too drained to argue. Sometime later, he'd removed the black cloth obscuring my vision and since then, he hadn't done anything that would keep me from knowing our location.

Not that it mattered right now.

My focus was elsewhere and like any other time I'd locked my attention onto something specific, nothing else was going to get in the way.

Not easily at least.

"Are you hungry?"

I heard him speak, but the words didn't exactly penetrate.

He couldn't just *kill* him.

"You're going to kill Tommy O'Halloran, aren't you? You're going to murder him."

The decidedly heavy silence instantly became heavier. He didn't respond for so long, I wasn't sure if he would answer. Looking over at him, I caught the way his mouth tightened on a grimace but as soon as he realized I was watching, his face smoothed out. "*Murder* is something that applies to humans, Tia. Tommy O'Halloran qualifies in only the most basic sense. He breathes, eats, bleeds. But he doesn't think like a human, doesn't feel, doesn't care. Humans, by nature, don't *enjoy* the suffering of others. They may not go out of their way to ease it, but that doesn't mean they derive pleasure from it. He does. He seeks it, chases it, avidly does whatever is necessary to cause it. Killing him is akin to killing a rabid dog, one that has started attacking other animals, but a dog doesn't think. Tommy does. A dog doesn't enjoy it. Tommy does. A dog with rabies will die. That's the course of the disease. Tommy doesn't have rabies. He's a sick, mean bastard and the cops can't seem to stop him. He needs to be put down."

I hated that it made sense.

A soft whining noise came from my left elbow. Looking down at Valkyrie, I rubbed her head and scratched around her ears. "Is that what you think?"

Her big eyes stared into mine, soulful and intense and I tried to think about how she would handle somebody who was crazy enough to kill and kill and kill. She was a dog. Dogs were animals and their instincts were basic and focused on things like life and food and sleep and attention...and I guess, if you weren't fixed like Valkyrie, getting screwed. If somebody tried to hurt you, then the instinct was to attack and defend and fight.

It was simple, in a way.

I didn't have what it took to fight somebody like Tommy and he...

"I don't know your name."

His shoulders hunched as I shot him an accusatory look. That made me *mad*.

"What the hell is that? You grab me from my home, made me think you're going to take me to Tommy, drag me across the country...and you *kissed* me. Then you get all pissy because I want to know your name? What the fuck?"

"In my line of work, how often do you think I tell people my name, Tia?" he snapped, irritation coming through loud and clear.

It amused me, satisfied something in me I hadn't even known existed and I found myself giving him a look of wide-eyed confusion and the sort of puzzled smile Bianca liked to give people when she was about to teach them a lesson in what she called Smart-Ass 101. "I really couldn't say because I'm not familiar with your line of work, Mr....?"

He snarled, then abruptly started to laugh. "You hid that sarcastic bitch very well. Call me Spectre."

"Is that a first or last name?"

"Neither." He shot me a level look. "And I expect you know it."

Instead of answering, I looked back out the window. I did it in time to see a sign, green and white, marked with the upcoming cities. "Where are we going?"

"I'd rather not tell you that," he said softly.

A headache started to pulse behind my eyes and I pinched the bridge of my nose.

"When are you going to let me call my brother?"

"I have a secure sat phone at our target destination. I'll call him from there and you can speak to him briefly." He shot me a narrow look before returning his attention back to the road. "You're not allowed to give him any information about where we are. I'll end the call the second you try."

"Perhaps you should try couching that in some other terms, Casper," I said sharply. "I don't respond to *not allowed* very well."

He was quiet for a long, long moment, so long that I shifted in my seat to give him a wary look. He had a puzzled frown on his face and after a few seconds, he asked, "Why did you call me Casper?"

"Spectre...ghost." I waved at him.

"I'm not following."

I blinked. "Are you serious?"

"Why wouldn't I be? What does Spectre, or ghost, have to do with the name *Casper*?"

"Were you dropped onto this planet by aliens?" I asked. "Or have you never seen cartoons before?"

My first comment had teased the start of a smile

from him, but by the time I finished talking, the smile had faded. And unless I was mistaken, there was a faint but unmistakable tension now, in the strong line of his lean shoulders, in the forearms, left bare by the rolled-up sleeves of a plain denim workshirt.

"My childhood didn't allow much time to indulge in cartoons, I'm afraid," he said.

There were entire untold stories there, delivered in those simple words, in his bland, emotionless voice.

But for some reason, they left a strange ache in my chest. *No,* I told myself. *He can't make things in your chest ache, damn it.*

"That's kind of sad. Explains a lot, though."

I directed my attention back to the front window and stared at the filthy back doors of a semitruck. Somebody had scrawled a giant smiley face through the dirt. Casually, I looked at the license plate and committed it to memory, then noted the time on the clock. It wasn't much of a reference point but if I could get enough licenses stored in my memory, and a rough idea of the time, I'd have something to give my brother. I didn't know how I'd pass the information on, but I'd worry about that later. Right now, I needed to focus on creating a moving path of breadcrumbs across the middle of America.

"What does it explain?"

His voice distracted me. Irritated, I looked away from the green Hyundai I'd picked out even as I'd tried to more carefully form a plan. Still in its abstract, the idea fell apart and I scowled at him. "What?"

"The cartoons I've never watched. What does it explain?"

This time there *was* something in his voice, an odd, almost wistful sort of curiosity and damn if that didn't make that ache in my chest expand. Irritated even more, I crossed my arms over my chest and glared at the filthy semi with enough intensity that my will alone should have melted through the steel.

"That's easy. It explains why you have more in common with a droid than a person. What kind of kid doesn't have time to *indulge in cartoons*? Was your daddy too busy trying to build you into the ultimate assassin or something?"

Spectre's mouth tightened. "No, Tia. His intentions were to make me into the ultimate monster. That's even worse than an assassin."

The ache in my chest was gone now, replaced by an awful cold.

I wished I hadn't flung that last bit out at him. But it was too late to take it back.

* * * * *

Two hours later, we stopped. He'd left the highway for a series of meandering side roads and he finally pulled into the parking lot of an old gas station that looked like it predated the start of the Cold War. Thanks to previous stops, I already knew what to expect and I sighed as he pushed a hat and a pair of glasses at me.

For a second, I considered refusing him but even as I pondered the possible outcomes, my mind drifted back to the images I'd seen on Leo's computer. Although I realized I'd been looking at what had once been a human, it was hard to really *believe* it—hard to process it. She'd been...destroyed. No other words for it. Fear shivered through me and this time it wasn't because of the man next to me, but because of the man who'd set Casper and me on this bizarre collision course.

Aware of his watchful eyes, I pulled on the hat, turning it backward and mashing my hair down before putting on the glasses. The lenses were plastic and too large for my face. When I put them on, they gave me a decidedly waifish look, making me look five years younger. Thanks the oversized jacket he'd given me, my own sweatshirt and leggings, I looked more like a college kid than a twenty-seven-year-old woman. Glumly, I checked my reflection and climbed out. He was halfway around the SUV before my feet hit the ground.

"In a hurry, Casper?" I asked sarcastically.

"You can use the restroom. I'll grab some food while we're inside. I'm hoping we won't have to stop again after this."

That got my attention. "Are we close?"

No answer. I wanted to punch him but settled for looking around in hopes of some sign of where we were. Before we'd pulled off, I'd been able to memorize thirteen license plates, strategically placing them out over a period of an hour, but after we'd left the interstate for the rural road, my chances to keep up that process had dropped drastically. I'd caught *one* license plate. Just one. *That* plate had been a Texas tag and I was almost positive we weren't in Texas. We really must be in the back half of beyond.

There were two cars parked but they were on the far side of the building, no way for me to get a look at the license plates and as we approached, I surreptitiously studied the little store's windows for some sort of identifier—*anything*. I couldn't even find a state lotto sticker. All I saw was one handwritten sign on cardboard, taped to the door.

It read:

If you come in here to rob us, you better be right with Jesus.

Charming.

"Are you right with Jesus, Casper?" I asked solemnly as he opened the door.

"No. But as I have no such intentions, it's a non-issue." He ushered me inside.

The smell of cigarette smoke wafted around us, thick enough to make me want to dash outside, but the panging in my bladder had grown noticeably more demanding since climbing out of the car, so instead of fleeing, I let Casper urge me to the back where the peeling *restroom* sign was located.

"You cain't use that toilet unless you're buying, girl!" a belligerent voice snapped.

My spine stiffened.

"We'll be buying gas," Casper said without breaking pace.

"I got cameras back there!" the guy at the counter shouted.

"They aren't even connected."

I looked over at him, gaping. "Are you *trying* to get him to call the police?"

Casper frowned at me.

Unwilling to discuss realities I'd started to understand only in the past few years, I shook my head and ducked into the bathroom. I wasn't going to bother trying to figure out where we were now. If the asshole owner was even remotely indicative of the typical citizen in this part of the country, I wanted to be gone before any cops showed. Nerves made my bladder lock up on me and I had to jerk my jeans up over my hips, go to the faucet and turn the water on to coax the damn thing into relaxing so I *could* pee, but finally, I managed. The closet-sized space was dank and dark, but mercifully clean, smelling sharply of bleach. If it had been dirty, there was no way I would have been able to take care of business in there.

The soap might as well have been pure lye, drying my hands out so bad they were itchy even before I dried them on my jeans. No paper towels and I didn't trust the wall-hung hand-dryer. Pulling the overlong sleeve of Casper's jacket down over my hand in a makeshift glove, I opened the door. He wasn't standing guard immediately outside, but I didn't even spare a glance at the emergency exist, partially blocked by a pallet stacked with cases of coke and shitty beer. Instead, I walked straight back into the main area of the store.

Casper stood at the counter, emptying a basket onto

the counter. His eyes met mine in the smudged, dirty mirror hanging behind the counter. "Do you need anything?"

Behind the counter, the man's lip curled as he stared at me.

My face flushed and I started to say no, jerking my gaze from the store clerk. His face went blank a split second later and I realized Casper had shifted his attention from me to the clerk with his scraggly beard, the brown giving way to gray despite the fact that he was probably only in his forties.

"Is there a problem?" Casper asked coolly.

"No," the clerk replied, his voice sulky.

He wasn't staring at me any longer though, so that was all that really mattered. Instead of approaching the counter, I wandered the small store. Spying a small personal care and hygiene section, I grabbed a package of elastics for my hair and a wide-tooth comb.

Then, feeling mean, I grabbed a box of tampons. They were the cheap kind I'd use only under threat of death, but that wasn't the point. I didn't even need them thanks to my IUD.

Bianca always told me I had to stop oversharing, it made people wig out. I used to tell her that was their problem, not mine, but had finally come to see that she had a point. People were much more comfortable talking to somebody who didn't mention extremely personal details within minutes of meeting of them.

Cradling everything against my chest, I made my way to the counter. "I need a few things."

Casper gestured to the pile. Dumping everything down, I looked at the clerk. "Those are crappy tampons. They're like sandpaper going in. You should buy a better brand for your customers."

He went stiff, face going red as his eyes jerked from the box up to me, then back to the dusty blue box that had probably been sitting on his shelf since before

Barrack Obama took office. "Nobody said you had to buy 'em, girl."

"It's that or bleed all over the place. I wasn't planning on starting my period out here in the middle of nowhere. I can't help if I'm early."

He opened, then shut his mouth. His cheeks puffed up and his Adam's apple bobbed, as if words were choking him in their effort to spill free. But a quick look at Casper had the blood in his cheeks fading away and he resolutely went back to ringing and bagging.

"I don't think that's none of my business," he said sourly, not looking at me as he jammed the keys on his old register with enough force to break the springs.

"I thought you might like to know there are better quality products out there."

He opened his mouth.

Next to me, Casper shifted.

The clerk's mouth snapped shut and he said nothing. As he slanted a quick look at me, I grinned.

The muscle in his jaw bunched up tight and pulsed.

Three minutes later, we were out the door, striding to the SUV, parked at one of the two fuel islands, the nose of the car pointing toward the store. Casper lingered a moment. "Do you need to use the restroom once more?"

"What?" I frowned at him.

He held up the bags of merchandise from the store, a brow cocked.

"Oh." Deliberately turning away, I went to the car door and waited for him to open it. A moment later, he thumbed the key fob and locks clicked open. "No. I have an IUD and I don't like that brand anyway. I wanted to screw with him. He's an asshole."

"Buying tampons was a way to screw with him?" Casper asked, sounding bemused.

Bemused...not uncomfortable. I couldn't help but

wonder at that as I glanced at him.

"Men generally shy away from discussing the realities of female biology." I paused and added, "Unless, of course, they're *you*. Now toss in the fact that I'm a black woman who rambled on about bleeding all over the place, then insulted his lousy buying choices...well, I'm surprised he stayed quiet. Although I think that was because of you."

He made no response, but I thought I saw a faint smirk on his lips as he carried the bags to the back-passenger door. I wondered about it as Casper opened the door and put the bags behind his seat where I could easily reach them. As he withdrew, I kept my attention on the store window, unease prickling inside me as the clerk darted looks out the window. "I think he's calling the cops."

I half-expected him to ask why.

Instead, he flicked a look at the grimy windows, a grim look on his face. "I'm not surprised. Don't worry. We'll be gone in a few minutes."

Chapter 13

I went straight back the way we'd come after we pulled out of the gas station. After five hundred yards, I took a county road to the north and settled into a leisurely speed exactly two miles over the recommended limit. Driving too fast caught attention but driving too slow could have the exact same effect. Aware Tia was watching with wide, strained eyes, I pressed my finger to the scanner on my phone, glad I'd deactivated the other security features for the drive, then tapped on the top left icon.

The phone's voice app came to life and I made my request.

A moment later, voices flowed over the Bluetooth earpiece I'd put in earlier.

I had to glance away from the road to change the app's location but a few seconds later, the police radio scanner app had locked in on the county sheriff's department, and local dispatch, who was still relaying the complaint from the gas station owner.

"What are you going to do if a cop catches up to us?" Tia asked, her voice tight.

"I'll handle it."

"How?"

From the corner of my eye, I saw her crossing her arms over her chest while tapping her fingers repetitively against her arm in a rhythmic tattoo—*da, da, da-da, da, da, da, da-da, da.*

Her lips pressed flat together as she kept shooting looks at the mirror.

She was terrified.

It wouldn't help if I told her not to worry.

"It's not likely to happen," I said, deciding to give her as much of the truth as I could. "I have an app that lets me listen in on the local police scanner. I turned it on and I'm listening. The sheriff's office is sending somebody out—" I paused, attention sharpening as the crackle of voices cleared and I heard an ETA, as well as a description of the vehicle. A *wrong* description. "But the nearest deputy is ten minutes out and coming from the southern part of the county. Plus the fool who called in the complaint reported this vehicle as some sort of *POS black Toyota, a RAV4.* He told the dispatcher he's about positive on that."

I shot her a look as I slowed at a stop sign. Tia blinked slowly and some of the tension left her shoulders. She took a deep breath, then the tapping on her arm stopped.

A few seconds later, she took another deep breath and looked at me.

"The insignia on this car looks nothing like the insignia on a Toyota."

"We know that. The idiot back at the gas station doesn't."

I pulled forward as a pair of headlights appeared on the horizon. Tia tensed, but after the car rolled past, she blew out a sigh of relief.

The tension remained for the next twenty minutes. I pointed out a sign on the right side of the road, announcing we'd just entered a new county.

She read it aloud. After a few seconds, she said, "I'm surprised you told me anything. You seem to be intent on keeping me in the dark."

"Don't worry," I said, surprised myself. "It won't happen again. I just wanted you to know you could stop watching the mirrors for flashing red lights."

She grumbled under her breath, but over the next few minutes, she did relax.

And within the next twenty, she dropped off into sleep.

She stayed asleep, too.

I stopped a few minutes after I'd noticed so Valkyrie

could piss in the scraggly, drought-ridden grass and drink some water from the bowl I'd brought along. She'd been whining off and on since we'd left the gas station, but I hadn't wanted to take a chance while we were still so close to the asshole behind the counter.

I'd known he'd call the cops. It had been written on his face, plain to see, and I'd considered sending Tia outside, perhaps to deal with the dog, so I could deal with the clerk. It wouldn't have bothered me to deal with him, even in a permanent fashion. Tia hadn't seen the way he'd leered at her as she walked to the back of the store, but I had. The mirrors placed advantageously around the store had given me a prime vantage point to witness it as he'd kept his eyes on her while she shopped, but it wasn't the security of his store and concern for petty theft that had been on his mind, not judging by the avid look in his eyes.

He'd caught me watching him as she'd shopped and he gave me a sly look as though we'd shared a mutual...appreciation, but he must have reconsidered fast because a dull red flush had spread over his cheeks and eye contact ended immediately.

I'm a predator. I'd been raised by one and forced to become one simply to survive. One learns to recognize another.

The man at the gas station was also a predator, one of a different class. While I could have dealt with him and not lost a moment's sleep, I also wouldn't have enjoyed it. It would be a matter of pragmatism and expediency.

He wasn't the sort of prey I took pleasure in. He was weak and foolish, easily cowed. Perhaps he preyed on others, enjoyed the scent of fear and pain, making those weaker than him cower. But he was also the sort who'd piss his pants when *he* was targeted.

He wasn't worth my attention and if it hadn't been for the way he'd treated Tia, I never would have noticed him. However, since I had, I wasn't sure why

I hadn't simply eliminated him.

Killing him would have been simple and possibly saved me some trouble.

I wasn't sure why I hadn't.

The only thing that made sense was Tia. I'd considered it, in those few seconds by the register as she'd taunted the old bastard with *tampons*. I'd wondered how it would affect her and I'd known immediately it would bother her.

So I'd pushed the idea aside.

Now, as Valkyrie paced around, stretching her legs, I looked back at the car. This job had proven to be much more complicated than I'd expected. I'd known it would be a pain in the ass as soon as Tommy O'Halloran laid out the details.

And yet I didn't regret any of it. I could have ignored his attempts to reach me. Then I'd know nothing about Tia and he would have eventually contacted another hit man and that would mean she'd probably die.

My hand tightened on the leash.

Valkyrie whined in her throat and looked at me.

"It never used to matter if anybody died. Unless it was Sarge," I told the dog.

She sat on her haunches and wagged her tail.

Sighing, I looked back at the car, barely able to make out her silhouette. "Come on. Let's get back in the car. Just a few more hours and we'll be at my cabin."

Valkyrie's ears perked and if the way she trotted back to the SUV was any indicator, I'd almost believe she understood.

* * * * *

I stopped at the Denver National Airport and parked the SUV. I lucked out and there was a spot next to the Escalade I'd driven to the airport. It was registered to one of the fake IDs I'd crafted, the legend complete with a credit history, job history and a vague educational background.

Switching out vehicles probably wasn't necessary, but I wasn't taking the SUV to my cabin. While Tia continued to sleep, I slid from the car and removed the plates. They weren't the first ones I'd stolen. I'd taken a second in the earliest hours of the day and Leo had provided me with another that wouldn't be tagged as stolen. He'd warned me the tags wouldn't hold up under intense scrutiny as they were counterfeit but even being pulled over for speeding shouldn't be enough to raise flags—at least not after he worked some magic online.

The biggest problem was Tia, like everything else over the past few days. I was oddly reluctant to take the steps I knew were necessary, but I couldn't risk her realizing where we were. She was too sharp, too observant. So I did what was required—injected her with a stronger dose of the sedative, one that would keep her asleep for the lengthy drive to my cabin and then some.

Four hours later, the moon's full light shining down on the cabin, I turned the engine of my truck off and tried to release the clenching of my jaw.

Valkyrie made a low growl in her throat.

"Okay, dog." I got out and opened the door to let her out.

She immediately ran a few yards to the side and squatted.

I needed to address my own bladder, but first, I had to get Tia inside. But before I could that, I had to do a quick check of the security measures. The sensors along the road that would have alerted me to the presence of another vehicle hadn't been activated until I'd arrived, but I still did a quick look at the cameras placed within the home.

All was quiet.

Once I had her inside, I'd do a perimeter check but it would have to wait until I had her indoors. It was getting cool and I wasn't leaving her out here exposed. There was a bite in the air already, even though it was only early September. Opening the door, I undid her seatbelt, then pulled her into my arms.

Immediately, all the instincts I'd been trying to smother since that stupid kiss surged to life. The scent of her hair filled my head, the softness of her curls brushing my cheek. The solid, warm weight of her in my arms. The way she mumbled under her breath, then turned into me. Locking my jaw, I moved from the truck, nudging the door shut.

Don't look at her, I told myself as I strode toward the wide porch. Then she turned her face into my chest.

"Casper?"

Her sleepy voice was a pure, erotic tease and I knew it shouldn't be.

"What?" I said. *Don't look at her.*

"Why're you carryin' me?"

"Because it's time for you to sleep."

She mumbled something else I couldn't understand and I slipped up. I looked at her.

She was staring at me from under the fringe of her lashes. "I was already asleep."

"I know. But now you can sleep in a bed."

"'Kay." She relaxed against me and was asleep before I got to the door.

* * * * *

The exhaustion of the past few days caught up with me.

My bedroom was on the second floor and had a large window that faced westward so I could enjoy the sunset...when I was here. I had a custom-made recliner there, along with a small table that usually held a book.

In my bed, Tia remained quiet and still. She'd slept longer than I'd expected, but after checking her pulse and pupils, I could only assume it was exhaustion. It was also possible she was more sensitive to sedatives than some. The dose I'd given her should have kept her asleep for four to six hours and we were coming up on the outer edge of that by the time I'd done a perimeter check and gone over the other various security measures to ensure nobody had encroached on my property or triggered any of the cyber-security measures I had in place.

Once that was done, I detoured by the bathroom and stripped out of the clothes I'd been wearing for well over twenty-four hours. The thick black material of the cargo-styled pants were left of the floor—they were bloodied and ripped, thanks to Tia attempting—and partially succeeding—to fillet my thigh. I tossed the rest of the clothing into the hamper, then broke out my first aid kit. After a cursory look, I decided the wound was healing well enough so I cleaned it and left it alone.

Too tired for anything else, I pulled on a pair of loose cotton workout pants, then took the destroyed black cargo pants to the bin just outside my backdoor for the next burn pile. Returning to my room, I looked Tia over as I dragged the recliner closer to the bed and sat. Valkyrie paced around, sniffing at the bed, then poking her nose around my feet. After a few seconds, she jumped up on the bed and stared at me, the look in her eyes one of challenge.

"I don't think you're supposed to be on beds," I told her.

She pricked her ears.

I shrugged.

She wasn't my dog.

Satisfied I wasn't going to chase her off, she lay down and put her chin on her paws.

After checking the time, I set my mental alarm clock. Five hours. Or until she stirred and the sounds woke me.

* * * * *

Sound woke me.

I tensed, hand going to the Sig Sauer P226 I'd tucked between my thigh and the side of the recliner, while my brain continued to process that faint, unfamiliar sound.

Clicking.

Something nudged my hand. Warm and damp.

The tension melted from my shoulders as I looked down and light reflected eerily off Valkyrie's dark-brown eyes. It had an otherworldly effect.

"You're a brave animal, approaching me like that," I told her.

The look of disdain she gave me spoke volumes and she turned away, giving a dismissive flick of her tail. Sarge had adopted a cat a few years after I'd moved out. The cat's dismissive attitude reminded me a *lot* of Valkyrie.

"Maybe you're a cat/dog hybrid."

She sat down in the doorway and stared at me again, impatience in her eyes.

I sighed, giving Tia one last, lingering look before rising.

I couldn't complain too much really. I hadn't gotten the full five hours I'd hoped for but even without looking at a clock, I knew it was a little past seven, so I'd gotten well over four hours. I could go another twenty-four or thirty-six hours without rest if I had to. Following the dog out of the room, we walked down the floating staircase. At the bottom step, I looked at her. "Are you hungry or do you want out?"

In response, she went over to the door.

Out of habit, I checked each window before opening the door. Birds chirped merrily as she trotted outside and I watched her ears swivel, but she didn't give chase. I followed her out and pulled my phone from my pocket, going online to access the anonymous, secure email server I used. It loaded quickly thanks to satellite internet access and the list of emails there caused no small level of amusement, although it was tempered with some concern.

I'd deal with Tommy, then Tia would go back to her life. She wouldn't appreciate it if Tommy uprooted that life because he was pissed off he couldn't get to her. I read through the emails, an idea already working in the back of my mind. I deleted all the emails without response then punched in a number. It took several seconds to make the connection, bouncing its way around the world in a trail too tangled for even the best hacker to follow.

It rang four times before she finally picked up and before she said a single word, she let out a long, weary sigh.

"Boy, you are causing trouble, you know that? You have any idea how many dumbasses have reached out to me, trying to charm me into giving information about you?"

"A few. But you answered my call, so I'm assuming they're not worrying you too much."

She chuckled, the sound long, low and husky. "Shit, Spectre, they'd have to do a lot better to get anything out of me."

"Not paying enough?"

"Nah. It ain't that. First of all, I'm not inclined to do any work for Tommy O'Halloran. He's a prick of the highest order and I'm not doing shit to help him or his dickhead of a brother." Anger sharpened her voice, piquing my interest but I decided not to push that spot.

She wasn't the kind of woman who'd appreciate it. "Theo, I need a favor."

"D'you now?" Theodosia, aka Theo, made another noise of amusement, but there was far more cynicism to this laugh. "Why am I not surprised to be hearing those words out of your pretty mouth?"

"Theodosia—"

"Don't you go *Theodosia-ing* me," she said, cutting

me off. "Just tell me what you want. Does it have to do with whatever bullshit is going on with his brother down in Georgia?'

"Tangentially." Skimming a hand over my scalp, I felt the rasp of stubble, and pondered how much to tell her, then decided I needed to give her enough information, otherwise, she'd dig it up on her own, which would waste time. I couldn't afford that. "O'Halloran wanted me to kill the sister of the cop who helped put the younger O'Halloran in jail. I decided not to. But I know his type. He won't let it go. He'll send somebody else and he's offering enough money that somebody will say yes."

"And that's why I'm getting tags about where in the hell one might find you." She huffed out a breath. "What did you do, kidnap the poor girl?"

I was surprised to feel a rush of blood to my cheeks. Tia had managed to evoke that reaction from me a couple of times, but I had assumed it was something related to her. She managed to evoke reactions from me, period. Yet here was Theo causing the reaction.

Apparently I didn't answer fast enough, because Theo hissed out a breath and said, "You did, didn't you?"

"What in the hell was I supposed to do? Let him kill her?" I demanded, my temper snapping. Something in her voice grated on my nerves, adding to my irritation, although I couldn't explain what pushed me over that edge.

"Spectre..." Theo's voice softened. "Honey. I think I'm proud of you. You didn't just take a principled stand there. You went out of your way to protect somebody. Sweetheart. Sarge would definitely be proud."

My face flamed and a hot, miserable sensation raced through me, one I couldn't identify. "It's not principles, Theo," I said stiffly, staring blindly at the dog. "I've got rules I go by, same as you."

"Okay, honey." The tempered, gentle amusement underscoring her voice didn't do much to soothe my rattled nerves. "What do you need from me?"

Uncomfortable, I rubbed the back of my neck and started to talk, taking care to keep my voice neutral.

I'd barely finished before Theo said, "I'm on it. I've got a few buddies from my Navy days who live in the area. I'll ask them to keep an eye out until I'm there. Shouldn't take more than a day or so. Just got to outfit myself for the job."

"Aren't you going to argue money with me?" I asked warily.

"Nah. How about this—you'll owe me a favor later down the road. Okay, I'm gone." She disconnected the call.

Lowering the phone, I looked down as Valkyrie sat on her haunches and stared at me for a long moment before her big, dark eyes moved over to the large window. Even before I looked back over my shoulder, I knew I'd find her watching me. The sun was breaching the horizon as I turned.

Tia stood there, the first rays of dawn glinting off the glass to cast half her face in shadow. The skin on the back of my neck drew tighter as our gazes locked.

After a moment, she looked down and studied my phone. When she shifted her attention back to me, there was a clear challenge in her eyes.

Yeah, she hadn't forgotten. Not that I'd expected her to.

* * * * *

The four hours of sleep I'd grabbed earlier was the most rest I'd gotten since the night I'd told Tommy I needed more time for *surveillance*. I'd grabbed four hours that night after finishing my research on Mackenzie Bailey, Tia's older half-brother.

Mac Bailey was as straight as an arrow, as far as cops went, had even saved a kid's life in high school at a party. The reports I'd read hailed Bailey as a hero, although he refused to do any interviews. Some of his friends had, clearly not as camera-shy as the dark-haired man who had the same eyes as Tia.

The boy, two years older than the then-seventeen-year-old Bailey, had been abusing cocaine for some time and was a person known to both local high schoolers and the cops, for the same reason. Chase McConnell had always been ready to sell a dime bag to kids looking to party, and from what I'd unearthed, he had enjoyed getting in on the party himself.

That night, the party had been at the home of Bailey's girlfriend, and neither Bailey nor the girlfriend had wanted McConnell around. McConnell had caused some hell and tried to start a fight with Bailey. From what I could piece together, the girlfriend had decided she'd rather the druggie hang around than have Bailey get into a fight, so she'd let it go. Bailey had backed down.

Shortly thereafter, panic ensued out by the pool when McConnell collapsed.

Bailey had apparently calmly approached and assessed, then started CPR while everybody else was panicking and screaming. He'd even managed to keep his girlfriend calm enough so she could call 9-1-1.

He'd gone on to college on a track scholarship, and judging by the photos I'd seen of him, he'd stayed in shape. He was something of a celebrity in Atlanta, one who'd developed an avid female appreciation club, so there was no scarcity of photos. That would either amuse Tia or confound her. Probably both.

Two of the men involved in the investigation surrounding Brian O'Halloran had been cops. Mac Bailey hadn't swayed course. According to everything I'd been able to dig up, he'd gone above and beyond, reaching out to supervisors and internal affairs...and the FBI. The ensuing joint investigation between the police department and the federal government had ended with a near-ironclad case against those involved.

How would a police detective, one apparently as clean as a whistle, handle the fact that his sister had been kidnapped by an assassin hired to *kill* her?

I needed to contact him and let him know she was safe.

Chapter 14

C asper came inside, bare chested, wearing a pair of cotton pants that rode low on his hips, giving me a view of a flat stomach that looked way too hard, way too muscled, to be real. The delineation of his chest, the sculpted set of his shoulders and arms, his entire body looked like he'd been crafted by a master artist.

I had to lock my jaw to keep it from falling open and if not for the bite of my nails into my palms, I might have forgotten what I wanted to say.

Fortunately, he held up the phone and my memory snapped into place.

"Are you going to let me call my brother?" I demanded, taking a step toward him.

He held out the phone.

I grabbed it.

He tightened his grip on it, not letting me take it out of his hand.

"Let *go*."

"In a moment," he said, voice cool. "Do not give him *any* indication of where you are."

I glared.

"Agree or I won't let you call."

"How do you know I won't lie?" I demanded, glaring at him.

"You don't do it very well," he commented. "You try, but it's obvious when you're not telling the truth. If you agree but plan to pull one over on me, I'll know. So don't bother."

I'd never been good at lying, but it pissed me off that he'd already figured that out. His green eyes cut into me, so penetrating, so compelling, and I jerked my gaze away, unsettled.

His bare chest and those muscles that didn't even seem real caught my attention. My heart skittered in my chest. Heat crashed through me and even though it was *such* a bad idea, I kept looking...lower...lower, until I found myself staring at a *massive* erection. The hard, heavy length of his cock pressed against the thin cotton of the heather-gray pants he wore and even as I watched, the damn thing pulsed. I felt an answering pulse in my pussy as a hard burst of air exploded out of me.

"Do you want to call your brother?" he asked, the words rough and raspy, almost foreign.

I jerked my gaze up, cheeks flushed. The blank mask of his face was gone and I found myself staring at a hungry predator. It should have terrified me. I should have backed the hell up, found something, *anything* to put between us—anything more substantial than the fucking phone he still held out to me.

"Answer the question, Tia."

"What the flying *fuck* does it matter to you? What does *any* of this matter to you?" I shouted.

It was a dare, a challenge. To both of us and I needed some sort of answer before I did something crazy. Like reach out and press my hand to his cock. Just the mental image was enough to have me clenching my thighs in an effort to still that unnerving ache.

"You don't *know* me. So you didn't take the job to kill me. *Thank you.* You could have gone merrily on your way. What's the point of any of this?"

I let go of the phone and moved closer, glaring at him.

Something flickered in the depths of those hungry, *hungry* eyes and I wondered if maybe I had lost my mind completely. He closed his eyes for a brief second, then looked at me, the remote, severe expression firmly back in place. "I've already explained. I don't have any intention of letting Tommy O'Halloran have you killed. If I didn't take the job, somebody else would have."

"So? What does that matter to you?" I shoved my chin up and stared at him, frustration, fear, and all the insanely confusing sensations crashing through me so intensely, it made it hard to think. Why did he get to me like this? Why did his response matter?

The noise, the rushing in my head, the crazed arousal I suddenly felt, *none* of it made sense and part of me wanted to run and hide from it, bury myself in my bedroom with a blanket and my sketchbooks and pencils and draw some logic into my life again.

The other part of me...well, she just *wanted*. And she wanted what was right in front of her.

"Do you want to call your brother?"

"*Stop* it!" I shoved him but he didn't even budge. The heat of him sank into me, feeding that hungry need burning within. "Answer the fucking question, you robot! What in the hell is this? Why do you care if I call my brother, if I live or die? Why did you drag me and my dog across the country?"

He didn't answer and I shoved him again, harder.

This time, he moved. But not because of anything I did.

He hurled the phone away, reached out and grabbed me. I collided against his chest. His hard, hot, *naked* chest. I sucked in a breath, shocked at the impact, at the solid feel of his body, the hot, smooth feel of his skin, the carved, sinewy play of muscles already imprinting on my hands as he shoved one arm around my waist.

"What in the *fuck* do you want?" I shouted.

That frenzied, confusing lust inside me exploded. So did fury. The two emotions tangled and whirled together to form a maelstrom that threatened to consume me.

Casper stared at me, eyes wide, the green of his

irises nothing but slivers against the stark black pupils. The cool, calm, controlled man who'd responded to me so often was all but gone.

Without thinking, I tightened my hand and didn't realize *what* I was gripping at first. Then smooth, warm flesh gave way and his lids flickered.

It was his shoulder. I had curled my hand into the flesh of his shoulder and now he stared at me, the bright green of his eyes skewering me.

"Agree," he said, his voice practically soundless. "Agree to what I asked, damn it, and call your fucking brother."

"I'm not *here* to do whatever the fuck you *tell* me, dumbass!"

"That's obvious."

I sneered at him, a reply forming but it never made it past my lips. His hand curled around the back of my neck and I felt the impact all the way down to my toes. But there was *nothing* cruel or domineering about—it was...gentle. Protective, even.

But then he moved and his next action wasn't even close to gentle or protective. He pressed me back against the wall and wedged himself between my thighs, let me feel, up close and personal, that big cock I'd noticed moments earlier.

I sucked in a startled gasp, then let out a hungry mewl before I could stop it.

"Keep pushing," he whispered against my ear. "Just...keep pushing, Tia."

He moved against me and I shuddered as his cock dragged over me—thick, heavy, demanding

"Keep pushing." He bit my earlobe. "You're not in your nice, safe world right now with some nice, safe guy you met for drinks at the bar near the aquarium."

He moved against me a second time, then a third.

I squeezed my eyes shut against the onslaught of sensation. Sensation too intense, too consuming.

I'd never felt *anything* like it.

"Those nice boys will walk away, Tia." He reached between us then, cupping me.

I sucked in a breath as he ground the heel of his hand against me.

I *tried*. I tried to brace myself against the impact of what was coming. His fingers slid lower. Defenseless, I clamped my thighs around his hand and dragged my lids up, staring at him.

"I'm *not* a nice boy. I'm not nice at all."

He went to pull away.

And that greedy, needy part of me wailed in denial.

Curling one leg around his hips, I moved my hips against his. "If you're so fucking not *nice*...then do it already."

Casper went rigid.

Before he could pull back, I curled my free arm around his neck and glared at him.

"Stop it," he said.

"No." I leaned in and kissed him. I wasn't very good at kissing. At least, I didn't think I was. I'd never enjoyed it before. The only time I *had* enjoyed it had been in the SUV with him—just *hours* earlier—when he'd been distracting a trucker. I wanted to pretend it was something other than what it was, but I was a lousy liar.

Not even to myself. He was right about that.

I kissed Casper the way he'd kissed me, tracing the line of his mouth with my tongue, catching his lower lip between mine and sucking it between my teeth, then biting down when I felt him shudder.

The heat between us sparked, grew, flamed. He thrust against me again and again and I was *starving* for more, to have him naked inside me, fucking me hard and deep.

He lifted his head and watched me, withdrawing before rocking against me again, slow and steady, letting me feel the full, heavy weight of his cock dragging over me, the folds of my pussy, my clitoris, *all* of me, making it clear he knew *exactly* how to bring me to climax.

"You're playing a dangerous game," Casper said, one hand palming my ass, lifting me, adjusting the angle so that when he passed over me *again*, the sensations were that much more intense.

I might have bit my lip bloody to keep from responding...except I realized that was what he wanted. He didn't *want* the response. He didn't *want* the reaction. It was safer, for him, if he could pretend I didn't react. Not to him. Not to this. Which made it that much more laughable. I'd *never* felt such a strong reaction to a man before, and everything *about* him made it harder to control my response.

He slid over me again and the cotton material of my leggings dragged over my wet, engorged clitoris. I sank my nails into his shoulders and shoved closer.

Fuck safety. Fuck logic.

Fuck everything.

I wanted to *come*.

He tensed.

"Tia..."

I dragged my lids open and stared at him, lashes heavy, body lax. "I want to *come*. Stop *telling* me what kind of game I'm playing when you have your cock wedged up against my pussy, Casper. Stop talking about...*whatever* it is you're talking about unless you're going to do something about it. In case you haven't *noticed*, I'm a mess right now. I can handle it by myself but it will be a lot easier if you're not fussing at me."

A hard breath shuddered from him.

He shoved a hand into my hair.

Then, even as I tried to center myself, he shoved his other hand into my panties and cupped me, the heel massaging my clit while his fingers thrust deep. "You want to come?"

I sucked in a breath. I should be able to answer,

right?

Casper screwed his wrist, flicked his thumb.

I convulsed before I realized what was happening and his mouth, always there, swooped down on mine to swallow the sobs. But he wasn't happy with *one* climax. He spun me around and jerked my leggings and panties off before bending me over the table near the door. I grabbed on, clutching for dear life. "You want to come, Tia?"

I whimpered and clamped my thighs together.

It was a waste of time.

He pushed two fingers into my cunt and twisted them, then withdrew, surging back inside while he bent low over me. "Tell me when you've had enough, love. But you'll have to speak up. Because when it comes to your sweet cunt, I don't think I can *have* enough...there..." He grunted and twisted his fingers again. "You feel that? That's your G-spot. I can make you come endlessly. Just playing...*right...here!*"

He repeated the action and I came again, hard.

I'd thought I'd learned the cues of my own body, because it sure as hell seemed like nobody else was going to. But in moments, he'd done it. I scrabbled against the table, not certain if I wanted to cling tight and beg for more or twist away from him...*if I could.*

Insanely enough, the utter helplessness of the last part was so arousing, I grew even wetter.

I *was* helpless, completely helpless...and yet I knew—*I knew*—in the very deepest part of my soul that he wouldn't hurt me.

Casper bit my shoulder, and behind me, I felt him straighten, then...*oh, fuck...*he'd shoved his pants down and I whimpered as he rubbed the swollen head of his cock through my slick folds.

"I'm two seconds away from fucking you, Tia. Right like this. Your chance to tell me to stop is now."

I squeezed my eyes shut, my pulse echoing through me in a way that it seemed like I felt *every* heartbeat with *every* second that passed by...more. How did I respond to this?

A wild, wanton woman I'd never realized existed rose inside me and she whispered, *How do you* feel *like responding?*

Well, *that* was easy. I wanted to tell him to fuck me, to even *beg* him to *please* fuck me and see if maybe, *oh, maybe,* some of the fantasies were real, that maybe the shit I read about was possible.

If *anybody* could make those daydreams come to life, it had to be him, right? This enigmatic man who turned my insides to lava and made me wonder what was *real* and what wasn't? But at the same time...*how* could I trust it? How could I trust anything I felt around him?

He shifted away and when he returned, I felt the brush of his clothing again. He'd dragged his pants back up, the bastard. He smoothed a hand over my ass, then before I had any idea what was coming, he spanked me. Hard.

"This isn't what you want, Tia," he said, voice cool and incisive. He took my wrists, using his free hand to stretch them over my head. "It's not even close."

But he was wrong. So, so, *so* wrong.

"Fuck me," I said, the words spilling out of me without any conscious decision on my part.

Behind me, Casper stiffened.

"What?" he demanded, one hand gripping my hip in a near-punishing grip.

"Fuck me, damn it. *That* is what I want and fuck *you* for thinking otherwise.

Chapter 15

Her words were like a dream. Gossamer in the rain. But even when I tightened my grip, demanded she repeat herself, Tia was calm...resolute, even. "*Fuck me.*"

This was wrong. So, so, *so* wrong.

I sputtered out...something, my hand tightening on her hip. I barely even realized I'd spoken, much less understood the words. But I heard *hers*.

"Fuck me, damn it. *That* is what I want and fuck *you* for thinking otherwise."

I looked down at her, at the flushed imprint of my hand on the soft, pale-brown of her skin, the full curve of her hips. She still wore her T-shirt—another one with comic book characters on it—this one a blond man with a hammer—emblazoned over her braless breasts.

Idly, I slid my hand from her hip to the mark I'd left on her skin, stroking. She shivered. "Have you ever had a man spank you before?"

She went stiff, then in a tight voice, she said, "No."

"You liked it."

I'd heard the broken sob she hadn't been able to control, one of sheer, feminine passion.

"I think it's pretty clear I'm liking a lot of stuff right now." She twisted against the hold I had on her wrists. "Just not the talking."

"Too bad." I let her go and watched as she straightened slowly, turning to face me. Her lower lip was swollen and I could see teeth marks where she'd bitten it.

Her cheeks were red and as I stared at her, she went to look away.

"Don't do that," I said.

"Do what?" she said sourly.

"Look away. You're aroused. I want to see it."

She narrowed her eyes and opened her mouth but before she could speak, I cut her off. "Get undressed."

Her lips parted. "Wh..." She stopped and cleared her throat. "What?"

"Get undressed. If I'm going to fuck you, I want you naked."

Her eyes darted downward to the cotton workout pants I'd pulled on after my shower. "Are you going to get undressed, too?"

"Do you want me to?"

She nodded, a quick, jerky motion that lacked the brazen quality she'd showed seconds earlier when demanding I fuck her. Still watching her, I shoved the pants down and kicked them away.

My cock, already painfully hard, bobbed and pulsed as she stared, her tongue coming out to wet her lips. She blinked slowly, as if coming out of a daze. "You're...um...you're really big."

I'd been told that before. "I don't make a habit of going around comparing my cock to others, so I'll take your word for it. Get undressed, Tia. Now. Or we're not doing this."

Her eyes slanted up to meet mine, a flicker of that snarling she-dragon from moments earlier rising again. "I'm starting to think you're not as in control as you think, Casper."

She was entirely too correct. Control and I had parted ways when she'd started staring at my chest, then looked lower and realized I'd been aroused, that my cock was hard, that I hurt...for *her*. It would be easier all around if she backed away. I could deal with sexual frustration. I only rarely indulged, making arrangements at a brothel in Europe where the women kept themselves clean and prided themselves on their jobs as professional sex workers. Everything was very cool, controlled and neat.

Nothing with Tia was. And I'd lost even the ability to care about what a fucking disaster that was.

She gripped the hem of her T-shirt, stripping it off. Her soft, wildly curling mass of hair settled back around her shoulders as she tossed the shirt down on top of my pants.

Her breasts were big and full, nipples already tight. They both had a faint tilt to them, pointing slightly outward and I was fascinated by that. She shifted, her arms, moving restlessly and I said, still studying her lovely tits, "Don't cover yourself. You've spent several minutes staring at my cock. I'm going to enjoy staring at your tits before I taste them."

And those lovely tits rose and fell on a shaky sigh. Finally, I dragged my eyes upward to meet hers. "I'm also going to stare at your cunt and taste you there. Does that pose a problem or do you still want me to fuck you?"

She nodded.

"Say it, Tia. I want you to be clear about this."

"I want you to fuck me." Her voice was whisper soft, but the words were steady and she stared me straight in the eye.

"Could I spank you again? Hold you down?"

Her mouth opened, a strangled laugh escaping. "Do you always have an inquisition before you fuck somebody, Casper?"

"I pay for sex. The basics are already pre-arranged."

Her eyes widened.

"I only use one place, where all the workers are tested monthly and condom use is required for any sort of penetration." I cocked my head as I studied her. "You haven't even mentioned protection."

"When you say you *pay* for sex, does that mean you've only *ever* had sex with prostitutes?" she asked, skipping the protection question entirely.

"Sex workers," I said. "Does that pose a problem?"

"I think you *want* there to be a problem." She licked her lips, then, letting her eyes glide over me, she gave my cock another lengthy perusal. "I'm going to the bedroom. If you're done playing games, come join me. And...yes, we're using protection. I assume a man who pays for sex keeps condoms handy."

I didn't, at least not here. Usually. It wasn't like anybody else had ever been to my cabin with me.

But some insane impulse had overtaken me at the gas station where that prick had been giving Tia a devil's glare and I'd pointed to a box of them behind the counter. *The Magnums*. He'd switched his sneer to me as the bathroom door opened and I'd watched Tia circle around the shop as he rang them up. I'd pocketed them before she reached the counter, telling myself I'd throw them out.

I hadn't.

On my way to the bedroom, I retrieved the box and found her curled up in the bed, the covers up to her chin.

I went to her, tossing the box of condoms onto the nightstand before crawling across the bed. I grasped the covers, half-expecting her to hold onto them in a ridiculous tug of war.

But she didn't so much as touch them as I dragged them down.

She shivered as I bared her body, then stretched out next to her. I stared into her eyes as I slid the flat of my hand down her arm, her hip, then up to cup her breast. A disquieting sensation spread through me as I palmed her, pinching the nipple lightly. Goose bumps broke over her flesh and she shivered.

"Are you cold?"

"Cold?"

The word sounded strangled and I looked up to see her with her eyes squeezed tightly shut. She must have felt me watching because her lids flew open and she glared at me. "No, I'm not...I'm not *cold*! What happened to the pissed-off asshole downstairs who had me bent over a table?"

"I'm still an asshole." With sudden insight, I said, "Intimacy scares you."

"I..." She blinked, then threw my hand off, rolling onto her back. "Intimacy *doesn't* scare me. I'm not the one who goes to pros—wait, I'm sorry, *sex workers*, to get my rocks off." She scooted closer to the other side of the bed and sat up.

I was right behind her and moved in, bracketing her waist with my hands before sliding them up. She stiffened, then groaned, wiggling her butt against me. "I've never concerned myself with intimacy because deeper emotions aren't something I feel, Tia. Sex is a release for me. That's all this is for you as well—a release. Too much adrenaline in your system for too long, too much fear and anger. You want an outlet. But it bothers you that I'm not..." I dipped my head and nudged her hair aside, biting her where neck curved into shoulder. Her spine arched, thrusting her tits into my hands then she sagged back against me. "Bending you over a table and fucking you. It bothers you that I decided to take my time and enjoy this sexy body."

She said nothing so I slid one hand down between her plump thighs. Hooking my ankles around hers, I spread her legs open, exposing her. "I told you I wanted to look at you. Taste you." Circling her clit, I rested my chin on her shoulder, looking down her body over the slopes of her breasts, the slight pouch of her tummy to where my fingers penetrated. "Look, Tia...watch while I touch you like this. Watch and tell me it doesn't make you even hotter than you already are."

She'd already been watching, but at my words, she shuddered and spasmed, tightening around me. I kept pumping and twisting until I had her hovering on the edge, then I wrapped an arm around her belly and hauled us back onto the bed, rolling until I had her pinned under me. Pulling back, I urged her onto her knees and spread her open, baring the slickly wet folds of her cunt.

"Your pussy is perfect," I muttered as I went lower and pressed my face against her.

She jolted and cried out. With my left hand, I tightened my grip, then I spanked her right cheek. "Hush, now."

She didn't. But I didn't really want her to. I craved the raw, rough sounds of pleasure falling from her lips. My cock practically howled in jealous rage, wanting to be where my mouth was, where my fingers had been. But her taste was rich, spicy and she moved against me with feverish intensity, her body vibrating. I wanted her hovering right on the edge, until she was lost in need, so I didn't hurt her.

I was big, too big for some women's comfort and the control I needed was shaky, too shaky. I couldn't even begin to gather the threads of it. The more ready she was...

A high, keening sound slid from her and she went rigid. I rose over her, watching as her spine flexed, then bowed up.

She swore in frustration and went to shove back against me. I spanked her again. She whipped her head around to glare at me.

"I thought you wanted me to fuck you."

"You're *teasing* me."

With a shrug, I slid from the bed and walked around it to get the box of condoms. She sank back onto her heels, cheeks flushed and eyes glassy, staring at me as I opened the box. I tore off one of the condoms. From the corner of my eye, I saw her moving and glanced over. She took the condom from me and swallowed, hard. "I want you in my mouth."

The box crumpled in my hand at those words, then

fell, mangled, to the floor.

Her eyes lit with smug female satisfaction and she looked incredibly beautiful in that moment. If my breath hadn't already been stolen by her previous words, then the expression on her face would have done it.

She caught my arms and nudged me around and I was stupefied enough to let her. She backed me up to the bed and I sat down. We stared at each other as she went to her knees in front of me.

I closed my eyes.

"Don't do that," she said, her words lightly mocking. "You're aroused, Spectre. I want to see it."

I went to snap at her—*Call me Casper.* I bit it back just in time, because how fucking stupid was that? Demanding she call me the name she'd plucked out of the air, most likely to annoy me.

I did look at her, though.

I watched as she wrapped her hand around the base of my penis, watched as she licked her lips, then darted a look up at me.

"I've never done this," she whispered.

"You don't have to do it." *Please don't stop.*

"I want to." She moved forward, then paused again. "How do I..."

"I can't help you, Tia. I've never done this, either."

Her eyes widened.

"I told you that I don't bother with intimacy. Sex is nothing more than a release and I don't need particular methods to obtain it."

Her fingers tightened slightly while curiosity and questions burned in her eyes. "I guess we'll figure it out then." She leaned forward and I grunted as her mouth, hot and wet, wrapped around the head of my cock. Her lips stretched to accommodate me and she jerked back after a moment, eyes watering, but she didn't stop. I wrapped my fist around my dick, marking her limit, shuddering as she slid back, then up. The reddened flesh of my penis grew wet and she fell into an easy rhythm that had my balls drawing tight, while sensation shot down my spine in prickling waves.

She moved faster. Pushing my fingers into her curls, I tried to slow her down. I didn't want to come yet and if she kept it up, I was going to. Nothing had ever felt like this—having Tia suck my cock while hungry little noises fell from her lips. She wouldn't slow. Swearing, I pulled her off but when I tried to stand, she pushed me back down and dragged her hand up over my wet cock.

"Move, Tia," I said harshly, catching her wrist.

"Why?" She squeezed.

My cock pulsed and I groaned, gritting my teeth.

She picked up speed. Swearing, I closed my hand over hers, and squeezed harder, tightening her grip. She swayed backward, watching. I looked down at the same time. One more rough stroke and I came, thick jets of white exploding out. It splattered on her chest and she shuddered, a faint smile curling her lips. She pumped until nothing else came out, then she leaned forward and kissed the head of my cock.

I was already aching for more.

She went to stand and I helped her, breathing hard, as if I'd just run ten miles uphill. "Do you want to clean up?"

Instead of answering, she leaned forward and pressed her mouth to mine.

"I'll take that as a no." Grabbing her around the waist, I pivoted and spun, planting her ass on the edge of the bed. The stark black condom packet stood out against the simple white duvet and I grabbed it, tearing it open.

Tia lay on her back, watching me, eyes roaming over me before locking on my hands as I dealt with the condom.

Snapping the bottom edge into place, I hooked my

left elbow under her right knee. "Tell me if I hurt you."

Her eyes widened. Her mouth fell open, but she said nothing as I rubbed the head of my cock against her clit before tucking it into her entrance. She yielded slowly, shuddering breaths escaping her.

I kept my eyes on her, watching for any sign I *was* hurting her but all I could see was her swollen mouth, her flushed cheeks, her gray eyes going so dark they almost looked black.

I started to withdraw and she whimpered.

Muscles quivering, I bent lower.

She made a tentative movement, clenching around me and I stiffened, the sensation electric. My cock liked it, too. Too much. It jerked inside her cunt and her eyes widened, a cry spilling out of her. "Please..."

I sank deeper inside, clutching the shreds of my control. "Please what...?"

"More." She reached up and caught my neck, pulling me down and pressing her mouth to mine.

Her breasts went flat under my weight and the slick fluid of my semen, still drying on her, had our bellies and chests sliding together. Her pussy gave another one of those milking clenches. I let go of her knee, fisting my hand in the sheet to ground myself but that was a mistake because as soon as she had her leg free, she wrapped *both* of them around me and pulled me deeper. Mindless, starving for her, I let her, feasting on the honey of her lips as I withdrew, then thrust back inside.

Body going rigid, she jerked her head back and wailed, squeezing my hips harder, lifting hers to meet me and grinding against me. "More...*more*..."

Control crumpled, withered into dust.

I lunged, filling her.

Tia's mouth opened in a soundless cry, her eyes wide and locked on my face. And she started to come, spasming around me, milking me, her cunt getting so tight it was work just to withdraw...and *sweet, sweet* torture to fuck my way back inside her.

But damn if I wouldn't submit to it. I rode her through the orgasm and she clung to me, demanding everything, even the dead remains of the control I tried to gather. The slick wet heat from her pussy bathed my balls and they drew tight against me, warning me of another climax.

Tia was nearing her third. Untwining her legs from my hips, I lifted her and took a few steps, putting her back to the window. I'd constructed the home to be safe, while still allowing me to enjoy the wild beauty of Colorado's Rocky Mountains. But this was the best view, and the best reason yet for the bullet-proof glass that now supported us.

The sight of her lovely face, flushed with passion, mouth open and eyes wide, imprinted itself on my mind.

Remember...

I had a visceral need to freeze this moment in time, a snapshot—not just how she looked, but everything. From the sounds rising from her throat, to the silken glove of her pussy clenching around me, the scent of sweat rising from our bodies.

Remember...

She gasped at the cool chill, arching into me. Her weight drove her down completely on my cock and she wiggled, flexed, moaned around me. Catching both her legs behind the knee, I lifted up, pinning her against the thick pane of glass, staring into her foggy eyes before letting my gaze drop down to where I had her impaled on my cock.

She did the same, moaning, the sound turning into a keening noise as I retreated, then rising to a sharp cry as I filled her again. She gripped my shoulders, nails biting into my skin, yet one more sweet sensation, a brand I didn't want to ever fade. But it would. *She* would. She'd disappear from my life and soon, I'd have only this...memory.

The idea infuriated me and I moved quicker, faster, shoving us both into climax.

Chapter 16

He carried me into the bathroom, putting forth proof that those sleek muscles of his weren't just for show. As he collected towels, I looked around, absently gathering up my hair.

"What's wrong?"

"I need something for my hair."

"Something...as in shampoo?"

I rolled my eyes at him. "In case you didn't notice, I'm half-black. I only wash my hair about twice a week. Black people don't have the same kind of hair as white people." Then I glanced at his scalp where the faintest hint of blond stubble showed. "At least when those white people let their hair grow."

He smoothed a hand over the left side of my hair and I could feel a flush burning my cheeks. I had no idea how crazy my hair must look after falling asleep without wrapping it or anything. The flush deepened as he leaned in and nuzzled the thick curls, murmuring, "I love your hair. Thick and soft...and it smells nice. I'm guessing you don't want it wet then. Wait here."

I was about to tell him I wasn't too worried about my hair getting damp, but he'd already walked away and when I turned to look at him, I got caught up in watching the flexing muscles of his ass and legs.

Wow.

My artist's brain immediately went to work, capturing every detail, because damn if I didn't plan to draw him. I jerked my eyes upward to get an eyeful of his back, but he'd already turned out of sight. Damn. Oh, well. I'd look later. Besides, that ass had been worth every second I'd spent staring. He was physical perfection. Squeezing my eyes closed, I made a mental snapshot to pull up when I had my charcoals and a sketchpad. Black and white. I'd draw him in black and white. It was the only medium that could capture the stark perfection of his body.

Already picturing how I'd start, I opened my eyes and it was in time to see him re-enter the bathroom and now I had another mental snapshot to capture, only I worried if my brain might shut down from overload.

He was all long, sinewy muscle and pure, masculine perfection. Wide shoulders gave way to a deep chest before tapering to a narrow waist and hips, like an artist's dream—and I should know. His thighs were solidly built and I shivered, thinking of how it had felt to have him driving into me, the contained power I'd felt inside him. Damn it, even his calves and feet were perfect.

His body wasn't without flaws, though. There were scars. Seeing them made my mind go blurry, so I blocked them out—all save one. That ugly red one on his right thigh was too new, too fresh.

And I'd put it there.

Guilt crept through me and I shoved it aside, unwilling to dwell on it right now.

He was so much better to dwell on.

"Men like you shouldn't be allowed to exist," I said.

"I'm aware." He held out a scrunchy. It was mine. I recognized the pattern.

Snatching it from his hand, I made a face at him. "Arrogance isn't sexy."

"Was I being arrogant?"

Scooping my hair up with practiced motions, I held his green eyes. "You're too fucking pretty, you're hung like a horse, and your body looks like something a master sculptor created in a fever dream. Men like you exist to make others feel inferior while giving visual orgasms to women. It's not fair to the human race, therefore you shouldn't be allowed to exist. And your comment? *I'm aware.* Yes, you're being arrogant."

His lids drooped, his gaze on my hands as I finished tucking up my hair. But he finally met my gaze again. "I'm glad you like my body. I'm strong because it serves me to be strong, considering the life I've chosen to lead. My body is a weapon. Like all weapons, it performs best when kept in prime condition. As to my cock..." He shrugged. "That's genetics. I think I've more to be arrogant about when it comes to how I made you scream when I went down on you. I don't give a shit if I make anybody feel inferior or if I give...how did you put it..." His lips quirked. "Visual orgasms. Although perhaps it's an interesting idea, watching you come, I'd much rather be more...directly involved, Tia."

I opened my mouth, then shut it. After a few more seconds, I finally said, "I think you're the only person I've ever met who is blunter than I am. Okay, if you being a walking orgasm and the unfairness to all other men isn't a reason against your existence, what were you talking about?"

"I'm a monster, Tia," he said, his eyes going cold and remote again. "Why don't you shower?"

He turned to go. I grabbed his arm. "With you."

He wanted to refuse. I saw it in his eyes.

But there was something else, something I'd realized was lurking behind that cold, icy remoteness.

He was lonely.

Stop it with your Stockholm/Casper fixation, Logical Tia said.

Usually, Logical Tia won arguments like this. Instinct wasn't as reliable as things that could be proven with simple fact, after all. But what facts backed up his claims of being a monster?

A monster would have taken the job and killed me. Or left me alone so somebody else could do the job. His methods were...odd, but I wasn't sure I could see the *monster* he thought I should see.

"With you," I said again, walking backward and drawing him along with me.

And he let me.

The shower was a thing of pure luxury, multiple jets from multiple angles. There was a larger one overhead, but he made a few adjustments and it turned off completely, allowing me to keep my hair out of the water. Yet another small kindness that so many would overlook. Sleek dispensers in the wall held soap and I sagged against the wall as he worked a thick lather over my body. When he would have done the job for himself, I pushed his hands aside and washed him, then before he could rinse off, I slid my hand down between us and wrapped it around his penis. He was hard, had been since he'd started slicking the soap over me. Pivoting us around, I nudged him toward the wall until he was leaning against it, then I began to pump.

"I've never had a man come on me before until you did. I think I liked it."

His lashes dropped until I could see only a sliver of green.

"I want to make you do it again."

His arms hung loose at his sides, but now his hands curled into fists. "Keep it up and that's what will happen."

His cock jerked in my hand, as if to add emphasis and I smiled, rather delighted with the way he reacted to me.

A shudder racked him from head to toe as I passed my thumb over the head of his cock, then stroked him again, keeping the pace slow. He slid his hand down and gripped his balls, tugging. My mouth went dry and my pussy, still swollen and slightly sore from earlier, pulsed in hunger. "Why did you do that?"

"It feels good."

I met his slitted gaze. "Then let me do it."

"I'm not stopping you." His hand fell away and I covered his sac with my hand, squeezing as I'd seen him do.

"Like this?"

"Harder." He covered my hand with his, squeezing down in instruction. "Pump me harder, Tia. Squeeze my dick."

I did, my knees going weak as raw hunger thickened his voice.

He shoved off the wall, but before I could protest, he had me pinned in the corner, my hand between us, still gripping his cock and he began to thrust into it, fucking my fist.

"Tighter...fuck, yes. Like that." He muttered the words against my lips before kissing me, his tongue demanding entrance, stabbing into my mouth in echo of the way he thrust his penis into my hand.

It was erotic and edgy and every bit as intense as what we'd shared in the bed, even if I wasn't on the receiving end. My clit pulsed and I echoed his movements with my own hips, hungry for him, but hungrier to make him come. He shoved back abruptly and grabbed my shoulder. "Look...watch. See what you do to me."

I looked down, breath stuttering out as he ejaculated, heavy white jets of come ribboning out onto my belly, breasts and hands. We weren't in the criss-crossing sprays of water so the semen slid slowly down my body.

"Fuck, Tia..." The words came in a low growl and he dragged me against him. "Give me your mouth."

I whimpered as he kissed me, a drugging kiss that left me feeling as if he were trying to reach the very core of my soul. When he broke away, I tried to pull him back but he had started on a path downward, kissing the slope of my neck, down to my collarbone, then lower, lower. He kissed his way through the lingering trail of come on my belly and kept going, kneeling in front of me as he grabbed my left knee and pushed it up, opening me.

"Casper..." I gasped as he slid his tongue around the swollen bud of my clit. His teeth scraped across it and it was like being lashed with velvet lightning.

Then he tugged my clitoris into his mouth and began to suck.

The strength drained out of me and he caught my other leg, bringing it up. He draped my thighs over his shoulders as he knelt there on the marble floor of the shower, feasting on my pussy. Liquid heat flowed from me and he lapped it up, groaning in appreciation. He slid his fingers over the sensitive patch of skin separating my pussy from my ass and I jerked, startled at the touch.

He did it again, then again, stroking the wetness from backward and I tensed, wondering if he was going to—

He pressed against my anus, gently.

I squeaked in surprise.

He lifted his head and stared up at me over the length of my body. "Do you want me to stop?"

"I..." Swallowing, I considered, then said honestly, "I don't know."

His eyes held mine as he pressed more firmly. My body took over and I pressed down, yielding to him. Aided by gravity and the lubrication from my own pussy, I sank down, taking just the tip of his thumb. I shuddered.

"Now do I stop?" he murmured, leaning in to flick his tongue over my clit.

"Nuh...nuh...no. Please don't."

He licked and sucked at my clit, stabbed his tongue into my pussy, and slowly penetrated my ass with his thumb, again and again until I was the one rocking against his hand and seeking more.

The climax was quick and rough, my brain snapping another one of those mental portraits, him kneeling in front of me, supporting all my weight while I practically rode his face and shoved my pussy against his mouth and he penetrated my ass with his thumb. I'd get wet later on just thinking about it.

* * * * *

"You're never sticking your cock in my butt," I told him after we washed a second time. "You're too big."

"You might not be able to take all of me, no. But the muscles stretch and if done right, there's pleasure in it. But you'd have to want it, to trust me and be willing to learn. If not, it would only bring you pain." A ghost of a smile tugged at his lips, although his eyes had gone remote again on me. "If it causes you undue pain and little to no pleasure, it holds no appeal for me."

He turned off the water and grabbed a towel from just outside the shower, wrapping it around me.

It was heated and I shivered at the small luxury, then all but melted as he began to rub me dry, even kneeling in front of me to stroke the towel over my lower legs.

Monster, my ass.

He wrapped the towel around me then stepped out, holding the door for me. I glanced over and saw the towel bar and the small light on the end, glowing red. There wasn't a second towel. Heat still clung to the one around me and I went to offer it but he'd grabbed a folded one from a bamboo table a few feet away, drying off with a few cursory motions. There were about a hundred things I wanted to say to him, but I didn't even know where to start.

"I...um...I'm going to get dressed," I said, averting my face.

"Wait in here a minute." He left and I breathed out a sigh, both grateful and resentful as he walked out. I needed to get my head on straight. I was also developing an insane fixation—*Stockholm Syndrome,* Logical Tia insisted—that demanded I be around him so I could figure him out.

He was back within a few minutes, carrying a large tote bag. He angled his head in a *follow-me* gesture and I padded out of the bathroom, clutching the towel at my breasts. He put the bag on the bed. It gave under the weight.

"What's in there? A baby elephant?"

"I didn't see one in your house so I didn't think you needed one," he responded in that cool, neutral voice that revealed so very little.

I didn't need to puzzle out his words, either, because he had the bag unzipped and stepped aside so I could look.

"My stuff," I said, looking inside to find the compartmentalized interior full of rigidly organized piles of my belongings—who could organize a tote bag like this? There were five pairs of shoes in one compartment, the plastic caddy that held my hair stuff in another and the spare satin scarf I used when I washed my favorite one, along with the toiletry kit from my bathroom closet. The last two compartments held art supplies.

"Your suitcase for fall is over there."

I looked up and saw the carry-on that depicted an autumn scene sitting by the door.

Before I could say anything, he turned and disappeared into the bathroom, closing the door behind him.

* * * * *

Twenty minutes later, face washed and moisturized, my hair dealt with, I was dressed in a bright-red tunic and my favorite pair of leggings— black and emblazoned with miniature *Mjölnirs*. I found him in the kitchen, with Valkyrie standing guard at the door.

She pricked her ears at the sight of me and came ambling over. I knelt in front of her, studying Casper from under my lashes while talking to my dog in a low voice.

She watched, listening to every word.

I was convinced she understood each one. Leaning in closer, I murmured to her, "I'm glad you're here. This whole thing is driving me crazy, girl."

She deigned to lick my wrist as I pulled away and padded along at my side as I went into the kitchen area. The main part of the cabin was open, the living, dining and kitchen areas flowing into one with no walls to obstruct the view. There were windows everywhere, offering a panoramic vista all around.

A large set of double doors opened out into the back, showing a deck with a firepit.

A ladder went up one wall at a slight angle to a lofted platform that went around the entire room, a mezzanine-like effect. A doorway on one wall led to the bedroom and bath, which were located above the garage. There were windows on that level, too, identical to the ones below on the ground floor.

It was an unusual design, as open as the man who lived here was contained.

As curious as I was to explore, the man in the kitchen held too much of my attention to let me. He'd shaved his scalp bare again and he wore lethal, deadly black. Facing away from me, he stood at the stove, but I knew he was aware of my presence.

Something about the set of his shoulders made me tense and the unsettled feeling got worse when I saw several black cases spread out on the coffee table.

"I've got breakfast," he said.

He was back to his I'm-Spectre-the-Assassin-and-you-will-do-as-I-say voice.

Wrapping my arms around my middle, I looked over at the plate next to where he stood at the counter. "Thank you."

I grabbed it and the glass of juice next to it, then went over to the table to eat, my mind whirling.

"Tommy sent two of his men to your house looking

for you."

I jerked at his words.

He slid into the seat across the table from me and stared at me, his gaze compelling me not to look away.

"I guess it was a good thing I wasn't there." Picking up the juice, I took a sip. My throat had gone dry and I wanted to guzzle it, but decided that would be a bad idea. Putting it down, I scooped up a small bit of scrambled egg and took a bite, chewing mechanically, not really tasting it. "Is this where I say thank you?"

"I'm not looking for your thanks, Tia."

Tucking my hands into my lap, I stared at him. It was hard again. I hadn't thought about it, but for a while there, it hadn't been so hard to meet his gaze. It was now.

"There's something you want to tell me. Get it over with."

"Eat first."

I started to argue, but decided it wasn't worth the effort.

I was stubborn, but I had learned long ago, after a lifetime with my mother, that it was important to pick your battles. I needed to eat. I needed to drink something. I didn't do my best when I was running low on energy anyway.

Five minutes later, I'd eaten a little more than half of the food on my plate, but ignored all the pile of bacon. Normally, I loved bacon, but the eggs and toast were all my nervous belly could handle right now.

"You don't like bacon," he said as I carried the plate to the sink.

"I love bacon. I'm just not in the mood for it."

He said nothing to that, only extended his phone with an implacable look on his face.

I sighed and took the phone, half-expecting him to remind me of the *no-details* rule, but he only said, "Keep it short. You're safe and you'll be home soon."

"Mac won't like the lack of a firm date," I hedged.

He cocked his head. "Within ten days. Probably less."

"Ten…" I blinked and shook my head. I'd asked. The tension creeping into the air was weirding me out and I suddenly wanted to be alone in one of the rooms here in this big cabin, or maybe up on that mezzanine-like platform, alone with my sketchbook and charcoals, losing myself in broad strokes and shadows. "Okay."

"One more thing."

I glanced at him.

His jaw was tight, a muscle pulsing in his cheek. "You have a friend, Bianca."

"I…what?" My hand was suddenly slick with sweat and I tightened my grip on the phone.

"She went to your house to look for you while Tommy's men were still there."

I lunged for him, swinging out.

He could have dodged the blow. Mac had taught me how to punch, but that wouldn't mean much to somebody who'd bluntly said that his body was a weapon. He didn't dodge, taking the hit on his chin and rocking back slightly before grasping my arms. "She's alive, Tia."

"I'm going to kill you!" I shouted, his words falling on deaf years.

Next to me, Valkyrie started to growl and I knew she was confused but I didn't care.

I wrenched against his hold, trying to twist away so I could hit him, hurt him. *Bianca…*

He moved and we were pinned against the wall, me pressed up against it with my back tucked to his front, while one steely arm pinned mine in place. I bellowed at him and he covered my mouth with his hand.

I bit. He didn't even show a reaction.

"She's alive, Tia," he said. "I had a contact of mine watching the house. The men were watching the house, waiting for you. Your brother was there, too. Police had already been called and your house is a crime scene. It was processed and your brother was the only one there when she showed up. She must have heard something because my contact told me Bianca looked panicked. She tore the crime scene tape off the door and was in the middle of unlocking it when your brother stopped her. He'd been in his car, watching the house from the street. Tommy's men had been hiding in the woods where the road ends in a cul-de-sac. They came out to rush your brother and friend and my contact took two of them out. Your brother saw what was going on right before the first of the group, the only one still alive, reached them. He drew his weapon and ordered the man to stand down, but the man pulled his weapon and your brother shot him in the shoulder."

At some point, I'd started to listen. "If Mac was shooting, he must have planned to hit him in the shoulder, then. Mac doesn't miss."

"Mac would have wanted them alive for answers so you're likely right. Bianca is safe."

I shuddered and pressed my head against the wall.

"She's never even met Mac," I whispered. "I'm selfish. She's the only friend I've ever had and I don't like sharing her at all. I don't like sharing my brother, either. Now both of them are scared and worrying about me and Bianca could have been killed because of me."

He shifted behind me and the brutal strength of his grip eased, his hand sliding to stroke my arm for the briefest moment. "Not because of you. Not because of your brother. This is all on Tommy."

He stepped away.

I sagged at the abrupt loss of support and realized how weak my legs had gone. "They would have killed her."

"Yes. But that wouldn't have been your fault,

either."

"You knew something like that could happen. That's why you had...a contact watching my house."

He didn't answer and I turned around, keeping my back braced against the wall because, damn it, I still needed the support.

He bent over and picked up the phone I'd dropped, his attention on it.

"Answer me."

He lifted his head. It was Spectre who answered— Spectre. Not Casper. "You didn't ask a question."

He held out the phone.

Utterly exhausted, I took it and dialed my brother's number.

"Hello?"

The sound of his voice, so sharp and ragged and underscored with worry, had me sucking in a hard breath. "Mac."

"Tia!"

"Hey."

"Son of...Sweetheart." His voice gentled instantly. "Sweetheart, listen to me. It's okay. I know you're scared, but I'm going to get you out of this. Okay? Help me out. Can you talk or is he listening?"

I didn't have to look to know where he was. He stood so close, it was like being in front of a freezer on full blast. I had no idea how somebody could radiate heat one moment, then turn arctic the next. "He's listening, but Mac...I'm not hurt. He hasn't hurt me. I'm fine, so can you worry about Tommy and Brian O'Holloran for now?"

Mac didn't answer immediately. Long, interminable seconds ticked by. I counted ten of them before he finally said, "If you can't get any measure of privacy, let's try to this. Did you go north? Yes or no."

"Stop it. I'm not doing this. No word games or shit, Mac" I snapped. I shoved off the wall. Spectre still stood in front of me and didn't move away so I shoved past him. He backed up and I was relieved he didn't follow as I stormed over to the double doors that faced out over a panoramic view of staggering mountains. Soaring, stunning peaks and evergreen trees spearing up into the sky as far as the eye could see.

Do not give him any *indication of where you are.* The echo of Spectre's warning loomed in the back of my mind and I was tempted to do it just to piss him off, to see if I could infuriate him enough that the ice shattered and Casper came back out.

But I wasn't going to. Not after what he'd said about Bianca. I wanted to ask about her, and *him*— but his warning, *keep it short*, loomed in my mind.

"Word games..." Mac laughed in disbelief. Fury underscored his words when he continued, although his voice remained fairly level. "Maybe you've forgotten something here, but *you were kidnapped*. What the *fuck* is going on? Where are you? What's his name? What's he look like?"

He stood behind me. I could see his outline in the glass and the blast of cold emanating from him pissed me off.

"His name is *Casper*," I said, turning to glare at the tall man behind me.

He didn't blink.

"Casper." Mac, unaware of my sarcasm, shifted back into cop mode. "Age? Race?"

"This isn't what you need to be worrying about, Mac," I said softly.

"The fuck it isn't, Tia."

Spectre held out his hand. I stared at it for a long moment, then swallowed. "Mac, listen. I'm fine. I'm not hurt. I'm safe. He hasn't hurt me and I want you to concentrate on dealing with Brian O'Halloran."

"I...Tia, what the fuck—"

My nerves stretched to the limit, I shoved the phone into Spectre's hand and walked away. I heard him talking behind me, and for the first few steps, I even heard Mac's enraged voice. But I didn't stop. I just kept going until I stood by the bed. Digging through the tote bag, I looked at the art supplies he'd packed. Taking what I wanted, I also grabbed my fat, fluffy hoodie and paused to shove the metal box of pencil and charcoals into the hoodie's pouch, then grabbed the sketchbooks. Valkyrie nosed my thigh and I paused to stroke her. Puffs of dog hair followed in the wake and I dragged my hand up again, then smoothed it back down, sending even more doggie fluff flying. It landed on the pristine wooden planks and for some reason, it made me smile. "I need to get you a brush. Still."

Drained, I hugged her. She rested her doggie head on my shoulder and I hugged her tighter, rocking to calm myself. Tears threatened and I fought them back, but I didn't know how much longer I could do it. A floorboard creaked and I pulled back from the dog, smoothing the hair from my clothes. Without looking behind me, I grabbed the sketchbooks I'd dropped and headed to the door.

Spectre didn't move. I glared at him. I needed *space*. I needed to *breathe*. I needed something that felt *normal* to me.

And he stood there, in my way, staring at me, *completely* unaffected.

"What?" I demanded through clenched teeth.

"He's telling me that he's doesn't give a fuck about the parole board and won't go if he doesn't believe you're safe. Apparently, he needs to speak with you alone in order to believe that."

I suppressed the urge to scream.

"If I give you the phone, are you going to tell him where you are?"

I had the urge to hit something. I wanted to hit *him* and reach through the phone and hit my brother. I snatched the phone. "No."

Spectre shut the door, leaving me alone.

"Go to the fucking parole hearing," I said into the phone, not waiting for Mac to say anything.

"How am I supposed to concentrate on *that* when my sister is missing? Where's the fucker who kidnapped you? Is he in the room?"

"No." I fisted my hand in Valkyrie's fur. "I already *told* you that he hasn't hurt me. I'm *not* in danger. Look, my dog even likes him."

"Your dog." A rough sigh escaped him. "Tia, sweetie, sometimes, you still make my head hurt, trying to keep up with you. Since when do you have a dog?"

"Since the day after I talked to you about it. Bianca helped me picked her out. She's a Golden Shepherd and I named her Valkyrie. Now shut up and listen to me. You *have* to go to the parole hearing. Brian O'Halloran isn't going to get away with serving a couple of *years*, Mac. Not after what he did." My voice hitched as I thought of the picture Leo had showed me. "And that fucker, Tommy, doesn't get away with trying to fuck this up by using *me* to get to you. Go to the hearing!"

"And what if something happens to *you*. How do I live with that?" he asked, his voice ragged. "We've only had each other a few years, kid."

"Nothing's going to happen."

"You don't know that. Some sick fuck grabbed you—"

"He was offered money to kill me, Mac." Even as pissed as I was as Casper, it pissed me off to hear Mac call him that. "I'm alive because of that sick fuck, okay? He went through a lot of trouble to keep me alive. He's not out to hurt me...so do your job. Make sure Brian stays in jail."

"You think Tommy will let it all go after the hearing, sweetheart?" Mac asked.

"No. But we'll figure that out after." I didn't

mention the man who probably lurked outside my door. I hadn't forgotten what he'd told me, but it wouldn't help my cop brother's peace of mind to hear that the man who'd kidnapped me was planning to kill the leader of an organized crime group.

Chapter 17

That sick fuck.

Her words still echoed in my ears.

I should have walked away—I likely could have trusted her, but trust wasn't in my makeup and I stood there listening. The words cut deep and left me with an odd ache that left my chest feeling hollow and empty.

Hearing movement behind the door, I strode away, stopping at the end of the balcony with my back to the bedroom. The lower living area sprawled out in front of me and I could see Valkyrie sitting at the base of the steep, ladder-like steps, staring at me, ears pointed forward slightly. Her head cocked to the side, then swiveled to the left as we listened to Tia coming up from behind.

The dog wagged her tail hesitantly as she glanced at Tia, but the wagging stopped and she slid her eyes toward me.

I clenched my jaw, staring not at the dog, but the open layout of the room below me.

Even as Tia came to a stop, barely visible in the outer edge of my peripheral vision, I didn't look away.

Conflicting urges burned inside, confusing me. This hollow emptiness in my chest was an uncomfortable, unfamiliar feeling, one I'd only experienced twice before—when Sarge had told me he was dying, and one other time, back when I'd still been too young and stupid to understand how cruel life was—the day my father had found that little stray dog and killed it right in front of me.

Logically, I could identify the sensation as emotional pain, but I couldn't make sense of it and I didn't have time for it.

I also didn't have the...*ability* to figure this out, or even understand why any of this mattered enough to cause me pain.

Despite Sarge's best efforts, I'd become a monster. Perhaps I wasn't the mindless weapon my father had been intent on creating, but I killed dispassionately and with no remorse.

"Here."

I glanced down and saw the phone. Wrapping myself in ice, I faced her. Her gaze held a mutinous look but it faded quickly, her lashes flickering as another expression crept into her gray eyes. Uncertainty.

Taking the phone from her, careful not to touch her, I walked away and went downstairs without saying anything.

She followed me and I sensed her hesitancy. It was uncommon for her to hesitate on anything and that pricked at me, but I pushed the thought aside. I couldn't afford to worry about it—worry about *her*.

"Thank you," she said, the words uncharacteristically soft.

They stopped me dead in my tracks. Standing in the middle of the floor, I turned my head until I saw her out of the corner of my eye. "What?"

She circled around and my gaze lasered in on her, trying to make sense of what I'd heard.

"Thank you, Casper," she said again. Her tongue slid out, wetting that full, perfect, perfectly fuckable pair of lips, distracting me for a heartbeat. Then she took a deep breath and came closer.

I tensed.

She noticed, but didn't slow.

Her lips brushed the corner of my mouth and she eased back, still staring at me with that uncertain look.

"What are you thanking me for?"

Her brows knitted together and she cocked her

head. "Everything? I mean, it's kind of obvious that you've put yourself out there to save me and I still can't understand why. I'm only now starting to figure it out, to be honest. And on top of all of that, you went above that and made sure Tommy couldn't hurt those who matter the most to me. I...I don't understand why you're doing any of this. You don't have to and I...well, I just..." Abruptly, she scowled and glared at me. "Can't I just say thank you and you be decent and respond with *you're welcome*?"

"Sick fucks don't do *decent*, Tia." The comment leaped from me without any real conscious thought behind it. I would have yanked it back in a heartbeat if I could. Humiliation wasn't an emotion I'd let myself feel in years, but I felt it now, all-consuming and gut-shriveling.

Heat bloomed in her cheeks and her eyes fell away. "I..."

I cut around her and went for the rug in the middle of the wide, sprawling living area. "There's no need for you to continue speculating about the why," I said, pulling the rug back to reveal the trap door. Fuck knows, I speculated enough myself. As I dealt with the biometric lock, I continued to speak. "Even among monsters, there are degrees of evil. Some of us even have a sense of morality, skewed though it might be. Tommy O'Halloran, for instance, has no sense of morality. He sees, he wants, he takes, caring nothing for those who are harmed in the process. Those are among some of the things that make him a monster."

I could feel her staring at me as I lifted the heavy door but I didn't look at her. Swinging my legs over the edge of the small armory I'd built, I pondered the differences between me and men like O'Halloran.

If it wasn't for Sarge, would there have *been* any difference?

I wanted to think so.

Jaw clenched, I thought back to the day when I'd killed my father—I'd hated that fucker so much. But even then, I hadn't enjoyed it. I'd just wanted him gone. Out of my life. Out of *everybody's* lives.

No, I decided. I wouldn't have been like O'Halloran. But that didn't mean I wouldn't have crossed the lines Sarge helped me find.

Tia still watched me.

I lifted my gaze and stared at her. "Both of us are killers, yes. But he does it for pleasure, for fun, for sport. He doesn't care who his target is. He could easily kill a child. He's ordered the deaths of families for those who've crossed him, as you well know. And that is where he and I differ."

"Casper—"

"Stop it." I couldn't let myself feel this softness for her, had to eradicate it, destroy it. "That's not my name."

Dropping down into the armory, I took a few steps into the room. The motion-activated lights came on and I looked around, taking stock.

"Fine, *Spectre*."

Hearing her footsteps on the ladder had me swearing under my breath. "Get out of here."

"I wasn't done talking to you," she said, ignoring my order.

Pivoting to face her, I opened my mouth to snarl at her. If I had to chase her out, terrify her—

The words trapped in my throat.

Her cheeks were flushed, eyes glinting bright with suppressed emotion and her breasts rose and fell, unrestrained, under the thin material of her tank top.

Fuck, I wanted her. Even knowing what she thought of me, I wanted her. In all my life, I'd never *wanted* anything, not really. Except maybe not to be what I was—what I'll always be.

But I wanted *her* with every fiber of my being but it was more than a physical need, although that was a gut-wrenching thing, one that might end me. I wanted everything about her, from the way she laughed, to the way she spoke to her dog to the solemn way she surveyed everything.

You can't have her. You'd destroy her.

Harshly, I said, "I don't give a fuck if you're done talking to *me*. I'm done talking to *you*. Just because I wasn't inclined to let O'Halloran kill you doesn't mean I'm inclined to listen to every rant or petty grievance you feel like airing."

"Rant..." Her mouth dropped open.

But I'd miscalculated if I thought I could infuriate her into backing off or walking away.

"Rant," she said again in a low voice. "*Petty grievance*. You *kidnapped* me. That was *after* I thought you'd shown up to kill me *and* my dog. Then I learn you're there because somebody *wanted* you to kill me. *Then* I learn that the bastard behind it is somebody who *dismembered* a girl who was brave enough and strong enough to get away from him. I'm all but *trapped* in this situation and I hate it, but I've also finally realized you saved my life, possibly saved my brother's life *and* you also saved my best friend and protected her. You think me talking about this is a *rant*? A *petty grievance*?"

Her stormy gray eyes had grown darker, her full lips drawn so tight they'd all but disappeared as she stared at me.

"What, *Spectre*? No response?" With a curl of her lip, she gave me a scathing look that took me in from the top of my head to my naked feet. "I guess to a hired killer, a lot of things seem petty. I mean, you hold the power of life and death in your hands. If I piss you off enough, are you going to decide I'm not worth the trouble?"

Tell her yes.

That was the logical answer. If I scared her, if I terrified her, she'd back away and it would protect us both. It would hurt...*me*. In the end, she'd be better for it, though. It would keep her out of my way, let me focus on the task at hand, so she could go back home to the life she missed.

"Well?" Her sharply pointed chin angled up and she sneered at me, daring me. Challenging me. Taunting me.

Destroying me. Like I'd known she would do.

"Go back upstairs." Was that really my voice? That harsh, hoarse whisper? Practically broken?

Her lids flickered. Her lashes drooped as she cocked her head to the side, studying me. Speculation drifted across her face, then she moved in closer, lifting her chin even more. She stood so close, I could feel the heat of her skin on mine. "Answer the question first...Casper."

I shot my arms out and grabbed her. "Go upstairs."

"What's the matter?" Her head fell back, eyes staring into mine, the foggy, lambent gray so compelling it could have been some enchanted fog cast by a witch. Her tongue slid out, dampening her lower lip before disappearing. Each breath came in slow, ragged exhalations, as if she had to work hard to fill her lungs. "Can't you answer that single, simple question?"

Her gaze drifted to my mouth again and my neurons imploded.

Question?

"What question?"

I didn't realize I'd even asked it out loud.

"I asked if you were going to decide to put me out of my misery if I got too annoying," she said, hitching up her shoulder, delivering the cold, rational comment like we were discussing whether I'd make soup for dinner.

Discussing her *life* like it meant next to nothing.

My temper snapped.

Hauling her against me, I grabbed the back of her

neck, soft, springy curls meeting my fingers. I spun around, moving on instinct and backing her up until I had her cornered against the wall.

"Don't you think that's a fucking dangerous question to ask a man like me?" I put every drop of menace I could into my voice.

Tia let her head fall back against the wall as she gazed into my eyes. "Well, I don't know yet. You haven't answered the question. Are you going to get fed up and put me out of my misery...Casper?" She angled her chin. "Come on...my neck's right there. It can't be that hard for a man like you to break it. Or maybe you prefer something bloodier. I saw an entire wall of knives. Would you prefer to slit my thr—"

I slammed my mouth down on hers, unable to listen to another word.

She made a noise, caught between satisfaction and dismay as she reached for me. I caught her wrists and pulled them behind her back. Ripping my mouth from hers, I pressed my forehead to hers. "Damn you, Tia."

"What did I do now?" she asked, rubbing her lips against mine.

What had she done?

The list was endless.

She'd yelled at me.

Attacked me when she'd thought I'd hurt her dog.

She'd begged me *not* to hurt her dog.

Then she'd attempted to end her life to be kept out of O'Halloran's hands.

She'd smirked in the face of a racist old prick and challenged him by buying a box of tampons.

She talked to her dog like it was a person.

She'd made me laugh.

Fuck her, she'd made me feel.

And I couldn't tell her any of that without the risk of exposing far more than I could afford.

Knowing that would be the one thing that damned

us both, I did the only thing I could do.

I played dirty.

Grabbing the short, stubby tail of her hair, I tugged it back and exposed the arch of her neck, raking it with my teeth.

A hard shudder racked her body.

I didn't stop.

Chapter 18

For a minute, I'd thought he was going to say something. Tell me something. My heart had rabbited out of control and I'd braced for whatever might fall from his lips.

But there was nothing.

Instead, he put his mouth to work in other ways, pressing it to my neck, then scraping his teeth along the arch, lingering where I was the most sensitive. I gasped, instinctively going to grab him, only to remember he still held my hands behind my back.

That was when he spoke.

"What do you think this is, Tia?" Cool, emotionless voice a soft murmur, he trailed his lips back up until he could nuzzle the sensitive spot behind my ear. "Do you think this is some fucked-up, twisted version of Beauty and the Beast? Do you have some pitiful idea that you've developed feelings for me, that perhaps I've come to do the same for you? Do you think that when this is all over, tied up nice and neat with no bloodshed or violence, of course, that I'll find some remnant piece of humanity within me and that the love of a good woman is all I've needed in my life to fill the raging void within?"

It was almost impossible to concentrate on his words, because as he spoke, he *stroked*. One hand slid under the loose tank top I wore with my pajama bottoms, his rough fingertips gliding over the sensitive skin of my side, then upward.

His free hand still held the loose ponytail I'd gathered my hair into, pulling my head back and exposing my neck.

He looked down at me and the cool distance in his eyes made one thing very clear.

Maybe I'd caught glimpses of Casper earlier, but he'd shoved those traces aside and buried them. I was looking at the same coldly efficient man who'd broken into my house, tranquilized my dog and me, then calmly threatened to kill a trucker.

He cupped my breast and a startled moan escaped as he tugged my nipple. I felt the answering pulse in my cunt immediately and clenched my thighs together.

And he noticed.

Still gripping my ponytail, he slid his other hand down my torso, leaving my breast aching and bereft, while my pussy practically did a tap dance, clitoris swelling and pulsing in gratitude. I jerked against his hold and he merely increased the pressure, drawing on my wrists in a manner that bowed my shoulders backward.

"No answer, Tia?" He bit my lower lip and rubbed me through my pajama pants. "Maybe you know what this is, then. It's sex. We're physically attracted and sexually compatible. Some part of your brain is likely responding to the danger you know is out there and you're drawn to the person you sense can protect you. Yes, I'm dangerous, but O'Halloran is worse."

He applied more pressure this time, targeting my clitoris, and my brain went into overload, misfiring and sending out messages that translated to *Oh, hell* and *please, more* and *wait a damn minute...*

Logically, a part of me realized he was doing something shitty—using my own body against me in an effort to keep me from pushing him about...*something*? But I was already so wet, the material of my pajamas slid back and forth over me, the sensation driving me even higher.

"More than likely, that's all this is." He bit my lower lip and I shuddered. "But if this is some sort of Stockholm issue you're developing, I recommend you get over it. You'll hate yourself for it once this is settled and you're back in your nice, safe, normal life."

He peered at me again, green eyes cool, as he slowly let go of my wrists. "Go on now. Back upstairs before I take what it is you're offering."

As he presented his back to me, I stood there, shaking.

"*Normal*," I spat out, glaring at him hard enough that he should be *bleeding* from it. "You don't know a fucking *thing* about my life, *Spectre*. But let me tell you...it's never been *normal* and up until a few years ago, it was pretty fucking far from *nice*, too. I wouldn't know normal if it bit me on the ass. I used to *want* normal more than *anything* and it took a damn long time for me to accept that I was better off finding my *own* normal."

"You're right. I apologize. I know nothing about your life. However, that doesn't change the reality of the situation you're in. You're not thinking clearly."

Oh, you son of a bitch...

Frustration, both sexual and emotional, still churned inside, but they paled next to the anger, the hot, red blur of it blasting through me. It was so overwhelming, I swung my head around, looking for something to throw.

The first thing I saw was a series of knives, mounted on a wall.

The light gleamed off them and that managed to penetrate the fog of fury enough that the other rumblings in my head had a chance to break through.

Okay, we're not throwing knives. I wasn't *that* pissed. A heavy, blunt object maybe, but not knives.

I told you not to go pulling any Stockholm shit, Logical Tia said, looking down her nose at me and pursing her lips.

Bizarrely enough, *another* Logical Tia appeared. She was different, though. Her voice was less righteous and domineering. She sounded almost like Bianca.

If he's a monster and all these bad things, why would he care if you Stockholmed on him? Wouldn't he fuck you and enjoy the side bennies while he could? And why the hell would he care about any of this? Even if he really believes he's only doing it because he isn't as monstrous as Tommy, then why didn't he just dump you and go? Why does he care if you worry about your brother or if you brother worries about you? And why would he apologize?

I stared at his naked back, a million thoughts circling through my mind.

Now the bitchy Logical Tia was quiet.

"You don't make sense," I said.

He stilled.

The muscles in his back were already so rigid, if he tensed any more, he might shatter into a million pieces.

My heart hitched as understanding bloomed inside my head.

Neither of the Logical Tias in my head said anything to dissuade me as I took a step toward him.

He braced his hands on the table in front of him—a big worktable that would have looked at home in Mac's garage where he fiddled and messed with all the DIY projects he claimed to hate. But there weren't any half-built wooden cabinets or sawed-off two by fours in here.

My brain couldn't make sense of the pipes and tubing and containers of chemicals and I didn't really care. My focus was locked on the tall man with his wide shoulders, bowed forward now as he bent over the table, muscles bulging as he gripped the edge. It was focused on the way he lowered his head, the way his hands convulsively tightened as I took another step toward him.

Slowly, I lifted a hand and placed it on his back, between the taut, rigid muscles. He flinched.

"Why would you even care...Casper?"

He didn't respond, didn't even move.

Raking my nails down his skin, I took in his odd, unnatural stillness. How could a human be that still? How could any living thing stand so motionless, like he was made of stone?

It was as if he were frozen in time. Waiting. Wary. Watchful.

Sliding my hand all the way down, I moved to his hip, right above the waistband of the worn, heather gray workout pants. Bringing my other hand up to grip his other hip, I moved in and pressed my lips to his shoulder and my breasts to his back.

"Nothing to say now? You were all full of words a minute ago, big, scary Spectre."

He spun around, moving with a speed and force that had me staggering back, but even as I fought to find balance, he caught my arms and steadied me, then kept on moving until I was trapped between him and the table.

He caught my chin in his hand and arched my face up to meet his.

"What are you doing?" he demanded.

I relaxed in his grip and met his eyes. "I'm trying to figure you out."

"There's nothing to figure out!" He half yelled it and as his voice bounced off the walls, his eyes widened, as if he was shocked by the sound of his own voice.

I couldn't stop the smile that spread over my lips.

His hands tightened convulsively on my hips.

"You know...usually in the Stockholm scenario, it's the hostage taker who has more control," I told him. He hadn't been entirely wrong earlier. This was a dangerous risk I was taking, but for different reasons than he'd meant. He wanted me to think he was a threat to me, that he was dangerous and might harm me.

There was no doubt he *was* a threat. In some ways, he was the biggest threat I'd ever known.

But if I did nothing, I ran the risk of doing myself more harm.

It was the craziest thing and something that logically shouldn't make any sense at all.

But looking at him *made sense.*

Touching him *made sense.*

Listening to him speak *made sense.*

Gazes locked, I saw the war waging in his eyes, followed by the resolution as he made his decision. His rejection cut all the way to the bone when he jerked his chin toward the ladder.

"Go." His expression became colder, features harder, and words more clipped. "Get the fuck out of here unless you're really ready to start playing by the rules of this game, Tia. And in case you haven't figured it out yet—you're *not* ready."

He practically wrenched himself away and turned back to the table.

"You're such a liar," I said, the words coming out in harsh, ragged bursts. I leaned in and pressed my mouth to his back, then traced my lips over the hot, smooth surface of his skin, like silk stretched over steel. I breathed him in. "I think *you* are the one who isn't ready, Casper."

Catching his hips and squeezing, I pressed myself more fully against him.

A hard shudder racked through him, then he went still again—that strange, predatory stillness that made the hindbrain whisper, *Be still, freeze, don't move, don't breathe...*

Only that message fell on deaf ears.

In the past few minutes, I'd gone and turned into some brazen, ballsy hellbitch with no limits, no boundaries and no sense of self-preservation.

Without thinking, I shoved between him and the table. There was barely enough room and the heat of him scorched me. Before he could jerk back, I grabbed the cheeks of his ass and hauled him against me. His cock was a brand against my belly and I moaned as the want rolled through me.

An answering noise, too animalistic to describe, emanated from him.

I couldn't hold him where he didn't want to be, and despite his pretenses otherwise, he most definitely wanted to be right there. He had no willpower when it came to me. There, at least, we were on equal footing.

His chest crushed into my breasts and I could feel the rapid beat of his heart, the heavy, hard rush as he struggled to catch his breath.

Tipping my head back, I stared at him.

His eyes were too wide, too dark.

"If this is just sex, why are you so concerned about anything other than fucking me, Casper?"

He grabbed my head between his hands, staring at me wild-eyed.

"Damn you," he muttered. "Damn you for making me feel."

Chapter 19

That void in my chest cracked open and things I hadn't known I *could* feel spilled out.

I needed to shut this down. Shut her down and end this, before it got out of hand, but it already was and I had no idea how to wrench matters back under my control.

"If this is just sex, why are you so concerned about anything other than fucking me, Casper?"

She stared up at me, taunting, challenging, *unafraid*—and so damn sexy, so erotic, so unexpected. So everything.

Grabbing her, I cupped her skull between my hands, staring into her hazy, beautiful gray eyes.

"Damn you." Damn us both. "Damn you for making me feel."

A faint smile curled her lips. "You think you haven't made me do the same thing, Casper?"

I groaned, burying my face in her soft, sweetly scented, crazy curls. "You should have walked away when you had the chance."

"I don't know if I ever did. I mean, you saved my dog, my brother and my best friend, Casper." She turned her face into my neck and brushed her lips over my skin.

That soft touch sent a flood of sensation flying through me and I tightened my grip on her, aching. It was a gut-deep, visceral ache—a thirsting, the kind that might never been quenched, or eased.

She kissed her way along my collarbone, then lower, lower.

A hard breath shuddered out of me and I looked down as she started to kneel, only to jerk my eyes away. The thought of stopping this was no longer even possible, but if I kept watching—

My gaze landed on the wall behind her.

It held my collection of automatic rifles. Blood roared in my ears.

"Get up."

She didn't move quickly enough so I caught her arms and pulled her upright. I had to get her out of this room. If I had someplace safe to take her—someplace other than *here*—I would haul her out to the SUV and drive her off my mountain just so I didn't have to think about her in this room ever again.

But I'd damn well get her out of *here*.

"Casper—"

"Stop," I said, barely able to squeeze out the word. Everything about her was life and warmth. Bewildering things I couldn't understand. What I understood was this room—cold, sterile death. And I wasn't going to have her hands on me in here. Nor mine on her.

I urged her toward the ladder and she must have sensed something was wrong because she didn't argue—for once.

Her shoulders slumped a little.

Do it. She thinks you're pushing her away again. Let her.

But I wasn't that strong.

When she realized I'd followed her up the ladder, she looked back at me, eyes widening, but I didn't look directly at her. I focused on closing the concealed room, securing the door and locking it. My hands were shaking by the time I was done—yet one more erratic, out-of-control oddity, one more reason I should push her away.

"This will never go anywhere," I said harshly. "My life, your life, they'll never be compatible. I am who I am. I can't change."

"Can't?" She took a step toward me. "Or is it won't? Or could it be...you don't know how?"

"Can't. If that's something you can live with, if you still want me to take what you're offering..." I stopped, unsure how even to proceed.

"Do you even know what I'm offering?" she asked, that challenge in her voice once more. "I'm not even sure *I* know."

I caught her hips just before she would have pressed her body to mine. Under my hands, her skin was soft and warm and everything about her called to me.

And I was tired of fighting it.

I stooped and caught her up, tossing her over my shoulder. From her perch on the couch, Valkyrie growled softly. "Sit," I said, not even looking at the dog as I walked by.

I climbed the steep steps to the loft and strode to my room, heart racing impossibly fast. By the bed, I lowered her to her feet. As soon as I straightened, I cupped her face in my hands and lifted her mouth to mine.

She lifted to meet me, lips parting, her hands gripping my sides, her short, neat nails scoring my skin.

Then she slid a hand between us and curled her fingers around my cock.

Groaning, I backed her up to the bed and half-lifted, half-pushed her down onto it, falling on top of her. She pushed the thin cotton workout pants down my hips.

I tore her shirt off and shoved onto my knees so I could strip her pajama bottoms away, then push her thighs wide.

She lay with her hands at her sides, staring up at me, mouth parted.

Still watching her, I stretched out between her legs and lowered my head until my mouth hovered just a breath away from her pussy. She whimpered and lifted her hips.

The scent of her filled my head and I pressed my mouth to her cunt, flicking my tongue against her clit.

She arched up again and I cupped her ass, angling her upward as I feasted.

My cock and balls ached, jealous of the slick honey I'd found, but I wasn't about to stop until she was moaning and begging for more.

Her hips rolled and pumped and her hands cupped my head, holding me against her. She dug her heels into the bed and pushed up.

"Please...Casper. I want more..."

I pulled back and rolled her onto her hands and knees, tugging until her legs dangled over the side of the tall bed, her toes barely touching while her ass and cunt were exposed to me. I knelt behind her again and spread her open with my hands, spearing my tongue into her pussy, then stopping to spank her and listen as she squealed and rocked.

Slick moisture flowed from her. I gathered it and worked it upward to her ass.

She quivered.

Rising, I bent over, gathering her hair in my free hand and brushing it aside so I could see her face as I pressed my index finger to the tight entrance. She whimpered as I stroked, the frantic rocking of her hips slowing to nothing. I twisted my wrist and she gasped. Pain pinched her features and I went to pull back, but then she moaned and pushed down on me, the tight muscles yielding to me.

The thought of feeling this hot, silken hole yield and take my dick was almost more than I could bear, but I'd suffer it happily as long as I could watch the erotic pleasure on her face as she softened and flexed and rocked against me.

But soon it wasn't enough for either of us, the frenzied movements of her hips demanding more and my cock leaking clear drops of fluid as I watched her ass bounce and rock as she took a part of me in a place where she'd allowed no other.

When I stopped, she groaned and swore at me. I left

her, bent over and quivering, while I went to wash my hands and get a condom, then came back and flipped her onto her back and lifted her legs into the air, hooking them over my elbows.

Her eyes widened as I pressed against her, then she jolted and shouted as I filled her, hard, fast and completely.

"Casper!"

I surged in and leaned over her, watching as her lashes fluttered and she shuddered, convulsing around me. "I want to fill you so completely, you feel me in every part of you."

"I think you succeeded." Her cunt tightened around me, a slow milking contraction that had my balls drawing in tight.

"It's not enough." I scooped her and rose, pacing over to the wall, once more hooking her knees over my arms. "This isn't enough."

But it was all I'd ever have.

"We'll make it enough." She pulled me close and kissed me.

I wanted to tell her she couldn't.

But the urgency was too strong. She flexed and tightened around me again and my cock ached and swelled and my control was shattered. Thrusting into the wet, snug glove of her body, I buried my face against her neck and she clung to me.

The orgasm grabbed both of us, slamming into us without mercy. I drove into her and she raked her nails down my shoulder, biting my lip as she writhed against me. I gripped her, hard and tight, forgetting about the soft satin of her skin, lost to everything but the strength of her passion and the certain, sure grip of her arms as she held on, steadying me.

Emptied, drained, I pushed away from the wall and staggered a step or two before I steadied myself.

I managed to make it to the bed and spill both of us onto it.

She was the one who snagged the covers and pulled them over us.

"It's not going to be enough, Tia," I said.

I didn't even know what I was talking about.

But she didn't question me.

She curled in closer and wrapped her arm around my waist. "We can make it enough. We just have to trust that we can do that."

"I don't know how to trust. And you shouldn't trust me."

She kissed my chest and pressed her fingers to my lips. "Go to sleep, scary, spooky, mean Spectre. You sound punch-drunk."

Chapter 20

W e both slept but I woke up well before he did. It was weird, lying there next to him without him rousing. I had a feeling it wasn't normal for him to lie there lost in sleep while somebody else lay next to him.

Was it a sign of trust?

Or just exhaustion?

I lay there, thinking about it until my head hurt, and then something else took center stage—my bladder. I had to pee. Shifting in the bed, I eyed the bathroom. Casper stirred.

"I need to go pee," I told him, not bothering to whisper. My gut told me that trying to sneak or be quiet around a guy who lived and died by violence wasn't the smartest move.

His eyes opened. There was no gradual awakening for him. He went from asleep to instant alertness and I was glad I hadn't tried to slip out of the bed. "You know where the bathroom is," he said.

His voice was back to that neutral tone.

"Yeah, but you were asleep. I've got a feeling you're not used to having somebody moving around in the bed with you when you're not awake."

To my surprise, a faint smile curled his lips. "No. I'm not." He cupped my face in his hand, brushing his thumb over my lip. "This wasn't supposed to happen, Tia. None of this."

"What?" I gave him a deadpan look. "You mean after you got that call from Tommy and laid eyes on my rocking bod, you didn't instantly decide that you and me were going to twist up the sheets every chance we got?"

"I never expect that smart-ass sense of humor to make an appearance. I don't know why, but it always hits me as a surprise."

Grinning at him, I bent over and kissed his nose. "It took me a while to figure out how to make jokes but I do have a sense of humor, you know."

"I know that." He stroked my face again. "I never doubted it. It's just...surprising when it slips out. I thought you had to go to the bathroom."

"I do. I just like talking to you. I don't always like taking to people."

His lashes drooped, concealing his gaze once more. "I'll be here when you're done."

Because the panging in my bladder had grown insistent, I hopped up and rushed off to take care of business. The soap left my hands feeling itchy so I dug through the toiletry case for my lotion. A pink bottle caught my eye and I went still, thinking back to what I'd told him earlier—and what he'd told me.

I'd told him to trust me.

I don't know how to trust. And you shouldn't trust me.

He'd mentioned trust to me one other time. Granted, it had been about something completely different, but was it really? I put the bottle down, cheeks heating just thinking of it. It was a crazy idea. I wanted him to trust me enough to take some sort of chance with me.

A chance at what? I asked as I put lotion on my hands, taking far more time with the task than necessary.

He'd already made it clear that a life together wasn't going to happen.

And it wasn't like we could stay *here*.

My brother was already frantic. Bianca must be, too.

I had a life. It had taken me a long while to build that life and I loved it.

Yet the idea of leaving him behind left an almost visceral pain in me. Did I love *him*?

You can't love him. You barely know him.

And it was true.

But maybe I *could* love him. Warmth settled in my chest. It was a comfortable kind of thing, too. Like I'd found the answer I'd been looking for. Sensing Logical Tia had something to say, I braced myself for the argument.

You won't be able to talk him into it, sweetie, she said, almost sadly. *He already said he didn't know how to trust.*

Looking into the mirror, I met my gaze.

"Then we'll teach him," I said quietly.

I hadn't always known how to trust, either. But I'd figured it out. There was no reason he couldn't do the same.

It hit me, then, that there might be reason why I felt so...*comfortable* with him. Even safe, when that was the last thing I *should* feel.

I saw parts of me within him.

I'd glimpsed it in the long drive here, when I first realized he was lonely, and during the odd comments he'd let slip about his childhood, which clearly had been far more screwed up than my own.

We could fit...somehow. I just had to make him see it.

Now I had to figure out the next thing.

How did I seduce the deadly guy in the room out there, and just how I should I go about telling him I was ready to let him try to fuck me in the ass?

After all, he'd told me it would take trust and if that was a way to show him that I could trust him, maybe it would help him learn to trust me.

"This sounds crazy, Tia."

Logical Tia agreed silently.

But both of us were a little excited, just thinking about it.

Excited, and maybe a little nervous. Okay. A lot

nervous. I thought about trying to sneak out and see if I could get his phone, research a bit. Or maybe I could talk him into letting me online. He had access. I knew he did. If I could just—

Stop stalling. It was surprising to hear Logical Tia urging me on, but maybe Logical Tia was just smarter or braver than I was.

I'm part of you, weirdo. Now get out there.

* * * * *

Five minutes later, I did just that. I didn't consider the extra five minutes stalling. I wanted to brush my teeth, then I decided since I'd done that, I should wash my face and maybe put lotion on all over. He seemed to like how I smelled and then it dawned on me that he might try to do other stuff, which made me think I should probably wash up some.

This seduction thing required way too much thought and preparation. It also allowed way too much time to think and I didn't want to chicken out, so instead, I thought back over all things he'd done to me so far...and how much I'd enjoyed, it, all of it.

Every single bit.

By the time I'd finished washing my hands—again—and putting lotion on them—again, I was already wet and aching. Earlier, he'd slicked back the juices from my pussy to lubricate his way as he fucked his fingers into my butt and I had no doubt I was wet enough for that now and he hadn't even touched me.

It was crazy the things he'd done to me, how he'd changed so much of...well, everything, and in such a short time.

Now I just needed to make him see that *we* could change things even more.

Hell, I *hated* change. If I could handle this, he should be able to do the same.

Squaring my shoulders and holding the bottle in my hand but cupped so he couldn't see it, I left the bedroom.

Instantly, I deflated.

He wasn't in the bed.

"Took too long," I mumbled.

"For what?"

Yelping, I turned and found him standing near the doorway of the large closet, wearing yet another pair of loose-fitting workout pants, this pair in black. He wasn't wearing underwear, either. That ought to be a crime, really. But then again, maybe the real crime was when he covered up that body, that ass. That cock.

"What took too long?" he asked again.

"Um…" Focusing, I recalled what I'd been grumbling about. With a sheepish shrug, I said, "Me. I took too long. I was planning on coming out and seducing you. Or trying to. But you're out of bed. And wearing pants."

His gaze slid down my body, lingering on my naked breasts, before moving lower. "Would you rather I be naked?"

"Always."

His dark-gold brows shot up at that, amusement tugging at the corners of his mouth.

"Well, maybe not always. You'd get arrested—or mobbed—if you went out in public naked. But while you're here with me…" I bit my lip and stroked over him with my gaze. My breath caught when I realized he'd grown erect. "You're hard."

"You're standing there naked. You told me you wanted to seduce me. And you're staring at me like you can't wait to start." He had a shirt in one hand, but with those final words, he lowered his fist and uncurled his fingers, letting the material fall to the floor. "Yes, I'm hard. You're so blunt. I don't know quite what to make of it sometimes."

Uncertainty flickered inside. Biting my lip, I glanced away from him and decided I'd feel better in the bed. Somehow, I'd managed to keep the bottle in my hand hidden but my nerves had just jacked up, which meant I was likely to drop it, because I got clumsy when I was nervous.

Hurrying over to the bed, I slipped under the sheets, tucking the bottle in next to my thigh so it stayed out of sight.

Casper had prowled closer, his gaze probing.

"Does it bother you?" I asked him. There were still so many social cues I didn't get, didn't understand, and I'd come to accept I might never really get *all* of them. No, I wasn't going to go talking about his dick being hard in public, but was it wrong to mention it to him?

"Why would it bother me?" He slid onto the foot of the bed, crawling across the massive expanse until he'd straddled my legs to kneel above me, face just a few breaths from mine.

"I...well. It bothers some people." Feeling defensive, I said, "I can't help it. Not all the time. I've got Asperger's. I'm...different, okay? A lot of people think I'm weird and I guess I am to them. Neuro-atypical is one of popular words. My brain doesn't work like others do." Fisting my hands in the sheets, I looked away from him only to find my eyes returning, trying to see how my words affected him. "I'm not *broken* or *wrong* or anything."

"No." He dipped his head and nuzzled my curls, nothing but tenderness in the gesture. "You're definitely *not* broken or wrong."

The first around my chest eased...a little. But it was enough that I had the courage to keep going. "It's taken a long time, but I'm comfortable with who I am. But some people can't deal with it. I don't have the sort of filter a lot of people have, so I say weird things, I blurt things out that make people uncomfortable. I didn't even get diagnosed until I was seventeen and I never could figure out why I had a hard time making friends or why people didn't want to talk to me. My thoughts are a mess sometimes and it's like I can't even keep up with myself. I can be awkward and I—"

His mouth closed over mine.

It was the gentlest kiss I'd ever experienced.

Not just from him, but ever.

It was like a blessing, a balm, a promise, all in one. His tongue traced along the curve of my lips slowly, as if he wanted to memorize their shape, their feel, their taste. Swaying closer, I reached for him just as he broke contact.

"You're not weird. You're funny, you're kind, you're mouthy and brave and gentle and amazing. You're you and you're perfect."

Tears burned my eyes as he lifted up.

"The next time you call yourself a monster," I told him. "I'm punching you."

A rusty sound escaped his throat, one that took a moment to place.

"Wow. You know how to laugh." Curling my arms around his neck, I urged him to come with me as I lay back. He followed me down, weight braced on his elbows.

"I rarely have reason." A shadow fell across his eyes.

I'll give you all kinds of reasons. I wanted to tell him that. But I almost felt like I was dealing with Valkyrie at the shelter, only he was far more leery than she'd been. Unwilling to trust, unwilling to yield.

That's fine, I told myself. I'm stubborn. I'll wait him out.

I nudged his shoulders. "Roll over. I'm supposed to be doing the seducing, remember?"

The resistance I'd half-expected didn't come and he went willingly. The bottle moved along with us, still unnoticed by him. I caught his wrists and pushed them up over his head, a heady sort of power rushing through me as he followed the silent command.

"What would you let me do?" I asked, holding his

wrists in place as I bent over him.

"Does it involve you naked in bed with me?"

"Yes." I licked his lips, the way he seemed to like to do to mine. I know I enjoyed being on the receiving end of that.

He responded with a shaky breath, opening his mouth.

But I didn't kiss him, just waited for an answer.

"I think I'd let you do anything you wanted, Tia." A line appeared between his brows as he said it, followed by a faint smile. "I've never let a woman on top of me like this before, never let anybody even try to restrain me."

Something dark flitted through his green eyes then. I didn't want to think about what might have caused it and I wouldn't ask. But it made my belly hurt.

I went to let his wrists go but he laced our fingers together. "I said I'd let you do anything. I meant it," he told me as he rocked his hips upward, letting me feel the full, heavy length of his cock. "Does it feel like I'm not enjoying this?"

"Oh, I'd say you're enjoying it." I shuddered as he pulsed against me, the thin cotton the only barrier between us. I rolled my hips against him, the sensation intensely erotic. "You feel amazing. Your cock is...wow."

"It will feel better inside you."

The heated promise in his voice was almost enough to make me forget my goal.

But...not quite.

Tugging my fingers from his, I trailed them down his wrists, along the skin on the inner area, to his elbows and upward to the sensitive skin exposed under his arms before gliding on to his chest. There, I pinched his nipples. He grunted and rocked under me.

My clit throbbed, my pussy clenched.

"What would you do to me...if I asked?" I whispered

to him, my voice almost unrecognizable.

His gaze locked on my mouth for long seconds before he finally looked up and met my eyes. The green was so hot, it seemed to glow. "If it's something that you want, that will bring you pleasure...you need only ask."

"And if it brings you pleasure?"

"Your pleasure is my pleasure."

"Put your hands on me, Casper," I said, a red haze of lust gripping me, ensnaring me. It was going to drown me and drag me under, I knew it.

He sat up, the muscles in his belly contracting in a powerful display that would have been distracting if he hadn't cupped my breasts in his hands a second later, plumping them together and pinching my nipples.

"More."

He obeyed, squeezing harder until pleasure and pain blurred. I covered his hands with mine, rocking feverishly. The contact wasn't enough and I wiggled and shifted until I could wrap my legs around him and grind against him. He rolled forward, spilling me onto my back and I whimpered at the loss of contact, but stopped once I saw what he was doing. He stripped out of his workout pants, his thick, heavy cock springing forward.

Running my gaze over him, I shivered, hardly able to believe the sheer beauty of him. My eyes fell on the fresh wound on his thigh and the heat inside started to fade. "Your leg..."

"It's nothing." Then an odd smile curved his lips. "No. That's not right. It's the only mark on me that means anything—it's *your* mark and I treasure it."

"I..." Shaking my head, I stared at him, not sure what to say.

Then he kissed me and thoughts of speech faded.

He moved closer and I shifted my legs wider to accommodate him.

Cool plastic brushed my leg.

Oh.

"Wait..." Blinking, trying to clear my head, I held up a hand just as he went to bend over me.

He froze instantly, retreating as if pulled by strings. I sat up and couldn't help but think how my abdomen didn't do sexy contractions like his had done.

"What's wrong?" he asked.

"Nothing." Nervous again, I squeezed the bottle of lubricant in my hand. I darted a look at him, but it was nerve-racking meeting his eyes now. I had no idea why, either. I could be naked in front of him and talk about his dick being hard and...

"Tia..." He cupped my face in his hands and dipped his head low, pressing another one of those gentle kisses to my mouth.

"I want you to do something," I whispered against his lips.

"Anything."

Rolling to my knees in front of him, I shoved the bottle into his hand. He didn't look down, simply curved an arm around my waist as he looked at me.

The silence was heavy, too heavy.

"Well?"

"Well, what?" His lashes, too thick and perfect and curly for a man, lowered briefly over his eyes. "You haven't asked for anything."

He was going to make me *say* it. My cheeks heated. Why was that a problem? We'd just discussed my bluntness, hadn't we? Yes, yes, we had.

"You said yesterday that you could..." My mouth had gone dry and I had to stop and clear my throat. "You told me you can fuck my ass and it would feel good if I trusted you and was willing to let you teach me. So...teach me."

Chapter 21

The words echoed in my head.

Blood pulsed and thrummed in my veins, nerve-endings firing as if I'd been tazed, only instead of incapacitating me, it had the opposite effect—charging me, fueling me, filling me.

Her gray eyes locked with mine, mouth unsmiling, cheeks flushed while her pulse fluttered in her neck.

I eased away and looked down at the small, round object she'd pushed into my hand. I'd been more focused on her than it, thinking maybe she'd had a sex toy in her toiletry case. I hadn't gone through it extensively and could have missed something small.

This *was* small—a pink bottle of personal lubricant, the kind branded for women.

Not the kind for anal sex, but that wouldn't pose an issue.

Dragging my eyes up to hers, thoughts racing, cock already issuing demands, I asked, "Do you carry personal lubricant in your toiletry case all the time?"

"Well..." She bit her lower lip. "Yes. Usually. Orgasms are good stress relievers. And I get stressed when I travel."

"So why not have sex?"

She made a face. "Because I don't socialize very well and in order for me to find somebody I'd be interested in having sex with, I'd have to socialize. You *made* me socialize with you."

Guilt slithered inside. "Tia—"

"You made me *socialize*. Not have sex. I pushed that." Her brows arched. "And I guess I could have ignored you. I'm good at that. Now...we were discussing something else entirely."

"We were." Shoving the guilt aside, I studied her. The guilt would wait. It would always be there, after all. She wouldn't. Curving my hand around her neck, I tugged her close enough that I could catch her lower lip in my mouth. "Just a day ago, you told me I wasn't ever going to stick my cock in your butt. Now you're asking me to do just that. Are you sure?"

"Yes." She shivered a little. "If...if it hurts too much, you'll stop, right?"

"Just say the word." But I could make sure that wasn't an issue. I'd introduced several women to this sort of sex play, the primal dominance of the act somehow able to quiet the howling voices in my head...for a time.

But that wouldn't be the case with Tia.

This was for her.

I slid from the bed, adjusting my pants back up to cover my hips as she watched.

"Lay down and spread your thighs," I told her.

She did so, self-consciousness making her movements stiff.

I brought her knees up, staring at the exposed folds of her pussy and making no attempt to disguise my hunger. "You're soaking wet. Are you sure you don't just want me to fuck you? Fill that sweet cunt with my cock until you've screamed yourself hoarse?"

"I..." A shudder went through her, one that had her limbs trembling before she got control. "No. I mean, can't we do that, too?"

Instead of answering, I bent over her and flipped open the bottle, drizzling cool lubricant over the naked, vulnerable folds of her labia. She gasped, her hips bucking from the contrast of cool fluid over her hot, exposed flesh.

"Touch yourself," I told her. "Show me how you play with yourself when you need to come, when it's just you."

"Why?"

"Because I told you to. The thought of you masturbating makes my mouth water. I want to listen while I take care of something. Don't try to be quiet, either."

"What do you have to take care of?" She frowned even as she slid her hand down her belly.

"Do you want me to spread your cheeks and fuck your ass or not?"

She rolled her eyes and huffed out a breath, then, as I fought a smile, she slid her fingers down and ran them through the lubricant. "You didn't need to use any lubricant. I'm already wet."

"Maybe I wanted to see it drizzling through your curls. Remember, I want to hear you."

I walked away and wondered if she'd do it.

I didn't have to wonder long.

A hitching gasp escaped, followed by a sigh.

"It..." Her breath hitched again before she finished. "It feels better when you do it."

Opening the closet, I went to one of the built-in drawers and tugged on the handle. It opened to reveal gags, various restraints and several tubes of the thicker, longer-lasting lubricant she'd need if I wanted to do this properly. The whorehouse I visited in Germany provided all the accoutrements one might need, but I never did like to let somebody else provide my tools so I always brought my own.

Taking one of the tubes, I turned back, but lingered in the doorway, staring at Tia, what I could see of her. Her head faced my direction and the view allowed for me to stare at the full, round curves of her tits, plumped together by the position of her arms, since she had both of her hands between her thighs. I couldn't see what she was doing with those hands, but a hungry moan escaped her lips and the sound had my balls drawing tight against me.

Crossing back to the bed, I stood so I could watch her and saw that she'd closed her eyes. But a smile curled her lips as if she'd sensed me.

And she had.

"It's better when you do it...but I like knowing you're watching me and that it turns you on." Her lashes fluttered up. "I bet I'd like watching you, too."

"If that's your subtle way of making a request, I'll keep it in mind." Mesmerized by the play of her fingers over her clit, and how she dipped them into her pussy, I moved closer to the bed. Dropping the lubricant down, I dealt with my pants before climbing back onto the mattress. I straddled her thighs with my knees and braced my hands over her shoulders. That curious mind of hers never stopped working, never stopped questioning, and I could already see thoughts flickering. "I'm going to tell you what I plan on doing, because you are more relaxed when you know and the more relaxed you are, the easier this will be. I plan on going down on you and getting you close to orgasm. Then I'm going to stop."

Her eyes popped wide. "What?"

"Then I'll do it again. And I'll stop. I might make you suck my dick before I eat your pussy again."

Her mouth opened and closed soundlessly as she processed this and I continued. "I'll keep doing this until you're nearly to the breaking point, Tia, because that's where I want you. And while I'm licking your pussy, while I'm sucking your clitoris and biting it and driving you crazy, I'll be fucking your ass with my fingers, opening you and getting you ready. If I don't think you can take me without it hurting you, I'm not doing it." I licked her lips, exactly the way I planned to lick the entrance to her cunt. "But the closer you are to coming, the more you need to orgasm, and the more you want it, the easier this will be."

"I..." She stopped and clenched her jaw. After clearing her throat, she tried again. "You just told me you plan on basically tormenting me out of my mind just so you can fuck my ass. Do I have that right?"

"Yes." I couldn't help but smile.

"You look like you plan on enjoying every bit of it."

"I will. If you still want me to do it. But...if we do it, you'll enjoy it, too. I'll make certain of it."

That delicious pink color returned to her cheeks, her lips parting. Finally, she nodded. "Okay. I trust you."

Something about those simple words grabbed me, grabbed tight and sank in, refusing to let go. Shoving the sensation down, burying it, I lowered my mouth to hers. Just before I kissed her, I whispered, "If it hurts, tell me and I'll stop. Remember that."

She shivered and nodded, reaching for me.

But I caught her hands and pushed them down to her sides, holding them there until she relaxed in acquiescence.

"You've done this before, right?"

Slanting a look at her, I said, "Yes."

"You enjoy it."

I stroked a hand down her hip, cupping her ass. "I...crave it. I have ugly things in me, Tia. You're too intelligent not to know that. Having somebody submit, yield in such a way is..." I paused, searching for the right explanation. "It's not sexual healing. I can't *be* healed. But when the ugliness gets too loud and the darkness tries to take over, I have limited options that allow me to burn it out. I can kill. I can work myself into exhaustion...or I can fuck it out. When I choose to fuck it out, I want submission from my partner. I want to dominate. This isn't a lifestyle where I expect obedience and to be called Master while my partner is a pet or slave. It's simpler and more basic. I fuck and they yield. I dominate and they submit. And nothing is more submissive than allowing a man to fuck you in this manner."

"Or a woman," she said when I went quiet. "I mean, strap-ons."

I think she expected a laugh.

"I was wrong," I said softly as dark, ugly memories washed in. "That is one thing I could never allow you to do."

She didn't ask. I didn't expect she would. But her hands smoothed over my arms and she said, "It's not something I want anyway. Others do, and if that works for them, fine. But...I just want you."

"Even after what I told you? That I fuck sometimes just so I don't kill?"

"Is that why you're with me?" That challenge in her voice again. Like she knew something I didn't.

"I..." Gripping her thighs, I looked at her, more exposed than I'd ever been. "I'm with you because I can't stay away."

"Good." A seductive feminine smile curled her lips and her lashes drifted low. "Now...you have some sexual torment to deliver."

I hesitated.

She shrugged and I watched as she slid a hand down her belly once more. "I guess I can get started myself. I mean, you got me all hot and bothered with that talk about making me suck your cock."

"Witch," I breathed out, pressing my mouth to hers.

She laughed against my lips, but the sound broke off into a gasp by the time I'd trailed my lips down a path to her neck. Her collarbone was next, followed by her breasts, and each large, swollen nipple. "I love your tits. So round and perfect and soft. And your nipples...delicious."

Burying my face between those gorgeous, ripe curves, I mounded her tits around my face before continuing my downward path.

She was panting by the time I reached my target, her hands twisting in the sheets.

Lying flat against the mattress was torment, my cock pinned between cool sheets and my belly, pulsing in time with her ragged breaths and my own racing heart.

I worked the slick honey from her cunt lower, using only that to ease my way for now. She was so wet, it was almost easy and she yielded without my prompting, pushing down and crying out when I twisted and screwed first one, then two fingers inside the silken sheath of her ass.

Sooner than I'd planned, her body tightened as her orgasm drew near and I had to stop, tearing myself from the delicious sweetness of her pussy. She moaned and grabbed my head, trying to pull me back, but I ignored her, kissing the fragile crease of skin where thigh met hip.

"Casper...please..."

"I'm just getting started, precious."

"Damn it," she choked out, grabbing the sheets again and jerking at them.

I trailed my mouth across her belly, gauging her breathing, the tension in her body and once she'd calmed, I went back and started flicking my tongue against her clit. She jolted and jerked upward, her hands coming down to close around my scalp in a viselike grip, tugging me closer as she begged, "Don't stop, don't stop...please, please, fuck, don't..."

I stopped. She wailed in disappointment, but soon moaned as I settled back into place, lubricant slicking my fingers now. "You're so close, I'm afraid you'll come just from me getting you ready," I said as I adjusted her position, dragging her knees over my shoulders, opening her, lifting her.

"I won't...please...just...don't stop...oh!" She bucked, startled as I pushed three fingers in this time, flexing them. Soon, she was crying out and begging as I went back to eating her cunt, drinking down that delicious honey even as I made her wet with more.

And again, too soon, she clenched up, body closing in on that edge once more.

I stopped.

Tia glared at me as I pushed up onto my knees. One hand was wet from her and the lubricant and I rested it on my thigh while I used my other hand to wipe my mouth and chin where her sweetness coated me. Staring into her eyes, I licked my palm, seeking out every last bit of her essence.

"I told you how this would go," I said after licking my lips, taking in the last bit of her taste. I slid from the bed and went into the bathroom to wash my hands.

She was sitting up and scowling when I came out.

Grabbing a pillow, I tossed it onto the floor, then pointed.

"Now get on your knees."

Chapter 22

If I'd ever been this turned on, I couldn't remember. If I'd ever been this exposed, I couldn't remember. If I'd ever been this desperate, I couldn't remember.

And I *knew* I'd never been this needy before. This kind of need, this kind of want—it just wasn't possible to feel something like it and *forget*.

Casper had me on my knees at the side of the bed without me even realizing I'd moved.

He speared his fingers into my hair and I groaned as he cranked my head back and pressed the head of his cock to my mouth.

It was the most carnal, the most intimate thing I'd ever experienced, taking him in while he stared down at me and told me to suck, to take him deeper and swallow his dick.

Such crude words.

Such naked need.

The head of his cock bumped the back of my throat. Gripping his hips, I moaned and pressed against him, hungry for more.

Casper swore, his fist gripping my hair while cupping my chin with his other hand.

"That's it, precious," he muttered, settling into a rhythm I'd already grown accustomed to. "Take it...take me...I want to come down your throat. Will you swallow it? Will you swallow me?"

I keened, the sound smothered around his penis. The ache in my pussy was so overpowering, I had to clench my thighs together just to cope with it.

He pulled me off, holding me in place as he started to pump his dick. "You'd let me come like this, Tia," he murmured. "Wouldn't you? I could stroke myself off and you'd swallow it and love it."

I swayed forward, wanting to wrap my lips around him again, but he didn't let me, forcing me to stay there as he stroked himself and waited for my answer.

"Yes." Panting, I looked up at him. Everything in me hurt. For all of him, for everything he could give me. "Please...don't stop now, Casper."

Vivid green eyes locked on mine, he dragged his fist up his cock, then down. "Open your mouth."

I did, unable to do anything else.

He tucked the head of his cock between my lips and I shuddered as he pumped his fist slowly—once, twice, three times.

"I'm tempted to come here and now, right down your throat," he said, his voice distant and cool. His fingers spread wide over my neck, curving around, then arching my head upward. "Let you suck me off and give you exactly what you're begging for."

He thrust faster, harder, until the head of his cock hit the back of my throat in a frenzied, bruising rhythm.

I grabbed onto his thighs, my nails digging into his flesh.

His cock jerked hard and fast and I moaned, taking him deeper without any conscious effort of my part.

Then he had me on my feet, spinning around and bending me over.

"But that's not what I want."

He spanked me. *Hard.*

I jumped, caught off guard.

A split second later, the cool, slick fluid of the lubricant slicked over that darker, almost completely untried entrance. He pushed into my ass with his fingers, determined, unrelenting, penetrating and demanding surrender.

He hunkered over me at the same time, whispering into my ear, "Yield for me, Tia. Take it..."

A low whine escaped my throat. He had me bent

over and I gripped the comforter in my fists as he pulled back. Sapped of strength, I sagged over the bed. I couldn't see him, but I felt his every movement as he straightened behind me, kicking my ankles apart to widen my stance before he moved in closer.

"Last chance, precious," he said, the words both a promise and a threat.

I shivered as he tucked the lubricant-slick head of his cock into place, probing against my ass.

"We're past that, aren't we?" I whispered.

He didn't say anything for long, interminable moments as he bumped, teased and toyed with me, rubbing against that tight resistant entrance with a confident knowledge that left me shaking.

"Casper," I whispered, flexing and pushing down. I reached back and caught the curve of my ass, not even thinking about what I was doing, going on instinct and nothing else. I tugged and felt him more intimately, and it left me shuddering.

"Tia..." He groaned and shifted.

I felt him roll against me and I almost swallowed my tongue at the intimate sensation, the blunt, fat head of his cock bumping closer, then closer...*closer*.

He gripped my other cheek and shoved, opening me, exposing me until I couldn't be more vulnerable.

A split second later, I sagged and sank back onto him.

Casper went stiff and groaned.

"That's...fuck...do it again. Take my dick, Tia. Ride it, take it... Do that again..."

It was as if I had no control. Instinct and biology and need took over and I sank back on him, opened and yielded and collapsed...

We both cried out as my body submitted to his, taking the head of his cock inside.

He froze after breaching the tight ring of muscle just inside my entrance.

I locked up at the same time, shoving up onto my

hands and rising on my toes to ease the pressure of him inside me, panicked and hungry and terrified and aroused, caught on the blade's edge of pleasure and pain. His hands gripped my hips, holding me steady and as I shuddered, hips rolling and spine undulating, he bent over me, lips pressing to my spine.

"That's it...come on, precious," he murmured. "Open...relax...*give* it to me..."

I moaned.

He brought his hand down sharply on my ass and I cried out, spine arching.

Casper withdrew until I held just the swollen, flared head of his penis, right at the clenched entrance of my butt.

He slid his hands down my back, then gripped the cheeks of my ass again, spreading me open. "Take it again, precious. You know you want it."

I did, but I was still wrecked from the new sensations, from that sharp, biting knife's edge that whispered of pain and pleasure.

"Casper...please..."

"Push down on me, Tia, just like you did the last time. Ride my dick." He rocked against me as he spoke, teasing nudges that did nothing to ease the ache and everything to fan the growing fire inside. He tugged my hips at the same time.

With a cry, I pushed down and gave in to him and he filled me again, then again. I dropped forward, strength gone as I took him. I had no idea how much—he was so big and I already felt overwhelmed by him. Sagging onto the mattress, impaled by his cock, all but pinned on him with my ass up and exposed, I shivered and twitched and tore at the sheets as he withdrew, then flexed, sending his length stroking deeper inside me.

"Do you want this?" he asked as he retreated.

"Yes..." I gasped my response into the sheets. "Please...fuck...yes, Casper. Don't stop...I need..."

The words choked in my throat, then strangled.

He grabbed a handful of my hair and pulled me upright. It changed the angle entirely and I sobbed as the movement impaled me on that massive cock.

Spine arched, breasts lifted and my nipples swollen and vulnerable, I stared out the window into the coming night. He slid a hand around my hip as I continued to rock and shudder. I held my breath, half-expecting relief from the torment.

But all he did was flick his fingertip over the aching, pulsating knot of my clit.

"You hurt," he whispered into my ear. "Don't you?"

"Yes," I whimpered, rocking forward.

"Tell me where. Exactly. I want to know how desperate I've made you, precious." He rolled forward with his hips and I groaned as his cock swelled inside me—so big, so thick, so rude and demanding now that I thought I'd die if he didn't give me relief.

"Everywhere. My pussy. My ass. My nipples." There was an ache in my chest, too. But I didn't tell him about that.

"These nipples?" He let go of my hair and reached around to pinch one, then the other.

"Yes." I groaned and tried to push against him, but I was straining on the tips of my toes, pinned on his cock like a butterfly pinned to a wall, and had no leverage. But he sensed what I needed and pinched me again, going back and forth between my breasts until they ached and burned nearly as badly as my swollen clit.

"And here..." He trailed his hand down my center. "You hurt here, too, don't you?"

I gasped as he spanked my pussy, a hard, sharp blow that sent a jolt of fire rushing through my veins. Writhing against him, I reached back and curled one arm around his neck while grabbing his thigh with the other, nails digging in.

"Answer me, Tia," he ordered, spanking me again, then again.

"Yes. I hurt there. Do it again, Casper. Please...spank me again...that feels so good..."

"Not yet. Do you want me to fuck you more?"

"Please. Fuck, yes. Spank my pussy again. Please. Nobody's ever..."

He pulled out and a second later, I was facing him, one hand cupping my chin almost brutally.

"Don't tell me what anybody has or hasn't done to you," he bit off. "You've had lovers. I know that. But the thought of anybody else touching you, you touching them— Don't mention them while I'm fucking you, do you understand? It makes me..."

He stopped, sucking in a breath. His green eyes were bright and hot, sharp enough to cut.

"It makes you what?" I asked, ignoring the need that screamed inside me. *He cares...*

Instead of answering, he boosted me up and kissed me, his mouth coming down on mine almost brutally. As his tongue thrust into my mouth, he fisted his hand in my hair and yanked, arching my neck for a kiss that was both punishment and promise.

I was panting when he tore away. He half-tossed me onto the bed then flipped me over, jerking me onto my knees.

I wasn't surprised when he spanked me, although the vicious curl of satisfaction *was* surprising. It wasn't from the spanking. That almost hurt. No, it was from the emotion behind it. *He cares...*

He spanked me again and again, then pulled me up and around, kissing me, nearly as rough before. "Nobody else exists now. Just you and me. Do you understand me, Tia?"

"Yes." The hot green glitter in his eyes were terrifying, exciting and haunting. I pressed against him. "I'll never mention another lover again."

His eyes widened. "Tia..."

I bit his lip.

"You're insane," he breathed.

"You've made me this way. If I mention another lover again, will you spank me?"

"No. I think I'm going to tie you up and finish fucking that ass just like you've begged me to do."

I rolled my eyes, but he had already left the bed and I sat back on my heels, confused. He disappeared into the closet and reemerged in under a minute, something thin and black in his hands.

"What is...oh. You're serious...?" My gaze darted from the cord in his hands up to his face.

"Unless you tell me no, right now."

I stayed quiet.

"Bend over then. Show me your ass...prove to me you still want it."

Shaking now, I bent over and he came up behind me, using the flat of his hand between my shoulder blades to push me lower until my cheek was against the bed. He caught my wrists and dragged them behind my back.

"Since you seem to enjoy taunting me, I'll do the same. The first time I tied a woman up, it was at the brothel in Germany. She kept touching me while I fucked her and I didn't want her to. I don't like being touched—ever. I grabbed her hands without even thinking about it. That was years ago. She giggled and said something about how she knew I'd be a rough one. That laugh grated on my ears and I tuned her out just so I could finish us both off. It was my first trip there and when I was done, I was disgusted and disappointed."

He talked as he worked, pausing from time to time and I'd feel a tug on my wrists.

"The madame of the house saw me leaving and she knew something was wrong. She takes great pride in her services and stopped me, asked me to join her for a drink. I did and when she asked what had displeased me, I told her. She suggested another girl and that I tie her up. There...you look perfect."

I tried to move my wrists. There was enough give for me to wiggle, but there was no way I could get free.

He fisted his hand in my hair and pulled me upright, the pressure more intense than it had been before, but it didn't hurt.

He bit my ear, then scored my neck with his teeth.

"Until you, Tia, I've never fucked anybody without tying them up—not since that night. I bind my partner, bend them over and fuck. Sometimes their pussy, sometimes their ass. I'm never careless and I take care to give pleasure, although not because I give a flying fuck if my partner enjoys it. I don't want to hurt whoever I've selected for the night, but their pleasure isn't my concern. I just do it so I can continue to have a wide variety of partners to choose from." He rubbed his cock against the seam between my buttocks. "And I don't care if it's a man or a woman. I don't know if you could consider me bisexual because sexual attraction doesn't weigh into my need to silence the screams in my head. I just request whoever is available and willing to take what I mete out—being bound, submitting and kneeling so I don't have to look at them as I fuck."

He cupped my breasts and plumped them together, fingers seeking out my nipples and squeezing until I gasped.

"Does it bother you hearing that I've fucked men as well as women? That I *enjoy* bending a man over and listening to him groan and gasp as I sink my dick into his ass?"

"Um..." Blood rushed to my face, turning my skin painfully hot. "No...it doesn't bother me."

At least not the way he thought, but if he didn't stop *talking* about sex while I waited here...

"I do believe you're the first person I've ever truly

felt sexually attracted to. Everybody else has just been...fuckable. Do you like hearing about past lovers?"

"They weren't lovers," I whispered without thinking. "I'm the only lover you've ever had. Everybody else was just...fuckable."

He tensed.

I braced myself for his reaction, mentally and emotionally. He'd push me away again, treat me to that cold, cool wall of his—

"Yes," he whispered against my ear. "You are."

My mind went blank.

"You're the only lover I've ever had, likely the only one I ever will have. So don't talk about the ones you've been with before, Tia. I don't want to hear it." He tugged and pulled until he could kiss me, but this time, it was gentle and sweet. He kept kissing me even as he stretched us out, him lying on top of me, nudging my thighs apart, then cuddling his cock against my ass.

I sobbed when he pulled away, jerking at the cord binding me, desperate to touch him.

"No," he said, almost thoughtfully. "I think I like you tied up and desperate."

"You ass. Please...Casper, I'm dying..."

He moved behind me. I couldn't see anything and the brush of his mouth over the curve of my butt was a shock. I whimpered, then shivered as he kissed his way higher, pausing to brush his lips over the bindings at my wrist.

"You're dying...why, Tia? What do you need?"

"You. Inside me. Please."

"Then beg me for it."

"I..." Swallowing, I clenched my hands into fists, nails biting into skin. "Fuck me. Please...I'm begging you."

"Here..." He pressed lubricant-slicked fingers against my ass.

Already tender and sensitive, I cried out, the shriek muffled against the bed. "Yes...damn it! Do it!"

He spanked me. "That's not begging."

But he didn't stop touching, working the lubricant deeper and deeper. I moaned when the head of his cock replaced his fingers.

"You can't play with your pussy now. It's going to be nothing but my cock filling your ass while you shudder and moan and beg. Are you ready for this?" he asked.

"Yes..." Whimpering, I pushed down as he'd instructed before and gasped as he sank deeper inside. It was easier this time, and there was an odd sensation. "I...it feels different."

"It's the lubricant. It has a faint numbing quality."

"I'm not numb," I whispered. Far from it.

"I did say faint." The words were raspy now, followed by a grunt as I pushed down even more, taking him deeper. "Do you want more, Tia? Tell me."

"Yes...oh, yes..." I twisted and arched, trying to take just that, but his hands kept me pinned in place and the cord binding me kept me from finding the needed leverage.

"Then beg me...tell me to fuck you. Tell me how. Harder? Deeper?"

My muscles were clenched, everything tight and desperate. I shuddered, feeling his cock throb inside me. "You're already fucking me. Why am I begging for it?"

"Because I want to *hear* it." He grabbed the cord and pulled, dragging me upright. I cried out as the position forced me farther down on his cock. My head sagged and he bit my neck. "Tell me to fuck your ass, precious. Say it. Tell me how you want it."

"Please...Casper. Fuck my ass. I need more...please, oh, please...give me more..."

Something between us moved and I realized he had his fist wrapped around his cock, preventing me from taking all of him.

"How much more do you want, Tia? I want to know how much more you can take. Should I give you more? Am I being too gentle? Too rough?"

With his free hand, he spanked my exposed pussy and I bucked, whimpering as lightning bolts of sensation tore through me.

"No...you're not being too rough. Give me more," I demanded. Drunk on him, on the need I felt, and emboldened by the lack of pain, I pushed back on him. "Give me more. I want you. I want *everything* however you want to give it to me."

Chapter 23

I want everything...
The words hit with an impact I wouldn't have thought possible and I couldn't shake the odd feeling that she meant something deeper than sex, something more than this intimate connection.

If it wasn't for the hot silk of her ass clenching around my prick, I might have tried to understand the tightness in my chest. Or I might have pushed her away. Again.

But the seductive perfection of her shuddering, the view as I stared down over her shoulder—those perfect, beautiful tits lifted up, soft brown nipples peaked and swollen, her spine undulating against mine as she fought to adjust to my invasion, it was more than I could handle already.

Tossing thought into the mix wasn't going to happen.

I spanked the open, wet folds of her cunt again, taking care to hit her clit. She jerked in shock, the movement setting her to bouncing on my cock. I eased my fist lower and spanked her again.

This time, she sank farther down and we both groaned.

A second, then a third swat of my hand against her pussy and I either had to pull my hand away completely, or change tactics. The hungry beast inside wanted to pull my hand away, grip her hips and thrust up into her, high and hard.

But as soft as she was, as much as her body worked to accommodate my width and length, I didn't want to hurt her, and even with the numbing lubricant, she wasn't ready for the wild, rough hunger tearing me up inside. She had yet to yield completely and the idea of causing her real pain was unbearable.

Bending her back over, I gripped one hip and withdrew before sinking deeper inside, slowly, enjoying every shuddering roll of her hips and the whimpering moans rising in her throat. She keened out and bore down on me, yielding even more.

A red haze of pleasure washed over my eyes. I almost lost it.

"Please..." She thrust herself back, then went rigid, spine arching. "Oh...*ow*..."

"Damn it, Tia." I gripped her hips, swearing as the tight inner walls of her ass flexed and milked my cock. It damn near killed me, but I started to withdraw. "You're moving too fast."

"You're moving too slow! Don't you dare stop." She flexed her fingers, seeking to grab something. I trailed my fingers over hers and she latched on, squeezing tight. "Just...do that thing..."

Instead of telling me, she started to rock back and forth in increments. Taking the hint, I settled into the teasing rhythm I'd used earlier to coax her into relaxing.

She whimpered, still shuddering, spasming around me as I sank deeper and deeper. Then she groaned and pushed down and her body finally yielded, completely and utterly.

I swore, lapsing into German, shuddering as she took every last, swollen, aching inch of my cock. The sensitive, fragile skin of her ass stretched tight around me and still she wiggled and moved, panting and begging.

"More...more...please...Casper...fuck me...I need...I need..."

My control shattered and I lunged, filing her deep, hard and fast.

She cried out, pain and pleasure both coloring the sound.

"Tia?"

"Don't stop!"

I flexed and filled her again, but this time, I caught her hips and held her still, staring down at where we joined.

"What's...Casper, please...don't stop..."

"You took all of me, precious...look at that..." I groaned, tingles racing down my spine, the pleasure more intense than anything I'd ever known. Gripping her hips, I moved her forward, then dragged her back, the sight so darkly, beautifully sensual, I wanted to imprint it on my mind.

She tried to take control, pushing against my grip.

"You're moving too slow," she said on a breathy moan.

"Yes...because I want to watch this. Fuck, Tia...the way you look as you take my cock...it's beautiful."

"I can't see," she said, a sulky pout in her voice. "Tell me..."

The petulant demand surprised a rusty laugh out of me. "Tell you..." I stroked a finger over the dusky skin where our bodies joined and she shivered. "Your hot, sweet ass is stretched wide around my dick. You're on your knees, lifted for me, with your hands tied and face buried in the sheets."

I shuddered, feeling like I was seeing it anew as I told her.

"Do you feel like you're submitting to me, Tia?"

"I feel like I'm being *tortured*! Move, Casper...*please*!"

I did, slowly.

"I feel like you're the one in control, precious. Like you're holding the reins." Gripping her hips, I braced myself for the ugly black rage, but it didn't come. "Why doesn't that bother me?"

"If I was holding the reins, I'd be coming by now." She moaned and flexed around me, squeezing, milking, while her hands opened, fingers seeking, reaching.

"This isn't enough," I muttered.

"What...?"

I shook my head, not thinking that she wouldn't see. Sinking down on top of her, I stretched out, bearing her weight until she was flat on the bed, then I rolled us half onto our sides.

Now I could feel more of her. I wasn't as deep, but it didn't matter. She whimpered and rocked, a mewl escaping her. Rising onto my elbow, I looked down as she twisted her upper body so we could see each other.

Now it was enough.

Gazes locked, I started to move.

Tia's mouth opened on a gasp.

I reached down, seeking out the slick heat between her thighs. Her lashes fluttered as I thrust into her, cock and fingers, filling her, ass and pussy.

"Better?"

"Yes...no...I don't know...what are you *doing* to me?" she whispered, staring at me with lust-fogged, hungry eyes. "I need more."

"I'll give it to you." I shifted again, sliding a hand under her hip as I moved my own, filling her more fully as her mouth parted on a gasp.

Her neck arched, eyes widening as I did it again, and again.

"Yes...please...oh, *fuck*, Casper! More, more, more...*oh*!"

Each word shoved me higher and the urge to rut on her like a madman grew stronger every second. I pushed onto my knees, grabbing her thigh and bringing it up a few inches. At the same time, I shifted position, straddling her lower leg.

With my leverage increased, I searched her face, watching her for signs that I was causing her pain, but there was nothing but her moans and cries, her breasts lifted and arched up, nipples so swollen my mouth watered just looking at them.

My only lover...

The slick wet heat from her cunt flowed out, coating my dick and balls, easing my passage even more.

Her eyes were glassy, mouth parted.

"Cas..." she gasped.

Pinpricks of sensation raced down my spine but I lashed my climax down, fighting it back tooth and nail.

On the next stroke, she started shuddering. "Please," she whispered, staring up at me blindly. "It's not... I want to come so bad, but it's not enough."

Mouth-watering, I slid my hand down her thigh until I found her wet, waiting cunt. "You're so juicy and wet for me, Tia..." I plunged two fingers into the wet well of her pussy and she clenched down, crying out.

"Spank it," she begged, voice barely intelligible.

I did and a split second later, her body locked up in climax and she started to pulse and twist and moan, working herself on my dick, squeezing, clenching.

I bent lower and slammed into her, caution, control gone.

She cried out my name, begged for more.

And I kept moving, kept fucking her, kept riding her through her broken moans until the orgasm slammed into me with devastating intensity.

* * * * *

Showered yet again, the two of us lay in bed a half hour later. I'd gone downstairs to put Valkyrie out just moments earlier after Tia noticed the dog giving us an exasperated look from the doorway.

"She probably thinks sex is silly, especially since we haven't put her out much today," Tia said now, resting her head on my chest.

I covered her hand with mine, not responding.

There wasn't much to say, but I wanted her to keep

224

talking. The sound of her voice centered me. It did a lot of other nice things, too—soothed and relaxed me.

"Hey."

She pulled her hand from mine and I flinched when she poked me in the side unexpectedly. Her eyes widened and she jerked upright so suddenly, it was as if she was pulled by springs.

"Are you ticklish?"

"No." I didn't think I was. But how would I know?

Tia dragged her nails down my side and I flinched again, grabbing her wrist.

"You are, too! Liar!"

She went to poke at my other side. Swearing, I moved and twisted, pinning her under me. My heart raced like it had never done before.

"I didn't lie," I said as an unfamiliar twist tugged at my lips. This lighthearted sensation she brought with her, the heat, the humor...how would I live without it when she was gone? "I didn't have a life where my father played games or tickled me."

Her face softened. "Let my hands go, scary Spectre. I'll play games with you."

I pushed my knee between her thighs. "There are better games to play."

"Yes..." Her eyes went smoky.

I rubbed against her but didn't enter her.

She wiggled around, then hooked her thighs around my hips, arching up.

Still, I held back. "I'm not wearing a condom."

"So? You didn't wear one when you fucked my ass earlier, either."

Heat rushed to my face. It took a moment to realize that I was blushing. "No. I didn't. I'm clean. I have a test after every visit to the brothel. I should have said something, though. I should have asked."

"Why didn't you?"

"Because I'm selfish and I wanted to have you yield and feel nothing between us."

A slow smile bloomed over her lips. "Then do it now."

I swallowed, hard. "There are other concerns if I'm going to take you like this, precious."

"No. I told you. I have an IUD. I won't get pregnant. And I want to have you inside me...no barriers. I want you—all of you, everything."

It was stupid and careless...and I didn't care. If she wanted me like this, then she'd have me. I'd given her every piece of myself that I could—*while* I could.

Rising onto my knees, I caught her thighs, pushing them high and wide. Then, staring down at her flushed face, I tucked the head of my cock against the naked, wet heart of her.

The first kiss of her pussy almost left my eyes crossed, she felt so good.

I sank in slowly, determined to commit every bit of this to memory, the expressions on her face, the scent of our bodies, the way her nails bit into my skin.

"More..." She moaned, trying to move against me.

I had her butt lifted for my claiming, though, and she could do little more than wiggle.

Or so I thought.

She closed around me in an internal caress, milking me.

I stiffened and the tensing of my muscles had me sinking deeper.

She groaned and slammed her head back against the mattress. "Yes...just like...no, don't pull...oh!"

I drove home, her slick cunt too much temptation to ignore.

She curled her arms and legs around me and I rolled onto my back, gripping her tightly as I fucked my way into her tight, wet pussy.

It was fast, wet and messy and we were sweating by the time we climaxed, our moans mingling.

"You've driven me insane," I said against her lips.

It wasn't until I slid my mouth upward and tasted

tears that I realized she was crying.

"Tia?" Panic filled me.

She clutched at my shoulders and shook her head. "Don't...I'm..." she hiccuped. "It's—it's just *me*, okay? I'm feeling a whole hell of a lot right now and sometimes...it's just a lot, okay?"

"I didn't hurt you?"

Her balled-up fist hit me on the hip and she gave a laugh that just as much sob as anything else. "No. Would you...just hold me a while, okay? I'm tired."

"All right." I withdrew and pulled her into my arms, tucking her back against my chest and holding her close. She shifted, wiggled, then sighed. After a few hiccupping breaths, she dropped straight into sleep.

I listened to the sound of her soft, steady breaths as I stared into the night.

I'm feeling a whole hell of a lot right now.

Yes, I understood that. Too well, in fact.

She'd done more than driven me insane.

Somehow, in the mere days since I'd first laid eyes on her, she'd done something I would have thought impossible.

My entire life, I'd lived an existence where I felt like I was masquerading as a person, wearing the mask of a human to conceal the monster my father had created. I'd never experienced the emotions I saw in others—happiness, pride, love. No, all my emotions were dark, ugly twisted shadows.

But Tia had made me laugh, had made me smile.

And she made me *want*. Not just sex, although for the first time, the act was about more than just a release.

No...Tia made me want *everything*.

She even made me want to trust her.

Chapter 24

I woke up smelling of sex and Casper and I smiled as I rolled onto my back, arms reaching overhead as I stretched.

Something cold poked my foot and I pushed up onto my elbows to see Valkyrie watching me balefully.

"Life's weird," I told her.

A week ago, I didn't have a dog, a lover or a clue that somebody wanted to kill me because my brother had done his job as a cop.

Now, all three of those things were true and here I was, breathing in the scent of the man who'd kidnapped me, flipped my world upside down...and told me I was the only lover he'd ever had. Ever *would* have.

"We're talking," I told Valkyrie. "That man and I? We're talking."

The house was strangely quiet, but not empty. As I pulled on a shirt—his—I could feel him, as if he were waiting for me.

A big, empty ache settled inside and I swallowed around the knot that had formed in my throat. I wanted to run and hide.

I found him on the front porch, four large black duffels lined up in a neat row. He sat on the top step, staring at the SUV. He didn't look up as I sat down next to him, although he was every bit as aware of me as I was of him.

"You're leaving," I said quietly.

"We both know I have to. There are things that need to be done before you'll be safe." He didn't look away from the SUV. "Until those things are done, you can't go back to your life, Tia. And you deserve to have that life, one where you're safe and happy."

Instead of answering that specifically, I said, "If it wasn't for my brother and Bianca, I could almost see myself having a happy one here."

I didn't look at him as I spoke.

But from the corner of my eye, I could see his reaction.

He'd finally moved, turning his head so he stared out over the eastern sky as the sun crept up over the horizon. "You should take care with what you say, precious. I don't give a damn about your brother or your friend. I could see myself keeping you here, even when this is all said and done. So don't tempt me."

"That you even admit you want to be with me is something." I leaned into him, closing my eyes against the knot in my chest. "Tell me you're not just going to completely disappear once this is over, Casper."

He was quiet for so long, I thought that was the answer—one I dreaded, one I hated.

Squeezing my eyes shut, I tried to breathe around the ache spreading through my chest and that just made it worse, like the very act of drawing in air, something necessary for life, exacerbated this visceral agony.

He turned his head and I shuddered as he buried his face in my hair, breathing me in.

"You know how impossible this is," he said, voice strangely gentle. "You have a family—your brother and your friend—people who love you. You have a job that brings you joy. You have a life. Where would I fit into any of that?"

Desperation shoved me into motion and I went to my knees in front of him, pushing my way between his thighs and grabbing his face in my hands.

That beautiful face.

That hard face.

"Exactly where we put you," I said stubbornly. "Where do you want to fit into it?"

He covered my hands with his. "That's just it, precious. I *can't* fit into it. Consider what I am, Tia."

My mouth started to tremble and I pressed my lips together. "I know what you are. And don't *tell* me you're a monster. You're *not* a monster. If you were, we wouldn't be having this conversation. A *monster* wouldn't care."

"Perhaps I'm not the monster I thought I was. But that doesn't change what I am." He arched a dark gold brow. "A killer. A murderer. I've killed people on six continents, in more than eighty countries. I never bothered counting, but I keep excellent records and I could give you a number if it would make it easier for you to understand."

A hard knot settled in my belly.

"You didn't kill *me*," I said, my breath catching in my throat as my control threatened to break.

His lashes swept down, hiding his eyes for a long moment, then he looked at me again. "It doesn't change the fact that I have blood on my hands. And I don't feel guilt over the lives I've taken."

A tear spilled out.

He brushed his lips over my cheek, catching the wet drop.

"How would you explain me to your brother, this cop who has led a Boy Scout's life?"

I went to wrench away from him.

His hands fell away but I stumbled and lost my balance and he caught me, steadying me.

"You understand now, don't you?" he said after I smacked off his hands and stormed away, standing at the far edge of the gravel walkway.

"I don't care what my brother thinks about you," I said.

But I heard the lie in my own voice.

So did he.

"I won't bring pain into your life, Tia."

"You *leaving* it will bring pain, you bastard," I said,

spinning around to glare at him. "If you don't want to bring me pain, find a way to make this work!"

He bowed his head, staring at the ground. "I can't change who I am."

"I don't want you to change." And I didn't. Somehow, I'd fallen for this scary, dangerous man. Scary, spooky Spectre...and I wanted him just the way he was.

And yet...

He lifted his head a fraction, staring at me through the veil of his lashes. "When I disappear for three weeks at a time and come back to you, when I slide between your sheets and press my body to yours, will it not bother you, thinking about where I've been, what I did...who I killed?"

"Stop." More tears fell now and I dashed them away, angry now on top of the misery. "Damn you, just stop."

"That is who I am, Tia. You cannot tell me you don't want me to change without considering what it is you'd be getting into if I was foolish enough to do this." He rose, the movement fluid and graceful.

I went rigid as he came toward me, his eyes pinning me in place. "And I'm tempted. More than you know, more than I even realized I could be tempted. But what will you tell your brother? How will your brother, this good, decent cop, react to the knowledge that his beloved sister is involved with a killer wanted by law enforcement agencies across the globe?"

"It's not like I plan on *telling* him," I muttered.

"He'll know," Casper said simply. "And you know that."

I did.

"Damn you." This time, it almost choked me and more tears fell, blinding me. I wiped them away but it didn't matter because a river of them continued to rain down. "Why can't you make this work?"

He reached for me.

I shoved him and his hands fell away. The anger exploded and I swung out. He didn't even try to move, his head snapping back as my fist smashed into his mouth. Then I grabbed him and pulled his head down to mine. "I'm sorry...I'm sorry..."

He wrapped his arms around me and let me kiss the small, bleeding cut and when I started crying again, he picked me up and carried me into the house, sitting on the couch with my head tucked under his chin.

He said nothing.

Perhaps there was nothing left to say.

His fingers stroked through my hair and after a while, exhausted by the emotional storm, I fell asleep.

When I woke, he was gone.

And I knew he wasn't just outside.

A piece of paper, folded and propped up, with my name written in elegant, neat script, waited on the simple table a few feet in front of me.

Valkyrie lay curled next to me on the couch, as if she'd known I'd need her.

Burying my face in her fur, I willed my mind to empty of anything and everything.

If I didn't think, I wouldn't hurt.

Chapter 25

Nine days had passed since I'd left Tia sleeping on my couch.

Nine long, empty days.

I'd never considered just how long and empty the hours of the day could be until I'd driven away from her.

Leo had arrived at the cabin twelve hours after I'd left and had sent me a few updates. She was angry with me and wanted to get the hell off my mountain, he'd told me in no uncertain terms. He'd taken the precaution of sealing the keys in the weapons vault, which she couldn't access. Yet I wouldn't be surprised if I soon received a message that he'd had to track her down after she decided to attempt walking.

I had one more name on my list to eliminate before I'd breathe easy, knowing she was safe.

Over the past three days, I'd killed the three men who made up the top echelon of Tommy O'Holloran's elite. This morning, I'd called him and told him he was next.

He'd reacted as expected, exploding into a fit of vitriol and rage, promising to hunt me down, piss down my throat after he tore it open and perhaps use my skull to bash Tia's head in.

I waited until he was done before telling him that I'd be emptying his bank accounts as well, since I'd paid a visit to his accountant.

"Listen, you stupid fuck," Tommy growled into the phone.

I hit *end* on the phone and pried off the back, removing the SIM card. The man next to me stared, petrified, as I wrapped the card in a strip of aluminum foil then held it over the flame of my lighter for a minute, effectively destroying it. "Normally, I'd just throw the card out in the nearest trash can and leave the area," I told him, watching him with a faint smile. "But I suspect if I got out of the car to dispose of it, you'd take off running, wouldn't you? Even if your condition."

Adrian Elmore shook his head and tried to smile, but it wobbled and fell away. "No, of course not."

"The condition of your pants says otherwise."

He'd taken off out the backdoor of his home three hours earlier when he'd shuffled into the kitchen to get a drink of water.

He had a gym physique, muscled and perfect, and yet when he saw me and I told him why I was there, he'd left, ignoring his wife of two years and their sleeping child.

Rather, he hadn't taken notice of their absence.

I'd been in his house twice already over the past five days, first looking for information on the best way to bring O'Holloran down, then to finalize my plan. His wife, sweet, ignorant thing, had no idea who she'd married.

She hadn't been in the mood to listen to me explain, either, but that was likely because I'd used the same tactic on her that I'd used on Tia, although with more success.

I'd drugged her and put her in my car, then fetched the sleeping baby, lingering only long enough to look for food to feed it.

Taking her to a hotel on the outskirts of town, I'd put in a call to Mac Bailey, who had gone through the roof. His shouting at me through the phone had woken the baby, and that had woken Ellis Elmore who'd screamed once the drugs cleared her system enough for her to realize the situation she was in.

Life had been much simpler before Mac Bailey's sister entered my life.

An FBI agent had arrived to take Ellis and the baby into protective custody after a long conversation with Mac, who had managed to gather himself when a crying woman started speaking rather than me.

I'd made another call to him after leaving the area, amused by the agents who'd been in place to watch for me, ready to arrest me no doubt. But they were looking for somebody in a car. I'd been a mile away, watching from the camera I'd left in the room.

Once Adrian's wife was safe, I was able to go back for him and had decided to make use of the well-stocked kitchen for a quick meal.

He came in just as I finished eating the omelet I'd made—I hadn't been quiet at that point. The bravado he'd shown had died at the sight of the gun I leveled on him. When I'd said Tommy's name, he'd lied, and done a fine job of it, but then I'd started listing account numbers.

That had been what sent him running out of the house wearing nothing but the pajama pants he still wore now. The urine and mud had dried. He now wore a faded NYU T-shirt, but he was a mess.

We'd left immediately after I'd hauled him back into the house and thrown a shirt at him. The FBI, no doubt, was already on their way.

"I would have thought more of you if you'd at least asked about your wife and baby," I commented, staring at the back door of the house I watched. It was located in a neighborhood that was struggling to stay in the lower middle-class. The classic Ford Mustang Shelby parked next to a shining Mercedes SUV looked out of place, and there was also a Ducati and Suzuki Hayabusa, two motorcycles that likely cost more than every house on this small block combined.

"You..." He cleared his throat. "You didn't hurt Ellis and Avery, did you?"

"It's a little late to ask that now, isn't it?"

He jerked against the zip cord holding his wrists.

Another cord secured him to the seat belt, restraining him quite effectively. "Listen, you fuck—"

"Be quiet. It's a sad thing that you ask about them now. Look, there's your boss, Elmore." I glanced over at him as Tommy came tearing out of the house, followed by several muscled men with thick necks. "At least you proved to have some use. I won't make you suffer when I kill you."

He paled, then swallowed.

"Look, buddy...I...you don't have to kill me. I can pay you. I can pay you a *lot*. I know where all Tommy's bodies are buried, too."

"Shut up." I backhanded him, more to silence him than anything else. A thought struck me a moment later and I glanced at him. "What will Tommy do to your wife when you're not home and you don't answer your phone?"

His phone sat in the cup holder, missing the SIM card.

"I..." Adrian turned gray.

Cocking my head, I studied him. That was curious. Perhaps he did care.

"You...fuck, man. Please. Let me call him. He can go anywhere else and you can do whatever you need to do. But if he gets there and can't find me..." His voice hitched and his blue eyes widened, blank now with sheer, blind terror. "He'll kill her. Her and the baby. He'll let his men do whatever they want. *Please*—"

He launched himself at me, regardless of the restraints and the seat belt jerked him back. Frenzied now, he continued to fight and something stirred inside me. I ignored it, though, lifting the Sig Sauer P210 and pressing it to his mouth, currently open with fury.

The tinted windows of the car made it difficult for anybody to see inside unless looking through the windshield and at this hour, few were awake. Still, the moment he went quiet, I withdrew the weapon and tucked it back into my lap.

"If you had such concern for them, perhaps you should have thought of them earlier."

Tears flooded his eyes, but surprisingly, he didn't plead. "If they die because of you, I'm going to kill you."

"If they die, it will be because of you."

Casper...

It was like she was there, shaking her head and scowling at me, exasperated.

I made no conscious decision to say it, but the words were out in the next second. "Your wife and daughter were already out of the house when you woke. I took them to a hotel. Your wife is now in FBI custody. If you don't piss me off, that's where you'll end up."

The strength drained out of him and he collapsed back against the door, gaping at me.

"I..." He stopped and cleared his throat. When he spoke again, his voice was hoarse. "I told Tommy you wouldn't take the job."

I didn't look at him, focused now on the taillights of the Mustang Shelby as the car swung into reverse. Tires squealed as he backed up, almost hitting the Suzuki. The bike's owner lunged for it and somebody grabbed him, otherwise he would have gone down because O'Holloran wasn't stopping.

"He's had your name for a while," Adrian said, voice thick. "Rumor has it you took out that Yakuza guy who was in New York."

I could feel him watching me, but I didn't speak. The car, SUV and two motorcycles were out of sight now, but somebody was still outside. I studied the cute, plump young woman standing in the backyard, arms wrapped around herself.

"Who is she?"

"Holly. Holly Boyd," Adrian whispered bleakly. "They were sweethearts in high school. She dumped him when she found out what he was involved in but he never got over her. She's married now...husband's a trucker. He comes over here once or twice a week while her husband's gone and..." He stopped for a minute. "He says she still loves him, but Holly knows if she doesn't do what he wants, he'll kill her husband. So she goes along."

Dispassionately, I watched as she bent over and picked up a rock, hurling it down the alley in the same direction of the vehicles.

"You work for this man who destroys lives. If that was your daughter, or your wife..." I stopped and looked over at him.

He was staring at his fisted hands.

"And still, you want to blame me."

His shoulders started to shake.

As the woman straightened, I started the car.

She spun around, startled. Her robe gaped open as she stared across the distance at me.

You're not a monster.

Tia, again. Haunting me like a ghost.

A monster wouldn't care.

Pulling out of the driveway of the vacant house where I'd parked, I turned.

But left...not right, which would have let me avoid passing by her.

She stepped into the alley, glaring at me.

I stopped.

When she stormed around the vehicle and slammed her fist against my window, I lowered it.

She bent down and sneered at me. "Tell that dickhead I don't want you assholes watching my house."

Her mouth was swollen. So were her eyes. It was clear she'd been crying.

Instead of addressing her comment, I said, "Make sure you watch the news today, Mrs. Boyd. I think you'll find your nights much easier in the coming days."

She straightened and backed away, her face blanking.

"You...you're not one of Tommy's boys. They..." She swallowed. "They don't talk like you. Who are you?"

"I'm nobody."

Then, before she could ask anything else, I punched the gas.

I wanted to be clear away from there before the fun started.

* * * * *

Even when there was relatively no traffic on the roads, the trip between Holly Boyd's house and the extravagant home where Adrian Elmore lived took more than forty minutes.

The differences between the two houses was stark.

The ramshackle house in Roxbury was small, so small, it could have fit into the large, open main room of my cabin in the mountains twice over.

Adrian's home, on the other hand, located outside of Boston on the other side of the city, was large and sprawling, on a lot of land that likely cost almost as much as the house itself.

The privacy had been perfect in a number of ways— from entering unnoticed to staging the scene to come.

But that long drive left many empty minutes for me to do nothing but wait and worry.

The cameras I had placed in the home and around the property gave me a perfect view and I'd seen when the police first arrived, followed by the FBI agents.

Casper...don't...

Her voice, again. Haunting me.

I could easily ignore it, and those law enforcement officers.

Yet, instead of doing that, parked in the garage of the house I'd rented just two miles from the neighborhood O'Holloran claimed as his own, I reached for my phone. As I did so, I caught sight of my reflection and studied it, not recognizing the man looking back at me. It wasn't just the disguise, either, although the round metal frames, the inserts I had in my mouth to alter the shape of my cheeks, the thicker brows I'd carefully applied, all of it worked to make my face look like somebody else entirely.

No, the difference was in the eyes.

Shaking the thought off, I made a call.

Mac Bailey picked up.

"Yes," he bit off, sounding like he was chewing through rusty nails.

"You have contacts on the ground in Boston."

A hard breath escaped him.

"Tell me that my sister isn't in *Boston*," he finally said.

"Of course not." Rattling off the address of the house I was staring at on the series of monitors in the van I'd moved to, I said, "There are county sheriffs, agents from the Massachusetts Bureau of Investigation and the FBI all milling around that house. Within the next twenty minutes, Tommy O'Holloran will arrive, hoping to locate his missing accountant. He should enter that house, Detective Bailey. Alone and unimpeded. Interesting information will come from what happens if he's allowed to do so. Enough, perhaps, to find out which dirty cops are involved in his network."

"You son of a bitch!" he shouted.

I sighed.

"I don't have jurisdiction over some house in fuck-all Massachusetts! Where the fuck is my sister?" he bellowed.

"Do you want Tommy O'Holloran shut down? His contacts rooted out and exposed?"

"I want to know where my sister is, you mouth-breathing, psychotic piece of shit!"

I smiled a little. "Once this is done, she'll be safe

and I'll tell you."

Instead of another explosion, he went quiet.

"You're telling me that all I have to do is call off the boys in blue up in Boston and I get my sister back?"

"You don't have jurisdiction in Boston," I reminded him.

"Suck my dick," he suggested. He went quiet again, then abruptly said, "I'll make a call."

Chapter 26

"**N**ine days."

The sun still wasn't up but I'd stopped trying to sleep after I'd woken the third time, just after three o'clock.

Valkyrie flicked an ear in the direction of my voice, but she didn't stir from her position at the foot of the bed.

I sat in the middle of the wide expanse, my notebooks open around me, charcoal pencils, pastels and pens making a mess.

Black from the charcoals smudged my pajama pants and the pristine white sheets. The sight of it made me smile. When he came back, he'd see signs of me everywhere.

Even if I wouldn't be here.

The knowledge of that filled my chest with a hard, leaden weight.

Downstairs, I could hear Leo moving around, preparing breakfast for now, but later, he'd be herding me out the door.

I knew that because he'd been advising me of that very fact.

Spectre has let me know his plan is going as expected.

Spectre thinks he'll have everything wrapped up within another seventy-two hours.

If everything goes according to plan, you'll be able to call your brother within thirty-six hours and he can make arrangements to pick you up soon. We'll be flying out within a day.

Not that he told me which city we'd be flying out from.

I knew the tags on the car Leo had driven up here

were from Idaho, but I also knew the vehicle was a rental so it could be from a city twenty miles away or from New York City. I had no idea.

What I did know was that my time here in this house, where I'd stayed with Casper, was coming to an end.

My hand moved across the heavyweight paper with near-frenzied energy, seeking to capture a moment that had been caught in my mind for days.

You decide what happens.

We'd been back at the rest area and the only other vehicle in sight had been the truck parked yards ahead.

If I'd been quiet, the other person never would have known there was a problem.

But I hadn't been quiet.

Casper had taken control of the moment, because that was what he did.

My fingers shook as they worked to freeze that moment, to capture it on paper, so somebody else could see what I'd seen.

You decide.

It had been too dark to see the green of his eyes, but that hot, brilliant glitter had been too intense, too compelling and I couldn't look away.

I rubbed my pinkie against the line of his cheekbone, smudging it slightly, then applying more pressure. Almost, but not quite. Still, I'd never capture the haunting beauty of his face.

And his voice, his eyes, in that moment as he'd looked at me.

He's ten feet away. You decide what happens, Tia.

He'd kissed me and, I swear, I could feel the tingling of my lips even now. Pressing them together, I shifted my attention to that part of the sketch—his mouth. Too perfect, really. At least for a portrait. There should be some flaw. Something to detract from the beauty of him.

But how did I take away from the sheer perfection of what he was?

Memory assailed me and I dropped the charcoal I held. His tongue, breaching my lips, tasting me while his hand clamped on my thigh.

It had been the first kiss I'd ever enjoyed. In my entire life, the first kiss that hadn't been faked or forced. And I'd wanted more. I still did.

Where was he?

Somebody knocked.

I ignored him.

"Tia?"

Long moments passed before he spoke again and I looked up with a snarl. "Go *away*."

Leo met my eyes solemnly. "I've heard from Spectre."

Surging up off the bed, I hurled the sketchpad at him. It made it halfway before falling to the floor. Valkyrie, already on edge, alerted to my mood and sprang between us, her lips peeling back from her teeth as she snarled.

"That's not his name!" I shouted.

Leo drew his head back. "No. It's not."

"Then don't..." A sob hit then, square in the middle of my chest. If he died, would anybody ever know him to be anything more than a ghost?

Yes, I told myself stubbornly. *I* would. Clearing my throat, I smoothed my shirt down, then my hair, and I finally met Leo's gaze.

"I don't want to hear whatever soothing bullshit you have, whatever lies you've concocted. His *name* is *not* Spectre. That name was manufactured, given to the person who was crafted, because a monster tried to kill the boy who *really* existed inside that man's body before he had a chance even to live. He's his own person, even if he's too scarred to see that." Looking him up, then down, I sneered. "He has reasons why he can't see beyond those scars, but you should be able to do it. Be man enough to try."

Leo rocked back on his feet, then to my shock, dipped his head.

"You're quite right." He looked around, taking in the bedroom's devastation, eyes lingering on the myriad sketches that littered the room. "We should talk, Ms. Jenkins."

Chapter 27

I wasn't surprised at the amount of surveillance. To be fair, I'd expected it.

I'd worked my way past more intense security measures in my time, including those put in place to protect a presidential candidate. The contract on him hadn't paid anywhere near what I'd invested to actually complete the job, but the more I'd dug into the son of a bitch's background, the more determined I'd been to complete the job, contract or not.

Compared to the dancing I'd done with the U.S. Secret Service, sidestepping some federal agents and U.S. marshals was a walk in the park.

That walk was made substantially easier by one Sam Collier, a man who vaguely fit my description, if you added in the fact that he had shaggy, reddish-blond hair and a scruffy beard to match.

Collier, effectively, would blend in and that was exactly what I needed, because the man I was after did the very same thing. He blended in as if he'd been doing it his entire life.

He was likely as at home in the posh luxury hotel as he was in a no-name motel that ran for fifty bucks a night, and I'd only have this one shot at him. If it wasn't for Theo, I wouldn't even have that.

Even now, she was perched in a protective position on the hotel across the street, watching.

If I didn't update her, she'd likely move in and it would be over.

At that point, I'd be dead and it wouldn't matter.

That was what I told myself, but I couldn't actually believe it.

It would matter to Tia, and no matter what,

whether I was here, it would matter to me. If it mattered to Tia, I'd care, even if I was dead and cold, nothing more than a memory to the few who even knew I existed.

"Thermo shows the room to be empty, Spectre," a voice murmured in my ear. "But I'm picking up radio chatter. He's on his way back. If he's not here in the next thirty minutes, I'll eat my hat."

"If you're that hungry, Theo, order some take-out," I said, working my way down the hall, carrying a stack of towels as part of my disguise.

"Did you just make a joke, Spectre? I think you did, but I can't quite believe my ears."

"Very funny." I stopped in front of the room and took one long, slow breath. "I'm here, Theo. I'm going in."

I pulled the card from my pocket as her voice crackled in my ear.

"Are you sure this is the way you want to handle it, Spectre? If things go wrong...hell, I won't be able to get there in time. We both know that."

I swiped the card and stepped into the room, easing it closed behind me so there was no heavy thud to announce my arrival. Once I ascertained that I was alone in the room, I answered, "If things go wrong, Theo, it won't matter. I have to do this."

Brittle silence stretched out between us, followed by the low, angry sound of her swearing.

"Hell. This is suicide, you know that, right?" she said abruptly. "Okay. I'm watching. There's a chair by the bed—big window, just like we thought. Make your play there. I've got good line of sight so if need be, I can take him out in a heartbeat."

"Remember what I said. No matter what happens." I put the towels away and moved around the room, taking in everything.

She swore over the line. "Damn it, man."

"You promised," I reminded her. Then I focused on

the area around me.

It was a nice suite, a sitting area that opened into a bedroom with a sprawling view of downtown Boston. The suite, coupled with the hotel itself, went hand in hand with what I'd learned about my target. He did like life's luxuries.

But he was by no means soft.

I couldn't afford to be off guard, not now. Not with him.

The chair was exactly where Theo had told me it would be, beside the bed. I took care of a few more things, then settled down to wait. The chair was surprisingly comfortable but despite my lack of sleep over the past few days, I had no worries that I might get *too* relaxed.

My blood rushed in my veins and my heart pounded with an urgency I was unfamiliar with.

Hearing the click in the lock out in the hallway, I breathed out slowly and closed my eyes.

Make this work. Those words, in Tia's low, sexy voice, had echoed through my mind so many times over the past week. *Make this work.*

It was nearly impossible.

Only one thing could be done for...*this*, for *us* to work, and in the next few seconds, I'd be making that call.

The door opened, then shut, the lock clicking as the man in the outer room turned the deadbolt. No lights were on, save for the single lamp he'd left burning earlier.

The lack of illumination, coupled with the dark night outside, turned the window into a dim mirror. I could see his reflection as he reached for the light switch and I heard him swear under his breath as nothing happened.

He moved deeper into the room and I watched as he moved out of sight. There was a faint click and he swore again. Two seconds later, he was back in my line of sight, hitting the switch for the lights in the small kitchenette area.

Nothing. He paused, then reached under the lamp shade.

He didn't show any confusion when he failed to find a light bulb. I had to give him points for that.

I gave him even more credit when he reached inside his jacket and he pulled out a weapon. With the lack of clarity in the window, I couldn't see the make but I had no doubt he would be more than proficient with it.

I also had no doubt he'd pull out another weapon soon—his cellphone.

"I'm hoping you won't need that weapon," I said calmly. I held my own, but instead of having it raised toward him, it lay against my thigh and I gripped it loosely, reluctant even to consider using it.

For the first time in my life, I actually had some concern the man would turn toward me and the weapon would fire, a bullet ending my existence in the next few seconds.

I'd never feared death until I found life. Damned if I'd give in so easily.

The man disappeared from sight.

My skin prickled. Instinct shouted, *Kill him.*

"It takes a phenomenally stupid person to break into a hotel room registered to a cop," Mac Bailey said, sounding remarkably steady.

"You're assuming I knew you were a cop when I let myself into your room. Why is that?"

Bailey snorted. "We'll call it a lucky guess."

Something shifted and I kept my focus on the door, for any flicker of movement in the shadowy depths lying beyond the door.

"We have matters to discuss, Detective Bailey. Shall we get down to business or are you going to continue creeping closer to the door so you can try to shoot me?"

There was a faint pause and I sensed his surprise, although none showed in his voice as he responded, "What sort of business do we have to discuss?"

"Put the weapon down and I'll tell you."

"And when are you going to put yours down?" he asked derisively.

I glanced at the Sig Sauer resting on my thigh. I could easily set it aside and found myself wanting to do just that. I didn't want to kill this man. I *wouldn't* kill this man, I told myself, resolved.

Theo was in place simply to make sure I had an escape if other officers arrived. I wasn't going to jail. That was my line there—I wouldn't go behind bars but I hoped it wouldn't come to that.

"Well?" he asked tauntingly, voice closer now.

"We could always come to a gentlemen's agreement," I suggested.

He made a noise low in his throat—laughter, perhaps. Or just a disgusted snort. I suspected it was somewhere in between.

"Sure," he said with grim amusement. "Why don't you outline the terms of this gentlemen's agreement?"

Sighing, I rose from the chair. Careful to keep out of Theo's line of sight, I approached the door. "Detective Bailey, it's going to be hard to strike any sort of agreement or even talk to you if you contact the police. I know when somebody is stalling. Please put your phone down."

Sensing more movement, I shifted as well, this time pressing my back to the wall just opposite of where I believed he stood.

"See," he said, false courtesy dripping from each word. "I'm having a hard time understanding just what kind of business I have with you. I'm pretty sure we don't know each other. And you showing up in my room without an invite has me a little edgy, especially considering some of the shit going on in my life lately."

"I understand your hesitation." He'd moved again. Wily prick, wasn't he? I hadn't even heard a sound.

Making a decision, I holstered the Sig, slipping the security strap in place so he wouldn't be able to disarm me—not that it was likely, but he'd already proven himself to be surprisingly competent. I listened for a few more seconds, then gave a quick hand signal to the woman watching from her perch, knowing she'd seen it clearly enough through her night-vision goggles.

Make it work, Tia's voice echoed inside my head. Focusing on that, I ducked low and moved forward, fast. Coming out of the shoulder roll, I ended in a crouch, having already spied him.

I launched myself at him.

He flung himself backward, moving with more speed than I would have expected.

Grudging admiration filled me as he twisted his body with agile dexterity and took cover behind the counter. If I was at all worried about anything but accomplishing my goal, I would have done the same thing—take cover.

But the longer I delayed, the more chance he would have to contact the local authorities and that meant I'd have to employ the last chance escape route.

The *final* escape.

I did have the advantage of surprise so I went with it, hurtling over the counter just as he started to peer above it. I saw him with barely enough time to pull back on my kick, but he still went stumbling back, sprawling on his ass before rolling all the way back from the momentum of my attack.

His cell phone dropped and I grabbed it. Picking it up, I checked the screen. He'd been mid-text. Fuck.

I'd deal with that in a minute.

Spying his weapon, I kicked it out of reach before he could grab it. He was still dazed so I picked it up.

With a few simple movements, I ejected the magazine and shoved the ammunition into a zippered pocket of my cargo pants.

He sat up slowly, wiping the blood from his mouth with the back of his right hand.

Setting his Glock down on the table, I grabbed a chair and spun it around. As I straddled it, I displayed the phone. "We can discuss that business as soon as you tell me what to say to assure this gentleman...ah, Agent Horton, that everything is perfectly fine here."

"Perfectly fine." His teeth flashed in the dim light, a sardonic smile that didn't look at all pleasant. "Okay. How about...*suck my dick*?"

"I didn't realize you swung that way, but I doubt an invitation like that is going to settle the matter, considering you just told him something might be up." Tapping the edge of the phone, I said, "Help me out, detective. We don't have much time before he contacts the local boys."

"Why don't you go fuck yourself?" A pained smile curled his lips but it was decidedly pleased at the same time, making me wonder what was going on in that canny mind. "I sure as hell hope you were smart enough to get a decent cut of the contract money up front. Because there's no way in hell you'll collect anything now."

Curious, I cocked a brow. "Meaning?"

"Meaning that your client is dead." Mac laughed and it was almost manic. "Really fucking dead. So dead, they won't even be able to scrape up body parts for a funeral. He was blown to bits a couple hours ago."

He shoved upright, then savage satisfaction gleamed in his eyes as he sneered at me. His gray eyes, so like Tia's, were hard and defiant as he spread out his arms. "So...go ahead. Do what you came for. I mean...that *is* why you're here, isn't it? Do it fast and make a run for it, then enjoy looking over your shoulder, because it's not that fucking easy to kill a cop and get away with it."

Understanding now, I smiled a little. "You're quite right about that. It's not all that easy to kill a cop and get away with it. It's much easier to...oh, say...make the top enforcer for the head of Boston's Irish Mafia overdose on the drugs he'd planned on slipping an underage girl at the strip bar he likes to frequent. A man will do most anything when you're holding a gun to his nuts after all. Especially if you catch him unawares in an...executive private booth and knock him out beforehand so he wakes up restrained, the same way he liked to restrain those underage girls he drugged and raped."

Mac went rigid.

"It's almost child's play to do that. It might be relatively simple, in theory, to slip into the home of said enforcer's girlfriend...the woman who helped recruit local girls for a particular group of thugs...and somehow she kept getting off."

"You're talking about Teddie Sessions and his girlfriend, Tammy Collins." His face had smoothed out fast, the cop taking over once more.

"I'm not *talking* about anybody. It's disturbing, theoretically, though, thinking that a woman could be engaged in such enterprises, even knowing what fate awaited such girls. Worse, don't you think, that one might find such a distasteful affair...arousing? Even enough to keep video of girls being forced and drugged? Hope lives eternal, of course, that she'd be an unwilling accomplice but hope's a fickle thing. Perhaps justice would be for her to share their fate. A broken neck really *is* too easy, and kind."

"You crazy motherfucker," Bailey said in a low, disbelieving voice.

"What's your opinion, detective? Would it be easy to swap out the steroids used by the goon O'Holloran called his second-in-command? Anabolic steroids are such a foolish drug. I wonder if those who abuse them kill their brain cells over time. Imagine..." I smiled at his disbelieving expression. "Injecting yourself and never once bothering to look at the vial of drugs. Not that it would be obvious at a glance, but still, if I were going to inject something into my body, I'd look at it first."

A harsh breath escaped him and I leaned forward. "I've heard that extremely high doses of strychnine can result in death within fifteen to thirty minutes...but it's still a brutal way to go. Brutal enough that it would almost be preferred to setting bombs in the place where the man who ordered the murder of an innocent woman lives. But even that was much easier than evading capture if one were so stupid as to kill a cop, isn't that right, Mac Bailey?"

"You..." He growled it out, the word seething and full of a venomous hatred.

Inclining my head, I said, "As I told you, we have business to discuss. Would you like to take care of notifying your agent friend...or should I just leave now? I have no desire to deal with the authorities."

Eyes cold and hard, Bailey came off the floor. He swiped the blood off his mouth, then spat some on the floor. Although I knew the cut on his mouth had to hurt like a bitch, he didn't flinch. "Text Horton. *Sorry, man. Head's still messed up over my sister. Seeing shit that ain't there, I think. I'll tag you in the morning. I need food and a drink, then a few hours horizontal.*"

"If this is code for something and law enforcement moves in, I will know." Tapping the weapon against my thigh, I added in a cold, hard voice, "I'm not dealing with the authorities."

"It's code for I need food, whiskey and sleep, dickhead," Bailey said with a sneer. "And your throat under my boot, but we'll leave that out since you don't want to invite him to the party."

After a cool, assessing glance, I dictated the words,

exactly as Bailey had spoken, giving the screen only a peripheral look before sending it.

That done, I silenced the phone and placed it facedown on the table.

He came at me hard and fast that very second. I took the first blow to my chin. I owed him that but I blocked the next and trapped his arm, maneuvering behind him before he could try again.

Letting my momentum carry me, I knocked his legs out from under him and almost had him on the ground, my arm around his throat, but he managed to get his knees under him.

"You're a fast son of a bitch, aren't you, detective?"

"Suck...my...dick," he rasped.

I smiled. He and his sister had a great deal in common. I suspected I'd like him, even if he wanted to kill me with his bare hands. "You're also strong, and clearly you have dedicated serious time to training yourself how to fight—more than just the typical scuffle, too. I have no desire to hurt you so I would appreciate it if you would stop this now so we can have that discussion."

"Go fuck yourself." He did stop struggling, though, his breath coming in choppier bursts. The tensing of his muscles was so slight, I barely had a second to adjust my stance. He almost threw me off and I don't know if it was because of my amusement at the predicament I was in or my determination not to cause him harm.

Tia wouldn't forgive that.

I squeezed harder, applying more pressure to his windpipe.

"You cannot beat me, Detective Bailey. As skilled as you are, I'm not a martial artist or anything else you've ever encountered. I'm a killer, born and bred. My father began training me for this before I was old enough even to understand what was expected of me, or why. I wasn't even nine years old before he forced me to kill the first time, leaving me alone in a room with a drunk pervert and a loaded gun. I had to choose...get raped or kill. You can imagine what I chose."

For a moment, he froze.

I don't know if it was because of anything I had said or simply a lack of oxygen. Easing up on the pressure, I asked, "Shall we talk? I'm sure you want to know about your sister."

Light flashing over the blade was the only warning.

Instinct took over.

Even as I heard the wet crack of bone breaking, I began swearing, first in German, then in English, only belatedly remembering that the language I'd first learned would be a clue to such a cunning bastard.

"You stupid son of a bitch." I hauled him upright, not knowing if I was speaking to him or myself. The light coming in through the windows was enough to see his features. His face was white as I shook him, trying to get a gauge on his status. I wasn't even surprised to see that he was clear-eyed—pale-faced and sweaty, but clear-eyed. "You've got to be one of the most stubborn people I've ever come across."

He tried to wrench away but I ignored him as I dumped him in the chair I'd vacated. Grabbing a fistful of his hair, I yanked his head back and glared at him. I was pissed off now, something that never happened while working.

Not that this was a job, but I hadn't expected emotions to come into play.

"I'm going to have to explain to her how you got hurt. Can you not make it any worse?"

"Explain it to who?" His voice was level, as if he wasn't sitting there with both bones of his lower arm snapped in two. "And where the fuck is Tia? If you hurt her..."

He shoved up out of the seat.

Covering his face with my hand, I pushed him back down.

He hit his broken arm and his already pale face turned gray.

"She's safe," I said, barely recognizing the growl of my voice. I looked around for something I could use to splint his arm. Even in the dim light, I could see well enough to know there wasn't much. At least nothing that I could see in immediate view. Turning to go into the bedroom, I took two steps but spun back and went into the living room area to grab the hotel phone. Holding his gaze, I yanked the cord from the wall, then tossed it on the couch across the room.

Then I went back to the little kitchenette and ripped that phone from the wall, as well, throwing it so that it fell next to its mate. With a cool smile, I grabbed his cell phone and shoved it into a zippered pocket on my hip, sealing it securely inside.

"Can't have you ruining our little party, now can I?"

"Not when you're just getting started on me, I guess." He stared at me with dead eyes, cradling his broken right arm but as I passed by him. He reached out with his left hand, his fingers digging into the sensitive nerves along my wrist with surprising strength and precision.

"Safe isn't good enough, pal. Where is she?"

As tempted as I was to wrench his hand away and break his arm at the wrist for grabbing me, I felt a weird kinship with him. I'd never loved anybody before, had never worried over anybody. Not until these past two weeks.

Reaching down, I caught his wrist, applying the same pressure and twisting at the same time. Standing over him, I had leverage, where he had none and soon, his grip relaxed.

"I told you, Detective Bailey. She's safe. By now, she's probably halfway back to Tennessee."

Disbelief was etched on his features but I ignored it. "You'll be able to talk to her soon and I will be walking out that door."

While he continued to stare at me with suspicion, I left him alone in the kitchen and went into his bedroom. I collected the light bulbs I'd removed from the lamps first. After a few seconds of searching, I found what I needed in the closet, a simple, well-made white dress shirt that I pegged as being custom-made. It would work. I grabbed the other thing I needed from where it lay draped over his neatly organized suitcase, propped half-open on the luggage rack.

I left the supplies I'd collected on the breakfast bar in the kitchenette, then replaced the light bulbs so I'd have light to work with.

In the kitchen, while he watched, I looked over the cabinets and drawers—three of the five were fake, nothing but silvery knobs on gleaming, cherry-stained wood. The next one was too shallow. The fifth, however, would work fine.

Dumping the basic kitchen utensils in the sink, I gave the drawer a hard pull to wrench it free from the moorings designed to hold it in place. Glancing over at him, I said, "You never know who might feel inclined to steal a drawer."

He didn't look amused.

Two hard blows knocked the sides of the drawer off, providing me with solid pieces to serve as splints.

I put them down and scooped up the knife Bailey had pulled on me. "May I use this?"

"Why the fuck not?" He eyed the pieces of wood and the shirt, something akin to disbelief in his eyes. "Either this is a new form of torture or you're planning on splinting my arm."

"I've had my arm broken before—both of them, in fact. In a manner just like that."

The first time had been when I was seven and I'd

been caught stealing. My father had been the one to order me to do it, while he was in the store. He had the money, of course, but it was part of my training. Every fucking thing he did had been part of my training, according to him.

Shaking off the memories that had become harder to ignore, I used the knife to cut loose the seams of the shirt sleeves, then ripped them the rest of the way off. "You'll be more...inclined to talk after your arm isn't hurting like hell, so we'll do that, then have our discussion."

When my arm had been broken, he'd left me to suffer with the pain all night, then set it himself, smiling cruelly.

"I'm not sure I want you setting my arm, Dr. Psycho," he said in a flat voice as I laid out the materials.

"I am setting the arm," I said. "Either you let me set it, or I'll pick you up, throw you on the ground and after you pass out from the pain, I'll do it while you're unconscious. Then we will talk. Frankly, it makes no difference to me."

"Because you have to explain this..." He gave his arm an irritated look before shifting his gaze to me. "To somebody. And who is that?"

There was a glint in his eyes that made me suspect he already knew.

He was proving to be a pain in my ass, so instead of answering, I met his gaze levelly and smiled. "Your sister, Detective Bailey. Tia is the reason I'm here after all."

The lines around his mouth went tight and his lids flickered.

"This is going to hurt."

He curled his lip. "No shit."

"It will be problematic if you scream."

"Just out of curiosity, are you part robot? A cybernetic organism from the future?" He gave me a disbelieving look. "Hate to tell you, but this is already sort of painful and it's about to get much worse."

"I'm aware." I wondered what he'd say if I told him I had bitten through my lower lip to keep from screaming. Even at seven, I'd known better. Screaming made the next punishment even worse. But nobody needed that in their head. Of course, nobody needed the torture of going through this unaided either. Hesitancy and doubt almost paralyzed me. Doubt. I was ill equipped to deal with it. My phone buzzed, but I didn't check it right away. I'd have a minute before she sent another.

There was a wet bar on the far wall and I went over to study the contents. Alcohol wouldn't help much but maybe the placebo effect would offer some comfort. Something would be better than nothing, I had to assume. The only bottle that had been touched was Johnnie Walker Blue so I opened it and filled two tumblers, each well over half full.

"You're full of surprises, aren't you?" Bailey said behind me, his voice strained and filled with an odd note I couldn't quite place. "You're a psychotic, murdering kidnapper with a knack for explosives and medical knowledge of some kind. But you've got fantastic taste in whiskey. Go figure."

After putting his glass in front of him, I pulled the phone out and texted Theo, letting her know there were no problems at present.

Mac had already tossed back half the liquor in the glass and I took a sip, staring at him over the rim.

"Do you need more?"

"No." His eyes gleamed as he downed the rest of the Johnnie Walker, then set the glass down with enough force, I wouldn't have been surprised if it shattered. "I want a clear head because I still plan on killing you if I don't like what you have to say about Tia."

"You sound like such a law-abiding cop, Detective

Bailey," I found myself smiling as I settled into the chair in front of him. Yes, I most definitely could find myself liking this man. I already respected him and that was an odd thing. He had nothing but a fierce need to protect his sister and what was clearly a deep love for her.

These emotions would have baffled me just a few weeks ago. But now, I appreciated them. Tia should have that kind of people in her life. More of them. Many more.

I wanted to be one of them.

Make this work...

I folded the belt in two and held it out to him. I wasn't surprised when he blew out a resigned sigh and accepted, putting the leather between his teeth and bracing his head against the wall at his back.

As he closed his eyes, I grasped his wrist with one hand, the upper part of his forearm with my other.

Other than a strangled groan low in his throat, he made no sound.

"It's a clean break, detective," I said as I splinted it. "If you don't injure it further before you can get it casted, it should heal without a problem."

Sweat drenched his face and he was still sickly pale. Yanking the belt from his mouth, he threw it, then grabbed my whiskey, mostly untouched, and tossed it back, leaving only a finger or so.

I sat waiting, listening as harsh breaths escaped him.

They slowed and Bailey opened his eyes. That bright, glazed look of pain was gone, replaced by a look of resolve.

"We can have that discussion now." Something hard nudged my knee.

I looked down and despite the circumstances, I couldn't help but smile at the sight of the small handgun he held. "I must really be distracted," I murmured. "I didn't check you for other weapons and you had two—a blade and a Baby Glock. Your clinch piece, I assume."

He bared his teeth in a parody of a smile, leveling the gut at my gut.

"Answer the question."

"Did you ask one?" I reached for the rest of the whiskey and drained it, staring at him with a smirk. "Unless you're talking about Tia, in which case, I did answer that one. She's safe and already on a plane, due to land in less than ninety minutes in Knoxville." I named the flight and airline number. "She checked in and boarded. She was worried her dog wouldn't meet the qualifications for an emotional support animal, but Valkyrie passed with flying colors, or so I'm told." Leo had taken care of the paperwork, including forging the needed documents, but such a task was child's play for him, even if he had been out of the game for some time."

"You sound rather certain on the details."

"Do I? Perhaps it's because I am." I eyed the empty glass and pushed back.

"Sit down." Bailey's voice was hard as steel.

"I just want more whiskey." I held up the glass. "You drank mine."

"It's my fucking whiskey and I told you to sit down."

This was getting tedious. Holding his gaze, I rose. The gun followed me, his eyes narrowing. I could only imagine the wheels spinning inside his head. It was a calculated risk to turn my back and walk over to the wet bar, but I took it. There, I refilled my glass and took a sip, holding his gaze challengingly in the mirror.

"You'd think a born-and-bred killer like yourself would know better than to turn his back on a man holding a gun on him, especially one who would have no problem shooting him."

"Ah, but you see, Bailey, you would have a

problem." I toasted him in the reflection. "You're not the sort to shoot a man in the back."

"If that man kidnapped my sister? Don't bet on it."

"I could point out that I did it to save her life," I said.

His mouth twisted in a sneer.

Turning, I strolled across the floor, gesturing with the hand that held the bottle. "We could discuss what I'm sure you feel are valid arguments—she could have stayed with you and some such bullshit," I said, coming to a stop in front of the bedroom door, right in front of the window.

"Sit your ass down," he growled.

"I'm fine standing." I took a deep drink of Johnnie, draining it this time and pouring another healthy serving. "You could have asked some of your Bureau friends to watch over her, but you and I both know O'Holloran has—or I should say *had*—a couple of agents on the payroll. His accountant has those names, by the way. And you're welcome."

"If you don't sit the fuck *down*..." he snarled, advancing on me.

I threw the now-empty bottle and pounced, taking him to the ground and disarming him. He grunted in pain as I shoved my knee into his right elbow, pinning that arm.

"I did tell you that you should avoid further injury," I said, giving the splint a critical once-over. It still looked secure, but I gave the cloth strips a few good tugs just to be sure.

Bailey closed his eyes, sweat popping out on his forehead once more. In a low, pained voice, he said, "I should have just shot you in the knee."

"I would have been dead a minute later, so it wouldn't have accomplished much."

Shoving off him, I held out a hand. He eyed me with disgust, but reached up and let me pull him to his feet.

"What the fuck does that mean?"

I pointed to the windows that ran the length of western wall, save for the narrow partition separating the kitchenette from the bedroom. "See the building across the way? Wave and smile. A contact of mine is watching. If any authorities show up, I get a nice, neat hole in the head."

"You're fucking with me."

I gave Theo a signal.

A second later, a red laser panned on the couch before slowing tracking over to me.

Bailey threw himself backward.

"What the *fuck*?"

I sent another signal. I didn't bother to look. Theo was already pissed I'd made her agree to this, had even threatened to kill me just out of pure spite, but she'd never do it.

Judging by the look on Bailey's face, he was still trying to figure out what was going on. Leaning against the armchair, staying in full sight of the window, I met his eyes.

"If you're that ready to die, why do you keep disarming me?" he asked. "I'd be happy to help you end it."

"But your sister wouldn't be happy. And...no, I don't think you'd shoot to kill, not unless you had no choice. It's not in your make-up. You...value life." I lifted a shoulder. "Personally, I'm in no rush to end up in a grave but...well, I had a feeling that talking to you would be a risky proposition and, as I've said, I'm not going to end up behind bars."

"You don't think you deserve it?" He shoved his back against the kitchen counter, shooting a look out of the corner of his eye at the window.

"That bullet isn't meant for you."

He laughed. "Yeah, I'm having a hard time buying that."

"I could have killed you at any time since you walked through that door." Holding his gaze, I drew the Sig Sauer and leveled it on him. "I could kill you now, if that's what I wanted."

His lids flicked to the weapon.

"Do you think that's what I'm here for? Really?"

Bailey's eyes narrowed. Taut moments stretched out. "You said Tia wouldn't be happy if I killed you. What the fuck do you mean by that?"

"Well, now. That's what I want to discuss with you. Are you ready to talk now?"

He shot a look over at the wet bar, then at the empty glass lying by his foot. "Get me a fucking drink, then yeah, I'll listen. I'm out of weapons for you to take away anyway."

Chapter 28

TIA

"**W**e need to talk."

I'd heard those words from Mac so many times over the past three weeks, I almost thought he'd forgotten how to say anything else. I stared at him over the easel, gripping my paintbrush like a blade and telling myself that if I threw it, the inky black clinging to the bristles would splatter all over the place and I didn't want the headache of cleaning up such a mess. Again.

I'd thrown any number of paintbrushes and canvases and palettes over the last month. The misery wasn't getting any easier and I doubted my temper would level out any time soon.

Bianca had suggested I talk to a counselor.

I'd suggested she kiss my cute brown butt.

The hurt in her eyes had made me regret it and I'd apologized immediately, but after our lunch was over, I hadn't talked to her and ended up canceling the next lunch date.

She didn't get it.

And Mac definitely didn't.

"Did you hear me?"

I stared at him, unblinking. The turbulent look in his eyes tugged at something in me, but I was already fighting more emotion than I knew how to handle. Looking back at the portrait, I struggled to control the sudden onslaught of tears.

"I'm not ready to talk yet, Mac," I said quietly.

"That's too bad." Steel edged his words.

The tone caught me off-guard and I looked up at him, surprised. He'd been handling me with kid gloves ever since he'd picked me up from the local FBI office in Knoxville. After landing, with Leo's watchful eye on me the entire time, I'd been whisked there from the airport without so much as a *what's up*?

I was glad Leo hadn't disembarked with me. He'd told me he wouldn't, that the Knoxville stop had just been a layover for him and I trusted the clever old bastard knew how to cover his tracks, so I hadn't worried about him.

Fortunately, the FBI didn't even seem to realize he was in the picture. Maybe his history with them made him fly under the radar.

Or maybe they'd been too curious about my *abductor*.

My head still hurt if I thought about those endless hours of questioning. Mac's intrusion had been a relief but I still wasn't ready to talk about the time in Colorado.

Not that they *knew* I'd been in Colorado. I hadn't even realized it until I'd spotted signs for cities like Fort Collins and Denver. At the time, I'd been too numb to wonder why Leo hadn't blindfolded or drugged me, but as we drew nearer to the sprawling Dallas-Ft. Worth airport, the old man had filled me in.

"Spectre says he trusts you not to tell anybody where you've been. I'm figuring he's right. Nobody can trace him to that house, except me...and now you. A world of hell would await that boy if anybody did track him down."

As far as warnings went, it hadn't been particularly subtle, but I didn't do subtle well. Even without the warning, I wouldn't have said anything.

Nobody would understand—

"Did you fall for this guy?"

At Mac's question, I dropped the paintbrush. Sennelier's Mars Black oil paint splattered across my feet and the material of my new green leggings that had the words *HULK*, *SMASH* in a textbook version of a comic font all over.

The question echoed in my head.

Did you fall for this guy?
Did you fall for this guy?

Swallowing the knot in my throat, I stared at Casper's face on the canvas, those high, carved cheekbones, perfect brows arching over intense eyes of green. The portrait was monochromatic, but my imagination filled in the color perfectly. His mouth, so brutally, powerfully sensual.

A face that could be beautifully cruel.

A face that could be cruelly beautiful.

Mine, my heart whispered as I stared at the canvas.

No, I thought dully. Because he wouldn't let himself be. The rage that lived under the surface tore through me and I slammed my hand down, scooping my fingers through the thick black oil paint, smearing it across his face, ruining the image.

Hand still coated with the viscous color, I picked up the canvas and threw it.

"Tia."

At Mac's gentle voice, I whirled on him. Hands clenched into fists, I glared at him. "I don't want to talk about this!"

He came to me.

In her place by my desk, Valkyrie stirred, looking at Mac with wary eyes. He gave her an annoyed look before continuing toward me, not stopping even when she sat up, ears pricking forward.

As my brother pulled me into his arms, I shoved him back. I didn't want comfort. I didn't want *anything*—

Liar.

Abruptly, I collapsed against him, crying.

"I don't even know if he's alive," I choked out through the tears. "I don't know how to call him. He didn't leave an email address or text and it's not like I can skywrite a message..."

Mac hugged me close, the rough material of his cast scratchy through the thin weave of my light sweater.

With his good hand, he rubbed my upper back.

He didn't speak, though.

The recriminations, the disbelief, the baffled dismay, everything I'd expected to hear—there was none of it.

When he picked me up, I shoved at his chest, still fighting tears, and losing the battle.

"Stop being so stubborn, little sis," he said sourly. "There hasn't been much I could do over the past few weeks, but from what I've heard, comforting you while you deal with a broken heart is sort of a brotherly prerogative."

He sat down and I was so tired, I gave up fighting, letting my head fall onto his shoulder.

"Okay."

He put a finger under my chin and tilted my head up. *Now* he looked dismayed. "*Okay*?"

"I'm too tired to argue with you." Tugging free of his hand, I dropped my head back onto his shoulder. I hadn't had more than a few hours sleep at a time since he'd left me.

Even then, my dreams were haunted by him.

Us, together on his mountain.

Us, here in *my* mountains.

Him, alone, on his mountain.

Him, alone, dying in a pool of blood.

Him, alone.

"I guess I got my answer," Mac murmured, pressing a kiss to my cheek before easing me off his lap.

He left me sitting there on the beanbag chair I kept in the corner of my studio and started scrounging around. Too disinterested to care what he was doing, I looked up through the skylight at the blue sky, dotted with fat, fluffy clouds.

Mac's shadow fell over me and I shifted my gaze to him as he knelt in front of me. He took my hands, both of which were smeared with the darkness of

Mars Black, and rubbed the excess paint away with a wet, stained towel. He went back to the deep sink and rinsed it out before returning and repeating the process a second time.

On his third trip back, he carried a trash can, a clear bottle and a roll of paper towels under his arm.

"You have a girlfriend who paints with oils?" I asked as he folded a square of paper towels and doused it with baby oil.

"No. Somebody closer than that." He glanced at me through the thick fringe of red hair that had fallen into his eyes. "It's not like I've never seen you paint before, Tia."

The sad smile on his face made me hurt inside.

"You notice everything about me," I said softly. "I don't think I do the same with you."

"You notice what matters." He shrugged and kept at the job until he'd cleared away all the oil except what had gotten under my nails. "I can't help with that. I'm not going to play manicurist."

"I'll survive." I took one of the leftover paper towels and dabbed it with the baby oil before going to work on my nails.

Mac stood by, watching, although I had little doubt it was because he was fascinated by the method I used to clean out the lingering oil paint.

"You know about what happened in Boston?"

Despite my desire not to react, I froze.

"Yes," I said.

"It was him."

"Is that a question? Cuz if it is, I can't help you. I already told the FBI agents, the guys with the Massachusetts Bureau of Intelligence *and* the Tennessee intelligence guys that keep hassling me, *I don't know anything about that shit.*" Jutting my chin up at him, I put as much attitude into my voice as I could. I'd gotten a lot of practice lately and I think I did just fine.

Mac hunkered down in front of me and his gray eyes, normally glinting with laughter or amusement, were dark. "No, it wasn't a question, Tia. It was a flat-out statement. It was him."

The certainty in his voice sent a shiver down my spine.

Judging by the way his eyes narrowed to slits, he saw my reaction, too. "That bother you?"

"Bother me?" Bending, I got to work on the paint still splattering my lower legs and feet. It was better not to look at Mac head-on. He saw the lies too easily. And the half-truths just as easily. "I don't know, Mac. The guy who wanted me dead is dead, and it sounds like the people who might have taken over and carried out the job out for him are also dead. I think I'm more bothered by the fact that people wanted *me* dead than I am by knowing that *they* are dead. But I can get why my cop brother isn't too happy that somebody blew them all up."

"If you think for *one second* that I'm not happy they're all in hell, vying to be Satan's righthand men, then you don't know me at all."

The hardness in his tone had me glancing up. Emotion, running far too close to the surface, had the knot swelling in my throat again. "Sorry," I mumbled.

"Fuck." He sighed and looked away.

I took advantage of it and did the same, busying myself with the few remaining traces of Sennelier's exquisite oil color staining my skin. Unable to waste any more time on it, I straightened. From the corner of my eye, I saw Mac and my heart froze when I saw what he held.

Aw, hell.

"This was a good piece," he said, facing away from me, holding the now-ruined portrait. With a shrug, he added, "Hell, you could still make it work. The swipes of yours could almost look like scars. Not that he has any."

My breath escaped me in a strangled sound. In the quiet studio, it was far, far too loud. Surging upright, I paced away from the beanbag chair and my brother, staring out into the late afternoon with a desperate urge to take off running. Valkyrie came over to me, whining low in her throat. Sinking my fingers into the thick fur of her neck, I clung to her.

He knew what Casper looked like.

Another one of those weird noises left me, and my petrified expression, blurred but recognizable, seemed to mock me from the window. Spinning away, I could see Mac now.

He'd turned to face me and watched me, a faint curve to his lips. "What's the matter, Tia? Cat got your tongue?"

I didn't bother wasting time asking how he knew what Casper looked like. There was only one of two ways, as far as I could figure. There hadn't been anything in the news, but there was all sorts of shit that didn't ever make it into the news, so that didn't mean much.

"Is he dead?" I asked, the fear I'd carried inside me the past three weeks making my voice quaver no matter how hard I tried to steady it.

Mac lowered the portrait to the floor, propping it against one of the shelves. "That's the second time you've made mention of that. Why do you think he's dead?"

"He's either dead or in jail if you know what he looks like." That familiar numbness started to seep through me again and I looked at the portrait, angry at myself now for damaging it. He'd looked that way the last day as we sat on the porch. Beautiful, fearless...*mine*.

My chest tightened and it got hard to breathe, each inhalation becoming more erratic and labored.

Dead. No...he couldn't be...

"Tia!"

I jerked when Mac closed his hands over my shoulders, shaking me.

"Look at me, sis," he murmured.

"No." *I don't want to…* I was terrified of what I'd see in his eyes, what he'd see in mine.

"Sweetheart." He cupped my chin and lifted, his grip gentle but unyielding. Once we were looking at each other, he pressed a kiss to my forehead. "Tia, if your reaction to my question didn't tell me that you have feelings for him, then looking at that portrait definitely would have. Do you really think I'd plunge into a conversation like this knowing you cared about this fucker if I knew he was dead?"

The band around my chest loosened, but only slightly.

"If he's not dead, then he's in jail. Is that why you're here? I am *not* testifying—"

"Good grief." He clamped his hand over my mouth and glared at me. "Stop jumping to conclusions, and please don't say shit that's going to make this harder on me, okay? I'm already questioning my sanity as it is." With that, he lifted his hand, but only a little. Brow arched, he said, "Are you going to pipe down and let me actually talk?"

"What are you going to talk *about*?" I asked, suspiciously.

"This guy…" He paused. "Fuck, I don't even know what to call him."

A knot in my chest eased. They couldn't have arrested him and not have a *name*, right?

"Casper."

Mac's brows shot up. "The guy who kidnapped you is really named *Casper*? I was convinced you were making that up."

"That's what I called him." With a shrug, I backed up, forcing my balled-up fists to relax. Valkyrie nudged her way up under my hand and a bit more tension faded. "I had to call him something, right?"

Mac's jaw bunched, then relaxed, conflicting emotions racing over his face. A hard sigh escaped him and he rubbed his hands over his face—or started to, the cast on his right hand impeding him. He gave it a disgusted look and lowered it to his side while scraping his stubbled jaw with the short nails of his left hand.

"Okay. *Casper*. You started feeling something for him. You know, there's a psychological reason behind—"

"Do you know what *sic 'em* means?" I asked, looking down at Valkyrie.

Her ears perked and she tipped her head back to meet my gaze, her big, brown doggie eyes connecting with mine. I couldn't say there was blind adoration there—yet. But we were definitely connecting.

"Sic 'em?"

She wagged her tail.

"Gee, Tia. Thanks," Mac said in a sardonic voice. "Nice to know my concern for you warrants a dog attack."

"I didn't think she knew what it meant." Shrugging, I curled my fingers in Valkyrie's thick fur. "But don't *tell* me that what I'm feeling is a psychological side effect."

Mac, looking like he wanted to argue, stood there, tongue pushing against the inner part of his right cheek while frustration darkened his eyes to near black. "I'm not going to tell you it *is*," he finally said, one hand up, palm toward me. "But how do you know it *isn't*?"

"Because I didn't *want* to fall for him. Because after the first few *hours*, I wasn't even afraid of him. I wasn't worried he'd harm me." A trucker, maybe, and yeah, that still unnerved me. The pervy old racist at the gas station? Yeah, I could see Casper planting a fist, or a boot, in that asshole's face. As far as the people in Boston? I wasn't going to cry over them being dead, either.

"You weren't?" Mac gave me a look so filled with skepticism, I burst out laughing.

It was the first time in *weeks* that I'd laughed, too. The sounds of mirth faded fast and left me feeling drained. Sinking back against the window seat where I often sat just to look out over the mountains, I thought back to those first, early hours with Casper, turning them over in my mind for what felt like the hundredth time. Or the thousandth.

"No," I said softly. Looking back at my brother, I hitched up my shoulder. "I wasn't afraid."

"He's *dangerous*," Mac bit out.

"Oh, I know that. *You* can be dangerous, Mac." Stroking my hand down Valkyrie's neck, I added, "She can be dangerous. Bianca could be, if she was pissed off enough."

He ground his teeth again. "I'm a *cop*. Hell, Tia, I'm a detective in Atlanta, Georgia! It's one of the worst cities in the country due to the high crime rate! You think I'm supposed to be a teddy bear?"

"Considering what Casper does, is *he*?"

"He's a fucking assassin!"

Shoving off the window seat, I stormed over to him and jabbed my finger into his chest. "He didn't kill *me*. In fact, he went out of his way to *protect* me—and *you*."

Mac jerked his head back.

"Yes, *you*. And Bianca. He had somebody watching this place the day people opened fire on my house, Mac. *That* is why you're both still alive."

Face going carefully blank, Mac gripped my wrist and eased my hand back. My finger was still digging a hole in his chest, which clearly annoyed him. I almost used my left hand, because he couldn't do much with a broken right hand. But it would be childish to stand around skewering him with my index finger, right?

"You know about that." Voice carefully neutral, Mac took a step back, then another.

Happy to see somebody else backing away this time, I said, "Yes. Casper told me not too long after it happened. He had...somebody there to watch my house because he was worried Tommy O'Holloran would send somebody back to my house and watch." My voice thickened and I looked away.

"Watch for...what?"

"For anything," I whispered. "For you, for Bianca. For anybody who might mean something to me."

"I'm not following," he said, shaking his head.

"What kind of detective are you?" Grumbling, I headed for the door, making a beeline for the living room and my nice, comfy couch, only to stop when the sticky feeling of residual oil through my leggings reminded me I'd have a mess—a permanent one—if I sat on my couch like this. Turning, I stared at Mac. He wore a white button-down, his standard clothing choice, apparently, and jeans. The jeans looked fine, but the shirt was trashed. "You've got clothes here. Get out of that shirt. I don't want oils on my furniture."

He muttered something but it was too low for me to hear and since he moved around me to head toward the room I kept for him, I didn't see the point in pushing. He was changing. That was all that mattered.

I headed up the steps to my bedroom, Valkyrie's nails clicking on the floor in a reassuring pattern that had already grown familiar.

In my room, I stripped off my ruined sweater and the leggings I'd bought mostly because the color made me think of Casper's eyes.

Not able to handle the emotional upheaval of yet more green, I settled on a pair of black cotton pajamas. Before going back downstairs, I wadded the ruined clothes up and threw them in the trash can in my bathroom. I'd deal with them later.

Back in the living room, I sank into the big, overstuffed armchair where I did most of my TV watching, my reading and lately...almost all of my sleeping. The big bed upstairs felt too empty with just me and my dog.

Mac was already there, crouched in front of the wood-burning fireplace I'd insisted on when I'd had the house built.

"You okay if I light a fire?" he asked, slanting a look at me.

"Yeah." I managed to smile. "Fires don't freak me much these days. Probably helps that I wasn't here when the big one tore through town."

He didn't respond to that, just went about laying the fire, then lighting it. Once it was blazing, he settled on his butt a few feet away from the hearth, staring into the dancing flames.

"If you knew your...friend, Casper, had somebody watching the house, then I have to guess he told you."

Mac didn't look at me, but I could tell from his profile that he still wasn't all that happy with whatever was going on inside his head.

"He told me not long after it happened."

"And that was...?" Mac slanted a look at me, the dancing flames casting his face half in shadow.

Twilight had settled. The living room was on the eastern side of the house, so most of the room was dark, the best illumination coming from the fire. The flames played over the lines of my brother's face and highlighted the rigid set to his shoulders.

The answer mattered to him. A lot. Swallowing the nerves, I told him.

Mac looked back at the fire, his head slumping.

I started to ask why, but he was talking again.

"And you were never afraid of him...not after the first few hours? Why the hell *not*?"

Valkyrie poked her nose against my thigh and I looked down at her, remembering the way I'd felt, seeing Casper bent over my dog. It hadn't been fear, not then. Even when we fought—or when I'd *tried* to fight—I hadn't felt fear. That had just been rage.

"He didn't hurt my dog," I said softly, staring into those big eyes.

Mac snorted.

I shifted my attention to him. "He didn't. And he didn't just leave her here where she'd go hungry. He took her with us—her food, her water bowl...her leash. And when I was..." *Unconscious.* "Asleep, he'd still stop so she could pee. Valkyrie liked him, too."

Mac blew out a hard breath. "Fuck."

"Why are you asking this?"

Getting to his feet, Mac braced his good hand on the mantle of the fireplace, his shoulders impossibly rigid. "What would it have done to you if I had come here and told you I'd killed him?"

A strangled cry ripped out of me. *No!*

I launched myself at my brother, fists slamming into him. He took the first couple of blows, but then I found myself pinned, his casted arm securing mine, while he used his good arm to hold me still. "I already told you he wasn't *dead.* I asked you what it would *do* to you!"

"That's just fucking cruel!" I shouted.

"Yeah, well, it's not easy for me to think about my baby sister being in love with a *fucking assassin*!" he shouted back, letting go of me so fast I stumbled.

Completely lacking Mac's grace, I wobbled, and if he hadn't steadied me, I would have fallen.

As it was, I didn't *want* his help and smacked at his hand. "You keep touching me, I'll break your other arm."

"Hell. You've always been mouthy and impulsive but violence? Really?"

"You're making me mad," I said.

"You're *driving* me mad." He spun away, one hand coming up to fist in his hair, fingers jerking at the strands as if he wanted to rip them out by the roots. "Can you...shit. Clearly, you don't want him dead and I get the feeling it would bother you if I *made* him that way."

"Is that what you're planning?"

"Life would..." He stopped, shaking his head, turning to look at me. "You're making this so fucking hard."

Another rush of emotion choked me. "What do you want from me?"

"Believe it or not, I'm trying to help." Under his breath, he added, "I think."

"Help?" Shaking my head, I flung out my arms. "In case you've forgotten, there are some things I just don't pick up on very well. Subtlety is one of them. Dancing around the bush? You're wasting your time. Whatever it is, you need to spell it out for me."

He pinched the bridge of his nose. "This is where we're coming up against a wall, sis. Because some of this shit, I *can't spell out*. Shit, I shouldn't even be asking. I ought to be writing myself up on some sort of ethics violation. So fuckin' stupid..."

The overbright look in his eyes made something flip over in my chest.

"You'd be...what...hurt, pissed? You half-expected him to be dead when I showed up here, but you didn't act like *that*."

"Mac, please..." I didn't want to beg, not my big brother who'd been the most important figure in my life almost since the day I'd met him. But my emotions already felt overused, stretched to the limit, wrung out and battered. The words came out, though. The answer to his question—I didn't think about it, didn't consider it. I just spoke. "It would tear me apart, okay? You're one of the most important people in my life and..."

A painful knot lodged somewhere between my throat and my chest.

"He knows that," I whispered. Tears burning my eyes, I stared at him beseechingly. "He knows...and I don't think he'd do anything that would hurt me. But you'd do anything if you thought somebody was trying to hurt me and..."

A strangled noise left his throat and I couldn't tell if it was a laugh or a sob.

I had no trouble understanding, though, when he snarled, "*Fuck!*"

Frowning, I wrapped my arms around my middle and stared at him. How was I supposed to react to this? Mac was pissed off, obviously, but I didn't know why. Was it at me? That didn't make any sense. Casper? Okay, *that* made sense, in a way, but at the same time—

"He saved my life!"

Mac's head swung my way.

Fisting my hand in the comfortable, worn cotton of my pajama top, I shifted endlessly from one foot to the other, all the while staring at my brother. "He saved me, okay?"

"Is that why you feel..." Mac gestured vaguely at absolutely nothing. "Whatever it is you feel?"

"No." I snorted. "Him saving me would warrant a nice thank-you note, I guess. I don't do the *rule* thing very well, you know that. But *you* do. He saved my life so why are you pissed off at him?"

He opened his mouth, then closed it, shaking his head.

"Why..." He laughed, sharp and dismayed. "Why am I pissed off at him?"

"Yes!" I dragged my hands over my hair, feeling the snarls I hadn't bothered to smooth out in days and not caring at all. "I'm *alive* because of him. I'll *stay* alive because of him! Are you so fucking hooked on rules and laws that you don't see that?"

"No." By contrast, Mac sounded almost abnormally calm. He stepped toward me and the look in his eyes was unsettling. "I'm pretty far from that point, actually. A sick bastard sent an assassin after my baby sister, the only person on earth I love—and I had to come to grips with the fact that there probably wasn't shit-all I could do to save her. At least, no way to guarantee that, and still make sure a raping, murderous thug didn't get out of jail, where he should stay for eternity, not just another pathetic ten years."

Rage flashed in his eyes as he moved even closer. "You think I didn't want to tear Tommy and that asswipe brother of his apart?"

"I know you did."

"Damn straight. No, I'm not pissed because he broke some laws to keep you alive. I'm *pissed* because he kidnapped you, and I'm *pissed* because you clearly fell for this guy, and I'm *pissed* because I don't know what the right thing to do is! Being a cop is black and white, Tia! Nothing about this is!"

"What is *this*?"

He opened his mouth, then closed it, shaking his head. "I've got shit to see to."

He turned and headed for the door.

"Hey!" Lunging forward, I grabbed his arm. "What the hell?"

Mac went still, turning toward me. He cradled my cheek in his hand and sighed. "He knew, Tia. I think that's what gets me. He knew it would tear you apart if I'd hurt him. And he went out of his way not to hurt me."

For a few seconds, I was too stunned to respond.

By the time I could? Mac was gone.

Chapter 29

I hadn't expected to receive the text.

It had come two days ago, just as I finished the last job I'd ever complete—one I'd assigned myself, to make sure there were no loose ends.

There were few—or there *had* been few—who could have tracked the Spectre. I hadn't expected there would be more than a handful, but even one was too many.

The job I posted had exactly four serious takers.

Of them, only one had even come close.

It had taken him nearly six weeks and none of the fail safes I'd set, save for the one that led him to me, had been triggered. I realized how he'd found me once I had his face up on the battery-powered laptop where I'd been hiding, just under a quarter mile away. Back when I'd been younger—and stupider—I'd been unaware a client had hired several others, desperate enough to see a rival dead that he'd been willing to pay the retainers to three different hitmen.

That man, Rene Broussard, and I had both ended up in the same hotel, under the same guise—gambling, and maybe a quick fuck with one of the prostitutes who liked to flirt with the winners of the high stakes floor.

We'd noticed each other, but he'd written me off, likely because I looked so young.

It was a mistake he'd have reason to regret as I completed the job while he was still in his room, fucking the woman he'd hired for a few hours. It wasn't until I'd collected my fee and was out of the country that I began to unearth his true identify, simply because he *had* noticed me—that had been another one of Sarge's rules.

You can't afford to be noticed, kid. Ever.

Broussard had set off a sensor alarm when he'd pulled off the main road onto the two ruts of dirt that led up to my home. Even though he'd left his vehicle behind and walked on foot, the alarm had picked him up and given me plenty of time to vacate the premises, all while setting up everything so he'd go inside.

It worked in my favor that Broussard had been a white man. He was ten years older than me, but nobody had any clue as to who I was, save for a select few, and only one of them had even a rough idea at my exact age. Even I didn't know for certain.

Leo, however, was a man I trusted with my secrets.

Should anybody else ever come looking, they could find his remains—or what was left of them—and a carefully crafted persona I'd been building for years. It now had connections to several unsolved murders and other crimes in Boston, Massachusetts. Most of the electronics were left in the unlocked weapons vault, my biometric data erased. The vault would withstand the small bomb that had been rigged to go on my signal and all I had to do was watch from a distance to make sure there wasn't any damage outside the structure. We'd have a great deal of rain and I had little concern there would be a fire, although I'd had a back-up plan if that hadn't been the case.

But everything went according to plan. Broussard went inside, certain I was there, thanks to heat-sensing technology. That tech had proven useful to me in the past, but I'd known it could be problematic. The solution for it had been discovered while reading a book—a sex doll, with an internal heating system that warmed the doll to body temperature.

He'd gone inside the house, made his way up the narrow steps to my bedroom, all because of a silicone sex doll with a dick that would put a horse's to shame.

After the debris had settled, I'd hiked back, checked

to make sure Broussard was dead. When he was found, *if* he was found, evidence would tie him to an elusive assassin some people didn't even think existed.

Spectre, effectively, was dead.

The only regret I had was leaving the cabin, the place where I'd first found some hint of life...with Tia. I'd had to spend hours eliminating the signs of her from the place, messy sheets that I'd burned out back, along with pages she'd torn from her sketchbook and left crumbled everywhere. It was like she'd wanted me to see signs of her everywhere when I returned. And I had. I'd slept in those messy sheets, streaked from dust from her pencils and smelling of her every night up until the last one. Watching the evidence of her presence in my life burn to ashes had torn at me even as I reminded myself it was necessary if I wanted to even have a chance at being with her.

Whether Meric had any chance at that was yet to be seen and the first hurdle lay directly in front of me.

I found him sitting by the entrance of the open-air café, sipping a beer, the sluggish breeze ruffling his hair. It might be nearing the end of October, but it was Atlanta and clearly autumn hadn't come. He spied me approaching and lifted his beer in greeting.

I'd already done two trips around the perimeter and hadn't seen anything out of the ordinary, except Mac Bailey, here an hour early for a one o'clock meeting. I'd arrived more than two hours early myself and had seen him saunter into the restaurant exactly sixty minutes before he should have been there, but he hadn't done anything more than place a thin, oblong object against the railing and order a beer. This was his third one.

As I sat down in front of him, he lifted the bottle in my direction. "You want one?"

"I think I'll go with Johnnie Walker." Giving him a thin smile, I added, "I've developed a taste for it."

"Weird. I've lost mine."

The server approached and I asked for bottled water, with the lid still on.

As she walked away, he asked, "Think I asked you here to poison or drug you?"

"Unlikely. But I'm not the trusting sort."

He took another sip of the beer and watched me with eyes that cut clear through me. "You trusted my sister."

"Yes." I had nothing else to say to that.

"For some fucked-up reason, you decided to extend some of that trust to me—a fucking cop." He drained the beer and put the bottle down. "I'm struggling to make sense of that."

"Don't overtax your brain. It was an action dictated by necessity, Detective Bailey, nothing more."

A wry smile tugged up the corner of his lips. "You're such a cold-ass piece of shit, but for some reason, there's something about you that I can almost find myself...well, not liking, but...I can't see myself hating you, either."

He rocked forward suddenly and braced his elbows on the table.

"You chose not to kill Tia. Why?"

Canting my head to the side, I watched him from under my lashes. "Is this being recorded?"

"No." His mouth turned down in a scowl and he looked away. "If I was the cop I thought I was, the answer would be yes, although I'd lie about that, too."

"And that is supposed to reassure me?"

A muscle pulsed in his jaw and after a lifetime, he looked at me. "If you had taken that job, my sister wouldn't be alive. And if I'd properly done mine..." his lids swept low and a hard sigh escaped him. "If I'd done what I should have, you'd be dead. Not because I did it, but because you would have had a sniper take you out, all so you could spare my sister the knowledge of knowing her brother had killed the only guy she'd ever really fallen for. That would have destroyed something inside her. And you knew that, didn't you?"

Drumming my fingers on the arm of the chair, I eyed him narrowly.

He had a smug look on his face and his gaze dipped to my hand—and the incessant beating. "Odd. I wouldn't have taken you for the sort of guy to fidget."

My hand froze. I tried to cover by shifting in my seat, but I did a piss poor job and I knew it.

"Is there a reason you wanted to speak to me, detective? Or am I here for shits and giggles?"

"Yeah, there's a reason. I—" He stopped speaking, a slow smile curling his lips as a woman appeared. "Hello, Natalie."

The server was Chinese, a pretty and petite woman, about five foot five with dark hair and large, dark brown eyes. Clad in a snug red T-shirt, she balanced a pizza that looked almost the same size as the table. As she put it down, she flashed a friendly smile at Bailey.

"Thanks, smells delicious."

"Did you expect anything less, detective?"

"Not from you, Nat."

"I aim to please." Natalie winked at him before shifting her attention to me. I wasn't surprised when her smile started to dim. It returned fast, but her polite expression lacked the warmth she'd directed at Bailey. "Is there anything you need, sir?"

"No, thank you."

She left in a hurry. Across the table, Bailey chuckled. "You make friends like that all the time?"

"Everywhere I go, as luck would have it." I eyed the pizza, then flicked my gaze to his. "What's this?"

"An extra-large pie. Double pepperoni. Their specialty, and yes, it tastes as good as it smells. I figured with all the prowling you did earlier, you hadn't eaten lunch yet. Dig in. I can't eat the whole thing myself."

The feeling that settled in my belly was one I'd felt several times over the past few weeks, but never this acutely. It was uncomfortable. No, I corrected myself. *I* was uncomfortable.

"Why?"

Bailey lowered the slice in his hand, a peculiar look on his face. "Why what?"

When I didn't answer, the perplexed expression shifted to one of speculation. "Let me guess...you haven't spent much time just sitting down to lunch with a big pizza, a couple of beers, just shooting the shit with somebody, have you?"

"My life doesn't lend itself to such...pastimes."

Bailey put the pizza down, the expression on his face making that uncomfortable feeling expand.

"I guess that makes sense. If you had a father who saw teaching you how to kill as family time, seems the rest of your life is going to be pretty damn fucked up, too." He grabbed the beer in front of him and took a sip, then put it down and lifted his pizza once more. "Eat some food...*Casper*. That, at least, is something you know how to do, unless you are a robot like I first suspected."

Moments ticked away while I watched him eat and he ignored me.

Was this some sort of test?

If so, I couldn't figure out the parameters or anything else. Bailey went for his third piece and gave the pie a pointed look.

Annoyed, I put a piece on the plate in front of me and scowled. The last time I'd eaten pizza had been with Sarge. He'd dragged me to a ballgame and insisted I have a beer, some pizza—the *experience*, he'd called it. Feeling Bailey watching me, I picked up the slice and took a bite. My diet consisted of food that was healthy, simple...and typically bland. The explosion of flavor that filled my mouth caught me off-guard and I had to work to blank my features. I ate one slice and had the urge to get another, but Bailey had settled back in his chair and the look in his eyes had me reevaluating.

"Why didn't you kill my sister?"

Involuntarily, I clenched the fist that rested on my knee. It took considerable effort to keep my voice level as I said, "There was no reason to kill her."

"You're an assassin. You've admitted as much. To an assassin, the reason is simple, isn't it—*money*."

"I don't *need* money."

Bailey's brows shot up, disappearing under the wavy fall of his hair. Leaning back, he gave me a pensive stare. "What *do* you need?"

Tia. I managed not to speak her name aloud.

But judging by the smug look on his face, he heard it anyway. He didn't say anything, though. Instead, he nudged the wrapped package on the floor with his foot, pushing it close to me.

I looked at it, deliberating, then finally picked it up.

What I found when I opened it left me struck dumb.

There were smears and splatters of paint across it, but the image—and the *resemblance*—was unmistakable.

"Tia did this."

"Yeah. She's damn good," Bailey said, pride in his voice. "Even if I don't care for the subject matter. Can't blame her that it got a little fucked up. I sort of pissed her off."

Looking away from the image—the painting of my face that was so perfect, it could have been taken with a camera—I stared at him. "Why?"

"Because I wanted to know how she felt about you, Dr. Psycho." He sipped his beer and leaned back in his chair. "Now...let's try this again. Why didn't you kill my sister?"

Chapter 30

I was awake.

Lying in the bed, I tried to figure out what had woken me. Eyes closed, I listened. Everything was utterly still and silent. As always. I started to close my eyes, then stopped, pushing upright. Valkyrie's bed was empty. I snapped my fingers but didn't hear the familiar click, click, click of her nails. I tugged the scarf from my head out of habit as I slid from the bed.

It was a little past midnight.

Absently, I glanced down the hall toward the backyard.

I froze.

It was too dark.

The bright light that illuminated the backyard wasn't on. An odd sensation settled in the center of my chest and I tried to swallow, but there was a knot in my throat, so big and massive, I could hardly breathe.

I heard a faint whine, a familiar sound, one I'd come to recognize over the past few weeks.

"Valkyrie..." I whispered.

The low, eager whine came again, followed by a yip.

Heart knocking hard against my ribs, blood roaring in my ears, I eased out of my bedroom and down the hall, ignoring the darkness of the backyard for the warm pool of light that beckoned from deeper in the house.

The kitchen was empty and beyond that lay the formal dining room that I never used. That room was empty, too, but there was light shining in from the living room and when a floorboard creaked under me, Valkyrie yipped and came running toward me, her long, fluffy tail wagging madly. Her eyes, black in the dim light, glinted at me, as if she were saying, *Hurry up*!

She looked back over her shoulder then darted toward me, coming up behind me to nudge me in the butt with her nose. Clearly, I wasn't moving fast enough for her.

Part of me wanted to run into the next room.

The other part wanted to tear back up the stairs, because if it wasn't him...

I practically collapsed against the frame of the wide, open arched doorframe, staring at the man sitting in a pool of shadows, despite the light that shone from the lamp he'd turned on.

I gripped the frame, squeezing so hard my fingers cramped.

Valkyrie nudged me again, then moved to sit at my side, her tail making a *swish, swish, swish* sound as she continued to wag it. All the while, she looked up at me eagerly as if to say, *Look! Look who it is!*

Curling my fingers in her soft fur, I held on tight.

"Let me guess," I said, my voice huskier than I'd like, but not shaking. That was a plus, right? "You were just in the neighborhood?"

Casper rose from the fat, overstuffed armchair and paced toward me.

He looked...different.

It had been close to two months since I'd seen him—months that felt like a lifetime. But that wasn't that long, was it?

Yet he looked...different. Still beautiful. Still deadly. And he still felt like...*mine*.

Short pale hair had grown in in the time since I'd seen him, proving that I'd been right—he was a blond. A scruffy beard didn't quite manage to hide those beautiful cheekbones or take away from the hard, sensual cruelty of his mouth. My hands shook with the need to touch him and I shoved them into the loose pockets of my pajama pants so I wouldn't reach out to do just that.

Touch had never been a need for me until he came along. When he left, the inability *to* touch him had caused an almost visceral ache.

His eyes glittered in the dim light, but he hadn't said a single word.

The penetrating look on his face left me feeling adrift and I tried to figure out which part of him I was dealing with—Spectre, the man who'd first appeared in my house, or Casper, the man who'd walked away from me.

"Are you going to tell me what you're doing here?" Clenching my hands into fists, I forced the words out. "Or am I just supposed to—Ummm..."

The rest of the words, whatever they would have been, faded as his mouth came down on mine.

He boosted me up, big hands grasping my butt and holding me snugly against him. Through the layers of clothing, I felt him, thick and heavy and hard. I could have cried, I needed him so bad.

The room spun around me in dizzying fashion as he carried me through the house, stopping every few feet to brace me against something hard so he could run his hands over me, or hold me steady so he could rub against me. Shuddering and aching, I caught his head in my hands. his short hair like silk against my palms.

"Don't make me wait," I begged as he went to pull away again.

"Bed, Tia," he muttered, his mouth fastening on my neck, teeth sinking into the sensitive curve.

"Fuck the bed. Right here. Don't make me wait..."

Here turned out to be the hallway, almost the exact position I'd been in the first time I'd seen him, although I didn't realize it at the time.

Neither did he.

He lowered my feet to the ground, yanked my pajama pants down, then boosted me back up.

The rasping sound his zipper made seemed horribly loud.

I shoved my hand between us, closing my fingers around his cock. As I squeezed him, he shuddered, muttering words in a language I didn't know. But then he wrenched my hand away with a force that might have frightened me if I hadn't been just as desperate.

He boosted me up and I wrapped my legs around him once more, whimpering as I felt the head of his cock nudging me.

He pressed against me. I buried my face in his neck, felt his big, strong body trembling. Pain burned as he went to push inside—as much as I needed him, I wasn't ready and he realized it almost instantly.

"I'm hurting you."

"I don't care..." I clung to him.

"I do." He pulled away, untwining from my arms and legs, pressing a gentle kiss to the corner of my mouth, then my chin, my neck—a hot, seductive path until he was kneeling in front of me. He brought one knee up over his shoulder and I gasped as he found me with his tongue, unerringly seeking my clit and teasing it to throbbing readiness.

My supporting leg trembled and I clutched at him. "I'm going to fall."

"I won't let you." He grabbed my other leg and moved in. Before I realized what he was doing, he had my legs draped over his shoulders while he gripped my ass in his hands, face buried between my thighs. "Come for me, Tia...show me you still want me."

Still want you... I might have laughed, but he'd already stolen the oxygen from my lungs. It was all I could do not to scream. But then he slid one hand down and plunged two fingers into my pussy, screwing them deep—once, twice, three times...and I started to come, crying out his name while rocking against him and clutching his face to my pussy as I begged for more.

"You're ready now," he whispered against the slick

wet folds, sliding my legs down. He rose in a fluid, rapid movement, caught me around the waist, and while I was still trembling from the orgasm, he lifted me, filled me.

The harsh keening that escaped sounded too animalistic to be me, but I knew it was because he was muttering in my ear, saying my name and other things in that unknown language while he thrust deep, then withdrew, only to fill me again, with slow, purposeful thrusts that stretched and filled me.

The second climax was almost as brutal as the first and I whimpered as he pulled out, still hard.

Dazed, I looked at him, watching as he hitched his jeans up and zipped them.

"What are you..."

He swept me up into his arms. "Making up for lost time."

* * * * *

"Don't." Eyes opened only to slits, I flapped a hand at him when he came out of the bathroom, his body, finally naked, was beautifully gilded by the silver moonlight shining in. "I can't handle any more."

He crawled onto the foot of the bed and pressed a kiss to my ankle, my calf, the back of my knee, working his way slowly up.

By the time his tongue circled my nipple, the pulsing between my thighs had grown strong enough to prove me a liar.

But he lay in front of me, eyes heavy-lidded, his short hair mussed from all the times I'd spent grabbing his head or clutching him closer as he kissed me.

"I can't believe you're here," I whispered, the words husky. Excessive shouting and moaning could be hard on the throat, apparently. Tears rushed to my eyes immediately after I said it and I wiggled forward, burying my face against his chest so I wouldn't blurt out what I'd just let myself think.

But he wasn't one to let me hide from my thoughts...or reality. In the short time since I'd known him, he'd never been anything less than brutally honest and unflinchingly direct. It was something I appreciated about him. But right now, that directness terrified me.

"Look at me, Tia."

"I don't want to," I said and as soon as I did, I wanted to kick myself. *Wait five seconds and think before you speak.*

His fingers curved around the back of my neck—strong, warm, impossibly gentle. "Why not?"

"Because if you're going to tell me you're leaving or more bullshit like that, I'd rather you just did it and not talk about it or make me watch. It was too hard last time." *Last time.* I'd dealt with it then, because as much as I'd hated it, I'd expected it, really. And I'd known he wasn't coming back.

But he had. He's here.

He's here, right here in bed with me. My emotions swung swiftly to anger and I jerked back, going to my knees so fast, it left my head spinning. "Fine." My voice came out clipped, but at least I wasn't yelling. "I'm looking at you. Just...just say it, okay? Whatever it is you came to say, say it and get out so I can cry about you all over again."

I crashed into his chest, hard. He speared a hand into my hair and his fingers snagged on the curls. He started to smooth his way through, but I yanked back.

"Be still," he said.

Narrowing my eyes, I said, "Don't tell me what to do."

For emphasis, I shoved against his chest.

"Why not? It's what you've been doing to me." He rolled then, pinning me under him.

Hurt and fury and fear tangled inside and I shoved at his shoulders, glaring. He caught my hands and dragged them over my head and my breath stuttered out of me as the shift caused him to press against me...intimately. I swallowed back the moan, refusing to let it out.

"I'm not leaving," he said quietly, kissing the corner of my mouth. "Not unless you tell me that's what you want."

He kissed my cheek next, my earlobe, then began to trace a path along my neck until he found the mad flutter of my pulse.

"I...what?"

He came back to my mouth and murmured those very same words. "I'm not leaving."

The light, hopeful feeling in my chest tried to break free of the chains I'd slapped around it, but I didn't dare let it happens. In fact, I added *more* chains, because there was nothing worse than dashed and smashed hope.

He kissed me, gentle and soft, and I lay there, clenching my hands into fists and struggling to figure out where the problem was...before the heat of his body, the persuasion of his kisses made thought utterly impossible.

He'd said something important...*not leaving*...I had to think about that and it wouldn't be possible if I didn't stop him soon.

He moved lower, mouth sliding along my collarbone and I groaned. "Casper...*stop*."

He nuzzled my neck and drew in a breath. I had the weird sensation he did it just to breathe in the scent of me and the idea left me feeling sort of giddy. "If you say so."

Pulling away, hands gliding over my skin as if he loathed breaking contact, he levered away from me and sat on the bed cross-legged with loose, boneless grace. *Immodest* grace. My mouth went dry as I raked him with a look, eyes lingering on the still-erect length of his cock.

"Unless you want me back on top of you, you

shouldn't look at me like that."

The rasp in his voice had me looking up at him. "Like what?"

He shifted on the bed, settling with his back against the elaborately carved wooden headboard. Eyes sultry and full of sensual promise, he stretched out one leg, while bringing the other up, knee bent. He slid one hand down and closed it around his cock, stroking lazily.

"Like you can't wait to put your mouth on me again." His voice dropped even lower. "And the way you just licked your lips makes me think that's exactly what's going through your mind."

"Of course it is, now that you went and talked about it." Grumbling, I wiggled away and grabbed blankets at random, burying myself in them so I didn't leap for him. When I looked back at him, my heart stopped and my mouth fell open.

He cocked a brow at me. "What?"

"You... Wow! You just smiled. Like...*really* smiled. Not just that little half-grin you do sometimes. But a real smile."

The smile had already faded but the memory shone crystal-bright in my mind and my fingers itched for my charcoals and paper. "You're serious, aren't you? About staying?"

His lashes drooped lower but he didn't look away.

"If you'll have me," he said in a rough voice.

"If I'll *have* you..." A half-wild laugh escaped me, but it stopped abruptly, all but choking me as it lodged in my throat when he rose and circled the bed. I watched, still huddled under the blankets, as he dragged on his jeans.

"I was asked to give you this," he said.

I shivered because it wasn't Casper's voice he spoke with now and when he looked at me, the cool, empty expression on his face was too much like Spectre's, the man who'd scared me shitless those first few hours. In his hand, he held out a piece of paper, folded into a square and worn.

Confused, I took it and opened it. I hadn't read more than two words before I jerked my head back up, already pissed off.

But he was no longer in the room. I hadn't heard him leave.

Swallowing, I looked back down at the note my brother had written.

> *Tia*
> *Apparently, this guy is what you want.*
> *I can't say I'm happy about it but from what I've uncovered, he's not the sick son-of-a-bitch I wanted him to be, although he is going to have to turn over a new leaf if you two are going to make this work.*
> *I only want what's best for you...and what will make you happy.*
> *So, if that bastard hurts you, I'll be doing some vigilante justice myself.*
> *Love you, sis.*
> *Mac*

Not quite sure what was going on, I slid from the bed and headed for the door. I didn't even think about being naked until I was halfway down the hall. Frustrated, I hurried back to my room and grabbed the first thing I saw—his shirt, lying on the floor. Dragging it on gave me a petty sense of satisfaction because he couldn't leave without a shirt, right?

I started into the kitchen but stopped when I saw the backyard light was on again. Veering in that direction, I paused when I saw him sitting on the porch, Valkyrie lying next to him with her head on his lap. She didn't look up, but her tail thumped when I opened the door and moved outside.

"When did you see Mac?" I asked warily.

"Which time?"

I blinked.

"You've seen him more than *once*?"

Broadly muscled shoulders rose and fell as he sighed.

Edging around him, I moved down the wide stairs so I could stand in front of him. I wanted to see him when he answered and I knew he wasn't going to turn to look at me.

The bright porchlight backlit him now, casting him into shadow so that I could only make out the dark glitter of his eyes, not their color, but I knew they'd be hot and intense, the green almost jewel-like in its intensity.

"Three times," he said in a remote voice.

"I..." The word squeaked out of me and I cleared my voice. "What do you mean, *three times*?"

Casper cocked his head. "Just that. I saw him three times. The first time was nine days after I left you in Colorado. I saw him again six weeks after that, when he texted me and told—"

"Hold up." I lifted a hand, index finger extended while I drew in a breath. "Just *how* did my *brother the cop* know how to text you...but *I* didn't?"

"Because after I left him in Boston—"

"After you left him in *Boston*?" I spun away from him and paced a few steps, yelping when my bare feet came in contact with the cold, wet grass.

Casper had his arm around me in a second. "What's wrong?"

"The grass is cold." I jabbed my elbow into his side and ducked out of his embrace and turned back to the porch. I wasn't ready to go back inside so I veered to the deck chairs and turned on the linear gas firepit with its high, deep walls—deep enough that it could act as a table, provided you didn't turn the heat up too high. Grabbing a blanket from the sealed outdoor storage unit, I wrapped it around my shoulders.

Mind whirling at what he'd revealed, I turned to Casper. "You went to Boston. To see Mac."

"No." He inclined his head. "I went to Boston for something else altogether. But Mac was there. I thought we should...talk."

"Talk. Yeah. Right. I bet Mac took that *real* well. How long did it take him..." I stopped as the realization hit, dropping down on me with the force of an anvil smashing into my head. Dazed, I sank onto the love seat, the cold damp not even penetrating this time. "You broke his arm, didn't you?"

A muscle pulsed in his cheek. "Yes."

"Did he pull a gun on you?"

After a brief pause, he nodded.

"Why on *earth* did you go talk to him? Especially without *me*? He could have killed you!"

"There wasn't a high risk of that happening," Casper said. "But it was one I was willing to take."

Pushing up off the padded cushion, I stalked across the porch and shoved him. "*Why?*"

"Because of *you*." He caught my shoulders, grip firm, but not cruel. His eyes held more emotion than I'd ever seen.

Heart racing, I grasped his wrists, but I didn't know if I wanted to peel his hands off or cling tight.

"You told me to *make it work*, Tia. And that wasn't going to happen with your brother standing in the way. There was only one option—see if he loved you enough to give *me* a chance."

Blood roared in my ears and my skin felt so hot, so tight, I thought I'd crawl right out of it. A million things raced through my head but when I spoke, I didn't say *any* of them.

"So you broke his damn arm?" I blurted out.

He *smiled*, the jerk. "In my defense, he pulled a knife on me."

"A..." Squeezing my eyes closed, I tried to block out the image. "You said he pulled a gun. Now a knife. So, a knife *and* a gun?"

When he didn't answer, I opened my eyes and glared at him. "Answer me!"

"Two guns and a knife," Casper said, saying it with such obvious reluctance that I knew he didn't want to tell me at all. "Perhaps if I'd been less distracted, I would have searched him after I took his first weapon and found the other two and I could have avoided breaking his arm. I'm sorry."

I blinked and shook my head. "I don't think I'm the one you're supposed to *apologize* to. You didn't break *my* arm."

"If it will help, I can call him and apologize."

Peeling my fingers from his wrists, I nudged him back and went over to the loveseat. My legs were wobbly and it didn't surprise me at all. "He pulled a gun on you, then a knife, then another gun but you'll call him and apologize."

"He's a cop who'd been worrying over his missing sister for several days." Casper stared at me unflinchingly. "He'd been worried about *you*. He loves you. I can't be angry that he did what he felt was necessary out of that love."

That tight, hot ball of emotion returned, lodging in my throat and rendering speech impossible. Covering my face with my hands, I struggled to control myself as too many feelings raged inside. Instinctively, I started to rock as I fought to untangle all the emotions, but there were just so many and I was spiraling, lost inside them.

Some of the things I felt right then, I didn't even know how to describe.

"Tia."

Casper's voice drifted over me and around me, but I couldn't quite focus.

Then he caught my hands and pulled them away and I had to look at him.

He knelt in front of me. The stark expression on his

face hit me dead center in my chest and I flinched from the impact.

"What's wrong?" he demanded. "What did I say? What did I do?"

"Idiot," I choked out. Nothing else came to mind, not word-wise, at least. I pulled free of his grasp, then caught his head, pulling him to me.

"Tia—"

"Shut up," I said against his lips. "Kiss me. I need you."

Pulling him closer, I slanted my mouth over his and wrapped my arms around the wide shelf of his shoulders, clinging tight. He came to his knees and pulled me to the edge of the seat and I gasped because now I felt him, thick and hard, through the layer of denim separating us. His jeans—*only* his jeans. I hadn't pulled on panties and the shirt I wore was already up to my hips.

"Get up." I urged him on by pulling at his belt loops and after a few more rough, hungry kisses, he rose but when he went to unzip his jeans, I knocked his hands away, rising to deal with the task myself, then turned and pushed him down. He pulled his jeans down to his knees but I found I couldn't get close enough. Shooting a look at the house behind me, I glanced back at him. "Did you notice if there were any cars in the driveway next door?"

He wrapped his hand around his cock, his other arm behind his head as he stared down at me.

"There was. I don't care." His gaze dipped to my mouth.

My pussy throbbed. Licking my lips, I caught the waistband of his jeans and dragged them down to his ankles. "In that case..."

After stripping the material completely off, I settled between his thighs, the blanket I'd dropped providing some padding between my knees and the wooden planks. Even before I bent over him, Casper had gathered my hair into a loose tail and when I moved in closer, he started breathing heavier and harder. With his free hand, he braced his cock, holding it at the base.

Part of me wanted to slow down and enjoy...tease.

But too much of me was desperate, that frenzied need roiling inside, fighting for release.

I took him in my mouth.

He grunted, a hard shudder racking his body. "More..."

I took more. I took him until he hit the back of my throat, then I swallowed and tried to take him even deeper. Only when my eyes were watering and my throat resisted did I pull back, and I pushed myself harder the next time. He tasted different and I realized with a flush it was because he'd been inside me. It made that pulsing ache in my core intensify.

I whimpered, shuddering. My nipples dragged over his thighs and that was more sweet torture.

Casper shifted. Knocked off balance, I fell back, my shoulders bumping into the wide lip of the stone firepit, the tall walls a barrier between me and the flames.

He rose, shoving the loveseat back. It only had six or eight inches, but it went flying until the railing forced it to stop.

Eyes wild, Casper said, "On your knees. Open."

Shaking, I complied with a whimper, opening for him as he aimed the hard, rude thrust of his cock for my lips. He fisted a hand in my hair and cupped my chin with his free hand, angling my head until he had me where he wanted—my gaze meeting his as he fucked my mouth.

My pussy clenched.

My nipples tightened.

And when he closed his eyes and shuddered, that tight, hard ball of emotion expanded, more and more...until it exploded—a different kind of release.

Almost bowled over by the emotional upheaval, my sense of self faded away for a few seconds. Minutes...maybe even hours. There was just that crushing, yet liberating sensation of everything I'd felt no longer trapped inside myself as I knelt there in front of him, his hands on me, urging me on.

Then he was lifting me and I was on my back.

He slammed into me, then went completely still.

"You were crying. Why?"

Arching closer, I rubbed against him. "It doesn't matter. Please!"

"It matters." He sounded bewildered. But he didn't make me wait. He filled me, again and again, hands cupping my face as he kissed away the tears, then covered my mouth. His voice raspy, he murmured, "Is this the *feeling-a-whole-hell-of-a-lot-thing* again?"

"Yeah." I sighed, relieved he remembered, that he got it. That I didn't have to explain. "Casper..."

"Meric." He pushed up onto his hands, hovering over me. "My name is Meric. Say it. I want to hear my name on your lips."

Stunned, I looked into his vivid green eyes. I hadn't realized I'd needed that from him. This piece—this *real* piece. But now that I had it, now that it settled into that place in my heart that he'd completely taken over, I couldn't believe how much I'd *longed* for it.

"Meric," I whispered, smiling up at him. "Mine."

Meric came back down over me then, one hand cradling my head, the other spread wide over my hip. "Tia...mine."

There were other words burning inside me, awkward ones that I was so bad at saying. But there was time for that later. Maybe he'd even be able to say it to me at some point. For now, I curled my arms around his neck and pulled him to me. "Meric..."

He shuddered and thrust deep, his cock stretching and pulsing and filling me.

So I said his name again and again, until we finally

crashed together.

He sprawled on top of me, half on the love seat, half on the wooden deck, face buried between my breasts.

"There's something I want to tell you," he murmured as my breathing finally slowed. Somehow, he managed to pull himself up, then me, levering me onto his lap and dragging the blanket over us as the cool night had me shivering.

Tipping my head, I looked into his eyes and somehow managed to smile. "As long as you don't say anything about leaving, you can say anything you want."

"No, I'm not leaving. Not if I have anything to say about it." His eyes held mine. "Tia...I love you."

Epilogue

"Sarge was basically like your dad."

Looking at her as she knelt over the grave of the man who'd saved me, I said, "Yes. In every way that counted. I didn't realize it in time to tell him."

Tia turned her head and gave me that sweet, half-smile that still made my heart clench up. "He knew, Meric. There's no way he didn't."

She rose and reached out, the emerald wedding ring, flanked by diamonds, flashed in the fading rays of the sun.

We'd gotten married four days earlier.

Mac had even been there to give her away. Other than that, and a brief visit at Christmas, I hadn't seen him in a year, not since the visit I'd made to his house when I went to tell him I was going to Tia.

If you fuck this up, I'll find another hit man, one just as mean and scary as you are, and I'll make you regret it.

I didn't doubt he meant it, but I had no intention of fucking this up.

As promised, I'd turned over a new leaf. It had been almost...simple, really. Walking away from that life had caused no regrets. Living with the rages that still flared up from time to time wasn't as simple, but Tia was always there and bit by bit, that cold, ugly knot of darkness seemed to fade away a little more all the time.

When the darkness got too bad, I took my camera equipment and disappeared into the mountains.

She understood—she'd even told me so. *Sometimes I need to be alone by myself, too, Meric. And I don't have as much ugly shit in my head as you do. It's okay.*

She murmured Sarge's full name out loud, calling

me back to the present. To her.

"I wish I'd gotten to know him," she said. But then she frowned. "Or maybe not. You weren't ready for me then."

I wanted to tell her I would have been, and it might not have been a lie.

"I sure as hell wasn't ready for you." She slanted a look at me, eyes crinkling at the corners.

"Really."

"Nope," she said, turning to me and wrapping her arms around my neck. "And I'm okay with that. Not because I'm patient."

"I never noticed."

She lifted a brow, dragging her fingers down my side in warning. "You're getting better at sarcasm."

"Don't do that." I caught her hand before she could do it again. I didn't mind when she played, but a lifetime of being wary in public wasn't an easy thing to let go of.

"Spoilsport." She kissed me then drew away to take my hand. "Are you ready?"

I looked down at Sarge's resting place once more. I hadn't been back here since the funeral. When I'd told Tia, she'd insisted we come here before we took our honeymoon. Hawaii, she'd decided, since I had no particular interest. As long as she was there, that was all I needed.

"Yes. I'm glad we came here."

"Me, too. We'll come back. Maybe even have a weekend or two in the beautiful old lighthouse." She smiled again and it was a wider, easier smile. She did it more often now.

So did I, because of her.

She tugged on my hand, but I lingered another moment, staring at the headstone.

"Thank you," I said, although I had no idea if he was floating around anywhere, capable of hearing. It didn't matter, either. I had to tell him, here and now, with her at my side.

He'd understand, too.

While Sarge had saved my life, I hadn't really started living it until Tia.

She wasn't my *second* chance—she was the first, the only, the always.

About

Shiloh Walker has been writing since she was a kid. She fell in love with vampires with the book Bunnicula and has worked her way up to the more...ah...serious works of fiction. Once upon a time she worked as a nurse, but now she writes full time and lives with her family in the Midwest.

She writes romantic suspense and contemporary romance, and urban fantasy under her penname, J.C. Daniels.

Follow her on Twitter, BookBub & Facebook.

Read more about her work at her website. Sign up for her newsletter and have a chance to win a monthly giveaway.

If you enjoyed this...

please consider leaving a review.

SIGN UP TO RECEIVE SHILOH'S NEWSLETTER
@
WWW.SHILOHWALKER.COM

Look for other titles by Shiloh

THE MCKAYS

THE BARNES BROTHERS

THE ASH TRILOGY

THE SECRETS & SHADOWS SERIES

THE **FBI** PSYCHICS

Wrecked

In the nineties, Abigale Applegate and Zach Barnes were the most beloved sitcom child stars in the world. Then they grew up and left Hollywood behind...

WHATEVER HAPPENED TO ABIGALE APPLEGATE? SHE'S BEEN WONDERING THE SAME THING.

With her Hollywood dreams long gone, Abigale now has a nice, neat, uncomplicated life—until the day her perfect fiancé *needs to talk.* Dumped, a little more than shattered, and totally confused, Abigale turns to Zach, her best friend since forever, to help her pick up the pieces. He does it with a gift—a copy of *Wreck This Journal.* She can vent her frustrations, and sketch out a new plan. Zach just hopes he's part of it. Because he's been in love with Abigale his entire life.

When the journal falls into Zach's hands, he discovers Abigale wants a new man. And fast. Nothing more than a hot distraction. Zach has a strategy, too. He's going to be that man. It's his last chance. Abigale might be out to shake up her life, but Zach's out to reinvent it. Now, all he has to do is convince Abigale that life *can* go as planned.

READ ON FOR AN EXCERPT FROM

Wrecked

THE FIRST BOOK IN SHILOH'S BARNES BROTHERS SERIES

"Hey, Zach."

She glanced down and he followed her gaze, saw that she had the journal he'd picked up for her. "Did you bring that here to beat me up with it or something?"

She laughed. "Well, there is something about an unexpected action..." Then she shrugged. "Nah. I actually figured out a plan. It's a weird one, but I'm here to ask you to help me do one of the things on the list."

"Okay..." He hooked his thumbs in his pockets and waited.

"I want a tattoo."

Zach closed his eyes. Reaching up, he rubbed his right ear and then said, "You want what?"

"A tattoo." She wiggled the book. "I wrote it down and everything. I did it last night and I've thought about it all day and I'm sure I want to do it, so stop looking at me like I've lost my mind, okay?"

"You wrote a plan that includes getting a tattoo," he said slowly. His mind was churning at the very idea of it and his blood was boiling. Putting his hands on her...*focus on the issue at hand, Barnes!* "And you want me to do it."

"Well..." She grinned at him and the dimple in her chin winked at him. "The tattoo part is in the plan. And who else would I ask? You're my best friend, right?"

He pressed the heel of his hand to his eye. "You sure about this, sugar?"

"Yes." She tapped the book against her leg, looking around. "Ah...does that mean you'll do it?"

"Like I'd let anybody else," he muttered. "Do you know what you want?"

She shrugged. "I hadn't really thought it through *that* far. I was kind of thinking you could help me figure it out."

He shoved a hand through his hair and glanced

around. The parlor was empty. "When did you want to do this?" He could take some time to think up some designs for her. Take some time to get a grip and—

"Now."

So much for taking time to get a grip.

"Okay."

Bent over the table, she watched as he sketched out another image. Keelie had left, locking up the front door and lowering the blinds. Zach seemed completely focused on the task at hand. "You got any idea where you want to put this?" he asked.

"Ah...well, I was thinking that I'd rather have one that doesn't really show. It's for me, not anybody else." She scooted back from the desk and went over to the design wall, studying some of the pictures. The back of her shoulder seemed innocuous enough, but this was something she was doing for herself. Not to show off and she wanted it personal. Completely personal. She saw one woman's picture—the woman was pretty damn clearly showing off—she was sexy as hell, Abigale had to admit, but did she really have to have her jeans open like that?

Although one thing was clear. She wasn't about to have him doing it on her hip like *that*. She'd have to all but pull up her skirt. Considering the way she was having trouble thinking clearly around him just now...? Yeah. Not happening. "I guess my lower back."

Glancing down at her skirt, she frowned and turned around to find Zach staring at her. His gaze dropped back down to the sketchbook in front of him. "Will this skirt work okay for this?"

"Yeah. You're fine. You wanna take a look at any of these?"

She crossed the floor to study the designs and frowned. They all looked so...simple.

"What's wrong?"

"Well...they're pretty, but..." She glanced at the

vivid color on his arms, the intricate detail and then back at the sketches. "Aren't they kind of plain?"

"Sugar, you've never had a tattoo before. Trust me. You want simple. They hurt. And the more intricate it gets, the longer it takes."

"Oh." Well, technically she *realized* it wasn't going to feel good. But having it pointed out to her made some of the nerves inside her flare to life.

A warm hand brushed down her arm and she turned her head, found Zach watching her closely. "You know, this isn't anything you have to do," he said quietly.

"Yes, it is. I want to." Tearing her gaze away from his, she looked at the designs. One in particular had caught her eye the second he'd drawn it. Simple or not, it was lovely. The stylized dragonfly made her smile. It was pretty, fantastical, and silly.

"I think that one is just about perfect," she said, tapping it with her finger.

"Okay." He checked the clock. "I need some time to get this ready. Don't suppose you feel like ordering us in some pizza or something, do you? You can put a movie in while I do this."

"Sure." She tugged her phone out and then glanced at him as he pushed back from the desk. "I...ah, well, I didn't know it was any more complicated than you just doing it."

A grin tugged at his lips. "Well, if you had the design in mind already or brought one with you, we could move a little quicker. But yeah, it takes a little while." He gestured down the hall. "The number for the best local pizza place is hanging on the fridge in the break room if you want to use them, or we can use Rosatti's."

Once she left the room, Zach dropped his head down on his desk and groaned. He had to do this. He knew he did. And he wasn't going to deny a very huge part of him *wanted* to do this—wanted it so bad, his hands were shaking from it, but how in the hell was he supposed to handle this without losing his damn mind?

"By doing your damn job." She came here because she wanted some ink. So that was what he was going to do.

As he pushed back from the desk, he kicked the chair she'd dragged over and knocked her purse over. The journal fell out as he scooped up the purse. He went to dump them both back on the chair, but found himself flipping through the journal. She hadn't done much of anything.

But then he stopped.

One page held her neat writing.

She'd titled it. That was typical Abby, although it made him a little nervous. *Wreck this life*. What the hell...

But the first few goals had him smiling. Tell off Roger. Cool. Flip off the photographers? He'd been telling her to do that for years. Stop worrying so much. Wonderful.

The tattoo...yes. She was serious.

But the last one had the blood draining out of his head.

Fffffuuuuuccckkkkk...

Snapping it closed, he dumped the book on top of her purse and shot upright. Have a fucking affair? *What the hell?*

Thunder crashed inside his head. At least it felt that way, although more than likely, he was having a stroke or something. His feet seemed to get in the way as he turned around and started for the door. They needed to talk.

Abby had just broken things off with that prick she'd been engaged to. She was upset and feeling a little lost, needed to do something crazy. He could understand that, he thought. And while he was completely on board with her learning to live a little, the idea of her having a fucking affair with some guy who wouldn't give a damn about her made him want to chew glass and break things. Lots of things.

Still, that journal was her personal property and he hadn't had any right to go rooting through it. He hadn't expected to find anything like *that* and how could he explain that he'd read it? He couldn't lie to her. But did he tell her that she needed to think this through?

Damn it.

Following the sound of her voice, he stopped in the doorway and made himself close his eyes while she finished placing the order.

Breathe, man. Gotta breathe. Gotta think. Gotta be calm.

First he had to explain just how he'd managed to see it in the journal. He hadn't exactly been prying...well, he had, but he was her best friend and he was nosy, and she knew that, and...

Feeling the weight of her gaze, he lifted his lashes, not looking directly at her. Not yet.

But Abby wasn't looking at his face.

She was eyeing his arms. Catching her lower lip between her teeth, she tugged on the soft curve and he almost went to his knees at the sight. A second later, she glanced away, but then she looked back.

The thunder that had been crashing inside his head grew louder and louder.

Have a torrid affair.

Damn it, if she was dead set on *that* idea, she could have an affair with *him*, he decided.

Even as the idea slammed into him, he tried to brush it aside. He'd kept what he felt wrapped up and buried deep for years. Spilling it now?

Just wondering if you're ever going to do anything about it.

It's complicated...

Hell. He was lecturing Abby about living life and letting go, and here he was, afraid to grab *on*.

The woman he wanted like he wanted his next breath was standing *right there* and he was afraid to even make a move.

She turned away as he stood there, still wrestling with the very thought of it, need burning in him and twisting him into tight, hungry knots. Damn it. *Damn it.* He needed to do this—

"It will take about an hour or so," Abby said.

I'm thinking longer—

"They're pretty busy."

"What?" Distracted, he dragged his eyes away from the curve of her ass and focused on what she was saying.

"The pizza place. They said it would be about an hour or so—asked if they should come around to the back and I told them yes."

"That's fine." He dragged a hand down his face. "Ah...I need to get back to work."

"I was thinking about going to grab some wine or something."

Good idea. Wait. "You can't." He turned around and headed back into the main area of the shop, found the consent forms he needed. Abby was behind him, although he hadn't heard her. When he turned around, she was just a foot away and the scent of her went straight to his head and Zach had to wonder just what in the hell he'd done to get this kind of torture thrown into his life.

"I can't go get wine?" A smile curved her lips as she tipped her head to look up at him.

"I can't do the tattoo if you do—I won't put one on anybody who has been drinking. Saves me trouble later on. And you need to read through the consent form and sign. Make it all nice and legal."

"Ahhh..." She took the paper and moved over to one of the seats, crossing her legs as she started to read. "I guess I should be totally clearheaded. Otherwise, I could end up having arms like yours."

"Nah. I might try to talk you into having *Forever Nate's* tattooed on your ass, but that's it." He gave her a strained smile and turned around. Distance. Serious distance was needed here so he could get back on track.

As he headed down the hall, she called out, "Yeah, sure. I'll do that when you have a heart with *Kate* somewhere on *you.*"

Once he was in his office, he rubbed the heel of his hand over his chest.

What in the hell would she do if she knew he already *had* her written on his skin?

Not Kate, of course.

He hadn't fallen in love with Kate.

He loved Abby and always had.

He'd loved her when she ran away from California all those years ago...and he'd waited until she stopped running, so he could follow.

He'd loved her when she came to him and told him she was getting married...to a man who didn't deserve her.

And now she was laying out a plan to go and have a torrid affair. With who?

Curling one hand into a fist, he crossed back to his desk.

"Why in the hell *not* me?"

Wine *would* have been a good idea, Abby thought. Maybe he didn't want her drinking *before* he got started, but after? Yeah, it would have helped.

Stretched out on her belly, she closed her eyes and tried to think about *anything* but the pain.

"You okay?"

Zach's hands on her weren't helping her zone out, she decided. It was one hell of a distraction, but it *wasn't* helping her zone out.

Swallowing the knot in her throat, she croaked out,

"I'm as good as I think I can expect to be."

"And how good is that?"

"Lousy."

He laughed a little. "Why don't you talk to me? We're halfway done," he said. "If you talk, you'll get distracted and it will be done before you know it."

"Okay." She scrunched her eyes tightly closed and tried to think of something to say. Her mind was blank. "I don't know what to talk about."

"You always have something to talk about," he teased, his voice low and easy and she knew even without looking at him that he was smiling.

"Not right now I don't." Well, she *could* think of a thing or two. But those weren't really things she could say. Were they? No. She'd thought this through. She wasn't going down that road with Zach.

"Okay. I'll help. What is this new life plan you've got laid out? Besides the tattoo?"

I plan on flipping my life upside down.

She bit her lip to keep from blurting that out. That would make him worry. She loved him dearly and she didn't need him worrying about her right now. "It's not a *life* plan exactly. It's just a *for now* plan," she said slowly. "Some things to keep me distracted until I figure out what I'm going to do with myself. There's the tattoo thing, which you're obviously helping with. I'm going to try to stop worrying so much. One of them, though...I plan on calling up Roger and telling him off."

He grunted. "Good plan." Something soft brushed against her lower back and she hissed a little.

Damn it, that hurt. It felt like something was slicing right through her skin.

Distraction. Talk, damn it. About anything.

"I don't get it," she said softly, some of the confusion and pain breaking free. "I mean...I thought he loved me. How could he love me and walk away like that? Over the life I *used* to have? That's what it's all about. I used to be an actress. I'm not anymore—I haven't been for *years* and I'm happy with that. How can he not see that? If he loved me, wouldn't he be able to see that I don't *want* to act anymore?"

Zach didn't answer.

Turning her head, she peered over her shoulder at him.

He had his head bowed, the gold-streaked strands falling down and hiding his features from her.

"Zach?"

He sighed. "Do you really want to hear what I have to say about this right now, sugar?"

"I always want to hear what you have to say."

"Okay." He used the cloth again on her back and then bent down, staring at her skin like there was nothing else in the world but her back and the design he was inking on her flesh. "He never loved you."

It was a strike, square to her heart.

She closed her eyes.

"If he loved you, he wouldn't treat you the way he did. When you walked into a room, it would have showed on his face...if he really loved you. Either he'd have been so busy staring at you because he just had to see you, or he would have been looking away so nobody *could* see it. Except he was going to marry you—you were his and he had every right to let the world see how he felt." Zach dabbed at her back again, still focused on the work.

She was almost glad of the pain now, because it was easier to think about how much it *hurt* than to think about what he had to say.

"But when you walked into a room, that fucking prick was too busy either messing with his damned gadgets or looking at everybody else to see what *they* thought about you. He was in love with the idea of having Kate the cutie on his arm—the son of a bitch just loved to talk about his fiancée, the *actress*...and don't tell me you never noticed. He might have loved the idea of being with *Kate...*but he never loved *you.*"

He paused what he was doing and for a brief second, the world fell away as he looked up and met her eyes. "He never loved you, and the son of a bitch sure as hell didn't deserve you, sugar."

Her heart slammed against her ribs as his blue gaze held hers.

And then, as it started to feel like all the oxygen in the room had dwindled away, he turned his attention back to the task at hand.

It felt like he was flaying the flesh from her bones. And she decided that was just fine, because now she needed *that* distraction.

Was he right, she wondered?

She'd noticed, and tried to ignore, Roger's fascination with her old life, but she'd chalked it up to him just wanting to *know* about her. They were getting married...they *should* know about each other. But what if Zach was right?

What if Roger had never really loved her at all?

And that thought, as much as it infuriated her, it also made her wonder one simple thing.

Had *she* loved him?

* * * * * *

"Okay, here are the important things," Zach said as he studied the design. It was cute and sexy as hell. If he found out another guy was the one who got to press his lips to that dragonfly where it curved low over the flare of her left hip, he thought he just might go insane. "I'll send you home with some instructions on how to care for it, but you need to make sure you keep it clean. No scrubbing at it or anything—you need to be gentle when you wash it. I've got some ointment I'll send home with you and I'll go into detail about using that, too."

She was still staring at it over her shoulder in the mirror. Worrying her lower lip with her teeth and eyeing the dragonfly like she expected it to take flight or something.

"I need to get the bandage on," he said softly.

"What? Oh."

She continued to stand there and he reached up, pressed his hand between her shoulder blades. "Lean forward a little."

Hunger screamed, jerking on the leash inside him as he eased the waistband of her skirt just a little lower so he could get the bandage in place. Bent over the table like that, he could so easily imagine pulling the hem of the skirt up. Slipping his hand between her thighs. Would she sigh? Moan?

No. This was Abby and she'd freak the hell out and then she'd run away and he'd lose her—

A soft, shaky sigh caught his attention as he smoothed the bandage down. Keeping his head bowed, he checked the mirror from under his lashes and his knees almost buckled.

Fuck.

Abby was staring at their reflection and her face was flushed.

What. The. Hell.

Abruptly, he stepped back and moved away. If he didn't move away *immediately*, he was going to grab her and do things he should never do to his best friend. The woman he loved. That was the problem. He'd loved her for too long and he was misreading the signals and—

"Do you really think all that's true? About Roger?"

Hearing that shithead's name on her lips snapped his temper. He turned around and glared at her. "If I didn't think that was the case, Abs, I wouldn't have said it. He's an egotistical, arrogant piece of work and he never loved you. You deserved a hell of a lot better and I knew it all along. But he was what you wanted so who in the hell was I to say any different?"

"You're my best friend," she said quietly.

"Shit." He went to pass a hand over his face and

stopped. He still had his gloves on. Stripping them off, he tossed them into the red trash can near the door and headed over to start cleaning up. "Yes. I am. You asked me what I thought and I told you. But I can't tell you what is in that fucker's head. You can always ask him when you call him to tell him off, although I doubt he'll tell you the truth. He doesn't even *see* the truth anyway."

"Have you ever been in love?"

In the middle of gathering up his supplies, he paused. Zach closed his eyes and started to mouth every single foul, nasty curse he could think of. He had four brothers. He could think of a *lot* of cuss words. Halfway through one that involved anatomical improbabilities and a goat, a hand touched his shoulder.

"Zach?"

Damn it, he couldn't do this. Moving away, he started grabbing his supplies at random. Dumping trash, slamming the tools here, there. Being fucking careless with them, but he couldn't look at her yet. If he did, she might see—

He went to dump the trash and turned around.

Abby was right there, dark brown eyes locked on his face, her shirt still knotted just under her breasts, leaving her belly bare.

"What is this?" she teased. "You make me play twenty questions all the time."

Edging around her, he focused on cleaning up. "I'm thirty-two years old, Abby. Yeah. I've been in love," he said, keeping his voice flat and his eyes on the task at hand. "It didn't work out."

"Why not?"

"She never seemed to notice that I was staring at her when she walked into the room."